T0249238

THE SAD END OF POLICARPO QUARESMA

LIMA BARRETO (1881–1922) is an iconic figure in the literary history of Rio de Janeiro. Prolific journalist, political commentator, literary critic and novelist, he is now recognized as one of the most important Brazilian writers of the early twentieth century. He was in many ways a victim of the racism of Brazil's ruling class and had to struggle with both his father's insanity and his own increasing mental confusion and decline into alcoholism, but this made his achievements all the more remarkable. *The Sad End of Policarpo Quaresma*, first published in instalments in 1911, and in book form in 1915, is considered his greatest achievement. Lima Barreto died in 1922, at the age of forty-one.

MARK CARLYON is a British writer and translator resident in Rio de Janeiro. Since 2009 he has researched and translated a number of Brazilian classics, including works by Manuel Antônio de Almeida, Machado de Assis and João do Rio. He is currently working on a number of literary projects, including José de Alencar's *Iracema*, one of the major works of Brazil's Romantic Indianist School.

LILIA MORITZ SCHWARCZ is Professor of Anthropology at the University of São Paulo, Global Scholar at Princeton and author, among others, of *The Spectacle of the Races: Scientists, Institutions, and the Race Question in Brazil, 1870–1930* and *The Emperor's Beard: Dom Pedro II and His Tropical Monarchy in Brazil*.

LIMA BARRETO

The Sad End of Policarpo Quaresma

Translated and with Notes by
MARK CARLYON
With an Introduction by
LILIA MORITZ SCHWARCZ

PENGUIN BOOKS

PENGUIN CLASSICS

Published by the Penguin Group
Penguin Books Ltd, 80 Strand, London WC2R 0RL, England
Penguin Group (USA) Inc., 375 Hudson Street, New York, New York 10014, USA
Penguin Group (Canada), 90 Eglinton Avenue East, Suite 700, Toronto, Ontario, Canada M4P 2Y3
(a division of Pearson Penguin Canada Inc.)
Penguin Ireland, 25 St Stephen's Green, Dublin 2, Ireland (a division of Penguin Books Ltd)
Penguin Group (Australia), 707 Collins Street, Melbourne, Victoria 3008, Australia
(a division of Pearson Australia Group Pty Ltd)
Penguin Books India Pvt Ltd, 11 Community Centre, Panchsheel Park, New Delhi – 110 017, India
Penguin Group (NZ), 67 Apollo Drive, Rosedale, Auckland 0632, New Zealand
(a division of Pearson New Zealand Ltd)
Penguin Books (South Africa) (Pty) Ltd, Block D, Rosebank Office Park,
181 Jan Smuts Avenue, Parktown North, Gauteng 2193, South Africa

Penguin Books Ltd, Registered Offices: 80 Strand, London WC2R 0RL, England

www.penguin.com

First published in Brazilian Portuguese as *Triste Fim de Policarpo Quaresma*
by the *Jornal do Commercio* 1911
This translation first published in a bilingual, illustrated edition by Cidade Viva Editoria, Rio de Janeiro, 2011
This English-only edition, with a selection from the original annotations, first published in
Penguin Classics 2014

007

Translation and notes copyright © Mark Carlyon, MINC/BN, 2011
Introduction copyright © Lilia Moritz Schwarcz, 2014
Translation of introduction © Mark Carlyon, 2014
All rights reserved

The moral rights of the translator and the author of the introduction have been asserted

Set in 10.25/12.25 pt Adobe Sabon
Typeset by Jouve (UK), Milton Keynes
Printed in Great Britain by Clays Ltd, Elcograf S.p.A.

ISBN: 978-0-141-39570-8

www.greenpenguin.co.uk

MIX
Paper from
responsible sources
FSC
www.fsc.org   FSC™ C018179

Penguin Books is committed to a sustainable
future for our business, our readers and our planet.
This book is made from Forest Stewardship
Council™ certified paper.

Contents

THE SAD END OF
POLICARPO QUARESMA

PART I

PART II

PART III

Introduction

An Ambiguous Encounter: Fiction and History in Lima Barreto's Masterpiece[1]

The first instalment of *The Sad End of Policarpo Quaresma* was published in the evening edition of the *Jornal do Comércio* on 11 August 1911. This was the most important paper of the time in Rio de Janeiro, with two editions published daily. Lima Barreto's text appeared in the section headed 'The *Jornal do Comércio*'s Feuilleton'.[2] This genre had become a craze in a city which, despite the abolition of the monarchy in 1889, continued to behave as if the court were still in residence, dictating fashions and behaviour.

The feuilletons were generally scandalous, offering the reading public a daily diet of complex plots and spicy episodes. The genre had originated in France and been adopted by writers such as Balzac, Eugène Sue and Alexandre Dumas. It had first appeared in newspapers in the mid-nineteenth century, when it occupied the *rez-de-chaussée*[3] at the foot of the front page. It also provided a useful format for unknown writers: if these novels in instalments proved a success they were published as books, attracting new readers for those starting out on a literary career.

In Brazil, Eugène Sue's *Les Mystères de Paris* had been published in the *Jornal do Comércio* between 26 September and 15 October 1843, almost doubling the paper's sales. José de Alencar's *O Guaraní*, which was published as a feuilleton between 1856 and 1857, also met with great success.[4] *Policarpo* was to be no exception. It had fifty-two episodes divided into three parts, each of which had a 'sad end': in the first, the termination of Policarpo's career as a civil servant, after his ill-received petition requesting that Tupi-Guaraní be adopted as the national language; in the second, the final collapse of his heroic farming venture; and in the third, when he volunteers to join the government forces and ends up under arrest and bitterly disillusioned.

Barreto was careful to keep the manuscript[5] safe – 254 handwritten pages in his notoriously illegible script. The foolscap pages bore the letterhead of the War Office, where Barreto worked as a clerk. His job was to write up the minutes, but in his spare time he worked on his literary projects. The work was not published in book form until 1915, the only edition that the writer lived to see. Barreto, who had paid for it himself, complained that the quality was poor and it was full of mistakes. In his *Diário Íntimo*, in March 1917, addressing himself in the third person, he noted: 'I only owe money to Lima for the publication of *Policarpo*; the sum of four hundred and forty two *mil-réis* . . .'[6] He also referred to the publication in 1916: '*Policarpo Quaresma* was written in just over two months. I borrowed money everywhere, even from Santos,[7] who lent me three hundred *mil-reis* . . . *Audaces fortuna juvat.*'[8]

The author also complained about the money he had to spend to promote the work. Despite his misgivings, the February 1916 edition of *A Época* carried an interview with the author on the front page, accompanied by a favourable review of the book. The article mentioned the author's unconventional lifestyle and his humble origins (when compared to those of other prominent writers). '*Policarpo Quaresma* is an ordinary book in which I attempt to show the diversity of our Brazilian expectations,' Barreto said in the interview. The journalist then described the writer:

> In Rio de Janeiro there is no one who doesn't know him. He frequents every district, every outskirt, every suburb: the street is his element. Ask anyone: 'Have you seen Lima?' and he will answer: 'I saw him today, this morning, playing billiards.' His erudition is beyond doubt. We imagine he reads on the trams, on the boats, on the trains. Lima Barreto is not young, he is over

thirty, but he is full of youthful vigour. He was born in Rio de Janeiro and is in awe of the dazzling beauty of his city. He studied engineering but abandoned the course – he escaped from being called 'Doctor', as he likes to say. He became a civil servant, to the despair of his bosses, it seems. We went in search of him. We went from bar to bar, from bakery to bakery, until we found him in a brasserie.

Barreto was characterized, and liked to characterize himself, as a bohemian writer, always drinking in bars, a realist, averse to the formalities of literature. He also defined himself as black in a country where, although most of the population was black, mulatto or mestizo, few of its public figures were, and where success had a 'whitening' effect, altering a man's self-image.

Afonso Henriques de Lima Barreto was born on 13 May 1881 (the date on which, seven years later, slavery was to be abolished) and died on 1 November 1922 (the year of the seminal Semana de Arte Moderna),[9] without living to see the success of modernism in Brazil. He was a journalist, activist and writer who never denied his past. His father, João Henriques de Lima Barreto, was a freed slave who had made a career as a typesetter. His mother, Amália Augusta, was the daughter of a slave who had been adopted by a doctor, Pereira Carvalho; she became a teacher and the owner of an elementary school, giving her son an unusually good education. But she died when Lima was only six, leaving João Henriques to provide for their children.

Perhaps it was this background, and the endless difficulties he met throughout his life, that led to Barreto's decision to become a counter-cultural figure: he would be a black writer (in life and in literature), badly behaved, opposed to the Brazilian Academy of Letters – everything that writers like Machado de Assis were not. However, like them, he wanted and intended to live from literature. As he said in the interview:

Literature is the purpose of my life. I only ask of it that which it can give me: Glory. I don't want to be a congressman or a senator; I want to be nothing but a writer. I don't ask literature

for easy conquests, I ask it for something solid and lasting. I
abandoned everything for it, and I hope it will give me many
things. It is the reason I live immersed in my grief, in my sorrows;
the reason we go and drink beer together.

And nothing seems to have tempered these expectations. His
choice of dedicatee for the 1915 edition is a good illustration:
João Luiz Ferreira. Whereas he usually dedicated his works to
friends, in this case he chose a member of the Piauí[10] elite. The
two men had studied together at the Escola Politécnica, but,
unlike Barreto, Ferreira had completed the civil engineering
course and gone on to become governor of the state of Piauí. He
was the brother of José Félix A. Pacheco, director and owner of
the *Jornal do Comércio*, congressman, senator and minister for
foreign affairs. Barreto cultivated influential friends on whom
he relied for the promotion of his literary projects.

By this time, however, he was far from unknown. In 1909 he
had published *Recollections of the Clerk Isaías Caminha*.
Although the book gained him a certain notoriety, he paid a
high price for its criticism of local racism and denunciation of
the press ('the fourth power of the Republic'). In the book Barreto revealed life behind the scenes at the *Correio da Manhã*.
He did not delude himself, affirming: 'I have no enemies, but
my book will have.'

Policarpo continued on the same track, as can be seen at the
outset with the epigraph from Renan's *Marcus Aurelius*. Renan
was a sceptic and a critic of the science of his time. Marcus
Aurelius and Policarpo would both be 'superior men', but sad
men too, misunderstood by their generation. A dedicated
reader of explorers' journals, given to the foibles of an amateur
scientist, Policarpo, like Barreto, was a misjudged patriot.

The First Republic:[11] an Uneasy Time

The novel was written in just two and a half months and is
characterized by its hurried pace and 'impatient tone',[12] which
reflect the tension of the historical context. Coincidence or not,
Policarpo symbolically marks the end of one phase of the

author's career and the beginning of another: before it Barreto mixed with writers, journalists and politicians; he had a circle of admirers. After it he became increasingly isolated by his growing dependence on alcohol.

But if the intention was to scandalize, the initial response was disappointing. The book received a further review, in *A Imprensa*, on 20 August 1916. The review defended the creation of an Academy for New Writers, denounced the exploitation of writers by editors and presented Lima Barreto as a fine example of the new generation of writers. It recognized him as the leader of the group that met at the offices of *Floreal* magazine and proposed engaged literature inspired by Dostoyevsky, and also writers like Tolstoy, Flaubert, Balzac, Taine, Stendhal, Voltaire, Eça de Queiros and Renan. Since the death of Machado de Assis in 1908, literary critics had found no writer that could rival him. Novels on the French model – sequences of little dramas – had come into vogue.

The first years of the Republic had been marked by constant political and cultural turbulence. In 1889, a year after the upheaval caused by the abolition of slavery, the Republic was proclaimed, with the promise of a modern, egalitarian society. But despite the new institutions the state was repressive and unpopular, controlled by the iron hand of the military in a virtual state of siege. Dissatisfaction was widespread.

Protests were constant, and there were serious uprisings, including the Revolt of the Armada[13] in 1893–4 and the Vaccine Revolt[14] in 1904. The mood of the country was divided; part of the population was sceptical. But the country was undoubtedly changing, with urban and industrial development and waves of migration. This was also the time when Pereira Passos, mayor from 1903 to 1906, undertook the rebuilding of Rio de Janeiro. The plan produced great improvements, but it also expelled the poor from the centre of the town. At the same time as the new Central Avenue was inaugurated, with its art nouveau façades, electric street lights, shops with luxury imported items and their Parisian-style clientele, surrounding areas were turning into slums. The forced demolition of homes led to the growth of shanty towns and the squalid hotels that Barreto referred to as *zungas*.[15]

In the years preceding the publication of *Policarpo*, the situation became tenser still. In 1909, with the death of President Afonso Pena, Hermes da Fonseca presented himself as candidate in a move that would return the military to power. Barreto wrote a letter of support to the opposition candidate Rui Barbosa, using the pseudonym Isaías Caminha, and set up his campaign headquarters in the Café Papagaio. It was here that he met the historian Antônio Noronha dos Santos, who was to become one of his greatest friends and collaborators. Together they published the magazine *Floreal*, and it was Noronha who took the originals of *Isaías Caminha* to Lisbon and delivered them to the editor who published the book. In 1909 the two men edited a pamphlet attacking Hermes da Fonseca's candidacy: *The Bogey – Weekly News from Behind the Scenes of Politics, the Arts and Candidacies*.

The campaign polarized the country. Whereas Fonseca represented a return to the military regime of Floriano Peixoto, his opponent, the civilian Rui Barbosa, was one of the country's most respected intellectuals and a brilliant orator. Tension between the civilian and military parties increased. Violence erupted when students took to the streets and conducted a 'symbolic burial' of General Sousa Aguiar (mayor of the Federal District[16] from 1906 to 1909, later promoted to marshal). Members of the military responded, killing two people and wounding a number of others.

The atmosphere remained tense when, in March 1910, Hermes da Fonseca defeated Rui Barbosa in the election. The result did nothing to appease public unrest. In September that year the trial of those responsible for the death of the students was held. Barreto acted not only as a member of the jury, but also as secretary of the legal counsel that condemned and sentenced the military culprits – despite the fact that he was an employee of the War Office, which paid both his and the defence lawyers' fees.

As we shall see, *Policarpo* does not only reflect the tensions of the time that preceded its conception, it also introduces a subtle dialogue between reality and fiction, where one is nourished by the other.

History Inverted

Barreto depicted these turbulent times in the book by transporting them back to 1893, when the Revolt of the Armada began. The events of that time held a great significance for Barreto. In 1890 his father, João Henriques, who was well established as a typesetter with the national press, was fired for alleged collusion with the monarchy. Due to the intervention of his longstanding benefactor, the Barão de Ouro Preto, a powerful politician during the Empire,[17] João Henriques received the post of bookkeeper at the mental asylum on the Ilha do Governador.[18] Meanwhile Barreto had been placed in a boarding school in Niterói[19] and visited the family at weekends. But these peaceful days were short-lived. The following year the military president, Deodoro da Fonseca, closed the Congress and, because of the resulting political pressure, resigned. His vice-president, Floriano Peixoto, seized power in what was effectively a coup d'état that prevented new elections.[20]

This event sparked the Revolt of the Armada. It was led by senior naval officers who felt politically eclipsed by the army and planned to prevent the illegal nomination of Peixoto. To the horror of Barreto's father, the rebels seized the Ilha do Governador; his letters from 1893 go from anguish to despair: 'Whatever will become of me?' Years later, in an article published in the *Almanaque d'A Noite* on 23 May 1916, Barreto described his life as a twelve-year-old and how the revolt affected it: 'Among the events of the revolt of '93, what most impressed me, without a doubt, was the landing of the rebels on the island of my childhood.' A few things stand out in his description: the weak figure of 'my unhappy father' and how, with the arrival of the insurgents, peace was destroyed. Although *Policarpo* is not restricted to this episode, it constitutes an important part of the story. The Ilha do Governador is described in the novel, and Curuzu, where Policarpo buys his little farm, 'The Haven', has many similarities to the Sítio do Carico, where the family lived.

The rebellion was finally put down in March 1894, and in November Prudente de Morais became the new president, promising to reorganize the country. Barreto, who had studied at the Ginásio Nacional, entered the Politécnica in 1907. He was not to complete the course. After being accused of a book-keeping error, his father suffered a mental collapse. Barreto had to bring him to Rio, leaving university and getting a job as a clerk at the War Office. From here on the writer and his character draw closer together. Both were civil servants, Policarpo a nationalist defending everything Brazilian, Barreto opposed to everything that smelled of 'foreigners' monkey tricks'. The revolt assumes a symbolic importance for both. For Barreto it signified the beginning of adult life, with the family moving to the suburb of Todos os Santos. For Policarpo it meant the beginning of maturity and the loss of his ingenuousness. And another of the novel's great characters, the minstrel Ricardo Coração dos Outros,[21] is conceived by Barreto as an inhabitant of the suburbs. Only in the suburbs was the simplicity of the old life still to be found: 'people appeared in the windows in their Sunday best. Blacks in white jackets smoking large cigars or cigarettes; groups of shopboys with gaudy buttonholes; girls in cotton dresses, very starched; old-fashioned top hats beside plump, lethargic matrons squeezed into black satin dresses.' It was Sunday 'adorned with the simplicity of the humble, the creativity of the poor and the ostentation of the foolish'.

Insanity would also become a recurrent theme in the novel, just as it had entered with full force the life of Barreto's family: João Henriques was diagnosed with neurasthenia, and Lima himself was later interned in the National Asylum on two occasions due to alcohol. In the novel Ismênia goes mad after her fiancé abandons her, and Policarpo is interned for several months after the rejection of his petition. But there is also madness in Floriano's headquarters and in the succession of events that blight 'The Haven'. Insanity constructs the narrative, and the portrayal of insanity was a theme ideally suited to the spirit of the feuilletons.

Characters and Types

In *Policarpo* Lima Barreto creates a gallery of unforgettable types. On the one hand Policarpo himself, 'a visionary', defender of 'all things Brazilian', so punctual that he serves as a sort of neighbourhood clock; on the other Floriano, with his 'sagging moustache . . . coarse looks and flaccid features' and a 'melancholy that was characteristic more of the race he represented than of the man himself'. Ismênia and Olga form a strong contrast. The former, fragile like Barreto's father, sinks into madness. The latter is a woman who embodies all the ethical standards of her godfather, Policarpo. Another strong contrast is that of the ever-faithful Ricardo Coração dos Outros and Genelício, a civil servant at the Treasury and master in the art of obsequiousness.

But the book also has its villains: the dissemblers, or 'perhapses', as Barreto so aptly calls them. General Albernaz and Rear-Admiral Caldas display their titles without ever having fought in a battle. Doctor Florêncio 'was more an inspector of water pipes than an engineer'. And so the story develops, with each of the characters expressing the dilemmas of a disintegrating modernity. Scepticism and optimism; honesty and dissimulation; sanity and madness; progress and decline – opposites that confront each other throughout the work. And what prevails is the ambivalence of the characters, a reflection of the ambivalence of the time, oscillating between great faith in the future, nostalgia for the past and uncertainty as to what was to come.

A highly significant moment in the story is when the ants finally destroy all of Policarpo's crops. With a touch of humour Lima Barreto quotes the botanist Saint-Hilaire (who travelled around Brazil between 1816 and 1822): 'Either Brazil destroys the ants, or the ants will destroy Brazil.' Policarpo's farm was overrun with ants: 'He wanted to drive them away. He killed one, two, ten, twenty, a hundred; but there were thousands, and the army kept growing.' The author never forgot this 'infamous enemy'. In 'The Ants and the Mayor', published in the *Lanterna* in 1918, he says: 'This business of ants has bothered me since I was boy, when my old friend Poli-carpo Quaresma told me the agonies they'd made him suffer.' These insects were frequently a real, as well as a metaphorical, obstacle. In his 1928 book *Picture of Brazil*, Paulo Prado includes them among the problems of tropical civilization, and in his classic of Brazilian modernism *Macunaíma* Mario de Andrade concludes: 'Lots of ants and little health are the evils of Brazil.'

Philosophical Melancholy

Today *Policarpo* is recognized as Lima Barreto's greatest work. After writing it, the author dedicated himself to building his career as a writer, even trying (without success) to get elected to the Brazilian Academy of Letters in 1917.[22] Although *Poli-carpo* was not recognized at first, it has since become an established Brazilian classic.

The most significant review the author saw in his lifetime was by the historian and diplomat Oliveira Lima, printed in the *Estado de São Paulo* on 13 November 1916. Lima called Major Quaresma a 'Brazilian Don Quixote' and concluded: 'both are incurable optimists as they believe that social ills and human suffering can be cured by the simplest, yet the hardest, treat-ment: the application of justice, of which both aspire to be the knight-errant'. Then both the book and its author disappeared for a considerable time. It was thanks to Francisco de Assis Barbosa, a journalist, writer and academic, that the book was later to reappear, followed by a major biography of the writer. Perhaps due to its irony, the parallels it drew with events of its time or the author's social origin, it took time for *Policarpo* to reach the public at large.

Works such as this deserve to be rediscovered by future gen-erations, approached in the light of the issues of their time. The pitfalls of patriotism and a sceptical view of nationalistic ven-tures are among the many inspired themes of this work, a work that is easy to read but has multiple interpretations. And its subtle, good-humoured criticism prevents it from becoming dated, or from being defined as folkloric or regional. There is even irony in the hero's name. *Policarpo* means 'he that produces many fruits'; but the hero's life bore no fruit worth mentioning. *Carpo*, from the Portuguese verb *carpir*, meaning to weep or lament, is a reference to the 'sad end' of the title. *Quaresma* also has many meanings: it is Portuguese for Lent, the forty days of fasting that precede the sacrifice of Christ – a sacrifice seen as an act of consecration, which is sad but at the same time constitutes the foundation of a pact with a new society. Policarpo is thus a kind of Brazilian Christ, the melancholy harbinger of a new dawn. And lastly *quaresma* is also a type of palm tree, the symbol that has been used to represent Brazil since the earliest maps of the sixteenth century. Ambiguity and ambivalence permeate the book, from its title and the epigraph to the final outcome of the story.

We do not know whether Lima Barreto read Flaubert's unfinished novel *Bouvard et Pécuchet*, published posthumously in 1881. What we do know is that he admired the French writer and that there are striking parallels between Policarpo and Flaubert's two clerks, lovers of science who dabble in many fields – agriculture, gymnastics, theology, chemistry and pedagogy – but who, like our hero, fail at them all. The fate of Policarpo is much the same: major, civil servant, historian and geographer, he ends up bankrupt and under arrest for treason. Flaubert's protagonists end up in an 'asylum and with no interest in life'. Policarpo was to die at the hands of his captors, equally disillusioned with the Republic of which he had dreamed.[23] And perhaps it would not be inappropriate to include Barreto himself among his fictional characters: he also saw himself as a knight-errant, a lone voice in the Republic of Literature.

Policarpo is a work full of hope, and yet one that disturbs us with the depths of its sadness and disillusion.

Lilia Moritz Schwarcz, 2014

NOTES

1. A slightly longer version of this text was published in Brazil in the 2014 Penguin/Companhia das Letras edition of the original novel.

2. *Feuilleton*: A novel printed in instalments.

3. *rez-de-chaussée*: A large space reserved for footnotes at the bottom of the front page.

4. *In Brazil ... met with great success*: This information on the feuilleton comes from Marlyse Meyer's history of the genre: *Folhetim: uma história* (São Paulo: Companhia das Letras, 1996).

5. *manuscript*: The manuscript is part of a large collection that includes many of Barreto's articles, short stories, essays, personal documents and notes.

6. *mil-réis*: *Réis* is the plural of the monetary unit that was used in Portugal, Brazil and other Portuguese-speaking countries. Due to its tiny value, a thousand *réis* (*mil-réis*) was later adopted as the monetary unit. According to an advertisement published on 3 March 1917 in the *Jornal do Comércio*, the rent of a 'modern house in the district of Botafogo, South Zone of Rio de Janeiro, with two reception rooms, six bedrooms, bath with heater, front garden etc.' was 253.9 *mil-reis*. Thus for Barreto, who lived in a modest house in the suburbs, this represented an enormous sum.

7. *Santos*: Barreto's friend Antônio Noronha dos Santos, who had facilitated the publication of his previous book, *Recollections of the Clerk Isaías Caminha*, in Portugal.

8. *Audaces fortuna juvat*: 'Fortune favours the bold'.

9. *Semana de Arte Moderna*: Modern Art Week was held in São Paulo in February 1922. Organized by painter Di Cavalcanti and poet Mario de Andrade, with the participation of composer Heitor Villa-Lobos and other leading young modernists, the event was an open challenge to the conservative cultural establishment and introduced the modernists' work to Brazilian society at large.

10. *Piauí*: A large state in Brazil's semi-arid north-east.

11. *The First Republic*: The 'First Republic' constitutes the period between the foundation of the Republic (1889) and the Revolution of 1930, when the populist dictator Getúlio Vargas came to power.

12. *'impatient tone'*: The expression is used by Lima Barreto's major biographer, Francisco de Assis Barbosa, in his *A vida de Lima Barreto* (Rio de Janeiro: José Olympio Editora, 2002).

13. *Revolt of the Armada*: Marshal Deodoro da Fonseca, who led the coup that founded the Republic in November 1889, was forced to resign nine months later after closing the Congress; his place was taken by his vice-president, Marshal Floriano Peixoto. The constitution required new elections if the president resigned before completing two years of his term. This served as the legal justification for the revolt led by potential presidential candidate Admiral Custódio de Melo along with Admirals Saldanha da Gama and Eduardo Wandenkolk, senior naval officers resentful of the increasing power of the army in republican politics.

14. *Vaccine Revolt*: In 1903 the director general of public health, Osvaldo Cruz (1872–1917), was granted sweeping powers to eradicate yellow fever and smallpox. Compulsory vaccination was decreed, allowing sanitary brigades, accompanied by police, to enter homes and vaccinate by force. The revolt coincided with an uprising at the Military Academy, turning the city into a virtual battlefield between 6 and 10 November 1904.

15. *zungas*: The equivalent of something like 'flea pits'.

16. *Federal District*: Rio de Janeiro was the Federal District until the transfer of the capital to Brasilia in 1959.

17. *the Empire*: The period between independence (1822) and the proclamation of the Republic (1889) is referred to as the Empire.

18. *Ilha do Governador*: Or Governor's Island, an island in Guanabara Bay. Rural and sparsely populated in the 1890s, it is now a densely populated district of Rio's North Zone.

19. *Niterói*: Rio's twin city, on the other side of Guanabara Bay, and capital of the state of Rio de Janeiro when Rio was the federal capital.

20. *a coup d'état that prevented new elections*: The constitution required new elections if the president resigned before completing two years of his term.

21. *Ricardo Coração dos Outros*: 'Richard Heart of Others', a pun on 'Ricardo Coração de Leão' (Richard the Lionheart) – an ironic reference to the heroism (in the singer's view) of his quest to be recognized as a patriotic singer/songwriter.

22. *trying . . . to get elected to the Brazilian Academy of Letters in 1917*: His first attempt was in August 1917. His application was not considered. In February 1919 he tried to get elected to the chair left vacant by the death of his friend Emilio de Menezes, also without success. In June 1921 he tried once again, after the death of Paulo Barreto (better known by his pseudonym João do Rio), but withdrew his candidacy on 28 September.

23. *We do not know whether Lima Barreto . . . dreamed*: The infor-
    mation on Flaubert's work and the parallels between it and
    Policarpo were taken from Silviano Santiago's essay included in
    the edition of Barreto's novel organized by Antonio Houaiss and
    Carmem Lúcia Negreiros (Madrid, Paris, Mexico, Buenos Aires,
    São Paulo, Lima, Guatemala, San José da Costa Rica, Santiago
    de Chile: AALLCA XX, Coleção Archivos, 1997).

Note on the Translation

'Death is not the only leveller: madness, crime and sickness also eliminate the distinctions we invent.'
The Sad End of Policarpo Quaresma, p. 62

The end of the nineteenth century was a time of great upheaval in Brazil. The new Republic, founded by an alliance between positivist idealists and the military with virtually no popular support, got off to a difficult start. Its unwilling first president lasted less than nine months in office. But the army had no intention of losing what it had gained. The vice-president, Marshal Floriano Peixoto, seized power, ignoring the recently promulgated constitution, which required new elections, and proceeded to confront rebellions on two different fronts. The first took place in the capital; it was led by three naval officers, who gained control of Guanabara Bay, from where they proceeded to shell the city. The second, in the south, was the re-emergence of an older problem: the aspiration of the southern states to break away from the Union.

Floriano, the usurper of power, the military dictator, the centre of a cult of authoritarianism, with his mediocre character and ruthless elimination of all opposition, is in many ways the central character around which Lima Barreto's story and its characters revolve. As he tells it, he gives us a vivid picture of the inhabitants of Rio de Janeiro in the early 1890s: Albernaz and Bustamante, promoted through the ranks to retire as a general and an admiral respectively, but who had somehow always avoided being sent to the front; Genelício, the pompous, self-serving bureaucrat; Doctor Campos, the populist politician who stops at nothing to keep his party in power; Coleoni, the Italian immigrant who made his fortune in Brazil but who is excluded from *carioca* society – and above all the introverted but determined Policarpo, who has made his love of his country into his life's central mission, a love for which he is to die in the deepest disillusionment. These lives are set in a city that in losing its monarch had lost a large part of its identity, a city traumatized by the struggle for power, against the constant background of a greater trauma still: the Paraguayan War, a war that left 60,000 Brazilian soldiers dead and thousands more crippled for life, that devastated the country's self-esteem and destroyed the spirits and the health of the emperor. Barreto's book denounces war, nationalism, military dictatorships, the system of political patronage and the abuse of human rights. It is as relevant today as it was when it was written.

Lima Barreto has become a Brazilian icon. The story of his life, with his father's insanity, his cruel rejection by *carioca* literary society, his poverty and alcoholism, is in itself as extraordinary as anything that could be produced by fiction. He is, however, by no means an easy writer for modern Brazilian readers, let alone for English-speaking ones. Certain passages, by contemporary standards, appear dispersive; and there are others where the ideas seem to lack precision or are left incomplete. There is also a certain lack of regard for maintaining the dramatic impetus, such as the introduction in the penultimate chapter of Felizardo's wife and children, three characters that are not developed. My overriding concern as translator has been to keep the readers with me, hoping that they will not get disheartened when the going is a little heavy, because when they reach the good bits, they are really good. This is, to my mind, a truly remarkable book.

A remarkable book, and one that presents remarkable difficulties to the translator. In many places it has been a great challenge to reshape the ideas and descriptive passages into a form that reads like authentic English while staying as close as possible to the meaning and character of the original text, a challenge which I hope has been worthwhile.

Mark Carlyon

To
JOAO LUIZ FERREIRA
Civil Engineer

'The major drawback in real life, and what makes it unbearable to the superior man, is that if one applies idealistic principles to it, qualitites become faults, so that very often distinguished men do not succeed as well as those motivated by selfishness or by mere routine.'

Ernest Renan, *Marcus Aurelius*

PART I

I

THE GUITAR LESSON

As always, Policarpo Quaresma, more commonly known as Major Quaresma, arrived home at a quarter past four in the afternoon. He had done so for more than twenty years. Leaving the Ministry of War, where he was undersecretary, he would pick out some fruit at the shops, buy a cheese occasionally and always the bread from the French bakery.

These tasks took him less than an hour, so that at around twenty to four he would catch the tram, never a minute late, and cross the threshold of his house in a distant street of São Januário at precisely a quarter past four, with the regularity of the appearance of a planet or an eclipse, a predetermined mathematical phenomenon, predictable and predicted.

His habits were well known in the neighbourhood: so much so that at Captain Claudio's house, where they dined at around half past four, as soon as they saw him pass, the captain's wife would shout to the maid: 'Alice, it's time; Major Quaresma has just gone by.'

And so it had been, every day, for almost thirty years. Living in his own house, with independent means in addition to his earnings, Major Quaresma was able to live more comfortably than a bureaucrat's income would permit, enjoying from his neighbours the consideration and respect afforded a man of wealth.

He never received anyone, living in monastic isolation. Although he was polite to his neighbours, they thought him odd and misanthropic. But if he had no friends in the neighbourhood, neither did he have any enemies; the only contemptuous remark about him had come from Sr Segadas, a well-known local doctor, who could not accept that Quaresma owned books: 'What for, if he has no degree? The pretension!'

The undersecretary didn't show his books to anyone, but it so happened that when his library windows were open the shelves could be seen from the street, crammed with books from top to bottom.

Such were his habits; lately, however, they had changed a little, and this had caused comment in the neighbourhood. In addition to his goddaughter and her father, previously his only visitors, a short, thin, pale gentleman with a guitar wrapped in a suede-leather case had been seen entering the house, regularly, three times a week. Suddenly the curiosity of the neighbour-hood was aroused. A guitar in such a respectable household! What could it mean?

That very afternoon one of the major's prettiest neighbours invited a girl friend, and together they spent some considerable time pacing up and down the street, straining their necks as they passed the eccentric undersecretary's open window.

Their spying did not go unrewarded. The major was seated on the sofa beside the newcomer, holding the guitar in the play-ing position and listening attentively: 'Look, major, like this.' And the strings vibrated softly with the note that was plucked. Then the teacher added: 'That's D. Have you got that?'

No explanation was needed: the neighbours realized at once that the major was learning to play the guitar. To think of it! That serious-minded man involved in such idle frivolity!

On a sunny afternoon – March sun, fierce and implacable – at around four o'clock, on both sides of a deserted street in São Januário, the windows were suddenly filled with people. Even in the general's house young ladies came to the window! What was it? A military parade? A fire? Not at all: Major Quaresma was coming up the street, at a little ox-like trot, head bowed, with the shameless instrument under his arm!

It is true that the guitar was appropriately wrapped in paper, but the wrapping didn't entirely conceal its shape. In the face of such a scandalous occurrence, the consideration and respect which Major Policarpo Quaresma enjoyed in the neighbourhood suffered to a certain extent. They said he was crazy, out of his mind. He, however, continued serenely with his studies; he didn't even notice the change.

Quaresma was a small, thin man who wore a pince-nez; his eyes were always downcast, but when he fixed his gaze on a person or an object they would gleam behind the lenses with a penetrating stare. It was as if he wanted to delve into the essence of what he was staring at.

However, he always looked down, as if his steps were guided by the tip of the goatee beard that adorned his chin. He always wore a striped morning coat – black, blue or grey, but always a morning coat – usually accompanied by an old-fashioned top hat, very tall with a narrow brim, from a time when he'd still kept abreast of what was in fashion.

When he arrived home that day it was his sister who opened the door for him:

'Are you going to dine now?' she asked.

'Not yet. Wait a little for Ricardo. He's coming to dine with us today.'

'Where's your common sense, Policarpo? A respectable man, of your age and standing, going around with that vulgar singer. It's not right!'

The major put down his parasol – an old parasol, with a wooden rod and a curved handle encrusted with small pieces of mother-of-pearl.

'How wrong you are, sister,' he replied. 'To think that every man who plays the guitar is a *persona non grata* is prejudice. The *modinha*[1] is the most authentic expression of Brazilian poetry, and the guitar is the instrument it calls for! It is we who have abandoned the genre; but it used to be held in high esteem, in Lisbon, in the last century with Father Caldas,[2] who played for ladies of the aristocracy. Beckford, a famous Englishman, praised it very highly.'[3]

'But those were different times; nowadays . . .'

'Nowadays what, Adelaide? Are we going to let our traditions die, our genuinely Brazilian customs?'

'All right, Policarpo, I don't want to annoy you. Carry on with your manias if you must.'

His sister went back into the house. The major went into a nearby room, undressed, washed, donned his house clothes and went into the library, where he sat down in a rocking chair and rested.

It was a vast room, all lined with iron bookcases, with windows that looked on to a side street.

There were ten or so of these, with four shelves, as well as smaller ones for the heavier tomes. Anyone who carefully examined this large collection would be astonished at what they revealed about the mind that had selected them.

In fiction there were only Brazilian authors or those considered as such:[4] Bento Teixeira's *Prosopopéia*, Gregório de Matos, Basílio da Gama, Santa Rita Durão, José de Alencar (complete), Macedo, Gonçalves Dias (complete) and many others. One could be assured that not a single Brazilian or naturalized Brazilian author of the 1880s was missing from the major's shelves.

The collection of Brazilian history was abundant: the chroniclers Gabriel Soares and Gandavo, Rocha Pita, Frei Vicente do Salvador, Armitage, Aires do Casal, Pereira da Silva, Handelmann (*Geschichte von Brasilien*), Melo Morais, Capistrano de Abreu, Southey, Varnhagen, as well as others that were rarer and not so well known. And books on travel and exploration, what an abundance! There were Hans Staden, Jean de Léry, Saint-Hilaire, Martius, Prince Neuwied, John Mawe, von Eschwege, Agassiz, Couto de Magalhães, and if these were joined by Darwin, Freycinet, Cook, Bougainville and even the famous Pigafetta, the chronicler of Magellan's journey, it was because all of these travellers had either briefly visited Brazil or stayed for some time.

And there were other books too: dictionaries, manuals, encyclopedias and compendiums in various languages.

This shows that his predilection for the poetry of Porto Alegre[5] and Magalhães[6] did not stem from a hopeless ignorance of the literary languages of Europe; on the contrary, the major had a considerable knowledge of French, English and German and, although he didn't speak these languages, he read and translated them correctly. The reason was to be found in the peculiar nature of his mind, in the powerful sentiment that guided his life: Policarpo was a patriot. Since he was a young man of twenty the love of his country had possessed him entirely. It had been no ordinary love, garrulous and void; it had been a serious, deep, consuming love. He had no ambitions in politics or government; what Quaresma wanted, or rather, what patriotism made him want, was absolute knowledge of Brazil, so that he could reflect on its resources and then point out solutions and progressive measures with a full understanding of his cause.

No one was sure where he had been born, but it certainly had not been in São Paulo, nor in Rio Grande do Sul, nor in Pará.[7] Those who looked for regional sympathies looked in vain; Quaresma was first and foremost Brazilian. He had no preference for any particular part of his country; his excitement was not aroused only by the plains of the south with their cattle, the coffee of São Paulo, the gold and diamonds of Minas, the beauty of Guanabara,[8] the height of the Paulo Afonso falls,[9] the inspiration of Gonçalves Dias,[10] the courage of Andrade Neves;[11] all these combined and merged into one, beneath the star-studded flag of the Southern Cross.[12]

At eighteen he had wanted to join the army, but the medical board judged him unfit. He was aggrieved, he suffered but he did not reject the fatherland. The government was liberal; he became a conservative, and his love for the land of his birth grew stronger than ever. Denied the gold braid of the army, he sought a career in government, and of its various ramifications he chose the military.

He was at home there. In the midst of soldiers, veterans, cannon, the names of rifles, technical terms for artillery, documents brim full with kilos of gunpowder, every day he inhaled the breath of war, of valour, of victory, of triumph: the very breath of the fatherland.

During his leisure time he studied, and his choice of study was the fatherland, its natural wealth, history, geography, literature and politics. Quaresma knew all the species of minerals, vegetables and animals that existed in Brazil; he knew the value of all the gold, all the diamonds exported from Minas,[13] the

Dutch invasions,[14] the battles of the Paraguayan War,[15] the sources and the course of all the rivers. With passion and acrimony he defended the pre-eminence of the Amazon over all the other rivers in the world. He even committed the crime of amputating a few kilometres from the Nile, the rival of 'his river' that most annoyed him. Heaven help anyone who mentioned its name! Normally calm and courteous, the major became ill-tempered and edgy whenever the lengths of the Amazon and the Nile were discussed.

For a year now he had devoted himself to the study of Tupi-Guaraní.[16] Every morning, before 'the rosy-fingered dawn for radiant Phoebus heralded the way',[17] until it was lunchtime, he grappled with Montoya's *Arte y diccionario de la lengua guaraní o más bien tupí*, studying the *caboclo*[18] language with dedication and passion. At the office, when the junior employees, clerks and copyists discovered he was studying the language of the Indians, they decided – heaven knows why – to call him 'Ubirajara'.[19] Once when the clerk Azevedo was distractedly signing the register, without noticing who was behind him, he said facetiously: 'Ubirajara's late today, isn't he?'

Quaresma was esteemed at the ministry: his age, his erudition, his evident modesty and honesty earned him the respect of all. Realizing that the nickname referred to him, he did not lose his dignity; he did not retort with insults and accusations. He drew himself up, straightened his pince-nez and, raising his forefinger into the air, replied: 'Don't be frivolous, Sr Azevedo. Do not presume to ridicule those who are working in silence for the greatness and emancipation of this country.'

That day the major spoke little. It was his custom during the break for coffee, when the employees left their benches, to share with his companions the fruits of his investigations, the discoveries of national riches he had made in his library at home. One day it was the petroleum that he had read somewhere had been found in Bahia; another it was a new species of rubber tree that grew along the Pardo River in Mato Grosso; another it was a well-known figure, an intellectual, whose great-grandmother had been Brazilian. And when he had no discovery to impart he would map out the country, describe the course of the rivers, the navigable stretches, the minor improvements required to make them entirely fit for shipping. He had a passion for the rivers; to the mountains he was indifferent. Too small, perhaps . . .

His colleagues listened to him respectfully, and none except for Azevedo dared attempt a joke or a wisecrack, or make the slightest objection while he spoke. But when his back was turned they took revenge for his lecturing by making fun of him: 'That Quaresma! What a bore! He thinks we're still at primary school! He never talks about anything else!'

And so he passed his days: half at the office, where he was not understood, and half at home, where he was not understood either.

On the day they called him 'Ubirajara', Quaresma said nothing, keeping himself to himself. He only decided to speak because, as they were washing their hands getting ready to leave, a colleague sighed: 'Oh God! Whenever will I get to Europe?' The major couldn't contain himself: looking up, straightening his pince-nez, he said amiably but forcefully: 'How ungrateful you are! With such a rich, beautiful country, you want to visit other people's! If ever I had the chance, I'd travel all over Brazil, from one end to the other!'

The man retorted that the country had nothing but mosquitoes and fever. The major contested this with statistics and even proved exultantly that the Amazon had one of the finest climates in the world, a climate maligned by weaklings who caught diseases there . . .

Such was Major Policarpo Quaresma, who had just arrived home, at a quarter past four in the afternoon, not a minute later, as he did every afternoon, except for Sundays, with the regularity of the appearance of a planet or an eclipse.

Otherwise he was a man like any other, except for those with ambitions for wealth or power, which Quaresma did not have in the slightest degree.

Sitting in the rocking chair in the very middle of the library, the major opened a book and started to read it while he waited for his guest. It was old Rocha Pita, the enthusiastic, effusive Rocha Pita of the *History of Portuguese America*.[20] Quaresma

was reading that famous passage: 'In no other region is the
sky so serene, nor the dawn so resplendent; in no other hemi-
sphere does the sun have such golden rays . . .' but was unable
to finish it. There was a knock at the door. He went to open it
himself.

'Am I late, major?' asked the visitor.

'No. You're just on time.'

Ricardo Coração dos Outros[21] had just entered Major
Quaresma's house, a man famous for his skill in singing *modinhas* and playing the guitar. At first his fame had been limited
to one small suburb of the city, at whose musical soirées he and
his guitar had played the part of Paganini and his fiddle at
ducal feasts; but gradually, as time went by, it spread to the
others, growing and establishing itself until it came to be seen
as an intrinsic part of the suburbs themselves. Do not think,
however, that Ricardo was just any old rogue, a run-of-the-mill
singer of *modinhas*. No, Ricardo Coração dos Outros was an
artist who frequented and honoured the finest households of
Méier, Piedade and Riachuelo.[22] There was hardly a single
night when he did not receive an invitation. Whether it was at
the home of Lieutenant Marques, of Doctor Bulhões or of Sr
Castro, his presence was always appreciated, and requested
insistently. In fact Doctor Bulhões had great admiration for
Ricardo, and when the troubadour sang he would go into
ecstasy. 'I love singing,' the doctor once declared on the train,
'but only two people measure up to my standards: Tamagno[23]
and Ricardo.' The doctor had a great reputation in the suburbs,
not as doctor – he never so much as wrote a prescription for
castor oil – but as an expert on telegraphic legislation, as he
was head of department at the Telegraph Office.

Thus Ricardo Coração dos Outros was held in general
esteem by suburban high society: a very *sui generis* high society,
that is, high only in the suburbs. It is mostly made up of civil
servants, small businessmen, doctors with limited experience
and lieutenants from the various militias, an elite that frequents
the potholed streets of these remote districts, as well as the parties and the dances, with greater pride than the bourgeoisie of
Petrópolis and Botafogo.[24] But this pride is put aside when one

of the suburban elite meets a person down on his luck. He looks him up and down, very slowly, as if to say: 'Pay me a visit and I'll give you a plate of food.' Because the pride of the suburban aristocracy is to have lunch and dinner every day: lots of beans, lots of dried meat, lots of stew – this, it considers, is the true hallmark of nobility, distinction and good breeding.

Away from the suburbs, at the opera, at the elegant gatherings in the Rua do Ouvidor,[25] these people wilt and fade away; they become invisible. Even the beauty of their wives and daughters pales; the same beauty that dazzles the handsome young men at the endless rounds of dances in the suburbs.

Ricardo, once the poet and the singer of this curious aristocracy, had outgrown the suburbs and was moving towards the city itself. His fame had already reached São Cristóvão,[26] and soon (he hoped) Botafogo would invite him, as the newspapers were already mentioning his name and discussing the impact of his work and his poetry . . .

But what had he come to do there, in the house of a person of such high purpose, of such austere habits? It is not hard to guess. He certainly had not come to help the major in his studies of Brazilian geology, poetry, mineralogy and history.

As the neighbours rightly guessed, Coração dos Outros had come there to teach the major to sing *modinhas* and to play the guitar. No more than that.

In accordance with his overriding passion, Quaresma had reflected for a long time on what the poetic musical expression of the national soul should be. He consulted historians, essayists and philosophers and became convinced that it was the *modinha* accompanied by the guitar. Assured of this truth, he did not delay: he set about learning this genuinely Brazilian instrument and the secrets of the *modinha*. In all this he was a complete beginner; so he inquired as to who was the greatest expert in the city and started lessons with him. His aim was to shape the *modinha* into a great new form of artistic expression.

Ricardo had indeed come to give him his lesson, but before this, at the special invitation of his pupil, he was to dine with him. That was why the famous troubadour had arrived early at the undersecretary's home.

'Can you play D sharp yet, major?' Ricardo asked as soon as he had sat down.

'Yes.'

'Let's see.'

With these words he started to remove his sacred guitar from its case. But Dona Adelaide, Quaresma's sister, came in to say that dinner was ready. The soup was getting cold; they should come!

'Excuse the simplicity of our dinner, Sr Ricardo,' the old lady[27] said. 'I wanted to make a chicken with petits-pois, but Policarpo wouldn't allow it. He said that these petits-pois are foreign and that I should use pigeon peas[28] instead. Whoever heard of chicken with pigeon peas?'

Coração dos Outros ventured that it might be good; it would be a novelty and there was no harm in experimenting.

'It's an obsession with your friend, Sr Ricardo, this business of only wanting Brazilian things. And the stuff we have to eat! Ugh!'

'You're just prejudiced, Adelaide! Our country, which has all the climates of the world, is capable of producing everything that the most demanding stomach requires. It is you who are being unreasonable.'

'For example: the butter that goes rancid . . .'

'Because it's made from milk. If it was like the foreign butter you see, made from fat from the sewers, perhaps it wouldn't go off! You see, Ricardo, they don't want anything that's Brazilian . . .'

'Most people don't,' Ricardo agreed.

'But they're wrong! They should protect Brazilian industry. That's what I do: if there's a national product, I don't use anything foreign. The clothes I wear are Brazilian, so are my boots, to give just two examples . . .'

They sat down at the table. Quaresma picked up a small cut-glass decanter and poured out two glasses of *cachaça*.[29]

'That's part of the national programme,' the sister said with a smile.

'Certainly, and it's a magnificent aperitif. Not like these awful vermouths. This is pure, good alcohol, made from sugar-cane, not from potatoes or maize . . .'

Ricardo picked up his glass with delicacy and respect, raising it to his lips, as if he were putting the whole of his heart into drinking the national liqueur.

'Good, eh?' the major said.

'Magnificent,' said Ricardo, smacking his lips.

'It's from Angra.[30] And now you'll see what magnificent wine we have from Rio Grande.[31] Burgundy – fiddlesticks! Bordeaux – fiddlesticks! We have far better wines in the south!'

And the dinner continued in this vein. Quaresma praising Brazilian products – the lard, the bacon, the rice – the sister making minor objections and Ricardo saying: 'Yes, yes, of course,' his small eyes rolling around as he frowned, his tiny forehead frowning as it disappeared beneath his wiry hair, making a tremendous effort to mould his small, harsh features into a genuine expression of courtesy and contentment.

When dinner was over they went to see the garden. It was wonderful: not a single flower . . . Certainly the forlorn rose-balsam and gladiola, the mournful lent bushes, the melancholic *manacás* and other fine specimens from our fields and countryside hardly merited such a description. As in everything else, in gardening the major was strictly Brazilian. Not a sign of roses, chrysanthemums, magnolias – exotic flowers! – our soil produced others, more beautiful, more striking, more sweetly scented, like the ones he had there.

Ricardo agreed yet again, and the two entered the living room as the dusk gradually fell, very slowly, unhurriedly, as if bidding a long farewell to the sun as it left the earth, covering everything with the sombre poetry of its dying light.

As soon as the gas was lit the maestro picked up his instrument, tightened the strings and tried out a scale, leaning over the guitar as if he were going to kiss it. He strummed a few chords, as a test, then he turned to his pupil, who already had his in position:

'Let's see. Play the scale, major.'

Quaresma flexed his fingers, tuned the guitar, but his playing of the scale lacked both the confidence and the elegance the master had displayed.

'Look, major, it's like this.'

And he showed him how to hold the instrument, resting in his lap, lightly secured by the right hand, with his left hand outstretched. Then he added: 'Major, the guitar is the instrument of passion. It speaks through the heart. We hold it against the chest, but gently, lovingly, as if it were the woman we love, our bride, so that it can express what we feel . . .'

When he talked about the guitar, Ricardo became eloquent, even dogmatic; he actually shook with emotion for the instrument that was treated with such disdain.

The lesson lasted for about fifty minutes. Then the major felt tired and asked the master to sing. It was the first time Quaresma had asked him, and, although he was flattered, his professional pride required him at first to refuse.

'Oh! I haven't got anything new – no new composition of mine.'

So Dona Adelaide suggested: 'Sing one by somebody else.'

'Heavens, no, madam! I only sing my own. Bilac[32] – do you know him? – wanted to write a *modinha* for me. I didn't accept. You don't understand the guitar, Sr Bilac. It's not a question of writing fine verses that say beautiful things; the essential thing is to find the words that the guitar is appealing for. For example, if I'd said, as I wanted to at first, in "The Foot" (a *modinha* of mine), "your foot is a leaf of clover", it wouldn't suit the guitar. Let me show you.'

And he sang in a low voice accompanied by the instrument: '*your-foot-is-a-leaf-of-clo-ver*'.

'You can see,' he went on, 'how it doesn't fit. Now listen: *your-foot-is-a-rose-of-myrrh*. It's far better, don't you think?'

'There's no doubt about it,' said Quaresma's sister.

'Sing that one,' the major requested.

'No,' said Ricardo. 'It's old. I'll sing "The Promise". Do you know it?'

'No,' both brother and sister replied.

'Oh! It's as popular as Raimundo's "Doves".'[33]

'Then sing it, please, Sr Ricardo,' Dona Adelaide said.

Ricardo Coração dos Outros finally tuned the guitar yet again and began in a soft voice:

> I promise by the Holy of Holies
> That I will be your love . . .

'You will see,' he said during a pause, 'so much imagery, so much imagery!'

And he continued. The windows were open. Young men and women began to crowd on to the pavement to listen to the minstrel. Aware of the interest from the street, Coração dos Outros began to sing out more clearly, assuming a fierce expression that he supposed was one of tenderness and enthusiasm. When he finished applause came from outside, and a girl entered, looking for Dona Adelaide.

'Sit down, Ismênia,' she said.

'I won't stay long.'

Ricardo sat up in his chair, looked at the girl for a moment and then continued to hold forth about the *modinha*. Taking advantage of a pause, Quaresma's sister asked the girl: 'So when are you to be married?'

It was the question they always asked her. She turned aside her sad little head, with its magnificent chestnut hair tinged with gold, and replied: 'I don't know . . . Cavalcânti graduates at the end of the year, so then we'll decide.'

She spoke the words slowly, with a remarkable lack of enthusiasm.

She was the daughter of Quaresma's neighbour, the general, and was not bad looking; in fact she was quite attractive, with her delicate, uneven features and good-natured air.

Her engagement had gone on for years. Her fiancé, Cavalcânti, was studying to be a dentist, a two-year course that he had dragged out for four, and Ismênia was forever answering the same old question: 'So when are you getting married?' – 'I don't know . . . Cavalcânti graduates at the end of the year and . . .'

In her heart she didn't mind. For her there was only one important thing in life: to get married. But she was not in a hurry; she had no reason to be. She had got herself a fiancé; the rest was a question of time.

After answering Dona Adelaide, she explained the reason for her visit.

She had come, at her father's request, to invite Ricardo Coração dos Outros to sing at her house.

'Father loves *modinhas*,' Dona Ismênia said. 'He's from the north. As you know, Dona Adelaide, folk from the north admire them greatly. Come with us.'

And so they went.

II

RADICAL REFORMS

It had been ten days since Major Quaresma had left the house. In the peace and quiet of his home in São Cristóvão he spent the days engaged in those pleasant and useful activities that so suited his temperament and inclinations. In the morning, when he had washed and breakfasted, he sat on the sofa in the living room and read the papers. He read a variety of these, always with the hope of finding some interesting piece of news that would inspire him with an idea that would help his beloved homeland. He lunched early, according to his civil service routine which, although he was on holiday, he continued to observe, taking his first meal of the day at half-past nine in the morning.[1]

After lunch he took a walk around the orchard, an orchard almost entirely predominated by Brazilian fruit trees, where the guavas and *pitangas* were treated with every possible care, as though they were cherries or figs.

The walk was leisurely and philosophical. Talking to Anastácio, the black man who had served him for thirty years, about things of the past – the marriage of the princesses,[2] the crash of Souto[3] and others – the major was unable to forget the questions that had recently been weighing on his mind. After an hour or so he went back to the library and pored over the magazines of the Historical Institute, the letters of Cardim[4] and Nóbrega,[5] the historical records of the National Library, von den Stein,[6] taking note after note, which he placed in a small folder beside him. He was studying the Indians, or, it would be more correct to say, he had been studying them for a long time: not only their language, in which he was almost fluent, but also ethnographical and anthropological aspects. He was recording (or rather, reaffirming) certain ideas from his previous studies, as he was planning a system of ceremonies and festivities that was based on the customs of Brazilian Indians and included all social dealings.

To understand the motive for this one must bear in mind that after thirty years the major's meditations, reflections and studies of his country were about to bear fruit. The conviction he had always had that Brazil was the leading country in the world, and his great love for his homeland, could no longer be suppressed and drove him to contemplate great undertakings. Inside he felt the overwhelming urge to act, to work for the implementation of his ideas. These were minor improvements, small adjustments, because in itself, in his opinion, the great fatherland of the Southern Cross needed nothing but time to be superior to England.

It had every climate, every fruit, every usable animal and mineral, the best arable land and the bravest, most hospitable, most intelligent and kindest people in the world – what more did it need? Time and a little originality. And thus in his mind he was no longer prey to doubts. He was certain that as far as the original traditions and customs were concerned, they had not disappeared, but rather been transformed. This was confirmed after he had taken part in the *Tangolomango*[7] at a party that the general had given at his house.

It so happened that the visit of Ricardo and his guitar to the general's house had awakened in that worthy soldier and his family a taste for the revelries and songs that many consider our genuinely Brazilian traditions. All of them wanted to relive the old popular customs, to give vent to their feelings, write verses . . . Albernaz, the general, remembered having seen such festivities when he was a child; Dona Maricota, his wife, even recalled some old verses about the Three Kings; and their children, five girls and a boy, seeing in this a pretext for parties, applauded their parents' enthusiasm. The *modinha* was not enough: their hearts desired the popular traditions, more authentic and reckless!

Quaresma was delighted when Albernaz said he was planning a festival, like the ones in the north, to celebrate the anniversary of his enlistment. That was how it was in the general's house. There was a party for every anniversary: at least thirty a year, in addition to Sundays, holidays and saint days, when there was dancing too.

Until then the major had thought very little about such things – traditional festivals and dances. However, he soon saw that the idea had great patriotic significance. He approved; he encouraged his neighbour. But who was to rehearse it, to produce the verses and the music? Someone remembered Maria Rita, an old black woman who lived in Benfica[8] and used to wash clothes for the Albernaz family. On a lovely, clear April afternoon, the two of them, General Albernaz and Major Quaresma, set off there, cheerfully and in a great hurry.

There was nothing soldierly about the general. He didn't even seem to have a uniform. Throughout the whole of his military career he hadn't seen a single battle, held a command or done anything related to his profession or his artillery training. He had always been an adjutant, an assistant in charge of this or that, a clerk, a stock-room supervisor. He was a secretary of the Supreme Military Council when he retired as a general. He behaved like a good head of department, and he thought very much as he behaved. He understood nothing about wars, about strategy, about tactics or about military history; his knowledge of these things was limited to the battles of the Paraguayan War, which for him was the greatest and most remarkable war of all time.

The exalted title of general, recalling the superhuman exploits of a Caesar, a Turenne[9] or a Gustavus Adolphus,[10] hardly suited that placid, kind-natured, run-of-the-mill man, whose only concern was to see his five daughters married and find someone with influence to ensure that his son would pass the Military College exams. It was not, however, advisable to doubt his military credentials. He himself, aware of his all too civilian appearance, would from time to time recount a military anecdote or his experience of war. 'It was at Lomas Valentinas,'[11] he would say . . . If anyone asked: 'Were you at the battle?' he would immediately answer: 'I couldn't be. I fell sick and returned to Brazil just before. But Camisão and Venâncio told me it was gruesome.'

The tramline that took them to old Maria Rita followed one of the most interesting routes in the city. It went through the Pedregulho,[12] an old port that was once the final stop of a route that led to Minas, branched off to São Paulo and provided access to the parish of Santa Cruz.

Along it, on the backs of mules, the gold and diamonds of Minas were brought to Rio, as were, in more recent times, our 'national products'.[13] It was less than a hundred years since the carriages of the king, Dom João VI,[14] like galleons, rocking on their widely spaced wheels, passed on their way to distant Santa Cruz. It can hardly have been an impressive sight: the king was slovenly and the court was short of money. Despite the soldiers with their ragged uniforms, ignominiously mounted on dispirited nags, the procession cannot have been devoid of all grandeur, not in itself but in the humiliating respects that all were obliged to pay to his pitiful majesty.

Everything with us is inconsistent, provisional; nothing lasts. There was nothing there that recalled the past. Even the old houses with their large, almost square windows and small panes of glass, were recent, less than fifty years old.

Quaresma and Albernaz travelled, without comment, along this route, as far as the final stop. Before arriving they glanced out at the racecourse district, a small part of the town full of stables and stud farms for breeding racehorses, where large horseshoes, horse heads, arrays of whips and other horse-racing emblems were displayed from gateposts, door panels and anywhere else where they might be decorative and could be clearly seen.

The old black woman's house was past the final stop, in the area surrounding the Leopoldina station. They set off in that direction. They walked past the station, past a wide plot, black with coal dust, filled with piles of wood and sacks of charcoal. Further on was a rail yard, where trains were being shunted along the tracks, groaning under their burden.

They finally came to the path where Maria Rita's house was located. As the weather had been dry, they were able to walk along it. Beyond lay the vast region of marshlands that stretches away, ugly and forlorn, to the far end of the bay, where the horizon fades into the foothills of the blue mountains of Petrópolis.

They arrived at the old woman's house. It was low, whitewashed and covered with heavy Portuguese tiles, set back a little from the road. On the right was a rubbish heap: kitchen scraps, rags, mussel shells, pieces of household china – a trove to rejoice the heart of some archaeologist in the distant future; on the left, a papaya tree, and on the same side, next to the fence, a bush of rue.[15] They knocked. A young black girl appeared at the open window.

'Can I help you?'

They came up and explained why they had come. The girl shouted into the house: 'Granny, there are two men who want to speak to you. Come in, be so kind,' she then said, turning to the general and his companion.

The room was small and had no ceiling. The walls were cluttered with a profusion of coloured prints from calendars, pictures of saints and illustrations from newspapers that clambered up towards the roof. Beside an Our Lady of the Peak there was a picture of Victor Emmanuel[16] with an enormous bushy moustache. A sentimental sketch from a calendar – the head of a dreaming woman – seemed to be looking at a St John the Baptist beside it. Above the door that led to the back of the house a gas lamp on a corner shelf had covered a china figure of Our Lady of the Conception in soot.

It was not long before the old woman arrived. She came in wearing a lace blouse that revealed her bony chest, adorned with a double string of beads. She limped with one foot and, in an apparent effort to aid her progress, placed her left hand on the corresponding leg.

'Good afternoon, Maria Rita,' the general said.

As she replied, she gave no sign that she had recognized who was speaking. The general came to her aid: 'Don't you know me any more? I'm the general, Colonel Albernaz.'

'Ah! It de colonel! It been so long! How Missus Maricota?'

'She's well. Maria Rita, we'd like you to teach us some songs.'

'What songs would *I* know, massa?'

'Lots of them! You never forget anything. You know "Bumba-meu-Boi",[17] don't you?'

'No, massa, I forget dat.'

'And "Boi Espácio"?'[18]

'Dat *old*, from de slavery time – what massa wanna know dat for?'

She spoke in a drawl, smiling meekly, with a blank expression in her eyes.

'It's for a party . . . Which song do you know?'

Her grandchild, who until then had listened in silence, decided to speak, briefly revealing a flash of immaculate, shining white teeth:

'Granny doesn't remember.'

The general, whom the old woman called colonel, as that was his rank when she'd known him, ignored the girl's remark and insisted: 'What do you mean, forgotten? You still remember some things, don't you, Maria?'

'I only know "De Bogeyman",' the old woman said.

'Then sing it!'

'But massa know it. He know it!'

'No I don't. Sing it. If I knew it I wouldn't have come here. Ask my friend, Major Policarpo, if I know it.'

Quaresma nodded his head in agreement, and the old black woman, perhaps nostalgic for the time when she was a slave and nanny at some great household where nothing ever lacked, raised her head to help her remember, and sang:

> De bogeyman come
> From behin' de hill,
> To eat liddle massa
> Wid a moutful o' meal.

'Really!' the general said testily. 'That's just an old song to rock children to sleep. Don't you know any others?'

'No massa. I forget dem.'

They both left disappointed. Quaresma felt disheartened. How could the people forget traditions of thirty years earlier? How could they forget their songs and their pastimes so quickly? What a sign of weakness, what a display of inferiority, compared to those resolute cultures that kept them alive for centuries! He must react: he must develop a cult of traditions, to keep them alive in the memories and customs of the people . . .

Albernaz was annoyed. He'd been sure he would find some good songs for the party he was going to give, but he hadn't. It was as if he were losing the chance of getting one of his four daughters married – four, as one was already catered for, thank God.

They reached home as twilight was falling, imbued with its melancholy mood.

But the disappointment lasted only a few days. Ismênia's fiancé, Cavalcânti, told them that there was a literary man in the neighbourhood who was a devoted admirer of Brazilian folklore and songs. They paid him a visit. He was an old poet who had been well known in the 1870s, a sweet, simple soul who had abandoned the life of a poet and now dedicated his time to publishing collections of stories, songs, maxims and popular sayings that nobody read.

He was delighted when he learned of the purpose of their visit. Quaresma was encouraged and spoke with enthusiasm. And Albernaz too, as he saw folklore songs at his party as a means of attracting attention, and people, to his home – and thus of marrying his daughters.

The room where they were received was large, but it was so full of tables and shelves, weighed down with books, folders and tin boxes, that one could scarcely move. One of the boxes was labelled 'Santa Ana dos Tocos', and one of the folders 'São Bonifácio do Cabresto'.[19]

'You have no idea,' the old poet said, 'how rich our popular poetry is. What surprises it has in store! Just a few days ago I received a letter from Urubu-de-Baixo[20] with a beautiful song. Would you like to hear it?'

After rummaging around in the folders, he finally produced a paper, from which he read:

> If God ever noticed the poor,
> He wouldn't ignore my plea,
> He'd find within her heart
> A little place for me.

My feelings for her are such,
I cannot contain my love;
It escapes from me through the eyes
And flies to the clouds above.

'It's beautiful, isn't it? . . . Very! If only you gentlemen knew the monkey stories, the collection of stories about monkeys that the people tell. Oh! It's an epic. A truly comic epic!'

Quaresma gazed at the old poet with astonishment and contentment, like someone who meets a fellow traveller in the desert. And even Albernaz, momentarily infected by the old man's enthusiasm, looked at him with greater interest.

The old poet placed the song from Urubu-de-Baixo in a folder; then he picked up another, from which he took several sheets of paper. Rejoining the others, he said: 'I am going to read you a little story about the monkey, one of many our people tell. I've already collected almost forty and I'm planning to publish them under the title of *Stories of Master Monkey*.'

Without asking whether they minded, or whether they wanted to hear it, he began: '*The Monkey and the Judge*. A band of screeching monkeys was jumping from tree to tree near the edge of a cave, when down at the bottom one of them saw a puma that had fallen in. The monkeys felt sorry for the animal and decided to rescue it. So they tore down some hanging vines and tied them into a rope, which they wound around each of their waists, and threw the far end down to the puma. With their combined strength they managed to haul it up. Then they untied themselves and fled. But one of them wasn't fast enough, and the puma grabbed him.

' "Monkey, my friend," he said, "what can I do? I'm hungry. Be kind enough to let me eat you."

'The monkey pleaded, insisted, wept. But the puma was obdurate. The monkey suggested that the question be put to the judge. So, without the puma letting go of the monkey, they went to the judge. In the animal world the judge is the turtle, who holds court on the river bank, sitting on top of a stone. The two arrived, and the monkey stated his case.

'The turtle listened and then instructed: "Clap your hands."

'Although the puma was holding on to him, the monkey still managed to clap his hands. Then came the puma's turn, who also stated his case. As before, the judge instructed the animal: "Clap your hands."

'The puma had no choice; he had to let go of the monkey, who made his escape; as did the judge, who threw himself into the water.'

When he finished reading the old man turned to the two.

'It's interesting, isn't it? Very! Our people are very inventive, very creative, wonderful material for interesting *fabliaux*[21] ... The day a genius appears who turns it into a great work of literature ... Ah! That will be the day!'

As he said this, beaming with satisfaction, two furtive tears appeared in his eyes.

'Now,' he continued, once the emotion had passed; 'let's see what we can use. The "Boi Espácio" or the "Bumba-meu-Boi" are too hard for you as yet. Let's take it slowly: begin with something easier ... Do you know the *Tangolomango*?'

'No,' they both said.

'It's fun. Get ten children, a mask of an old man's face, an exotic costume for one of the men, and I'll rehearse it for you.'

The day arrived. The general's house was full. Cavalcânti had come, and he and his fiancée, alone in one of the windows, seemed to be the only ones who weren't interested in the fun. He, talking a lot, eyes darting from side to side; she, rather reserved, glancing at him from time to time with a look of gratitude.

Quaresma played *Tangolomango*; he put on an old overcoat of the general's and a huge mask of an old man's face and entered the room grasping a walking stick in the shape of a shepherd's crook. The ten children sang in chorus:

> A mother had ten children,
> She kept them all in a pot:
> But the *Tangolomango* came,
> And then there were only nine.

At this the major came forward, banging his stick on the ground and saying: 'Oooh! Oooh! Oooh!' As the children fled he seized

one and took it back inside. So he went on, to the great delight
of the guests. But in the fifth verse he felt breathless, his eyes
clouded over, and he collapsed. But when they removed the
mask and shook him a little Quaresma came to.

The accident did nothing to diminish his love of folklore. He
bought books, read all the publications on the subject; but a
disappointment awaited him after a few weeks of study.

Almost all the traditions and songs were foreign – even the
Tangolomango! He realized that he must find something original, genuine, something that was a creation of Brazilian
customs and culture.

This idea led him to study the customs of the Tupinambás.[22]
And as one idea leads to another, he soon extended his research,
and that is the reason why he was compiling a list of relationships, greetings, domestic ceremonies and festivities based
upon Tupi tradition.

After ten days of devotion to this arduous task, one Sunday
his work was interrupted by a knock at the door. He opened it,
but instead of shaking the visitors' hands he burst into tears,
yelling and pulling his hair out, as if he'd just lost a wife or a
son. His sister rushed up, followed by Anastácio, and his goddaughter and her father – for they were the visitors – stood
stupefied on the threshold.

'What's happened, my old friend?'

'What is it, Policarpo?'

'Godfather, what . . .'

He continued to weep for a while. Then he dried his tears
and explained, as though his behaviour were perfectly normal:

'You see! You don't have the slightest idea of our national
customs. You wanted me to shake hands. That's not Brazilian!
Our national greeting is to weep when we meet our friends.
That's what the Tupinambás used to do.'

Vicente, his old friend, Vicente's daughter and Dona Adelaide glanced at each other; they didn't know what to say. Had
he gone mad? What eccentric behaviour!

'But Sr Policarpo,' his friend protested; 'it may be very Brazilian, but it's very depressing.'

'Indeed, Godfather,' the girl insisted, 'it's like a bad omen . . .'

His old friend was Italian by birth. The story of their friendship should be told. Some twenty years earlier he had been a greengrocer who sold from door to door and supplied Quaresma's house. Quaresma already had his patriotic ideas but nevertheless he would talk to the greengrocer, and even took pleasure in seeing him, sweaty, bowed down under the weight of his baskets, his pale European cheeks flushed and red. But one day, when Quaresma was crossing the Largo do Paço, distracted, reflecting on the architectural wonders of Master Valentim's fountain,[23] he happened to bump into the man. Speaking to him with his characteristic frankness, he saw that the fellow was seriously upset. Not only did he let out exclamations with no connection to the conversation, but his lips were tense, and he was grinding his teeth and clenching his fists in fury. On questioning him, he discovered that he had had an argument about money with a colleague and was ready to murder him, as he had lost his credit and would soon be reduced to utter poverty. He declared this so vehemently and with such unusual ferocity that it took all the major's kind nature and powers of persuasion to dissuade him from his plan. And he did not stop there: he also lent him money. Vicente Coleoni opened a greengrocer's shop, made a bit of money and soon became a businessman. He became rich, got married and had the daughter who was baptized by his benefactor. It hardly need be said that Quaresma was unaware of any contradiction between his patriotic ideas and what he had done.

It is true that these ideas were not yet established, but they were already taking form in his mind: the vague desires that, since the age of twenty, had filtered into his consciousness and before long would take shape, needing only time before they would manifest themselves as deeds.

It was this friend Vicente and his goddaughter Olga whom he had received with the most authentic Tupinambá greeting. And if he wasn't wearing the costume required by that interesting people, it was not because he did not possess one, but because he hadn't had time to change.

'Are you reading a lot, Godfather?' his goddaughter asked, gazing at him with her bright, shining eyes.

The two were very attached to each other. Quaresma was rather reserved; the embarrassment he felt at showing his feelings did not permit great demonstrations of affection. But it was clear that the girl occupied the place in his heart of the children he'd never had, and would never have. She was a lively girl, used to speaking her mind, who did not hide her affection for him, the more so as she was vaguely aware that there was something special about him: the search for an ideal, the tenacity in pursuing a dream, the quest, in short, of a man who aspired to the highest regions of the spirit, unlike anyone else she had met. This admiration did not stem from her schooling. She had had the standard education of girls of her class. It was a natural inclination, perhaps due to European influence, which made her a little different from our Brazilian girls.

It was with a bright, searching look that she had asked the question:

'Well, Godfather, are you reading a lot?'

'A lot, my child. You know I am planning great things: reform, the emancipation of a people.'

Vicente had gone into the house with Dona Adelaide, and they were talking in the library. The girl noticed there was something different about Quaresma. He was talking with so much self-assurance, he who had always been so reserved, who used to falter as he spoke. Good heavens! Could it be possible? Perhaps it could . . . And that glint of triumph in his eyes – the triumph of a mathematician who has solved a problem, or a scientist with a new invention!

'You're not going to get involved in some sort of conspiracy, are you?' the girl said laughingly.

'You don't need to be afraid about that. It will happen naturally; violence won't be needed . . .'

At that point Ricardo Coração dos Outros arrived in his long-tailed serge morning coat with his guitar wrapped in its leather case. The major introduced them.

'I already know you by name, Sr Ricardo,' Olga said.

Coração dos Outros was overcome with a feeling of absolute contentment. His shrunken features expanded, his eyes gleamed with satisfaction. His dried-out skin, usually as pale as old marble, now glowed with the softness of youth. That girl, so wealthy, so refined, so beautiful, actually knew him. How splendid! He was always clumsy and tongue-tied in the presence of girls, whatever their social standing, but now he took courage and started to talk; he became eloquent and loquacious: 'Then you must have read my verses, ma'am?'

'I haven't had that pleasure, but some time ago I read an article praising one of your works.'

'Was it the one in the *Tempo*?'

'Yes it was.'

'Very unfair!' Ricardo protested. 'All the critics insist on this question of metre. They say that my verses aren't verses . . . But they are: only they're verses for the guitar. I'm sure you know that verses for music are different from ordinary ones. So there is nothing to be surprised about if my verses, which are written for the guitar, have a different metre, use a different system. Don't you agree?'

'Of course,' said the girl. 'But it seems to me that you write verses for the music and not music for the verses.'

And she smiled slowly, enigmatically, staring at him unblinkingly, while he, suspicious, tried to fathom her meaning with his sharp little mousey eyes.

Quaresma, who until then had remained silent, broke in: 'Ricardo is an artist, Olga. He makes great efforts to achieve respect for the guitar.'

'I know, Godfather, I know . . .'

'Between us, ma'am,' said Coração dos Outros, 'in Brazil my efforts are not taken seriously, but in Europe the guitar is respected. Everyone supports it . . . Major, what's the name of that poet who wrote in everyday French?'

'Mistral,'[24] replied Quaresma, 'but it's not everyday French, it's Provençal, a separate language.'

'Yes, of course,' Ricardo agreed. 'But isn't Mistral highly thought of and respected? I am doing what he is doing, but with the guitar.'

He looked triumphantly from one to the other, and Olga, looking straight at him, said:

'Continue with your work, Sr Ricardo; it has great merit.'

'Thank you. You may be certain, ma'am, that the guitar is a fine instrument and is very difficult to play. For example . . .'

'Nonsense!' Quaresma abruptly intervened. 'There are others that are much harder.'

'The piano?' Ricardo asked.

'The piano! I mean the *maracá*, the *inúbia*.'[25]

'I don't know them.'

'You don't know them? That's a good one! Our very own instruments, the only ones that are truly Brazilian. The instruments of our ancestors, that valiant race that fought, and still fights, for the control of this beautiful land. The Indians!'

'An Indian instrument? You're not serious!' retorted Ricardo.

'Yes, Indian! What's wrong with that? Léry[26] says that they have a very melodious, harmonious sound . . . If they're worthless because they're Indian instruments, then the guitar is worthless too – it's a vagabond's instrument.'

'Vagabond, major! How can you say that?'

And the pair continued their heated argument, in front of the frightened, startled girl, who could find no explanation for the sudden change that had come over her godfather, until then so calm and tranquil.

III

GENELÍCIO'S NEWS

'So when are you to be married, Dona Ismênia?'

'In March. Cavalcânti has graduated and . . .'

At last the general's daughter had an answer for the question they'd been asking her for almost five years. Her fiancé had finally completed his dentist's course and had fixed the date for the wedding in three months' time. The family was delighted, and, as in such a situation a celebration was called for, a ball was announced for the Saturday after the groom-to-be had made the formal request.

Her sisters, Quinota, Zizi, Lalá and Vivi, were more pleased than the bride. They thought that she was now leaving them free to find husbands, as if it had been their sister that had prevented them from doing so until now.

After being engaged for five years, Ismênia already felt almost married. This, added to her lack of imagination, prevented her from feeling much happiness. Nothing had changed. For her there was no passion in getting married, no feelings, no sensuality: it was an idea, just an idea. To her simple way of thinking there was no connection between marriage and love, the pleasures of the senses, the gaining of freedom, being a mother, or even the bridegroom. Since childhood she had heard her mother say: 'Learn to do such-and-such, because when you're married . . .' or 'You must learn how to stitch buttons, because when you're married . . .'

Not a moment, not a day went by without this 'because when you're married . . .', and the girl gradually became convinced that the only aim of existence was marriage. There was no point in education, private joys and pleasures. Life came down to a single thing: getting married.

And it was not as if this concern were restricted to her family alone. At school, in the street, in the houses of friends, the only topic of conversation was marriage: 'You know, Dona Maricota, Lili got married. She hasn't done very well for herself, the husband's not up to much,' or else: 'Zezé's desperate to find a husband, but heavens, how plain she is!'

Life, the world, the intense variety of feelings, of ideas, the right to happiness itself, became more and more insignificant to that little mind of hers, and the idea of getting married assumed such importance that it came to represent a kind of duty, whereas not getting married, remaining single, an 'old maid', would be a crime, a disgrace.

Dull-spirited as she was, incapable of feeling anything profoundly or intensely, without the emotional capacity for passion or great love, the idea of 'getting married' had stubbornly embedded itself in her mind; it had become an obsession.

She was not ugly, with her olive-coloured skin, delicate features and nose that, though imperfect, was assertive. She was neither too short nor too thin. Her docile, innocent appearance, the apathy of her gestures and the sentiments she expressed made her the type of girl whom the lads would call 'cute'. The most beautiful thing about her, however, was her hair: luxurious chestnut hair, tinged with gold, silky even to the eye.

At nineteen she began her courtship with Cavalcânti. Given her lack of independence and her fear of not finding a husband, it was hardly surprising that she made such an easy conquest for the future dentist.

Her father disapproved. He kept abreast of his daughters' courtships. 'Always tell me who they are, Maricota,' he used to say. 'Keep an eye out! Better safe than sorry; he may be a scallywag!' When he found out that Ismênia's fiancé was a dentist, he was none too pleased. What's a dentist? he asked himself. Someone who was semi-illiterate, a sort of barber. He would have preferred an officer with an army salary and pension, but his wife convinced him that dentists earned well, and he gave his consent.

So Cavalcânti began to frequent the house. It was understood that he was the fiancé, although he hadn't proposed; it was not 'official' yet.

At the end of the first year, hearing that his future son-in-law was struggling to complete his studies, the general came generously to his aid. He paid for his enrolment fees and books, among other things. It was not unusual, after a long talk with her daughter, for Dona Maricota to come to her husband and say: 'Chico, let me have twenty thousand *réis*[1] for Cavalcânti to buy an anatomy book.'

The general was a good, loyal and generous man. Apart from his military posturing there was not a single flaw in his character. And the requirement of seeing his daughters married had made him even more attentive to their interests.

He would listen to his wife, scratch his head and give her the money. To save his future son-in-law expense he even invited him to dine with them every day. And so the courtship continued . . .

'At last!' he said to his wife when they had retired to their room the night Cavalcânti proposed. 'At last it's over!'

'Thank goodness,' she replied. 'That's one settled.'

The general's resigned satisfaction was merely a pose; he was in fact delighted. Whenever he met a friend in the street he would take the first opportunity to say: 'What a nightmare! On top of everything, Castro, I have a daughter's wedding to arrange!'

To which Castro replied: 'Which one?'

'Ismênia, the second one,' Albernaz answered, adding: 'You're the lucky one. You only have sons.'

'Ah, my friend,' the other said mischievously. 'I learned the recipe. Why didn't you do the same?'

After taking his leave, the old general rushed off to the stores: to the china shops to buy more dishes, fruit bowls, a centrepiece for the table . . . The party must be impressive, must display the abundance and wealth that reflected his great satisfaction.

On the day of the party to celebrate the engagement, Dona Maricota was singing as she got out of bed. It was unusual, but on especially happy occasions she would hum an old aria from her girlhood days, and her daughters, seeing what a good mood she was in, would run up to her and ask her for things.

Always active, always diligent, there was no housewife who was more economical, who made her husband's money go further or the work of servants yield more. As soon as she was up and about, she set the servants and her daughters to work. Vivi and Quinota were sent to make the desserts, Lalá and Zizi to help the maids cleaning the rooms, while she and Ismênia arranged the table, with a great show of luxury and taste, to be admired in all its elegance throughout the day.

Dona Maricota was extremely happy. She could not understand how a woman could live without being married. It wasn't only the dangers to which she was exposed, the lack of support; it seemed disreputable, a disgrace to the family. Her contentment did not stem only from having 'got one settled', as she would say. It stemmed from something deeper: her sense of motherhood and family.

The mother was agitated and cheerful as she set the table; the daughter reserved and distant.

'Child!' she said. 'Anyone would think you weren't getting married! What a face. You look like a dead fly!'

'What do you want me to do, then?'

'Well, it doesn't look good to laugh too much, or to be too chatty, like a flirt, but that expression on your face! You're a bride!'

For some time the girl made a great effort to look more cheerful, but her lack of imagination, her incapacity for any real feelings, meant she soon sank back into that state of unwholesome apathy that was so characteristic of her.

A lot of people came. As well as the girls and their respective mothers, Rear Admiral Caldas, Doctor Florêncio (the water engineer), the honorary Major Inocêncio Bustamante, Sr Bastos, a bookkeeper and relation of Dona Maricota, and other important people came at the general's invitation. Ricardo had not been invited, because the general was afraid of what people would think about his presence at a social event. Quaresma had been but had not come. Earlier Cavalcânti had dined with his in-laws to be.

At six o'clock the house was already full. The girls surrounded Ismênia, congratulating her, their glances not entirely devoid of a touch of envy.

Irene, a tall, fair-haired girl, advised:

'If I were you I'd buy everything at the Parque.'[2]

They discussed the wedding dress. Although single, they all had advice: the cheapest shops, the most important items, those that could be dispensed with – they knew everything about it.

Armanda suggested, with a malicious glint in her eyes:

'Yesterday I saw a double bed in the Rua da Constituição – ever so pretty! Why don't you go and see it, Ismênia? It wasn't expensive.'

Ismênia was the least enthusiastic. She hardly answered the questions and, if she did, she answered in monosyllables. There was a moment when she smiled, almost without inhibition. Estefânia, the schoolteacher, with a ring on her finger that had enough stones to fill a jewellery store, suddenly put her sensual lips to the bride's ear and whispered something secret. When she had finished whispering, as though she wanted them all to know, she opened her eyes wide and said loudly, with a lively, mischievous look:

'Just wait and see! They *all* deny it. They *all* deny it!'

She was referring to Ismênia's terse reply to her whispered confidences: '*Not on your life!*'

While they talked they all kept their eyes fixed on the piano. The boys and some of the men were standing next to Cavalcânti, who looked very grave in a large black tailcoat.

'So you have graduated, sir?' said one of them, as a way of introducing himself.

'Yes indeed! I studied hard. You gentlemen have no idea of the obstacles, the hardships – it requires real heroism!'

'Do you know Chavantes?' asked another.

'Yes I do. An inveterate reveller . . .'

'Was he in your class?'

'Yes he was, he was on the medical course. We joined the same year . . .'

But before he had had time to answer the first question, another guest interrupted: 'It's a wonderful thing, to graduate.

If I'd listened to my father I wouldn't be pouring over accounts books every day. But there's no good crying over spilt milk.'

'Nowadays it doesn't mean a thing, dear sir,' Cavalcânti said self-effacingly. 'With these private academies . . . There's already talk about a private Academy of Dentistry! It's the limit! A course that is difficult and expensive, that requires corpses, equipment, good teachers, how can it be private? The government can hardly cope . . .'

'Well, sir,' another put in, 'let me congratulate you. As I said to my nephew when he graduated: "Now carve your career!"'

'So your nephew has graduated?' Cavalcânti inquired politely.

'In engineering. He's in Maranhão, with the Caxias road.'

'A fine career.'

During the pauses in the conversation they all looked at the newly graduated dentist as though he were some sort of supernatural being.

For those people Cavalcânti was no longer merely a man, he was a man with something different, something sacred, something superior in essence. It wasn't what he might know, what he might have learned, that changed the way they saw him. It was not that at all. For many his appearance continued to be ordinary, commonplace. It was the substance that had changed, that was different from theirs, that had somehow been elevated above its earthly nature, into something semi-divine.

The people who approached Cavalcânti in the living room were of lesser importance. The general, who had stayed in the dining room, smoking, was surrounded by the older guests and those of higher rank. Rear Admiral Caldas, Major Inocêncio, Florêncio the doctor and Captain Sigismundo of the Fire Brigade were with him.

Inocêncio took advantage of the occasion to consult Caldas on a question of military law. The rear admiral was a very interesting man. In the navy he had come dangerously close to being as inactive as Albernaz had been in the army. He had never boarded a warship, except during the Paraguayan War, and even then only for a very short time. The fault was not his, however. After becoming first lieutenant he had begun to isolate himself, abandoning his circle of comrades, so that, without exerting himself and with no friends in high positions, he was forgotten about and received no commissions to embark. Military administration is a curious thing: commissions are granted on merit, but only to protégés.

Once, when he was already a lieutenant-commander, he was given a ship in Mato Grosso. He was appointed commander of the battleship *Lima Barros*. He set off, but when he reported to the commander of the flotilla he was told that no such ship existed on the Paraguay River. He asked around, and someone ventured the opinion that the *Lima Barros* could be part of the squadron on the Upper Uruguay River. He asked the commander.

'If I were you,' his superior said, 'I'd leave for the Rio Grande flotilla at once.'

So he packed his bags for the Upper Uruguay, where he finally arrived after an arduous, exhausting journey. But the *Lima Barros* wasn't there either. So where could it be? He wanted to telegraph to Rio de Janeiro but was afraid of being reprimanded, all the more as his reputation was hardly outstanding. So he spent a month in Itaqui, hesitating, without receiving his salary or knowing what to do. One day he had the idea that the ship could be on the Amazon. He boarded a ship for the north of the country, stopping in Rio, as was required, to report to the senior naval authorities. He was arrested and brought before the naval tribunal.

The *Lima Barros* had been sunk during the Paraguayan War.

He was acquitted but he lost favour with the ministers and their generals for good. He was seen as a dimwit, a commander out of an opera buffa searching for his ship across the face of the earth. They left him to his own resources, and it took him almost forty years to rise from midshipman to frigate commander. When he was retired – as a commander, advanced one rank in remuneration – he concentrated all his bitterness towards the navy into a tireless routine of studying the laws, decrees, permits, dispatches and resolutions referring to the promotion of officers. He bought catalogues of laws, compiled compendiums of legislation, of reports, and filled his house with all this laborious, tedious, administrative literature. The navy ministers were inundated with petitions for a reassessment of his pension. After months doing the endless rounds of the government departments they were always refused at the recommendation of the Supreme Military Court or the Naval Tribunal. He had recently hired a federal court barrister and spent his time going from one public notary to another, mixing with bailiffs, clerks, lawyers and magistrates – that ill-tempered rabble of the law courts that seems to have contracted all the woes of the world it inhabits.

Inocêncio Bustamante had the same fixation on lawsuits. While recalcitrant and stubborn, he was also submissive and servile. He had volunteered for the war and received the honorary rank of major. Not a day passed that he didn't go to Army Headquarters to check the progress of his petitions, and those of others. In one he requested a place in the Home for the Disabled; in another, recognition as lieutenant colonel; in another, some medal or other; and when there was no petition of his own he went to check on other people's.

He even espoused the cause of a maniac who petitioned for promotion to the rank of major, because he was an honorary lieutenant and also a member of the National Guard: as two stripes plus two stripes made four, the result was – a major.

Knowing about the admiral's meticulous studies, Bustamante put his question.

'I can't say offhand,' Caldas replied. 'The army isn't my speciality, but I'll find out. That's all in a mess as well!'

And he scratched one of the white sideburns that gave him the look of a naval inspector, or a Portuguese farmer; his Portuguese traits were very pronounced.

'But in my day!' Albernaz put in. 'What order! What discipline!'

'There's no one of any use any more,' said Bustamante.

Sigismundo then ventured his opinion:

'I'm not a soldier, but . . .'

'Not a soldier?'[3] Albernaz said heatedly. 'You gentlemen are the real soldiers, always confronting the enemy. Isn't that so, Caldas?'

'Of course, of course,' the admiral answered, stroking his sideburns.

'As I was saying,' Sigismundo continued, 'although I'm not a soldier, I do think that our armed forces are in a very bad way. Where are men like Porto Alegre[4] or Caxias?'[5]

'They no longer exist, my friend,' Doctor Florêncio murmured.

'I don't know why – isn't everything based on science nowadays?'[6]

This attempt at irony had come from Caldas. Albernaz was indignant and retorted hotly:

'I'd like to see these boys in their suits, with their mathematical formulas, at Curupaiti![7] Eh, Caldas? Eh, Inocêncio?'

Doctor Florêncio was the only civilian in the group. He was an engineer and civil servant, and time and a quiet life had made him forget everything he had learned at school. He was more an inspector of water pipes than an engineer. He lived near to Albernaz and came almost every afternoon to play solo with the general. He now asked: 'You were there, weren't you, general?'

The general answered at once; without hesitating or getting confused he said with absolute frankness: 'I wasn't there. I fell ill and returned to Brazil before it began. But I had many friends there: Camisão, Venâncio . . .'

They all fell silent and looked out at the dusk. From the window the mountains could no longer be seen. The horizon had closed in along the backs of the yards of the neighbouring houses, with their washing lines, chimneys and squawking chicks. A leafless tamarind tree was a sad reminder of the breezes and wide-open vistas. The sun had already sunk beneath the horizon, and the flicker of gas lights and household lanterns began to appear behind the panes.

Bustamante broke the silence:

'This country has gone to the dogs. Do you know that my petition for promotion to lieutenant colonel has been in the ministry for six months?'

'A disgrace!' they all exclaimed.

Night had fallen. Dona Maricota came bustling in, beaming with content.

'What are you all doing – praying?' And then: 'Excuse me, I need a word with Chico.'

Albernaz left the circle of friends and went into a corner of the room, where his wife whispered something to him. He listened, then returned to his friends, saying in a loud voice as he went:

'If they aren't dancing it's because they don't want to. Am I stopping anyone?'

Dona Maricota went back to her husband's friends and explained:

'You understand gentlemen. If we don't encourage them, no one takes a partner, no one plays. There are so many girls, so many boys. It's such a pity!'

'All right, I'll go,' said Albernaz.

He left his friends and went into the living room to start the ball.

'Come on, girls. What're you all doing? Zizi, a waltz!'

And he went round in person, pairing them off. 'No, general, I already have a partner,' said a girl. 'It doesn't matter,' he retorted. 'Dance with Raimundo. The other can wait.'

After starting off the ball, he returned to the group of friends, sweating, but contented.

'Having a family – anyone would think one was mad!' he said. 'You did well, Caldas: you never married.'

'But I have more children than you. I have eight nephews to support, not to mention innumerable cousins.'

Albernaz invited them to play solo.

'But there are five of us,' Florêncio remarked.

'But I don't play,' said Bustamante.

'So the four of us will play, and we'll take it in turn to deal,' said Albernaz.

The cards were produced, and a small three-legged table was brought. The partners sat down and cut to see who would deal. It was Florêncio. The game began. Albernaz had a determined look as he played: his head fell back and his eyes assumed an expression of deep concentration. Caldas sat very straight in his chair and played serenely, like a lord high admiral at whist. Sigismundo played very cautiously with a cigarette in the corner of his mouth, his head inclined to one side to avoid the smoke. Bustamante had gone to the living room to watch the dancing.

They had started to play when Quinota, one of the general's daughters, came across the room to take a drink of water. Caldas, stroking one of his sideburns, asked her:

'Tell me Dona Quinota, where's Genelício?'

The girl turned around proudly and with a click of her tongue said with affected ill-temper:

'How would I know? I don't follow him around!'

Caldas reprimanded her: 'There's no call to be cross, Dona Quinota. It's just a question.'

The general, who was examining his hand attentively, interrupted the conversation and in a grave voice said:

'I pass.'

Quinota left the room. Genelício was her fiancé. He was a relative of Caldas, and their marriage was thought to be certain by the family. Everyone favoured the match. Dona Maricota and her husband were constantly giving him parties. An employee of the Treasury, this young man, not yet thirty, at the outset of his career, held out great promise for the future. There was no one as servile, no greater sycophant than he. No sense of propriety, no sense of shame. He plied his bosses and superiors with every possible attention. He would linger around before leaving, washing his hands three or four times, so as to catch the director at the door. He then accompanied him, if he were going home, to the tram, discussing work with him, offering advice and opinions, criticizing some colleague or other. Whenever a minister came he would get himself appointed as spokesman and make a speech, which on birthdays always took the form of a sonnet that began 'Hail!' and ended 'Hail, thrice Hail!'

The words were always the same, he just changed the minister's name and the date.

The following day the newspapers published the sonnet and printed his name.

He had been promoted twice in four years. He was now working to be transferred to the Audit Office, into a higher post that was about to be created.

At flattery and working his way up, he was truly a genius. He didn't restrict himself to sonnets and speeches, he had other means and stratagems. One of these was articles in the daily papers. With the aim of impressing directors and ministers with his erudition, from time to time lengthy treatises on public accountancy would appear in the press. They were merely collections of antiquated decrees, sprinkled here and there with quotations from French or Portuguese authors.

The curious thing is that his companions respected him and had a high regard for his knowledge. In his department he was treated with the respect that was due to a genius – a genius for paperwork and for providing information. As well as his safe administrative post Genelício had a partially completed law degree, and so many qualifications could hardly fail to favourably impress the Albernazes, with their pressing matrimonial concerns.

Outside the department his manner was haughty, which appeared comical in one of such weak physique, but he sustained it by his conviction about the great importance of the services he rendered to the state. A model civil servant!

The game continued in silence; the evening wore on. At the end of each round there were a few brief comments, but at the beginning the only words heard were those required by the game: 'solo', 'kitty', 'double', 'pass'. After that they played in silence, while from the living room came the festive sound of dancing and talking.

'Look who's here!'

'Genelício!' said Caldas. 'Where have you been, my boy?'

He put his hat and walking stick down on a chair and greeted them. Small, already slightly bent over, thin-faced with a blue-tinged pince-nez, everything about him betrayed his profession, his tastes and habits: he was a clerk.

'I was just taking care of some business.'

'Is it going well?' asked Florêncio.

'Almost guaranteed. The minister promised . . . There'll be no problem. I'm well in.'

'I'm very glad,' the general said.

'Thank you. Do you know something, general?'

'What?'

'Quaresma's gone mad.'

'*What?* Who told you?'

'That guitar player. He's been taken to the asylum . . .'

'I saw at once,' said Albernaz, 'that that petition was from a madman.'

'But that's not all, general,' Genelício went on. 'He wrote a registered letter in Tupi and sent it to the minister.'

'That's what I meant,' said Albernaz.

'Who is he?' Florêncio asked.

'That neighbour, the one who works at the Arsenal.[8] Don't you know him?'

'A short fellow with a pince-nez?'

'That's him,' said Caldas.

'One could hardly expect anything else,' Doctor Florêncio put in. 'Those books, that fixation with reading . . .'

'Why did he read so much?' asked Caldas.

'A screw loose,' said Florêncio.

Genelício intervened sententiously: 'He didn't have a degree. Why get involved with books?'

'You're right,' Florêncio replied.

'Reading books is for scholars, for the wise,' Sigismundo observed.

'It should be forbidden for people without a degree to have books,' Genelício said. 'In that way these disasters would be avoided. Don't you agree?'

'Of course,' said Albernaz.

'Of course,' said Caldas.

'Of course,' added Sigismundo.

They were silent for a moment. Then their attention returned to the game.

'Are all the trumps out?'

'You should have counted, my friend.'

Albernaz lost. Silence fell in the living room. Cavalcânti was going to recite. He walked proudly across the room with a broad smile on his face and took up his position beside the piano. Zizi accompanied him. He coughed, and in a tinny voice, enunciating the final letters with great precision, he began:

> Life is a comedy without meaning,
> A story of blood and of dust,
> A darkling desert . . .

And the piano moaned.

DISASTROUS
CONSEQUENCES
OF A PETITION

The events referred to by the grave personages gathered around the solo table on the memorable evening of the party to commemorate Ismênia's engagement to be married had occurred with breathtaking speed. The strength of the ideas and feelings that had welled up inside Quaresma was revealed by a sequence of sudden, unexpected actions that had the force of a whirlwind. His first step, which provoked surprise, was followed by others and yet others, so that what at first appeared merely eccentric was soon shown to be outright insanity.

A few weeks before the announcement of the engagement, at the opening of the session of Congress, the secretary was obliged to read out an extraordinary petition, one that was to attract a profusion of comments and publicity that were most unusual for a document of its kind.

The uproar and mayhem that characterize the debates indispensable to the exalted task of legislating prevented the deputies from hearing it. The journalists, however, who were near to the table, burst into raucous laughter when they heard it, most inappropriate to the dignity of the setting. Laughter is contagious: by the middle of the reading the secretary was laughing quietly; by the end the president was laughing, the notary was laughing, the clerk was laughing – the entire table and everyone around it were in stitches at the petition, some with tears rolling down their cheeks, however hard they tried to stop.

Anyone who knew how much effort, hard work and high-minded altruism that sheet of paper represented could not but feel saddened and hurt at the sound of the dismissive laughter that greeted it. Perhaps this document that was now presented to Congress merited anger, hatred, the mockery of enemies, but not to be greeted with hilarity, to be taken so lightly, as if they were laughing at some sort of buffoonery – a circus parade or a clown pulling faces.

But those who were laughing didn't know this; they just saw it as an occasion for a good laugh. The session that day was dull, which was the reason why the next day the political columns in the papers published the following petition accompanied by comments of every conceivable kind.

The petition ran thus:

Policarpo Quaresma, Brazilian citizen, civil servant, convinced that the Portuguese language has been lent to Brazil; also convinced that, for this reason, speaking and writing in general, above all in the field of literature, find themselves in the humiliating position of continually suffering severe criticism from the proprietors of the language; aware, too, that within our country authors and writers, notably grammarians, do not agree on what is grammatically correct, observing the bitter controversies that daily arise among the most learned scholars of our language; invoking the right conferred upon him by the Constitution, hereby requests that the National Congress decree Tupi-Guaraní as the official national language of the Brazilian people.

The petitioner, leaving aside the historical arguments which militate in favour of his idea, begs leave to recall that a language is the highest manifestation of the intelligence of a people, its most brilliant and original creation, and therefore the political emancipation of the country requires as its complement and consequence linguistic emancipation.

Moreover, Honourable Members, Tupi-Guaraní, an extremely original, hybrid language, is the only one capable of expressing the beauties of Brazil, putting us in tune with our nature and perfectly adapting itself to our vocal and cerebral organs, as it is the creation of peoples who lived and still live here, and thus possess the physiological and psychological structure to which we incline; furthermore avoiding the sterile grammatical controversies stemming from a difficult adaptation to a language from a region that is foreign to our cerebral structure and vocal apparatus – controversies that so impede the progress of our literary, scientific and philosophical culture.

Confident that the wisdom of the legislators will find the means to implement the measure proposed and aware that the House and Senate will weigh its potential effect and usefulness,

Approval is hereby requested.

For days this petition of the major, signed and duly stamped, was the subject of every conversation. It was published in all the papers, with facetious comments, and not a single soul failed to make a joke about it or invent some witticism at the expense of Quaresma's suggestion. They did not stop at that: the prying and snooping went further. They wanted to know who he was, the source of his income, if he was married or single. An illustrated weekly published a caricature of the major, and he was pointed at in the street.

And the small, witty papers, the weeklies with their satirical articles, imagine the savagery with which *they* depicted the wretched major! With a frequency which revealed the editors' delight at having found an easy target, the texts were full of: 'Major Quaresma said this', or 'Major Quaresma did that'. One of them, among other references, dedicated a whole page to the topic of the week. The cartoon was entitled: 'The Santa Cruz Slaughterhouse, according to Major Quaresma', and the drawing showed a queue of men and women marching towards a chopping block on the left. Another depicted him as a butcher: 'Quaresma the Butcher'. In the subtitle the cook asked the butcher: 'Have you got any tongue?' To which the butcher replied: 'Only Portuguese. Do you want some?'

As Quaresma had no influence in journalistic circles, the jibes, some more amusing than others, continued unabated for far longer than was usual. For two whole weeks the undersecretary's name was constantly in print.

All this irritated Quaresma profoundly. Living for thirty years, almost alone, without coming into conflict with the world, he had acquired a heightened sensibility, and the slightest thing was able to make him suffer intensely. He had never been criticized, never exposed to publicity. He lived immersed in his dream, sheltered and kept alive by the warmth of his books. Apart from them he didn't know anyone; and with the people he spoke to he exchanged commonplaces, routine remarks that had nothing to do with passionately held beliefs.

Not even his goddaughter, for whom he had the highest regard, could penetrate this reserve.

This introversion gave him an indefinable air of being aloof from things – competition, ambition – because all such things that create hatred and rivalry were alien to his character.

With no interest in money, in fame or status, living in a world of dreams, he had acquired the frankness and the purity of soul that characterize men with single-minded purpose – the learned, the great scholars, the inventors, men who become more gentle, more ingenuous, more innocent than the damsels in the poems of bygone ages.

It is rare to meet such men, but they exist; and when one does, even though they may have a touch of madness, we feel more sympathy for our species, more pride in belonging to the human race and more faith in the happiness of mankind.

The longer the mockery continued in the papers, the more they stared at him in the street, the more exasperated he became and the more determined to stick to his idea. At every jibe he was forced to swallow, at every jest, his mind turned to his petition, meticulously evaluating its every aspect, comparing it to similar projects and recalling the authors and authorities who proposed them; and the more he reflected, the more convinced he became of how pointless the criticism was, how futile the jokes, and the idea took hold of him, dominated him, absorbed him more and more.

Whereas the press had greeted the petition with inoffensive jokes devoid of malice, the department was furious. The petty jealousy in bureaucratic circles regards superior intelligence that reveals itself in any way other than through official correspondence, neat handwriting and knowledge of the rules and regulations with great hostility.

It is as though such a superior mind represents a betrayal of the mediocrity, the anonymity of bureaucrats. It is not just a question of promotion, of higher salaries, it is a question of self-esteem, of wounded feelings at seeing a colleague, a fellow forced labourer, subjected to the same regulations, the same whims of the bosses, the same disdainful glances of the ministers, drawing attention to himself, acquiring the right to infringe the rules and regulations.

They look on him with the disguised hatred with which the common murderer looks on the marquis who murdered his wife and her lover. Both are murderers, but even in prison the aristocrat is surrounded by an air of finesse that resists the prison environment and wounds the pride of the commoner who is his partner in crime.

And so it is in the civil service when an outsider appears who is considered unworthy of his appointment. The venomous implications begin to appear, the whispered slanders, the veiled remarks, the whole envious arsenal of a woman who is convinced that her neighbour dresses better than she does.

Men from the press who are respected for their writing, their editorial skills, their dedication to their work, even doctors and academics, are friendlier, or at least more tolerant towards each other than towards those who have earned renown. There is no understanding whatsoever of a colleague's work or merit; no one accepts that so-and-so, that fellow clerk, could possibly do anything that could be of interest to outsiders, let alone become the talk of the entire town.

Quaresma's sudden popularity, his success and ephemeral renown irritated his colleagues and superiors. 'Who ever heard anything like it!' the secretary said. 'This idiot making a proposal to Congress! The pretension!' When he came into the office the director looked at him askance and regretted that the regulations had no provisions for sanctions in such a case. His least offensive colleague, the archivist, said at once that he was mad.

The major was well aware of the hypocritical atmosphere, the allusions, and they increased the desperation with which he clung to his idea. He never imagined that his petition would cause such a storm, such general resentment: it was well intentioned, a patriotic proposal that deserved and ought to have the consent of everyone. He pondered, mulled over the idea and examined it with greater attention.

The event received so much publicity that it reached the mansion in Rua Real Grandeza where his friend Coleoni lived. Now a rich widower from the profits of his building projects, the one-time greengrocer had retired from business and lived quietly in the spacious house which he himself had built and which had all the architectural features he loved the most: stone vases on the parapets, an immense coat of arms above the front door, two china dogs on the pillars that flanked the gates and other such details.

The house, which had a large basement, stood in the centre of the plot. At the front was a fair-sized garden which extended to both sides, dotted with bulbs of varying colours, a veranda, an aviary where the birds mournfully died in the heat. It was a bourgeois residence in the Brazilian style: ostentatious, expensive, ill-suited to the climate and devoid of comfort.

Inside the whims of the owner prevailed, in accordance with his taste for the baroque and a rash eclecticism. It was crowded with furniture, carpets, curtains, trinkets – and his daughter's embellishments, untidy and inappropriate, conferred even greater chaos on that hoard of costly things.

He had been a widower for several years, and an elderly sister-in-law ran the house with his daughter, who took him on outings and to parties. Coleoni readily submitted to this well-intentioned despotism. He wanted Olga to marry well, according to her wishes, and thus did nothing to curtail her plans.

At first he thought of marrying her to his assistant, his foreman, a sort of architect who didn't draw, but planned houses and large buildings. First, he probed his daughter. He met with no resistance; but neither did he meet with consent. He came to the conclusion that the girl's dreamy nature, her distant, heroic air, her intelligence and her fanciful temperament would not combine well with the rustic simplicity and country ways of his assistant.

She wants someone with standing, he thought – I'll see to it!

Naturally he won't have a penny, but I have, so things will work out.

He looked on high-ranking Brazilians like the marquises or barons of his native land. Every country has its aristocracy: there it is the viscount, here it is the graduate, the dentist or the doctor; and he thought it perfectly natural to purchase the satisfaction of ennobling his daughter with a few million *réis*.

There were times when his daughter's activities rather annoyed him. Fond of retiring early, he had to waste night after night at the theatre, at balls; loving to sit smoking his pipe in his slippers, he was obliged to walk the streets hour after hour, bustling in and out of fashionable stores behind his daughter, to have bought by the end of the day half a metre of ribbon, some hairpins and a bottle of scent.

It was amusing to see him in the stores with that look of a proud father who wants to elevate his child, giving his opinion about the fabric, finding this one more beautiful, comparing one with another, with such a lack of affinity for such things it was even apparent as he perused them. But he went, took his time and strove to acquire the secret, to understand the mystery, with a tenacity and candour that were purely paternal.

All this he could put up with. But what really annoyed him were the visits: his daughter's friends, their mothers, their sisters, with their airs of false nobility and their disguised contempt, showing the old contractor how far removed he was from Olga's colleagues and friends.

But he did not take it too much to heart: this was what he had wanted and what he had done; he had to accept it. When such visitors arrived, Coleoni almost always withdrew to an inner room. However, it was not always possible for him to do this: at the big parties and receptions he had to be present, and it was then that he most felt the thinly veiled disdain of the elite of the land who frequented his home. He had always been a contractor, giving little thought to anything beyond his work and, unable to dissemble, took no interest in all the chatter about weddings, balls, parties and expensive outings.

Occasionally one of the politer guests would suggest a game of poker. He accepted and always lost. He even formed a poker group at home, which included the famous lawyer Pacheco. He lost heavily, but that was not why he stopped the games. What had he lost? A few thousand – a trifle! The thing was that Pacheco played with six cards. The first time Coleoni noticed this he thought it must be just absent-mindedness on the part of the distinguished journalist and famous lawyer. An honest man wouldn't do that. But what about the second time? And the third?

It was impossible to be that absent-minded. Once he was certain Pacheco was cheating he kept quiet, restraining himself with (for a former vegetable seller) unexpected dignity, and bided his time. The next time they came to play, and he used the same ruse, Vicente lit a cigar and observed, in a perfectly innocent voice:

'Did you know that in Europe there is now a new system for playing poker?'

'What is it?' one of them asked.

'It's a small difference: they play with six cards, or rather, just one of the players does.'

Pacheco pretended not to have heard, went on playing and winning, said goodnight at midnight, extremely politely, made a few comments about the game and never came back.

As was his habit, in the morning Coleoni was reading the papers with the slow deliberation of a man unaccustomed to reading, when he came across the petition of his friend from the Arsenal.

He didn't really understand the petition, but the papers derided it and treated it with such contempt that he thought his one-time benefactor must be caught up in some criminal conspiracy, must have inadvertently committed some grave offence.

He had always thought of him as the most honest man in the world, and still did, but you never can tell . . . The last time he visited him hadn't he behaved so oddly? Perhaps it was a joke . . .

Despite the fact he was now a wealthy man, Coleoni had the highest regard for his anonymous friend. Not only did he feel the gratitude of a peasant who had benefited enormously, but also a redoubled respect for the major as a government employee and learned man.

European, of humble and rural origin, deep inside he retained the sacred respect of the peasant for those who have received the investiture of the state. And as, despite all the years in Brazil, he still had not learned to distinguish between knowledge and rank, he had the greatest esteem for his friend's erudition.

It is thus not surprising that he was upset to see Quaresma's name involved in events that were condemned by the papers. He read the petition again but did not understand what it meant. He called his daughter.

'Olga.'

He pronounced his daughter's name almost without an accent, but when he spoke Portuguese the words had a peculiar guttural sound, and his sentences were interspersed with little expressions and exclamations in Italian.

'Olga, what does this mean? *Non capisco . . .*'

The girl sat down on a chair beside him and read the petition and the commentaries in the paper.

'*Che*. Well?'

'My godfather wants to substitute Portuguese with the Tupi language. Do you understand?'

'What!'

'At the moment we speak Portuguese, don't we? Well, he wants us to speak Tupi from now on.'

'*Tutti?*'

'All Brazilians, everyone.'

'*Ma che cosa!* Can it be true?'

'Perhaps. The Czechs have their own language and were obliged to speak German after they were conquered by the Austrians. And the French speakers in Lorraine . . .'

'*Per la Madonna!* German is a language, but this Swahili, *ecco!*'

'Swahili is from Africa, Father; Tupi is from here.'

'*Per Bacco!* It's the same thing . . . He's mad!'

'But there's nothing mad about it, Father.'

'What? So this comes from someone sane?'

'Perhaps it's not wise, but it isn't mad.'

'*Non capisco.*'

'It's an idea, Father, it's a plan. It may be absurd at first sight, unconventional, but not altogether mad. It's daring perhaps, but . . .'

However much she tried she was unable to judge her godfather's act as her father did. In him it was common sense that spoke; in her, the love of great things, of courage and bold undertakings. She remembered that Quaresma had talked to her about emancipation, and if she felt anything other than admiration for the major's courage, it was certainly neither disapproval nor regret, it was compassion at seeing the gesture of the man whom she'd known for so many years, alone and unknown, obstinately pursuing his dream, thus misunderstood.

'This will cause him a lot of unpleasantness,' Coleoni observed.

And he was right. The archivist's verdict dominated the discussions in the corridors, and the suspicion that Quaresma was mad gradually assumed an aspect of certainty. At first the undersecretary took it all in his stride, but when he realized that they assumed he barely knew a word of Tupi, he was speechless with rage and could hardly contain his anger. How blind they were! He, who had studied Brazil in the minutest detail for thirty years, and as a result had been obliged to learn a language as obnoxious as German – he, not to know Tupi, the Brazilian language, the *only* Brazilian language – what an outrageous idea!

Let them think he was mad if they liked! But not doubt the sincerity of his assertions! He started to think of ways to rehabilitate himself. He became distracted, even while writing and doing his office tasks. He was divided in two: one part concerned with his daily routine, and the other with proving that he knew Tupi.

One day the secretary didn't come to the office, and the major stood in for him. There was a lot of work, and he personally drafted and copied a part of it. He had started to copy a report on Mato Grosso that discussed Aquidauana and

Ponta-Porã,[1] when, from the far end of the room, Carmo said with a note of contempt:

'Homero, people who *know* is one thing, but those who just *talk* . . .'

Quaresma didn't take his eyes off his work. Whether because of the words in Tupi that appeared in the text or because of the clerk's remark, the fact is that he unconsciously began to translate the official document into the Indian language.

When he had finished he returned to his customary thoughts, but then other clerks arrived with their work for him to approve. Other matters put it out of his mind and, forgotten, the document in Tupi went on its way with the others. The director didn't notice, signed it, and it was forwarded to the ministry.

It is hard to describe the uproar that it caused there. What language was it? They consulted Doctor Rocha, the most competent man in the office, about the matter. He cleaned his pince-nez, grabbed the paper, turned it back to front, turned it upside down and concluded that it was Greek because of the double *y*s.

Doctor Rocha was reputed to be a man of great learning, as he was a graduate in law and never uttered a word.

'But,' his superior objected, 'are authorities permitted to communicate in foreign languages? I think there's a ruling from '84 . . . Look into it, Doctor Rocha . . .'

They consulted all the regulations and catalogues of legislation, they went from desk to desk asking if anyone recalled any rule, but to no avail. In the end, after three days of reflection, Dr Rocha went to the boss and asserted, emphatically:

'The ruling of '84 is about spelling.'

The director looked at his subordinate with admiration: what a zealous, intelligent employee he was . . . what dedication! He was informed that the legislation was remiss with regard to the language in which official documents should be written; nevertheless, the use of any other than the national language did not seem correct.

On the basis of this information and further consultations, the minister returned the document and reprimanded the Arsenal.

What a morning that was at the Arsenal! Bells tinkled furiously, the porters bustled about in a terrible state, and everyone constantly asked for the secretary, who was late in arriving.

'Reprimanded!' the director muttered. There went his promotion to general. To live all those years with the dream of those stars, to see them slip away like that, probably due to a prank by a clerk!

Things could still change . . . But how?

The secretary arrived and went to the director's office. Informed of the reprimand, he examined the document and recognized the handwriting as being Quaresma's. 'Send for him,' the colonel ordered. As he came, the major was mulling over some Tupi verses that he had read that morning.

'So you are having some fun at my expense, is that it?'

'What?' Quaresma gasped.

'Who wrote this?'

The major didn't even need to examine it closely. He saw the handwriting, remembered his moment of distraction and confessed without wavering:

'I did.'

'So you confess?'

'I do. But sir, you don't know . . .'

'*I don't know!* What?'

The director rose from his chair. His lips were white, his hand raised to his forehead. He had suffered three insults: to his personal honour, the honour of his rank and the honour of the educational establishment that he had attended – the Polytechnic of the Praia Vermelha, the leading scientific establishment of the world! He had even written a short story, 'Nostalgia', for the *Pritaneu*, the college magazine, that had been highly praised by his colleagues. Having passed all the examinations with full distinction, he now wore the laurels of both scholar and artist. Such distinction, rarely found even in a Descartes or a Shakespeare, transformed that 'you don't know' from a clerk, into a grievous offence, a personal insult.

'Don't know! How do you *dare* say that to *me*! Have you,

by any chance, taken the course of Benjamin Constant?[2] Have you studied maths, astronomy, physics, chemistry, sociology and ethics? How dare you? Do you think, because you've read a few novels and learned a smattering of French, that you can take on a man who got nine in calculus, ten in mechanics, eight in astronomy, ten in hydraulics and nine in composition? Do you?'

And the man's hand trembled with fury as he looked ferociously at Quaresma, who already envisioned himself before the firing squad.

'But, colonel—'

'That's enough! No more! Consider yourself suspended until further notice.'

Quaresma was good-natured, kind and modest. He had never intended to doubt the wisdom of his director. He made no claims to be a scholar and had spoken the words to initiate an apology, but when faced with that torrent of knowledge and qualifications, hurled about in such fury, he lost his train of thought and was unable to utter a word, such was his confusion.

He slunk out of the director's office like a criminal, while the colonel continued to glare at him ferociously, indignantly, like a man who had been cut to the very core of his being. So he left. When he entered the office he said nothing: he took his hat and his walking stick and rushed out of the door, staggering about like a drunkard. He walked around for a while, went to the bookshop to collect some books. When he went to get the tram he met Ricardo Coração dos Outros.

'You're early, aren't you, major?'

'Yes I am.'

They said no more. An uneasy silence descended between them. Ricardo tried a few tentative words:

'You look as though you have something very important on your mind today, major.'

'I have, my boy, and not just today. It's been on my mind for a long time.'

'It's good to think. Aspirations are a consolation.'

'Perhaps they are, but they also make us different from others. They create an abyss between people . . .'

They separated. The major took the tram, and Ricardo wandered cheerfully along the Rua do Ouvidor with his awkward gait, his trousers rolled up to the knee, his guitar tucked under his arm in its leather case.

V

THE STATUETTE

It was not the first time she had been there. More than a dozen times she had climbed that wide stone staircase with its statues from Lisbon on one side and 'Charity' and 'Our Lady of Mercy' on the other; passed through that doorway with its Doric columns, crossed the tiled courtyard, leaving Pinel on the left and Esquirol[1] on the right, meditating on the anguishing mystery of madness; climbed another carefully polished staircase, and at the top found her godfather, downcast and absorbed in his dreams and obsessions. Her father would sometimes bring her on Sundays when he came, as the obligation of a kind and dutiful friend, to visit Quaresma. How long had he been there? She didn't remember exactly – three or four months, if that.

The name of the place alone inspired dread. The asylum! It is like being buried alive, a half burial, the burial of the spirit, of the reason that guides us, whose absence the body rarely resents.

Health does not depend on it, and there are many who even seem to acquire more vigour, to live for longer, when it departs, who knows through which orifice of the body, and to where.

With what terror, like the fear of something supernatural, the dread of some ubiquitous, invisible enemy, did the poor people refer to that institution on the Praia das Saudades! Better off dead, they used to say.

At first sight it was hard to understand this fear, this dread, this terror of the people for that huge, austere, severe building, half hospital, half jail, with its high railings, its barred windows, stretching for hundreds of metres, overlooking the sea, immense and green, at the entrance to the bay, on the Praia das Saudades. On entering, one saw a few calm, thoughtful men, meditating like monks on retreat, in prayer.

What was more, entering into that quiet, dignified silence seemed to belie the popular notion of madness: the uproar, the raving, the grimaces, the cacophony of gibbering from all around. There was none of this; everything was perfectly natural: calm, silent and orderly. But later, in the visiting room, as one looked more closely at the contorted faces, the bewildered looks, some gaping and expressionless, others absorbed, lost in an impenetrable world of their own, and at the agitation of others, in such contrast to the apathy of their companions, then the full horror of madness came home – the anguish of the mystery it contains, when the spirit takes flight from what we imagine to be reality and becomes obsessed with the illusionary appearances of things.

Whoever has witnessed this indecipherable enigma of our nature is filled with dread, perceiving instinctively that the seed of madness exists in all of us and with no warning may attack, overpower, crush and bury us in a frantic, absurd, inverted comprehension of ourselves, of others and of the world. Every madman has his own inner world, and for him his fellow men no longer exist: what he becomes in his madness is different, completely different, from what he once was.

And this change has no beginning, or rather one isn't aware that it is beginning, and it almost never ends. With her godfather, how had it happened? First, that petition ... But what was that? A whim, a fantasy, a thing of no importance, an old man's idea, of no consequence. And then, that document? It had no importance, a mere distraction, something that happens all the time ... And next? Outright insanity: tenebrous, enigmatic insanity that steals our soul and puts another in its place, that demeans us ... Yes, outright insanity, the fixation with self, the dread of going out, the mania of persecution, of seeing an enemy even in the closest of friends. How heartrending it had been! The first phase of his delirium, the deranged agitation, the incoherent rambling, with no connection with the outside world or with his past life; rambling that came from where, out of what, from what point of departure? And the dread that had possessed the gentle Quaresma! The dread of one who has seen a cataclysm that left him trembling from head to foot, left him indifferent to everything but his own delirium.

His house, his books and his financial affairs were all abandoned. They had ceased to exist for him; they no longer had any value or importance. They were shadows, illusions. What was real was his enemies, the terrible enemies whom his deranged mind was unable to name. His old sister, shocked, bewildered, was at a loss as to what she should do. She had always had a man in the house, first her father, then her brother; she had never learned to deal with the world, with business affairs, authorities, influential people. At the same time, in her inexperience and sisterly love, she oscillated between the belief that her brother had actually gone mad and that none of this was really true.

If it had not been for Coleoni (and for this Olga loved her rustic father all the more), who had taken charge of the family's affairs and succeeded in converting Quaresma's outright dismissal into early retirement, what would have become of him? How easily everything in life can collapse! That methodical, steady, upright man, with his safe job, had appeared unassailable. Yet it took just a drop of madness . . .

He had been in the asylum for a few months, but his sister could not bring herself to visit him. The shock to her nervous system, the horror of seeing him in that semi-prison, completely unlike himself, had brought on an inevitable attack.

Olga and her father came, sometimes her father alone and occasionally Ricardo. These were the only three to visit.

That Sunday was particularly beautiful, especially in Botafogo, near the sea and the high mountains, outlined against a silky sky. The air was soft, and the sunlight played gently on the pavement.

On the way her father read the papers while she pensively leafed through the illustrated magazines that she was bringing to please and amuse her godfather.

He was a private patient, but even so, at first she felt a certain embarrassment at mixing with the visitors.

She had thought that her wealth should protect her from

having to witness such wretchedness, but she had suppressed
this selfish thought and her social snobbery and now entered
unaffectedly, thus enhancing her natural refinement. She loved
these sacrifices, these acts of self-denial; she was aware of their
innate nobility and she was happy with herself.

On the tram there were other visitors who all promptly
descended at the gates of the asylum. As at the gates of all our
social infernos, there were people of every kind: high and low,
rich and poor, blessed and cursed. Death is not the only leveller: madness, crime and sickness also eliminate the distinctions
we invent.

The elegant and the shabby, the wealthy and the poor, the
handsome and the ugly, the clever and the simple, all entered
quietly and politely, with a glint of fear in their eyes, as though
penetrating an unknown world.

They greeted their relatives, and the packages were
unwrapped: there were sweets, tobacco, socks, slippers, occasionally books and newspapers. Some of the patients chatted
with their relatives; others remained mute in angry, inexplicable
silence. Others were indifferent. The receptions were so diverse
that the ill they all shared was forgotten, to such an extent did its
manifestations vary from one to the other, reflected in the whims
of each individual and the dictates of each one's will.

And she thought how diverse and varied life is, how it is
richer in sadness than in happiness and how in the variety of
life there are more varieties of sadness than there are of happiness and how sadness lies at the core of life.

She felt something akin to satisfaction at this reflection. Her
intelligent, inquiring mind found satisfaction in the simplest
discoveries that her spirit revealed.

Quaresma was better. The excitement had passed, and the
ravings seemed unlikely to return. Shocked at finding himself in
those surroundings, he reacted as best he could, and should. He
must be mad, because they had put him there . . .

When he greeted his goddaughter and her father, beneath his
moustache, already tinged with grey, there was even a smile of
satisfaction. He had got a little thinner, his black hair was a
little whiter, but in general he looked his old self. He had not

altogether lost his soft-spoken manner, but when the madness reappeared he became dry and suspicious. When he saw them, he said warmly:

'So you have come as always . . . I was waiting for you . . .'

They exchanged greetings, and he even gave his goddaughter an affectionate hug.

'How is Adelaide?'

'She's well. She sends her love. But she didn't come because . . .' Coleoni added.

'Poor thing,' he said, and he hung his head, as if trying to forget a sad recollection. Then he asked:

'And Ricardo?'

His goddaughter replied eagerly – overjoyed at seeing him safe from the death-in-life of insanity:

'He's well, Godfather. He visited Papa a few days ago and said that the paperwork for your pension is almost ready.'

Coleoni had sat down. Quaresma had too. The girl was standing, the better to watch her godfather more closely with her luminous eyes and steady stare. Guards, nurses and doctors came in and out with professional indifference. The visitors didn't look at each other; it seemed they didn't want to recognize each other later in the street. Outside it was a beautiful day: a light breeze, the vast sombre sea, the mountains outlined against a silky sky – the beauty of nature, majestic and unfathomable. Coleoni, although a more frequent visitor, noted the improvement in his friend, and his satisfaction was revealed in a smile that flickered across his features. After a while he ventured: 'You're much better now, major. Do you want to leave?'

Quaresma did not answer at once. He thought a little and then replied slowly and firmly:

'I'd better wait a while. I am feeling better . . . I'm sorry to give you so much trouble, but you who have been so good to me must pay the price for your kindness. A man who has enemies needs good friends . . .'

Father and daughter glanced at each other. The major looked up and seemed about to burst into tears. The girl interjected quickly:

'Godfather, I'm going to get married.'

'It's true,' her father added. 'Olga is going to get married, and we came to tell you.'

'Who is your fiancé?' Quaresma asked.

'He's a young man . . . '

'Obviously,' her father interrupted, smiling.

They both smiled too, happily and amicably. It was a good sign.

'It is Sr Armando Borges, who is doing his doctor's degree. Are you pleased, Godfather?' Olga asked kindly.

'So it will be early in the new year.'

'That's what we're hoping,' said the Italian.

'Do you love him?' Quaresma asked.

She did not know how to answer that question. She would have liked to feel she loved him, but she didn't. So why was she marrying? She didn't know . . . Something required by society, that didn't come from her – she didn't know. Did she love another? Again the answer was no. None of the young men she knew were distinguished enough to captivate her, none had that *something*, as yet undefined in her heart and in her mind, that would fascinate and conquer her. She didn't know exactly what it was; she had never analysed her feelings to discover what quality in a man attracted her most. Perhaps it was the heroic, the out-of-the-ordinary, the willpower to achieve great things, but in the confused state of mind of youth, when ideas and desires intertwine and intermingle, Olga was unable to clearly define this longing, the role she should adopt, the way in which to love a person of the opposite sex.

And she was right to marry a man who did not live up to her ideal. It was so difficult to discern whether a man of twenty to thirty had the qualities she dreamed of, she was in danger of throwing her pearls to the swine . . .[2] She was marrying because it was the custom, and also partly out of curiosity – to widen her horizons and heighten her sensibility. All this went quickly through her mind, and she answered her godfather without conviction:

'Yes I do.'

The visit didn't last much longer. It had to be short so as not to fatigue the patient. As they left it was evident they were both contented and optimistic.

At the gates some of the visitors were waiting for the tram. As none came, they walked further down the track, along the façade of the asylum. Halfway along they saw an old black woman leaning against the railings, weeping. The kind-hearted Coleoni went up to her:

'What's the matter, my dear?'

The wretched woman stared at him, her eyes moist with tears, with a look of irreparable sadness:

'Oh, sir!' she replied. 'It's terrible . . . My poor boy! Such a good boy!'

And she continued to weep. Coleoni was touched. His daughter looked at her with concern, and then asked:

'Is he dead?'

'If only he were, miss!'

And between tears and sobs she told them how her son no longer recognized her or answered her questions: he was like a stranger. She dried her tears and concluded:

'They put a spell on him.'

The two walked away sadly, deeply affected by the poor woman's grief.

The day was cool, and the breeze which began to blow wrinkled the surface of the sea with little white waves. From the froth the Sugar Loaf rose stiffly up, austere and black, as if casting a shadow across the brightness of the day.

In the Institute for the Blind someone was playing a violin, and its slow, plaintive sound seemed to emanate from everything around, from their melancholy and grandeur.

After a while the tram arrived. They took it and got off in the Largo da Carioca. It's pleasant to see the city on a Sunday, with its shops closed, its narrow streets deserted, where footsteps echo like in a silent cloister. The city is a skeleton: its flesh – the coming and going of carriages, carts and people – is not there. At the doors of some of the shops the shopkeepers' children ride bicycles and throw balls, highlighting even more the contrast with the city as it was the day before.

The habit of visiting the rural outskirts was not yet in vogue; they passed the occasional couple hurrying along on their way to pay a visit, as they were. The Largo de São Francisco was deserted and the statue which had once stood in a small garden seemed reduced to just an ornament. The trams drew sluggishly into the square with just a handful of passengers. Coleoni and his daughter caught one which went to Quaresma's house. They took their places. The afternoon was drawing on, and already people were appearing in the windows in their Sunday best. Blacks in white jackets smoking large cigars or cigarettes; groups of shopboys with gaudy buttonholes; girls in cotton dresses, very starched; men in battered top hats accompanied by lethargic matrons squeezed into black satin dresses. And so the Sunday appeared, adorned with the simplicity of the humble, the creativity of the poor and the ostentation of the foolish.

Dona Adelaide was not alone. Ricardo had come to visit her, and they were chatting. When Coleoni and his daughter knocked on the door he was recounting his latest triumph:

'I don't know how it will turn out, Dona Adelaide. I don't keep my music, I don't write it down. It's a disaster!'

It was a case that would upset any composer. A Sr Paysandón, from Córdoba in Argentina, a very well-known composer in that town, had written to him asking for some samples of his songs. Ricardo didn't know what to do. He had written down the words, but not the music. Although he knew them by heart, to put them all down on paper in a short space of time was beyond him.

'It's a disaster,' he repeated. 'Not for myself, but it's a lost opportunity to make Brazil better known abroad.'

Quaresma's elder sister took no great interest in the guitar. She had been brought up to see it as an instrument that was played by slaves and their like; she could not accept that people of a certain rank would take an interest in it. But out of consideration for Ricardo she supported his obsession. She had even begun to nurture a certain admiration for this famous troubadour of the suburbs. Her esteem stemmed from the dedication he had shown during the family drama. Small jobs, minor duties and running errands here and there had fallen to Ricardo, who had discharged them with goodwill and dedication.

He was currently in charge of making the arrangements for his former pupil's retirement. Dealing with the bureaucracy for a government pension was an arduous task. Once the employee has been officially retired by decree, the process goes through a dozen departments and civil servants before it is finalized. Nothing surpasses the gravity with which an official pronounces the words: 'I am still making the calculations.' And the case drags on for another month, or even more, as if it depended on the alignment of the planets.

Coleoni had the power of attorney, but with no experience in dealing with government bureaucracy he had handed this part of his duties to Coração dos Outros.

Thanks to Ricardo's popularity, and to his cordiality, he had conquered the resistance of the bureaucratic machine, and the paperwork was shortly to be finalized.

It was this that he informed Coleoni when he came in, followed by his daughter. Both Dona Adelaide and Ricardo asked for news of Quaresma.

She had never understood her brother, and the crisis did not help her understand him any better. But her sisterly devotion to him was very strong, and she sincerely longed for his recovery.

Ricardo Coração dos Outros was devoted to the major, in whom he had found the moral and intellectual support that he needed. The others enjoyed hearing him sing, but their appreciation was that of dilettantes; the major was the only one who realized the true significance of his efforts and the patriotic importance of his work.

And this was a moment of particular suffering – his fame, the product of years of slow, continuous work, was being challenged. A black who sang *modinhas* had appeared, and was becoming famous; his name was appearing alongside Ricardo's.

His rival annoyed him for two reasons: firstly, because he was black, and secondly, because of his theories.

It was not that he had any particular aversion to blacks. The danger he saw in a famous black playing the guitar was that it would diminish the instrument's prestige even more. If his rival played the piano and became famous because of it, there would be no harm at all. On the contrary, the young man's talent would achieve greater recognition through the means of that esteemed instrument. But as he played the guitar, it would be the reverse: the colour prejudice against him would demoralize the mysterious instrument Ricardo so highly prized. And the theories! To want the *modinha* to convey a meaning, to set it to verses! It was absurd!

And Ricardo brooded on this unexpected rival who had now come between him and the shining path to glory. He must get rid of him, crush him, show his indisputable superiority. But how?

Advertising was not enough: his rival advertised himself too. He needed the support of a famous person, a great writer, to write an article about him and his work; then his victory would be certain. But it wouldn't be easy. Our men of letters were such fools they spent their time absorbed in works in French . . . He thought of a periodical, *The Guitar*, in which he could challenge his rival and crush him with his arguments.

This was what he needed to find, and his hopes lay with Quaresma, who was currently in the asylum, but fortunately recovering. And this was why he was so delighted when he heard his friend was better.

'I couldn't go today,' he said, 'but I'll go next Sunday. Has he put on weight?'

'Very little,' said the girl.

'He talked a good deal,' Coleoni added. 'He was even pleased when he heard Olga is getting married.'

'Are you getting married, Dona Olga? Congratulations!'

'Thank you,' she said.

'When will it be, Olga?' asked Dona Adelaide.

'Towards the end of the year . . . There's no hurry . . .'

And they started to shower her with questions about her fiancé and suggestions for the wedding.

Olga was put out: she found the questions and the suggestions presumptuous and irritating. She tried to change the subject, but they kept returning to it, not only Ricardo but Adelaide too, who was more talkative and inquisitive than usual.

This torment, which was repeated at every visit, almost made her regret accepting the request. In the end she managed to find a way of changing the subject by asking:

'How is the general?'

'I haven't seen him, but his daughter often visits. He must be well. But Ismênia is very upset – broken-hearted, poor thing!'

And so Dona Adelaide recounted the drama that had turned the little world of the general's daughter upside down. Cavalcânti, that bastion of five years' duration, had left for the interior three or four months earlier and had sent neither letter nor card. She took this as meaning that the engagement was broken. And she, so incapable of deeper feeling, of applying herself to anything, felt very hurt. She saw it as something irreparable and could think of nothing else.

For Ismênia it was as if all the marriageable young men had ceased to exist. Finding another was an insoluble problem, a task beyond her powers. All that again? Flirting, writing little notes, making eyes, dancing, going on outings – she couldn't go through it again! She was obviously fated not to get married, to be an old maid, to put up, for her whole life, with what frightened her most – being a spinster. She hardly remembered what her fiancé looked like: his darting eyes, his prominent, bony nose. But despite having forgotten what he looked like, every morning, when the postman failed to hand her a letter, she remembered that she was not to be married. It was a punishment! Quinota was going to be married; Genelício was seeing to the papers; and she, who had waited so long and had been the first to get engaged, was to be cursed, demeaned in front of them all. They even seemed to be pleased about Cavalcânti's inexplicable flight. The way they'd laughed during Carnival, throwing her premature widowhood in her face! The relish with which they'd thrown confetti and squirted perfume, making such a show of their happiness at the prospect of getting married, that glorious, coveted condition, compared to her abandonment!

She successfully hid how she felt about their happiness, which she found indecent and hostile. But her sister's constant mockery – 'Have fun, Ismênia. He's a long way away, make the best of it!' – made her furious, that terrible fury of the weak, which corrodes from within as they are unable to let it out.

So to keep herself from brooding she took to looking at the frivolous decorations in the street, the multicoloured bunting and the gaudy streamers hanging from the balconies. But what most cheered her simple, oppressed soul was the groups of carnival revellers, banging their drums and clanging their tambourines. Surrounded by all the noise, she forgot the sad thoughts that had pursued her for so long, as if something were blocking them from entering her head.

What was more, the extravagant Indian costumes, the ornaments of an unashamedly savage mythology – the live alligators, snakes and turtles, so *very* alive – brought to her usually unimaginative mind scenes of clear rivers, immense forests, places of purity and calm which comforted her.

And the Carnival songs, shouted, bellowed out, with their relentless rhythm and almost entire absence of melody, helped to heal the hurt feelings that she had repressed, that begged to be released in an outburst of shrieking – an outburst for which she no longer had the strength.

Cavalcânti had left a month before Carnival; after the great *carioca* festival her torment became more acute. She had the habit neither of reading nor of conversation, she had no domestic activities at all; she spent the days lying down or sitting, brooding over a single thought: she was not to be married. It was a relief to cry.

She still perked up when the postman delivered the mail. Perhaps? But no letter came, and the thought that plagued her would return: she was not to be married.

When Dona Adelaide finished relating poor Ismênia's disaster, she added:

'There should be a punishment for this sort of thing, don't you think?'

Coleoni intervened with his usual goodwill:

'There's no reason to give up hope. Lots of people never get around to writing.'

'But it's been three months, Sr Vicente!' Dona Adelaide retorted.

'He's not coming back,' Ricardo pronounced sententiously.

'Does she still expect him to, Dona Adelaide?' asked Olga.

'I don't know, my child. No one understands the girl. She barely says a word, and when she does she doesn't make sense. She seems to have no spirit, no energy. You can feel her sadness, but she doesn't say a thing.'

'Is it pride?' Olga asked.

'No, no . . . If it were pride she wouldn't mention him every now and again. It's more lethargy, a lack of vim . . . It's as if she were afraid to speak in case something might happen.'

'And what do her parents say?' asked Coleoni.

'I don't really know. But from what I can tell the general is not too put out, and Dona Maricota thinks she should find someone else.'

'That would be the best thing,' said Ricardo.

'I'm afraid she's given up,' said Dona Adelaide, smiling. 'She was engaged for so long . . .'

And the conversation had already moved on to other subjects when Ismênia arrived on her daily visit to Quaresma's sister.

As she greeted them all they saw that she was hurt: her features clearly displayed her suffering.

Her eyelids were red, the pupils dilated, and the look in her small brown eyes was more intense. She asked after Quaresma's health, and they all fell silent for a while. Then Dona Adelaide asked:

'Has a letter come, Ismênia?'

'Not yet,' she replied in a voice that could hardly be heard.

Ricardo shifted in his chair. His arm hit the sideboard, knocking to the floor a porcelain statuette. It shattered into countless pieces, almost without a sound.

PART II

I

AT 'THE HAVEN'

The place wasn't ugly, but neither was it beautiful. It did, how-ever, have that tranquil, contented appearance of a person who is at peace with life.

The house was built on a terrace, a sort of ledge which pro-vided access to a small hill that rose up behind it. At the front, through the bamboo fence, a plain could be seen, stretching away to the mountains in the distance. It was crossed by a stream with stagnant, muddy waters that ran parallel to the front of the house. Further off, with its narrow strip of cleared track, the railway line streaked across the plain, and on the left a cart-track, with houses on either side, crossed the stream and meandered towards the station. Thus Quaresma's home had a wide, open view, facing the hillside to the east, its whitewashed walls giving it a certain lightness and gaiety. Entirely devoid, as all our rural houses, of any architectural merit, it was equipped, nevertheless, with vast reception rooms, spacious bedrooms, each with its own window, and a veranda supported by col-umns in a variety of styles. In addition to the house, 'The Haven', as Quaresma's little farm was called, had a couple of outbuildings: the old flour mill, with the furnace still intact and the wheel dismantled, and a stable with a thatched roof.

It had been less than three months since he had come to live in the house, in that secluded place, two hours by rail from Rio, after spending six months in the asylum on the Praia das Sau-dades. Was he cured? Who could say? It seemed so: the raving had stopped, his behaviour was that of a normal man. Never-theless there were signs that, although it no longer took the form of madness, he had not abandoned the dream he had

nurtured for so many years. These six months had served more
for rest and seclusion than for psychiatric therapy.

Quaresma had lived there, in the asylum, resignedly, talking
to his fellow inmates: the rich who said they were poor, the poor
who pretended they were rich, the scholars who cursed all schol-
arship, the uneducated who proclaimed their education. But of
all of them the one that struck him most was a soft-spoken old
tradesman from the Rua dos Pescadores who thought he was
Attila. 'I am Attila, did you know?' he would say. 'I am Attila.'
He knew virtually nothing about him – little more than his
name. 'I am Attila; I've killed a lot of people.' That was all.

The major left sadder than he had ever been. Of all the sad
things to see in this world, the saddest is madness; it is the
bleakest and the most heartrending.

Our lives carry on as normal, but this imperceptible yet pro-
found and almost always unfathomable disturbance renders
them entirely useless. It appears to stem from something that is
stronger than we are, goading us on, in whose hands we are no
more than puppets. There were cultures in the past that
regarded madness as sacred. Perhaps this is the explanation
why, when we hear a madman raving, we are overcome by a
sensation that he is not the one who is speaking – it is someone
else, seeing for him, interpreting for him, guiding him . . . someone who is invisible! . . .

Quaresma left, impregnated with the sadness of the asylum.
He went home, but the sight of his familiar things could not
remove the deep impression with which his mind had been
imbued. Although he had never been cheerful, his expression
was sadder than before, more downcast, and it was in an
attempt to raise his spirits that he had retired to that cheerful
house in the country where he spent his time on his modest
farming projects.

The idea, however, had not been his. It was his goddaughter
who had suggested that gentle form of retirement. Seeing him
so downcast, so withdrawn and sad, not daring to go out,
imprisoned in his house in São Cristóvão, one day Olga
broached the subject in her affectionate, daughterly way:

'Godfather, why don't you buy a little farm? How lovely it

would be to have your own orchard, your vegetable garden . . . don't you agree?'

His expression, so withdrawn and silent, immediately changed at the girl's suggestion. It was something he had always wanted to do, to plant his own food, to live off the land, to find his happiness in nature. And these old plans came to his mind as he answered his goddaughter:

'I do, my child. What a magnificent idea you have had! There is so much fertile land that is not used . . . Our country has the most fertile land in the world. The maize yields two harvests a year, four hundred plants in each . . .'

The girl almost regretted having made the suggestion. She feared it might reignite some of her godfather's old obsessions.

'But there is fertile land all over the world, is there not, Godfather?'

'But not like that in Brazil,' he retorted. 'Very few countries have that. I am going to do what you say: plant, breed, grow corn, beans, potatoes . . . and when you see what I grow, my vegetable garden, my orchard – then you'll realize how fertile our land is!'

Once planted in his mind, the idea soon germinated. The soil had been ploughed; all it needed was good seed. Although he had never been cheerful, the reticence disappeared, along with the depression, and the vigorous mental activity of his younger days returned. He inquired into the current prices of fruit and vegetables, potatoes and cassava; he calculated that fifty orange trees, thirty avocado trees and eighty peach trees, among others, as well as pineapples (what a gold mine), pumpkins and other less popular produce would provide an annual income of four million *réis* after expenses. There is no need to enter into the details of his calculations: they were all carefully based on statistics from the bulletins of the National Agricultural Association. He took into consideration production per hectare, the average production of the various fruit trees, as well as the wages and inevitable losses. As for prices, he personally went to the market to see what they were.

He planned his agricultural life with the thoroughness and precision with which he planned all his projects. He examined every aspect – the points in favour and against – and he was very pleased to find it potentially profitable, not because he desired to make money, but because this was further proof of the excellence of his native Brazil.

Such were the ideas that led to his purchasing that little farm, whose name – 'The Haven' – suited the new life he had adopted so well, after the storm that had rocked it for almost a year. It was not far from Rio, and he had chosen it, despite its abandonment and neglect, the better to demonstrate the power of perseverance and dedication in agricultural work. He expected abundant harvests of fruit, pulses and vegetables. From his example a thousand other plantations would spring, and shortly the great capital would be surrounded by flourishing farms. Imports from Argentina and Europe would no longer be required.

How happily he had moved there! He hardly gave a thought to his old house in São Januário, which now belonged to others, perhaps earning its keep as a rented home ... The vast living room which had calmly sheltered his books for so many years was now perhaps the scene of frivolous dances, squabbling couples and family feuds, that pleasant, comfortable room, with its high ceilings and plastered walls, impregnated with the desires of his soul, infused with the breath of his dreams – but he was not concerned.

He'd been happy to leave. How easy it was to live off our land. Four million *réis* per year, yielded by the land, joyfully, openly, generously! Oh blessèd land! How could so many people want to be civil servants, to rot behind a desk, to renounce their independence and self-esteem? How could they prefer to live in poky, dark, airless houses, eating unhealthy food, breathing air that spread diseases, when they could so easily choose a happy, healthy life, a life of freedom and plenty?

And it was only now that he had arrived at this conclusion – after enduring the privations of city life and the emasculation of public office for so long! It had come late, but not too late to prevent him from experiencing the sweet country life and the fecundity of the Brazilian soil before he died. He now thought that his desire for major reforms in institutions and customs had been a mistake: what was vital for the greatness of his long-suffering homeland was a strong agricultural foundation, a cult of its bounteous soil, on which the great achievements for which she was predestined could be built.

Indeed, with its fertile land and varied climate that made farming both pleasant and lucrative, this was obviously the path to follow.

And before his mind's eye he saw the rows of orange trees in flower, sweet-smelling, very white, lining the hillsides like a procession of brides; the avocado trees with their furrowed trunks, weighed down beneath the burden of the great green pears; the black *jabuticabas*[1] sprouting from the dry bark; the pineapples, crowned like kings, anointed by the sun; the pumpkin vines, creeping along the ground with their heavy, pollen-laden flowers; the watermelons, so perfectly green they could have been painted; the velvety peaches, the monstrous jackfruits, the *jambos*,[2] the vigorous mangoes; and amidst all this the figure of a woman, her lap full of fruit, one shoulder bare, smiling at him in gratitude, with a fixed, otherworldly smile: Pomona, the goddess of fruit trees!

Quaresma spent the first few weeks making a systematic exploration of his new property. It had a lot of land, ancient fruit trees and a large grass-covered plot covered with red sage, *parahybas*, prickly ash, *ipê* and other plants. Anastácio accompanied him. Recalling his days as a plantation slave, he taught Quaresma, so knowledgeable and widely read in all things Brazilian, the names of these inhabitants of the woods.

Quaresma set up a natural life museum at 'The Haven'. The specimens from the woods and fields were labelled with their common names and, whenever possible, their scientific ones. The plants were displayed in a herbarium, the wood in small blocks, revealing the cross-sections.

His passion for reading had led him to study the natural sciences, and in his self-taught zeal he had acquired a considerable knowledge of botany, zoology, mineralogy and geology.

It was not only the plants that merited an inventory, but the animals too. But as he didn't have enough space, and the preservation of these specimens was a more painstaking task, Quaresma limited his museum to documents, describing the various snakes, the armadillos, agoutis, cavies, wood rails, finches, grosbeaks, seedeaters and tanagers that lived on his farm. The land was not rich in minerals: clay, sand and here and there a few crumbling blocks of granite.

When this inventory was complete he spent two weeks organizing his agricultural library and making a list of meteorological instruments to help with the work in the fields.

He ordered Brazilian books, as well as books from France and Portugal; he bought thermometers, barometers, pluviometers, hygrometers and anemometers.[3] They arrived and were duly assembled and installed.

Anastácio was aghast at all these preparations. Why all this stuff, all the books, all the test-tubes? Had his old employer become a pharmacist? But his doubts were soon put to rest. One day, as he gazed in astonishment as Quaresma read the pluviometer, as though he were watching some magical rite, the master noticed his servant's amazement and said:

'Do you know what I'm doing, Anastácio?'

'No, masser.'

'I'm seeing how much it has rained.'

'What you do dat for, masser? We can *see* how much it *rain* . . . We gotta *hoe*, put de *seed* in de *groun'*, let it *grow* and den *harvest* it . . .'

He spoke slowly in his soft African voice, with its almost imperceptible *r*s, but with conviction.

While continuing to consult the instrument, Quaresma listened carefully to his servant's advice. His land was covered with weeds and brush. The orange trees, avocados and mangoes were in a dreadful state, full of dead branches and covered in the medusoid locks of a parasitic creeper, but, as it was not the right season for pruning and cutting branches, Quaresma restricted himself to weeding between the fruit trees. Every day at dawn he and Anastácio left with their hoes on their shoulders to work in the fields. The sun was fierce and relentless; summer was at its height, but Quaresma set off, determined and undaunted.

He was quite a sight, protected by a straw hat, grappling with an enormous hoe with a knotted wooden handle, small, short-sighted, striking blow after blow to uproot a stubborn broom-jute. His hoe was more like a dredge or an excavator than a small agricultural tool. Anastácio, at his side, looked on with pity and astonishment. To be out in that sun of his own free will, weeding without knowing how. Whatever would he get up to next?

And the two continued working: the old black clearing away the undergrowth swiftly and deftly with his experienced hand, his hoe gliding over the earth as it pulled up the weeds; Quaresma furiously tearing up great clods of earth, taking for ever over every bush. Sometimes, when he missed his aim he drove the blade of the instrument into the ground with such force, sending up such an infernal cloud of dust, that it looked as if a squad of cavalry had just ridden by. Then Anastácio would humbly intervene, but in a professorial tone:

'It not like *dat*, major. You don't *bury* de hoe! *Easy*, like *dis*.'

And he taught the inexperienced city-dweller how to put the ancient tool to proper use.

Quaresma took hold of it, positioned himself and tried his very best to use it as he had been taught. But it was in vain. The shaft struck the root, the hoe gave a jolt, while overhead a songbird let out a mocking *chickadee!*[4] This infuriated the major, who tried again, exhausting himself and starting to sweat, swiping furiously with all his strength. On several occasions he missed his aim and toppled over, falling face-down on the earth, the mother of fruits[5] and men. His pince-nez flew off his nose and smashed against a stone.

The major, more infuriated than ever, returned with renewed energy to the task he had set himself. This sacred, age-old task of deriving our sustenance from the land is so deeply embedded in our ancestral memory that it began to awake in Quaresma, and he gradually acquired the skill of using the venerable hoe.

By the end of a month he was clearing the land quite well: not continuously from dawn to dusk, but with long, hourly rests, as his lack of age and experience required.

Sometimes the faithful Anastácio would rest alongside him beneath the shade of one of the larger fruit trees, and they would contemplate the oppressive air of those summer days, as it wound its way between the leaves, leaving in its wake a brooding sensation of morbid resignation. It was then, shortly after midday, when everything seemed anaesthetized by the heat, the whole of life immersed in silence, that the old major perceived the very essence of the tropics and the incongruities: a bright Olympian sun blazing down on the death-like torpor of death it had wrought.

They had lunch in the open – food from the day before quickly heated on a stove that was improvised with stones – and so they worked on until dinner time. Quaresma's enthusiasm was sincere, the enthusiasm of an ideologist who wants to see his ideas put into practice. He did not allow the land's initial ingratitude, its unwholesome love of weeds and incomprehensible hatred of the fecundating hoe to nettle him. He kept hoeing and hoeing until it was time for dinner.

Dinner was a more leisurely meal. He talked for a while to his sister, giving his account of the task of the day that always consisted of an appraisal of the area cleared.

'You know, Adelaide, tomorrow the orange orchard will be cleared, there won't be a single piece of undergrowth left.'

His sister, who was older than he was, did not share his enthusiasm for country things. It was too quiet for her; she had come to live with him out of habit – she had always accompanied him. Although she was fond of him, she did not understand him. She understood neither his actions nor his inner restlessness. Why hadn't he taken a degree and become a deputy, as he should have done, as everyone did? Immersed in books for years on end, to end up a nobody, it was absurd! She had come with him to 'The Haven' and, to keep herself busy, raised chickens, to the delight of her farmer brother.

'That's good,' she said, when her brother told her about his work. 'Now be careful not to get ill ... Out in this sun the whole day long ...'

'Ill, Adelaide? Haven't you seen how healthy all these people are? If they get ill it's because they don't work.'

After dinner Quaresma would go to the window, which looked on to the chicken coop, and throw pieces of bread to the birds.

He enjoyed the spectacle, the fierce fight between ducks, geese and hens of all sizes. He saw in it a synthesis of life and the rewards it offers. He would then inquire about life in the chicken coop:

'Have the ducklings hatched yet, Adelaide?'

'Not yet. There are still eight days to go.'

Then his sister added:

'Your goddaughter's getting married on Saturday. Aren't you going?'

'No. I can't . . . I can't face it: the ostentation . . . I'll send a suckling pig and a turkey.'

'For heaven's sake! What sort of a present is that?'

'What's wrong with it? It's tradition.'

That day, as brother and sister were talking in the dining room of the old country house, Anastácio came to inform them that there was a gentleman at the gate.

No one had come to visit Quaresma since he had moved to the house, except for poor people from the surrounding area who came to ask for this or that – in other words, to beg. He himself had made no acquaintances, so he received Anastácio's announcement with surprise.

He hurried to the main room to receive his visitor, who had already walked up the few steps in front of the house and entered the veranda.

'Good evening, major.'

'Good evening. Please come in.'

The stranger came in and sat down. He was an ordinary-looking man; his only remarkable feature was that he was fat. He was not, however, disproportioned or grotesque, but he did appear dishonest. He looked as if he'd been stuffing himself with food until he could cram no more in, afraid all food might suddenly disappear, like a lizard who builds up layers of fat to live through the barren winter. Behind his chubby cheeks his inherent, normal slimness could still be perceived; he was too young, just a little over thirty, to have been able to become really fat. Despite his chubby cheeks, his hands were thin, with long, spindly, agile fingers. The visitor introduced himself:

'I am Lieutenant Antonio Dutra, notary from the tax department.'

'Is there any problem?' Quaresma asked nervously.

'None, major. We already know who you are; everything is in order, there are no legal pendencies.'

The notary coughed, took a cigarette, offered one to Quaresma and continued:

'When I heard that you plan to settle here, I took the liberty of coming to disturb you ... It's nothing important ... I do hope, major, that ...'

'Of course you're not disturbing me, lieutenant!'

'I've come to ask for a small contribution, for the festival of Our Lady of the Conception, our patron saint. I'm the treasurer of the fraternity.'

'Why certainly. It's a good cause. Although I'm not religious, I'm ...'

'That makes no difference. It's a local tradition that we must maintain.'

'That's good.'

'You see,' the notary continued, 'the people here are very poor, and the fraternity too, so that we are obliged to appeal to the goodwill of the wealthier inhabitants. And so, if I may, major ...'

'Just a moment please ...'

'Oh, don't get up, major. There's no urgency.'

He mopped his brow, returned his handkerchief to his pocket, glanced outside and then added:

'It's so hot! We've never had a summer like this. Are you settling in well, major?'

'Very well.'

'Do you intend to farm?'

'I do. That's why I have come to the country.'

'It's of no use now; but in the past! ... This farm was a glory, major! The quantities of fruit, the quantity of flour! But the land is tired and ...'

'Tired! Sr Antonio, there is no such thing as tired land! Europe has been cultivated for thousands of years, and still . . .'

'But there people work.'

'And why can't they work here?'

'Well, of course, they can. But Brazil presents so many obstacles . . .'

'My dear lieutenant, there's no obstacle that cannot be overcome.'

'Major, in time you will see. In our country the only thing that matters is politics. Anything else, forget it! At this very moment everyone's fighting over this question of the elections for deputy . . .'

As he spoke these words, the chubby face cast a furtive, crafty glance in the direction of the ingenuous Quaresma.

'What question?' he asked.

The lieutenant seemed to be expecting the question and answered gleefully:

'So you haven't heard, then?'

'No I haven't.'

'Well I'll tell you. The government's candidate is Doctor Castrioto, a fine young man, good orator, but certain leaders of municipal councils in the district have decided to oppose the government, all because Senator Guariba broke with the governor. And – *bang* – they've put forward this fellow called Neves, who's done nothing for the party and has no influence . . . What's your opinion?'

'Mine? . . . None!'

The employee of the tax department was astounded. Here was a man, who lived in the municipality of Curuzu[6] and, knowing the whole story, took no interest in the fight between Senator Guariba and the governor of the state! How could it be possible? Then he gave a sly smile. Of course, he thought, the cunning fellow wanted to keep in with both sides, to cover himself after the election. He was playing his cards with caution . . . How shrewd and ambitious! He would have to clip the wings of this 'foreigner', wherever he came from!

'You are a philosopher, major,' he said craftily.

'If only I were!' Quaresma innocently replied.

Antonio attempted to continue discussing the grave occurrence but, giving up hope of discovering the major's secret intentions, he assumed a vacant expression and prepared to leave, saying:

'So you have no objection to contributing to our festival, then?'

'Of course not.'

They said goodbye. Quaresma leaned on the veranda and watched as he mounted his lively, plump little chestnut, glistening with sweat. The notary rode off and disappeared down the road. The major reflected on the extraordinary interest such people took in political infighting, electoral intrigues, as if there was something immensely significant about them. He couldn't understand why a fight between two powerful men should create dissension among so many people who moved in entirely different circles. Wasn't the local soil good for cultivating and planting? Didn't it demand arduous daily labour? Why didn't they divert the effort they put into political fights and political meetings into enriching the soil so that it yielded new forms of life – wasn't that the creative work of God and of artists? How foolish it was to think of governors and Guaribas, when our lives depend entirely on the land, which demands our labour and our love . . .

What a scourge universal suffrage was, he thought.

A train whistle blew. He paused and watched it arrive. Watching a vehicle bringing people from the outside world is a special experience for those who live in distant places. It brings a mixture of fear and of joy. One thinks of the good news that it could be bringing, but also the bad . . . Thoughts that cause anguish . . .

The train, and the steamer, emerge from the distance, out of the Mystery, bringing with them not only news, good and bad, but also the touch, the smile, the voices of the people we love and who live far away.

Quaresma waited for the train. It arrived panting, in the glowing light of the setting sun, weaving its way like a reptile towards the station. It did not stay. The whistle blew, and it left

again, bearing news, friends, joys and sorrows to stations further off. The major thought briefly how ugly it was, how far
removed our modern inventions had become from the classical
concept of beauty bequeathed to us from two thousand years
ago. He glanced at the road that led to the station. Someone
was walking along it. He was coming towards the house. Who
could it be? He cleaned his pince-nez and directed it towards
the man who was walking in such a hurry ... Who was it?
That hat, like a soldier's helmet ... That long frock coat ...
Those short steps ... The guitar! It was him!

'Adelaide, Ricardo is here.'

THORNS AND ROSES

The buildings in the suburbs of Rio de Janeiro are the strangest of all the city. Part of this is undoubtedly due to the local topography, the capricious shape of the hills. The main cause, however, is the bizarre nature of the buildings themselves.

You can picture nothing as irregular, as erratic and as completely unplanned. The houses sprouted up like seeds that had been scattered by the wind, and the streets sprouted up alongside them. Some begin as wide as a boulevard and end as narrow as an alley; they meander along in fortuitous loops and resist being straightened out with implacable tenacity.

At times they run parallel, with irritating regularity; at others they draw away from each other, leaving large open spaces crammed with houses. In some places the houses are piled on top of each other, oppressively pressed together. Then suddenly a field opens out, stretching away as far as the eye can see.

The houses are laid out in this haphazard manner; and consequently so are the streets. There are houses for every taste, built in every possible style.

Walking down a street lined with mean, humble cottages, each with a street wall and a single door and window, one suddenly comes across a bourgeois villa, with stone vases atop an ornate façade, erected over a sturdy basement with iron-grilled windows. Recovering from the surprise, looking around, one sees a wattle hut with a roof of corrugated iron or even thatch, with people swarming around it and, a little further on, an old farmhouse with a veranda and columns of a style that is hard to define, which appears out of sorts as it tries to conceal itself from that onslaught of preposterous new buildings.

There is nothing in our suburbs that remotely recalls the famous suburbs of the great European cities, with their grand, placid villas and their well-cared-for, tarmacked streets and avenues, nor even those well-kept gardens, pruned and trimmed, because ours, when they exist at all, are usually ramshackle and ugly.

The local government services are also erratic and inconsistent. There are streets of which some sections have pavements and others have none. There are important connecting roads that are paved while others are left in a state of nature. You will find a perfectly good bridge to take you across a dry river bed and then, a short way ahead, a few rickety planks to get you across a fast-running stream.

In the streets there are elegant ladies in silks and brocades, cautiously avoiding the mud and the dust so as not to tarnish the splendour of their dresses. There are workmen in clogs,[1] dandies displaying the latest fashion, women in plain cotton dresses. In the evening, as they return from their work or their outings, this mixture of types can be seen in a single street or block, and rarely does the finest dressed enter the finest house.

In addition to the endemic flirting and the ubiquitous practice of magic,[2] the suburbs have other notable features, one of which is unique: the tenements (who would imagine them there?). Houses that scarcely have space for a tiny family are divided and subdivided, and the resulting minuscule quarters are rented out to the city's poor. It is here, in these human cubicles, that the most neglected fauna of our society is to be found, over whom a cloud of poverty hangs as dense as the fog that engulfs the London poor.

It is hard to conceive the humiliating trades by which the inhabitants of these cubicles live. Apart from office boys and government clerks, there are old women who weave lace by hand, men who trade in empty bottles, others who castrate cats, dogs and cockerels, witch-doctors, dealers in medicinal herbs; in short, a whole range of wretched occupations the very existence of which our middle and upper classes have not a single notion. Sometimes an entire family is squeezed into one of these cubicles, and on many occasions the parents have to walk to the centre of town for the lack of a nickel to pay for the train.

Ricardo Coração dos Outros lived in a wretched tenement house in one of the suburbs. It was not one of the sordid ones, but it was a tenement house in the suburbs.

He had lived there for years. He liked the house, which clung to a hillside and provided a view from his window of the built-up area that stretched from Piedade to Todos os Santos. Seen like this, from above, the suburbs have a certain charm. The tiny houses, painted blue, white or ochre, set amidst the dark green foliage of the mango trees, with here and there a coconut or military palm, tall and proud, make a fine sight, and the lack of any perceptible pattern in the streets imbues the landscape with a flavour of democratic confusion, of perfect solidarity between the people who live in them. And the tiny train nimbly crosses the entire scene, turning to the left, leaning to the right, very supple, its great vertebrae of coaches weaving their way like a snake through a rocky terrain.

It was at that window that Ricardo gave free rein to his contentment – his joys, his triumphs – and also to his pain and his resentment.

And there he was now, leaning over the sill, chin cupped in the palm of his hand, contemplating a wide stretch of that beautiful, grand and original city, capital of a great nation, of which he, he could not help but feel, was in a certain way the soul, giving form to its nebulous dreams and desires in somewhat dubious verses, which nevertheless the mournful guitar, if it did not endow them with meaning, endowed with a voice of its own, the plaintive voice of a child, of a country that was still growing up . . .

What was he thinking? Thoughts that made him sad. That black singer was still obsessed with giving meaning to the *modinha*, and he had followers. Some even referred to him as his, Ricardo's, rival; others were already saying he was far better than Coração dos Outros; and there were even some – ungrateful wretches – who had already forgotten Ricardo's work, his untiring efforts for the recuperation of the *modinha* and the guitar, and made no mention of his selfless labours.

With a glazed expression Ricardo thought of his childhood, of the village in the scrublands, of his parents' little house with its cattle pen and the mooing of the calves . . . And the cheese? As sturdy, as strong and as ugly as the land that yielded it, and yet vigorous too – so much so that one small slice would suffice for an entire meal! The parties . . . how he missed them. And the guitar – how had he learned it? Hadn't his teacher, Maneco Borges, foretold his future: 'You'll go far, Ricardo. The guitar wants your heart'?

Then why this enmity, this hatred directed at him – he, who had brought to this land of foreigners its substance, its essence, its very soul?

Hot tears began to stream down his cheeks. He looked at the mountains, straining his eyes to see the sea in the distance. The landscape was beautiful and majestic, yet wherever the ubiquitous granite, stark and impious, was not softened by the greenery of the vegetation, it appeared harsh and thankless.

And he was alone, alone with his glory and his torment, without love, without a friend to confide in, alone like a god, or like an apostle, in a thankless land that refused to hear his gospel.

He suffered for the lack of a friendly breast on which to shed his tears, which now fell to the impervious ground. He remembered the famous line:

If I weep . . . the burning sand my tears doth drink . . .[3]

As he cast his eyes down at this recollection, he caught a glimpse of a black girl doing her laundry in the communal tub. She was bent double over the clothes, bearing all their weight; she deftly soaped them, beat them against the stone and then began again. He felt a pang of pity for that wretched woman, doubly burdened by her class and her colour. A wave of tenderness came over him. He mused on this life, on its misfortunes, lost for a while in perplexity at the enigma of our wretched human destiny.

The girl had not seen him and began to sing as she worked:

Even the breeze is envious
Of the softness of your eyes

It was one of his. Ricardo beamed with satisfaction. He wanted to kiss that wretched woman, to hug her . . .

How strange life was! His consolation had come from that girl: in her humble, suffering voice, she had assuaged his torment! Then some lines of Padre Caldas[4] came to him, that predecessor of his on whom the aristocratic ladies of Lisbon had doted:

> Lereno made others happy,
> But happiness never knew . . .

So it was a mission! The girl stopped singing. Ricardo couldn't contain himself:

'Well done, Dona Alice, well done! I deserve an encore!'

The girl looked up and, seeing who it was that had spoken, said:

'I didn't know you was vere, sir; I wouldn't 'ave sung if I 'ad.'

'What nonsense! I assure you, it was good, very good. Sing!'

'Not fer ve world! Fer you to *larf* at me!'

Despite his continued insistence she refused to sing any more. But all resentment had now left Ricardo. He went back into the room and, sitting down at the table, he tried to write.

His room was furnished in the most rudimentary way. There was a hammock with lace fringes, a pine table with writing materials on it, a chair, a shelf with a few books and, hanging on one of the walls, the guitar in its leather case. There was also a device for making coffee.

He sat down with the decision to write a *modinha* about Glory, that fugitive quality that we think unattainable, as impalpable, as ungraspable as a puff of wind, that disturbs us, inflames us, that we yearn for, and burn for, like Love.

He set out the paper and prepared to start, but nothing came. The impact had been terrible; the idea that they were trying to rob him of his merit had shaken him to the very depths of his nature. He was unable to concentrate, pluck the words from the air, hear the music resounding in his ear.

It was almost midday. In the bare tamarind tree outside

crickets were chirping. It was getting hotter, the sky was a quivering, pale blue. He wanted to go out, to find a friend to share his concerns with. But who? If only Quaresma . . . *Quaresma! He* would console and comfort him.

It was true that his friend had shown little interest in the *modinha* of late, but nevertheless he understood the purpose, the meaning, the far-reaching potential of the work that he, Ricardo, had undertaken. If only the major were not so far away! He felt in his pockets. Not even two thousand *réis*! How could he go? He would arrange for a pass. There was a knock at the door; it was a letter. Not recognizing the writing, he excitedly tore it open. What could it be?

'My dear Ricardo,' he read, 'greetings. My daughter Quinota is getting married tomorrow, Thursday. She and her fiancé would be very pleased if you came. If you are free, get hold of your guitar and come here to take some tea with us. Your friend – Albernaz.'

The troubadour's features changed as he read. By the time he had finished reading the note the downcast, inconsolable expression had given way to a broad smile that covered his face from cheek to cheek. The general had not abandoned him: for the worthy soldier, Ricardo Coração dos Outros, was still the king of the guitar. He would go and he would arrange a free pass from Quaresma's former neighbour. He gave his guitar a tender, thankful look, as though it were some kind of deity dispensing its blessings.

When Ricardo entered the home of General Albernaz the guests had already drunk the last toast and were making their way in small groups towards the reception room. Dona Maricota was dressed in purple silk; her short trunk looked more than usually tightly squeezed into the luxury fabric that seemed intended for suppler, more elegant bodies. Quinota was radiant in her bridal dress. She was tall and had more classical features than her sister Ismênia, but a less interesting personality, despite her attractive looks. Lalá, the general's third daughter, fast becoming a woman, was wearing a large amount of face powder and constantly adjusted her hair while smiling at Lieutenant Fontes, generally considered her husband-to-be. Genelício, arm-in-arm with his bride, dressed in a badly cut tailcoat that emphasized his hunched-over stance, was finding it hard to walk due to his tight patent leather shoes.

Ricardo was too late to see them pass. As he arrived the general was the centre of attention, dressed in one of his uniforms from the grand old days, looking as ill at ease as a National Guardsman in Sunday dress. Beside him Rear Admiral Caldas had an air of great importance, both military and governmental. He had been the best man and was impeccably attired in full dress uniform. His insignia glistened like the brasses aboard ship at inspection time, and his sideburns, sprouting from his cheeks, scrupulously combed, seemed to yearn for the great winds of the open seas. Ismênia, dressed in pink, with her lack-lustre look, was moving listlessly from room to room, putting things in order. Lulu, the general's only son, proudly displayed his Military College uniform, covered with tassels and golden braid, as thanks to his father's influence he had passed the end-of-year exams.

Before long the general came to speak to Ricardo, and when he greeted the bride and groom they thanked him. Quinota even said, 'I'm so pleased . . .' as she leaned her head to one side and smiled at the ground – a smile that filled the troubadour's heart and transported him with joy.

The dances began, and the general, the admiral, Major Inocêncio Bustamante, who had also come in his uniform with its honorary purple stripe, Doctor Florêncio, Ricardo and two other guests went into the dining room, where they could talk.

The general was pleased. For so many years he had dreamed of a ceremony like this in his house, and now, for the first time, it was actually happening.

This business about Ismênia was a disaster . . . The ungrateful dog! But why think about it?

They greeted each other again.

'He's a fine young fellow, your new son-in-law,' said one of the guests.

The general removed his pince-nez, which was secured by a thin gold chain, and as he cleaned it, squinting a little, he replied:

'I'm very pleased.'

He put it back on, straightened the chain and continued:

'I think I have married my daughter well: a graduate, with good prospects, and intelligent.'

The admiral put in:

'And what prospects! It's not because we're related, but to be first clerk of the Treasury at thirty-two is something unheard of.'

'Isn't Genelício in the Audit Office? Didn't he pass?' asked Florêncio.

'Yes he did,' the other guest, who was a friend of the groom's, interjected, 'but it's all the same thing.'

Genelício had, in fact, got himself transferred; but this was not the only thing that had decided him to get married. He had written a *Synthesis of Scientific Public Accounting*, which, heaven knows how, had been heaped with praise by 'the press of this capital'. The minister, in light of the work's exceptional merit, had awarded him a prize of two million *réis*. The book had been published by the National Press, at the state's expense. It was a heavy tome of four hundred pages, in bureaucratic language, documented with a wealth of decrees and directives that took up two-thirds of the volume.

The opening sentence of the first part, the truly scientific, synthetical core of the work, had been widely commented and praised by the critics, not only for the novelty of the idea but for its beautiful turn of phrase.

It went as follows: 'Public Accounting is the art or science of appropriately entering the state's expenses and revenues.'

As well as the prize and the transfer, he had been offered the post of assistant director as soon as there was a vacancy.

After listening to all the comments by the admiral, the general and the other guests, the major was moved to remark:

'Except for the military, the best career is the Treasury, don't you agree?'

'Yes, of course,' said Doctor Florêncio.

'I don't mean to belittle our graduates,' the major hurriedly put in. 'Those who . . .'

Ricardo felt he ought to say something and said the first thing that came into his head:

'If one is successful, then all professions are good.'

'I wouldn't say that,' the admiral objected, stroking one of his sideburns. 'Not to disparage the others, but ours . . . eh, Albernaz, eh, Inocêncio?'

Albernaz raised his head, as if trying to recapture some vague recollection, and then he replied:

'Yes, but it has its drawbacks. When things go wrong, like at Curupaiti: enemy fire, people shot, soldiers dying, crying out . . .'

'Were you there, general?' asked the guest who was Genelício's friend.

'No I wasn't. I fell ill and returned to Brazil. But Camisão . . . You can't imagine what it was like – but you know, don't you, Inocêncio?'

'Of course . . . as I was there . . .'

'Polidoro[5] was ordered to attack Sauce. Flôres took the left flank, and our lot charged the Paraguayans. But the devils had used their time well, they were well entrenched . . .'

'That was Mitre,' said Inocêncio.

'It was. We attacked ferociously. That dreadful thundering of the cannons, bullets everywhere, men dying like flies . . . It was hell!'

'Who won?' asked one of the other guests.

They all stared in amazement, except for the general, who had great admiration for the skill of the Paraguayans.

'It was the Paraguayans. I mean, they repelled our attack. That's why I say that ours is a fine profession, but it has its drawbacks . . .'

'But that's not it. It was the same at the battle of Humaitá . . .'[6] the admiral was saying.

'Were you aboard?'

'No, I went later. I wasn't sent – political intrigue – going aboard was seen as a promotion . . . But as I was saying, at Humaitá . . .'

In the reception room people were dancing merrily. Very occasionally a guest would come into the room where they were talking. But the gentlemen did not permit the laughter, the music or the general merriment to distract them from their discussion of war.

The general, the admiral and the major astounded those placid civilians with accounts of battles they had not fought in and valiant combats they'd never seen.

No one appreciates stories of war as much as a mild, well-fed citizen after a few generous glasses of wine. He sees it as picturesque – what one could call the immaterial aspect of war and battles. The shots are fired in salute; if they kill, it matters little. Even Death, in such accounts, loses its tragic import: *only three thousand dead!*

And, as recounted by General Albernaz, who had never seen a war, it was all romanticized, a war seen through rose-tinted glasses, a war out of popular literature, where the ferocity, the brutality and the bloodshed remain untold.

As Ricardo, Doctor Florêncio – the one who was employed as an engineer at the waterworks – and Albernaz's two new acquaintances listened enthralled, both astonished and envious, to the imaginary exploits of our three heroes (one of whom was at least an honorary soldier, perhaps the only one who had ever really taken part in a war), Dona Maricota came bustling in. She was eagerly livening up the party. She was younger than her husband, and the hair on her tiny head, which afforded such a contrast to her enormous body, was still completely black. She was still breathless as she reproached her husband:

'What on earth are you all doing in here, Chico, while I have to run about, getting the girls to dance? . . . Everyone into the other room!'

'We'll come in a minute, Dona Maricota,' one of them replied.

'No!' the lady of the house retorted. 'Right now! Come along Sr Caldas . . . Sr Ricardo . . . all of you!'

And taking hold of their shoulders, she pushed them out one by one.

'Quickly, quickly! Lemos's daughter is going to sing. And then it's your turn, do you hear, Sr Ricardo?'

'Of course, madam. Your word is my command . . .'

As they went the general came up to Coração dos Outros and asked:

'Tell me something: how is our friend Quaresma?'

'He's well.'

'Has he written to you?'

'Occasionally. I was wondering, general . . .'

The general inclined his head and, adjusting his pince-nez which was about to fall off, barked:

'Wondering what?'

Ricardo was a little intimidated by the general's martial tone. He hesitated for a while, but then, afraid he would miss the opportunity, blurted out:

'I was wondering if you could arrange a ticket for me, a pass, to visit him.'

The general looked thoughtful and scratched his head:

'It won't be easy . . . but come to my office, tomorrow.'

As they continued on their way, Coração dos Outros added:

'I miss him. And I'm worried about a few things . . . As a man of reputation I have to protect . . .'

'Come tomorrow.'

Dona Maricota reappeared. She was annoyed:

'Well, are you coming or not?'

'We're coming!' the general retorted.

And then, turning to Ricardo, he said:

'Our friend Quaresma could be perfectly all right, but he *would* meddle with books! I haven't looked at a book for forty years!'

They now entered the room, which was vast. The only decorations were two large portraits in heavy gilt frames – garish depictions in oils of Albernaz and his wife – an oval mirror and a few smaller pictures. The furniture had been removed to make more room for the dancing. The bride and the groom were sitting on the sofa, presiding over the party. Low-cut necklines, tailcoats, a few frock coats and a lot of morning coats with striped trousers could be seen. Through a gap in the curtains Ricardo saw the street. The pavement outside was crowded; it was a tall house with a garden, so it was only from the street that onlookers could get a glimpse of the party. Lalá was talking to Lieutenant Fontes on one of the verandas. The general glanced at them approvingly, bestowing his blessing . . .

Lemos's celebrated daughter was preparing to sing. She went to the piano, put the sheet of music in position and launched

into an Italian *romanza*, which she sang with all the perfection
and lack of taste of a well-educated girl. When she finished
there was some perfunctory clapping.

Doctor Florêncio was standing behind the general:

'That girl has a lovely voice. Who is she?' he asked.

'She's Lemos's daughter, Doctor Lemos from the Sanitary
Department,' the general answered.

'She sings very well.'

'She's in the last year at the conservatory,' the general
explained.

Ricardo's turn came. He sat in a corner of the room, took up
his guitar, tuned it, played a scale and then, assuming the tragic
air of an actor about to play Oedipus Rex, he said in a grave
voice: 'Young ladies, ladies and gentlemen . . .' He cleared his
throat and continued: 'I am going to sing "Your Arms", a *modinha* with music and lyrics of my own composition. It is a fine,
tender composition, full of exalted poetry.' At this his eyes
almost left their sockets. He added: 'Please don't make a sound,
as it destroys the inspiration. And the guitar is a very, *ve-ry
de-li-cate* instrument. Now . . .'

The silence was complete. He began. He started softly with
a gentle moan, like the long-drawn-out sigh of a wave. Then
came a rapid, jerky section, with wild strumming on the guitar.
Finally, alternating between the two, the *modinha* came to a
close.

They were all profoundly moved; he had touched the hearts
of the girls and the aspirations of the men. The applause went
on and on. The general embraced him. Genelício rose and
shook his hand. Quinota repeated his gesture, immaculate in
her wedding dress.

Ricardo fled to the dining room to escape their praise. In the
corridor someone called out: 'Sr Ricardo, Sr Ricardo!' He
turned around.

'What may I do for you, madam?' It was a girl who wanted
a copy of the *modinha*.

'You must know,' she said sweetly, 'you must know that I
love your *modinhas* . . . They're so tender, so sensitive . . .
Could you give it to Ismênia to keep for me?'

Cavalcânti's fiancée was passing and, hearing her name mentioned, she asked:

'What is it, Dulce?'

The girl explained. She accepted the undertaking and then asked Ricardo in her plaintive voice:

'Sr Ricardo, when do you plan to see Doná Adelaide?'

'The day after tomorrow, I hope.'

'Are you really going to visit them?'

'Yes I am.'

'Then ask her to write to me. I would so much like to receive a letter . . .'

And she furtively wiped her eyes with her little lace handkerchief.

III

GOLIATH

On the Saturday of the week after the general's daughter took the grave, hunched-over Genelício, the pride and glory of our civil service, as her husband, Olga got married. The ceremony took place with the pomp and finery habitual to people of her social standing. There were some Parisian features, *corbeilles*[1] for the bride and other fashionable touches, that didn't bother her, but that gave her no more pleasure than they would have any normal bride. Even less, perhaps.

No clearly made decision lay behind her presence in the church. She still could not understand what it was that had made her take the step, but there was no indication that she had been influenced by anyone in her resolve. But the husband was pleased. Not so much due to the bride as to the life that he would lead. Being a doctor with qualifications and awards that attested his talent, now that he was rich he saw ahead of him the road to triumph: in the medical field and through the positions he would hold. He didn't have a penny but saw his routine qualification as an aristocratic title, like those of traditional European nobility used for the social elevation of the daughters of Yankee sausage tycoons. Despite his father being an important farmer, somewhere in the vastness of Brazil, his father-in-law had given him everything – and he had accepted without compunction, with the disdain of a duke, a duke with grades and scholastic awards receiving the tribute of a rogue who had never set foot inside an academic institution.

He believed that his bride had chosen him because of his magnificent title, his doctor's certificate. It was not for the title, but for the intelligence, love of science and overriding aspiration to knowledge that she thought he possessed. This illusion rapidly faded; then it was the inevitable course of events, the tyranny of society and her natural reluctance to break it off that led to the marriage. She even thought to herself that, if it weren't this one, it would be another just like him: it was best not to put it off.

These, rather than the constraints society imposed on her, of which she was unaware, were the reasons she had not entered the church that day entirely of her own free will.

Despite the pomp she was far from being a majestic bride. In spite of her purely European origins, she looked small, tiny in fact, beside the bridegroom, who stood tall and erect, beaming with joy. She seemed to disappear beneath the dress, the veils and the outmoded ornaments with which girls who get married deck themselves out. Moreover she was not a great beauty; she did not have those classical features society expects of a wealthy bride.

There was nothing Grecian about her looks, authentic or contrived, none of the majesty of grand opera. Her features were completely lacking in classical proportions, although they were deeply individual. The brightness of her large black eyes, which almost entirely filled their sockets, lit up her lively face, and her small, finely drawn mouth expressed a kind and witty nature. She had the air of a girl who was both thoughtful and inquisitive.

Contrary to custom they did not leave town but settled into one of her father's former residences.

Quaresma didn't go to the reception: he sent the traditional turkey and suckling pig and wrote a long letter. His whole attention was taken up by the farm. The heat was ending, the rains and the planting season were coming. He didn't want to leave his land. It would be a short journey, but, even so, it would be like deserting the battlefield.

The orchard was completely cleared, and the vegetable plots were ready. Ricardo's visit had distracted him a little, without, however, keeping him away from his agricultural duties.

Ricardo spent a month with the major, and it was a triumph. Everyone fêted his presence and vied for his attention.

First of all he went to the town. It was four kilometres past Quaresma's house, and there was a railway station there. Instead of taking the train Ricardo took to the road on foot, if 'road' is an adequate term for a path full of potholes that led up and down hills, across plains and over rivers at rickety bridges. The town! It had two main streets: the old one, which ran along the old army route, and the new one, which had been built to connect the old one with the railway station. Together they formed a T, the vertical arm of which was the road to the station. The other streets opened off them. At the beginning the houses stood side by side, but they grew gradually further apart until they reached the open country. The old street, formerly 'Imperador', was now called 'Marechal Deodoro', and the new one, formerly 'Imperatriz', 'Marechal Floriano'.[2] The Rua da Matriz[3] led from one end of Rua Deodoro to the church on the top of a hill, stark and unadorned in the Jesuit style. The Town Hall stood in an open space, the Praça da República,[4] reached by a street that was scarcely recognizable as such, the houses were so far apart.

The building was a mass of bricks, mouldings and windows with iron-barred balconies, of no architectural style; the lack of good taste would sadden the heart of any who knew the buildings of a similar nature in the small medieval communes of Belgium and France.

Ricardo went into a barber's shop in Marechal Deodoro Street, the Rio de Janeiro Salon, to have a shave. He introduced himself, and the barber told him about the town. One of the customers took him under his wing, and he was soon being introduced to people.

When he returned to the major's house he already had an invitation to the ball at Doctor Campos's the following Wednesday. Doctor Campos was chairman of the council.

He had arrived on Saturday and gone for his walk around the town on Sunday.

After mass Ricardo watched the congregation emerge.

Congregations are never large in the interior, but he watched a few of the country girls, decked out in bows, with downcast, listless expressions as they walked in silence down the hill from the church, spread out into the street and then immediately entered the houses, where they would spend a week of boredom and seclusion. It was as he came out of church that they introduced him to Doctor Campos.

He was the local doctor, but he lived outside the town on his farm. He had come to attend the service with his daughter, Nair, in their spider buggy.[5]

Our troubadour and the doctor chatted for a moment, while the daughter, very thin and pale with long, skinny arms, gazed down at the dusty street in feigned irritation. When they left Ricardo gazed after her for a while, this daughter of the great open spaces.

Doctor Campos's party was followed by others, which Ricardo honoured with his presence and animated with the sound of his voice. Quaresma did not go with him, but he savoured his victory. Although the major had given up the guitar, he continued to admire that essentially Brazilian instrument. The disastrous consequences of his petition had in no way shaken his patriotic convictions. He maintained his deeply rooted ideas, only now he concealed them so as not to suffer from the incomprehension and malice of others.

Thus he relished Ricardo's overwhelming victory, showing as it did that national sentiment was still strong enough in the town to resist the invasion of imported fashions and tastes.

Ricardo was showered with honours and favours without distinction of party. It was Doctor Campos, chairman of the council, who most plied him with tributes. That morning the councillor was sending one of his horses to take him on an outing to the Carico. Ricardo was talking to Quaresma before he left for the fields:

'Major, it was a fine idea to come to the country. One lives well here, and one can achieve success . . .'

'I have no desire to do that. You know how alien all of that is to me.'

'I know . . . Quite . . . I don't say one should seek it, but if people offer, one shouldn't refuse, don't you agree?'

'It depends, my dear Ricardo. I couldn't accept the burden of commanding a squadron . . .'

'No, nor could I. But listen, major: I love the guitar; I even dedicate my life to its acceptance and refinement. But if tomorrow the president said to me: "Sr Ricardo, I want you to be deputy," do you think that I wouldn't accept? Of course I would! Even knowing perfectly well I would have to abandon the guitar! One should never refuse an offer, major.'

'Everyone has his theories.'

'True. By the way, major: do you know Doctor Campos?'

'By name.'

'You know that he's chairman of the council?'

Quaresma glanced at Ricardo for a moment with a look of slight suspicion. The minstrel didn't notice and continued:

'He lives a league from here. I've already played at his house and today I'm going riding with him.'

'That's good.'

'He wants to meet you. May I bring him here?'

'Of course.'

At that moment a servant of Doctor Campos came through the gate, bringing the promised horse. Ricardo mounted, and Quaresma set off for the fields to find his two employees – two, as in addition to Anastácio (who was more a member of the family than an employee) he had hired Felizardo.

It was a cool summer morning, after several days of continuous rain.

There was a soft breeze, and everywhere the light was radiant. Quaresma walked along surrounded by the sounds of nature: the rustling of leaves in the woods, the chirping of birds. Red tanagers fluttered about, bevies of seedeaters, ani-birds perched in the trees, looking like little black specks against the greenery. Even the wildflowers, often so sad, had come out to bask in the sunlight, not only to propagate the species, but to display their beauty too.

Quaresma and his employees were now working a long way

off, clearing a field. It was to help with this work that Felizardo
had been hired. He was tall and thin, with long arms and legs,
like a monkey's. He had a copper-coloured complexion and a
wispy beard, but despite his fragile appearance there was no
more valiant hoer than he. He was also a tireless gossip. When
he arrived in the morning, at around six o'clock, he already
knew all the petty intrigues of the town.

The clearing was to regain land at the north end of the farm
that was overgrown with scrub. Once it was cleared, the major
planned to plant half a hectare or more with maize, interspersed
with potatoes, a new crop for which he had high hopes. The
scrub had been cleared, and the fire-break ditches had been
dug. But Quaresma had decided not to set fire to it, so as not to
scorch the soil and destroy its nutrients. His work today consisted of separating the thicker branches for use as firewood
and taking off the leaves and smaller branches to where he
would burn them later, in little bonfires.

This took time and cost him several falls, unused as he was
to the vines and tree stumps, but it was land that promised a
greater yield.

During the work Felizardo gossiped away to pass the time.
Some people sing. Felizardo talked, hardly caring whether anyone listened or not.

As soon as the major arrived, he remarked: 'Tongues are
waggin' everywhere.'

Quaresma would usually listen and ask Felizardo questions.
Anastácio would remain silent and serious. He worked away,
pausing from time to time to reflect, adopting as he did so a
priestly posture reminiscent of a Theban fresco.

'Why, what's up?' the major asked.

The good fellow placed a thick branch on the pile, wiped the
sweat away with his hand and replied in his soft, melodious voice:

'Politics ... Lieutenan' Antonio almos' *attacked* Doctor
Campos yesterday.'

'Where?'

'At ve station.'

'What about?'

'Politics. From what I 'eard, ve lieutenan' is fer ve guvner and Doctor Campos is fer ve senator . . . A right ol' pickle!'

'And which one do you support?'

Felizardo didn't reply at once. He took his scythe and cut through the rest of a vine that was wrapped around the trunk he was about to remove. Anastácio glanced at his loquacious companion. At length he said:

'I dunno! It ain't fer ve likes o' me t' decide. Vat's fer people like yerself, sir.'

'I'm the same as you, Felizardo.'

'Wouldn't I be ve lucky one! Why, jus' free days back I 'eard vat you was a friend of ve *marshal*.'[6]

He went off with the vine. Quaresma was very taken aback.

'Who told you that?' he asked when he returned.

'I can't say exactly, guv'ner. I 'eard it in ve Spaniard's grocery; and vey say vat Doctor Campos is all puffed up an' proud, wot wiv bein' a friend o' yours.'

'But it's a lie! I'm not a *friend* of the marshal! I've met him . . . But I've never told anyone here! How can they say I'm his friend?'

'So!' exclaimed Felizardo with a broad, knowing grin. 'Yer tryin' t' oil out of it, guvn'er.'

Despite all Quaresma's efforts, there was no way to remove from that simple mind the idea that he was a friend of Marshal Floriano. 'I met him at work,' the major would protest. Felizardo would grin suspiciously and say, 'Ve guv'ner! 'E's as cunning as a fox.'

Such insistence had a marked effect on Quaresma. What could it mean? And Ricardo's words, his insinuations that morning . . . He believed the singer to be a good man, a faithful friend who would be incapable of luring him into a trap; but his enthusiasm combined with his desire to be a good friend could have misled him and made him the instrument of some plot. For a while Quaresma was pensive and paused in his work of removing the branches. Soon, however, he forgot all about it and gave it no further thought. In the evening, at dinner, he no longer remembered the conversation, and the mood was normal – not particularly merry and not particularly sad, but not overcast by apprehension.

Dona Adelaide, as always in her cream housecoat and black skirt, was sitting at the head of the table with Quaresma on her right and on her left, Ricardo. It was she who always encouraged Ricardo to talk.

'How did you enjoy your outing, Sr Ricardo?'

She could not bring herself to call him simply 'Ricardo'. Her upbringing, as a lady from a different era, did not permit her to adopt this commonly used, vulgar form of address. Her parents, who were rigorously Portuguese, had always addressed people as 'senhor', and she continued to do so, without affectation.

'Very much. What a place! A magnificent waterfall! For inspiration, one must come to the country!'

His features assumed an expression of rapture, like a Greek tragedy mask, and his cavernous voice emerged like muffled thunder.

'Have you been composing a lot, Ricardo?' Quaresma asked.

'I finished a *modinha* today.'

'What is it called?' asked Dona Adelaide.

' "Carola's Lips".'

'Splendid! Have you written the music yet?'

It was Quaresma's sister who had asked. Ricardo was lifting his fork to his lips; he left it suspended between his mouth and the plate and replied with great conviction:

'The music, madam, is the first thing I write.'

'You must sing it to us soon.'

'Of course, major.'

After dinner Quaresma and Coração dos Outros went out for a walk around the farm. This was the only concession that Policarpo made that would allow his friend to observe the progress of his agricultural labours. He took the customary piece of bread that he crumbled and then threw the crumbs to the chickens to watch the cruel dispute between the birds. When he had finished he would remain for a while reflecting on the lives of those creatures that were bred, maintained and protected to sustain his own. He smiled at the chickens, picked up the chicks, featherless but very alive and greedy, and paused to marvel at the stupidity of the majestic turkey, strutting around, letting out its conceited cries. Next he would go to the pigsty, where he helped Anastácio pouring the rations into the troughs. The huge hog with floppy ears got to its feet with an effort and solemnly came to bury its head in the mixture. In the next compartment the piglets came grunting up with their mother to wallow in the food.

It was true their greed was repugnant, but there was a lingering softness in their eyes that was human, that made him like them.

Ricardo took little interest in these lower forms of life, but Quaresma would contemplate them for minutes on end, lost in silent, protracted speculation. They sat down at the foot of a tree, Quaresma watched the sky overhead, while Coração dos Outros recounted some story or other.

It was getting late. The surroundings had started to mellow after the long, burning kiss of the sun. The bamboos sighed, the crickets chirped, the doves cooed amorously. Hearing footsteps, the major turned around.

'Godfather!'

'Olga!'

They embraced and then stood, hands clasped, still staring at each other. There followed those meaningless, touching remarks that characterize all happy reunions: 'When did you get here?' 'I didn't expect . . .' 'It's so far . . .' Ricardo looked on, enchanted to see their fondness for each other. Anastácio had removed his hat and was gazing at the 'young missus' with that kindly, vacant look of the African.

Once the emotion had passed the girl examined the pigsty then cast her glance around the farm. Quaresma asked:

'Where's your husband?'

'The doctor? . . . He's inside.'

Her husband had resisted a great deal before accompanying her there. He thought such intimacy unsuitable; the fellow had no degree, no brilliant career, no fortune. He couldn't understand how his father-in-law, who despite everything was a wealthy man who moved in a different social sphere, could have maintained this friendship – and made it even closer – with a minor official of a second-rate government department, and made him her godfather too! He should have broken it off; it was a friendship that undermined the whole structure of Brazilian society! But when Dona Adelaide received him with such immense respect and special consideration, he was mollified; all his little vanities had been paid their due.

Dona Adelaide, an elderly lady from the time when the Empire[7] first established the academic elite, had a special reverence for doctor's degrees; and she naturally did not conceal this when she found herself in the presence of Doctor Armando Borges, of whose academic record she was all too aware.

Even Quaresma received him with every sign of admiration, and the doctor, enjoying such prodigious esteem, started to talk – slowly, sententiously, dogmatically. And as he talked, perhaps not to weaken the impact, with his right hand he gyrated the huge ring, the talisman, the symbol that covered the whole of the base of his left index finger.

They talked for a long time. The young couple told them about the political turmoil in Rio and the uprising of the Fort of Santa Cruz.[8] Dona Adelaide talked of the drama of the move, the broken furniture, the objects destroyed. Around midnight they all went very happily off to bed, while the toads in the stream raised their solemn hymn to the transcendental beauty of the deep, black, star-studded sky.

They woke early. Quaresma did not go to straight to work. He chatted with the doctor over breakfast. The post arrived, bringing him a newspaper. He tore open the wrapper and read the name. It was *The County*, a local weekly aligned with the government party. As the doctor had gone out, he took the opportunity to read it. He was on the veranda. The breeze rustled through the bamboos, which gently swayed. He put on his pince-nez, sat back in his rocking chair and, unfolding the paper, began to read. The main article was entitled 'Intruders' and consisted of a vicious attack on the residents who lived but had not been born there: 'complete outsiders who have come to interfere with the private and political life of the Curuzu family, disturbing its peace and tranquillity'.

What the deuce did it mean? He was about to put the paper aside when he thought he caught sight of his name. It was in these verses:

CURUZU POLITICS

Quaresma, my dear, Quaresma!
Quaresma of my dreams!
Leave the potatoes in peace,
Forget about the beans.

A farmer, my dear Quaresma,
That you will never be.
So go back to your old obsession
Of writing in Tupi.

ALERT EYE.

The major was stupefied. What could it mean? Why? Who was behind it? He simply couldn't find any reason, any basis for such an attack. His sister came up with his goddaughter. Quaresma held out the paper to her with a trembling hand: 'Read this, Adelaide.'

She saw at once how upset her brother was and read it with great concern. She had the maternal spirit of spinsters, whose concern for the sufferings of others seems to be all the more as they have no children. While she read Quaresma said: 'But what have I done? What have *I* got to do with politics?' And he scratched his greying hair.

Dona Adelaide said gently:

'Calm down, Policarpo. Is this all it is? Really!'

His goddaughter read it too and then asked:

'Have you ever interfered in local politics?'

'Never . . . I shall announce that . . .'

'Have you gone mad?' the two women exclaimed at once. His sister added:

'That would be dreadful! An explanation? Never!'

The doctor and Ricardo came in as the three of them were discussing the matter. They noticed how changed Quaresma was: pale, misty-eyed, constantly scratching his head.

'What's the matter, major?' the troubadour asked.

The ladies explained and gave them the verses to read. Ricardo told them what he had heard. Everyone in the town believed that the major had come to engage in politics; that was the reason he allowed the peasants to gather wood on his land, distributed medicine and gave out alms . . . Antonio had said that he was a hypocrite who must be unmasked.

'But didn't you deny it?' asked Quaresma.

Ricardo said that he had, but that the notary hadn't believed him and had repeated his intention of attacking Quaresma.

The major was deeply affected by all of this. But, as was his habit, he tried not to show his feelings and while his friends were with him he concealed his concern.

Olga and her husband stayed for about two weeks at 'The Haven'. At the end of the first week her husband already seemed bored. There were not many places to see. Our villages in general have very little beautiful scenery, but just like in European villages there are always one or two traditional sights to visit.

In Curuzu the most famous excursion was to the Carico, a waterfall two leagues from Quaresma's house in the mountains that crossed the horizon. Doctor Campos had already made the major's acquaintance, and thanks to him there were horses and a side-saddle so that Olga too could go to the waterfall.

They went in the morning: the chairman of the council, Olga and her husband and Doctor Campos's daughter. It was a fine sight: a narrow waterfall hurtled down the mountainside from a height of fifteen metres, in three separate streams. The water twisted and swirled as it fell, crashing down into a great rock basin with a thunderous roar. The surrounding vegetation gave the impression of closing it in beneath a vaulted roof of trees. With an effort the sun filtered through; small circles and oblongs of sunlight appeared, glittering here and there on the water and the rocks. The parakeets perched on the branches, a paler shade of green, looked like overlaid ornamentations in a phantasmagorical room.

Olga was left completely free to see it all, roaming from one side to the other, as Doctor Campos's daughter never uttered a word, while the doctor was getting news about the latest medical developments from her husband: how do they cure erysipelas nowadays? Is emetic tartar still used?

What she had noticed most during the outing was the poverty everywhere, how little was planted, the precarious houses, the downcast, dejected look of the poor. Brought up in the city, she had the notion that peasants were cheerful, healthy and happy. With so much clay and so much water, why weren't the houses built of bricks? Why didn't the roofs have tiles? There was nothing but that dreadful thatch and the mud-covered wattle with the criss-crossed stakes showing through, like the skeleton of an invalid. Why was nothing planted around the houses, vegetables or fruit? It would be so easy, just a few hours' work! And there were no cattle, of any size. Scarcely a goat or a sheep. Why? Even on the farms the picture was not more encouraging; they were squat and gloomy. No perfumed orchards, no succulent vegetable plots. Apart from the coffee and a maize plantation here and there, she could see no other crops or signs of agricultural activity. It couldn't be just laziness. For their own sustenance people are always prepared to work. Even those peoples who are most accused of sloth do a little work. In Africa, India or Indo-China, the families and tribes plant food to eat. Could it be the soil? Why? All these questions aroused her curiosity, her desire to understand, and also her compassion for those outcasts, dressed in rags, living in huts, possibly going hungry – doleful creatures . . .

If she were a man, she thought, she would spend months, even years, here and in other rural regions. She would inquire, observe and without doubt discover the reason and the solution. They were like peasants in the Middle Ages and at the start of the modern era, like La Bruyère's[9] famous animal with a human face and articulate speech.

The next day, as she was going to walk around the fields her godfather had cleared she decided she'd ask the talkative Feliz-ardo about it. The long and arduous task was nearly complete; the large tract of land which extended a short way up the hill-side behind the farm was almost entirely cleared.

Olga found him at the bottom of the hill, chopping the larger pieces of wood with an axe; Anastácio was at the top of the hill, at the edge of the woods, raking leaves. She greeted Felizardo.

'Mornin', ma'am.'

'A lot of hard work?'

'I does wot I can, miss.'

'Yesterday I went to the Carico, a lovely place . . . Where do you live, Felizardo?'

'On ve uvver side, on ve road t' town.'

'Is it a big place?'

'It's got some land, yes miss – *ma'am*.'

'Why don't you plant for yourself?'

'*Do wot*, miss! And wot would I eat?'

'What you plant, or using the money from selling it.'

'No miss, it ain't 'ow you're finking. An' while ve plants is growin', wot do we eat *ven*?'

He brought down his axe, but the branch escaped him. He placed it more firmly on the block and said, before striking again:

'Land's not for us. An' what about *ants*? We ain't got no tools. It's all for vem *Italians* an' *Germans*, 'oo ve guvment gives everyfing to. Ve government don' wan *us* . . .'

He brought down his axe, firmly and surely, and the rough-barked branch split almost exactly in two, pale, yellowish wood with a trace of dark heartwood emerging.

As she returned she tried to put his discontent out of her mind, but she couldn't. He was right. For the first time she real-ized that it was only Brazilians that the government left to fend for themselves; for the immigrants every assistance, every facil-ity was provided, in addition to the education they had received and the support of their compatriots.

And wasn't the land his? But to whom did all the abandoned land all around belong? She had even seen farms closed down with the houses in ruins. Why was all the land owned by so few? Why these vast, unproductive estates?

But her concentration was not good, and her thoughts soon wandered to other thoughts. She headed for home, all the faster as it was dinner time and she had begun to feel hungry.

She found her husband and godfather in conversation. The former had lost a little of his haughtiness; there were times when he was even quite natural. When she arrived her god-father was exclaiming:

'Fertilizers! No Brazilian would ever think of that. We have the most fertile soil in the world!'

'But it wears out, major,' the doctor observed.

Dona Adelaide remained silent, intent on her crochet. Ricardo was listening, wide-eyed. Olga interrupted the conversation:

'What has annoyed you, Godfather?'

'It's your husband who is trying to convince me that our soil needs fertilizers . . . It's an insult!'

'Make no mistake, major,' the doctor continued, 'if I were you I would try out some phosphates . . .'

'He's right, major,' Ricardo put in. 'When I started to play the guitar I didn't want to learn music. Music? What nonsense! Inspiration is all you need! Now I realize one has to. It's the same thing . . .' he concluded.

They all glanced at each other, except Quaresma, who spoke from the depths of his soul:

'Doctor, Brazil is the most fertile country in the world, the most richly endowed, and her soil requires no "assistance" to sustain her people. Be certain of that!'

'More fertile land exists,' the doctor put in.

'Where?'

'In Europe.'

'In Europe?'

'Yes, in Europe. The black soil of Russia, for example.'

The major gazed at the young man for a while and then exclaimed triumphantly:

'You are not a patriot! These young men . . .'

Things were calmer over dinner. Ricardo even made a few remarks about the guitar. In the evening the minstrel sang his latest work, 'Carola's Lips'. It was suspected that Carola was one of Doctor Campos's maids, but no one mentioned it. They listened attentively and applauded effusively. Olga played on Dona Adelaide's old piano, and before eleven o'clock they had all withdrawn.

Quaresma entered his room, undressed, put on his nightshirt and once in bed began to read a historical account that praised Brazil's natural wealth and resources.

Everything was quiet in the house; outside, there was not a sound to be heard. The toads had momentarily suspended their nocturnal symphony. As Quaresma read he remembered how Darwin had listened with pleasure to this concert from the marshes. Everything in this country is extraordinary, he thought. He heard a strange noise coming from the storeroom next to his bedroom. He listened hard. The toads started their hymn again. Some of the voices were deep, others were higher and shriller. They entered in turn, before coming together to sing for a while in unison. For an instant the music ceased. The major listened intently: the noise continued. What was it? There was a soft snapping sound as if someone were breaking twigs and letting them fall to the ground ... The toads began again: the conductor tapped his baton and the basses and tenors entered. They sang long enough for Quaresma to read five pages. The amphibians stopped; the noise continued. Quaresma got up, took the candlestick, and just as he was, in his nightshirt, went to the room from where the noise was coming.

He opened the door and saw nothing. He was about to examine the corners when he felt a sting on the back of his foot. He almost cried out. He lowered the candle to see more clearly and discovered an enormous ant furiously clinging to his scrawny ankle. He had discovered what was making the noise: it was ants. They had invaded the storeroom through a hole in the floor and were carrying away his supplies of maize and beans, whose containers had inadvertently been left open. The floor was black, and, weighed down with grains, in serried ranks, they dived into the ground in search of their subterranean city.

He wanted to drive them away. He killed one, two, ten,

twenty, a hundred; but there were thousands, and the army kept growing. One bit him, then another, and they kept on biting: his legs, his feet, climbing up his body. He could stand it no longer. He yelled, stamped and dropped the candle.

He was in the dark. He struggled to the door, passed through and fled from that infinitesimal enemy, which perhaps, even in the brightest sunlight, would not be able to see who he was . . .

IV

'STAND FIRM,
I'M ON MY WAY'

Dona Adelaide, Quaresma's sister, was four years older than he was. She was a fine-looking lady, of medium build, a complexion that had begun to acquire the glaze of advancing age, a thick head of hair, now entirely a yellowish grey, and an expression that was calm and gentle. Unemotional, unimaginative, objective and positive in her outlook, she was a contrast to her brother in every way. Although there was never any deep disagreement between them, neither was there any deep understanding. She neither understood nor tried to understand her brother's nature, just as her methodical, organized nature and plain, straightforward ideas had no effect on him.

She had already reached fifty, and shortly he would too. But they were both in fine health, with very few ailments, and promised to live for many years to come. The orderly, untroubled life they had lived until then was largely responsible for their good health. Quaresma's obsessions had not emerged until he was forty, and she had none.

Life was simple for Dona Adelaide: it meant living – that is, having a house, lunch and dinner, clothes, all modest and unassuming. She had no ambitions or passions. As a girl she had not dreamed of princes, fine possessions, adulation or even a husband. She never married because she had not felt the need to; she felt no need for sex. She was a person who was at ease with herself.

Within the family household her tranquil manner, her calm emerald-green eyes that shone with a lunar softness served to highlight her brother's restlessness and his anguished state of mind.

I am not implying that Quaresma was used to raving like a lunatic. Fortunately not. His appearance revealed nothing of the inner anguish that disturbed his spirit; however, a more careful observation of his habits, gestures and behaviour would soon reveal his troubled thoughts and his lack of peace of mind.

There were times when he would gaze into the distance at the horizon for minutes on end, lost in thought, others, when he was working in the fields, when he would stand stock still, eyes fixed on the ground, scratching one hand with the other. He would remain like that for a moment, then with a click of the tongue he would return to his work. And there were even some occasions when he would let out an unwarranted exclamation or remark.

On these occasions Anastácio would glance furtively at his employer. He no longer looked him in the eye, nor did he make comment. Felizardo continued his account of the elopement of Custódio's daughter with Manduca from the store. And so the work progressed . . .

It hardly need be said that Dona Adelaide did not notice any of this, for the obvious reason that, apart from in the early morning and at dinner, they were always apart, Quaresma planting in the fields, she supervising the running of the house.

Their other friends and acquaintances were not aware of the preoccupations that were gradually consuming the major for the simple reason that they lived so far away.

It was more than six months since Ricardo had visited him, and the last letters he had received from his goddaughter and her father had arrived a week earlier. He had not seen Olga since Ricardo was there, and had not seen her father for almost a year, that is, since he had moved to 'The Haven'.

During this time Quaresma's interest in how he could best put his land to use did not cease. His habits had not changed, and his activities continued as before, although it is true that he had lost interest in his meteorological instruments.

He no longer consulted the hygrometer, the barometer and his other companions, no longer entered the readings in his notebook. He was annoyed with them. Whether it was his own lack of experience and understanding of the theories, or for whatever other reason, every forecast that Quaresma made based on combining the data was wrong. When he predicted fine weather it rained; when he predicted rain it stayed dry.

As a result he wasted a lot of seed. Felizardo would smile about the instruments with his primitive caveman's grin:

'It's no use, guv'ner. Ve rain comes when God decides.'

The aneroid barometer still stood in a corner with its pointer swinging from side to side, unnoticed. The thermometer, a legitimate Casella, lay abandoned on the veranda, without so much as a friendly glance. The basin of the pluviometer was now in the chicken pen, being used as a drinking bowl. Only the anemometer continued stubbornly spinning, without the cable at the top of its mast, as if in protest against the contempt for science that Quaresma displayed.

Thus Quaresma carried on, sure that the campaign against him, although no longer in public, was being developed behind the scenes. With all his heart he desired to put an end to it – but how? How, if they didn't show their hand or accuse him of anything directly? It would be a fight against shadowy figures that would be absurd to take on.

Furthermore, the conditions around him, the extreme poverty of the country people that he had never imagined, the farms that were abandoned and unproductive, all this was a source of anguished reflection for his patriotic mind.

It saddened the major to see that there was no feeling of solidarity among these poor people, no mutual support. There was nothing that brought them together: they lived separately, isolated, in common-law families, without seeing the need to join together to work the land. And yet, close at hand, they had the example of the Portuguese, who managed by working together in groups of six or more, to plough and plant large areas and to live off the profits. Even the old custom of collective community work seemed to have disappeared.

How could this be solved?

Quaresma was in despair . . .

He thought that those who affirmed that there was a lack of

labourers must be either fools or liars, as was the government that imported them by the thousand without a thought for those who already existed. It was like putting three more cows into a field that could barely supply enough food for the half dozen already there, so as to increase the supply of manure!

He saw from his own experience the obstacles and difficulties in the way of making the land productive and remunerative. One particular incidence was an especially good example of this. After freeing them from creepers and the effects of so many years of ill-usage and neglect, his avocado trees began to bear fruit – not much, it is true, but more than his family required.

He was delighted. For the first time he was going to receive money produced by the land; his ever-constant, ever-fertile land. He planned to sell them, but how? To whom? A few local people were prepared to buy, but for virtually nothing. Undeterred, he went to Rio to find a buyer. He went from door to door. There were too many. Nobody wanted them. They told him to go to a certain Sr Azevedo, the largest fruit merchant in town. So off he went.

'Avocados! I've got so many . . . They're two a penny!'

'But,' Quaresma said, 'earlier I asked at a grocer's and the price was five thousand *réis* a dozen.'

'For a handful, but in bulk . . . Anyway, if you want to send them . . .'

He shook the heavy gold chain on his wrist, stuck his hand into his waistcoat and, with his back half-turned to the major, said:

'I'll have to see them . . . It depends on the size . . .'

Quaresma sent them, and when the money arrived he felt like a conqueror who has just won a decisive victory in battle. He stroked the grimy notes one by one, studied the numbers on them, the design, laid them out side by side on a table. It was a long time before he could bring himself to exchange them.

To see what his profit was, he discounted the freight, by rail and cart, the cost of the crates and the workers' wages. The calculation didn't take long: it showed that his profit was one thousand five hundred *réis*, no more, no less. For every hundred avocados Sr Azevedo had paid him the price of a dozen in the shops.

But he remained as proud as ever and that tiny amount of money gave him as much satisfaction as if he had earned some enormous sum.

And so he went back to work with redoubled vigour. The profits would be higher next year. He now set about pruning the fruit trees. Anastácio and Felizardo were still busy planting in the fields. He hired a new employee to help him with the old fruit trees.

So he started the pruning with Mané Candeeiro, sawing off the dead branches and the ones where parasites had embedded their roots. It was a long, hard task. Sometimes they had to climb right up to the top of a tree to cut off a branch. The thorns tore their clothes and cut into their flesh, and they were often in danger of tumbling to the ground, Quaresma, Mané and the saw.

Mané Candeeiro hardly spoke, unless it was to talk about hunting, but he sang like a bird. While he sawed he sang traditional farmhand songs. These were naive, and to the major's surprise made no mention of the wildlife or plants or local customs. They were faintly sensual, very tender and even sentimental. There was one in which a local bird was mentioned, to which the major paid special attention:

> I'll make my farewells
> The same as the hawk,
> One foot on the road
> And one on the stalk.

This reference to the hawk was particularly gratifying to Quaresma: the local people were beginning to take an interest in the environment around them. They were beginning to identify with it, which showed that our people were putting down roots in the vast country which they inhabited. He copied out the verse and sent it to the old poet in São Cristóvão. Felizardo said that Mané Candeeiro was a liar: all those stories about hunting boars, guans and panthers were inventions. But he admired his poetical talent, especially in contests: he was good!

Mané was pale-skinned with strong, firmly drawn classical features, slightly modified by his African blood.

Quaresma tried to detect the evil disposition that Darwin observed in people of mixed race, but, sincerely, he found none.

With Mané Candeeiro's help Quaresma managed to complete the pruning of the fruit trees of the old farm that had been abandoned for almost ten years. When the work was done he looked sadly at those old trees, amputated and mutilated, leafy in places and bare in others . . . Their suffering reminded him of the hands that planted them thirty or forty years earlier – slaves probably, downcast, despairing . . .

But it was not long before the buds sprouted and everything was green again, and with the renewal the joy of the wild birds that flew around seemed also to be renewed. In the morning red tanagers fluttered about, cheeping – a bird that seemed predestined to furnish its beautiful feathers for the decoration of ladies' hats – flocks of brown wood pigeons collecting food, pecking the ground . . . In the late morning cardinals sang from high branches, grass-peckers, clouds of seedeaters . . . and in the afternoon they all came together squawking, chirping, chirruping in the tall mango trees, in the cashews and avocados, singing the praises of the persistent, productive labours of old Major Quaresma.

But this happiness did not last long. An enemy appeared unexpectedly with the extreme daring and speed of a consummate general. Until then he had been cautious, only sending out a few scouts.

Since the attack on Quaresma's supplies, when they were driven off, the ants had not reappeared, but that morning, when he looked at his maize plantation, his heart almost failed. He stood motionless, and tears came into his eyes.

With childlike shyness the maize had poked its head above the surface, very green, and now stood two inches high. The major had already sent for the copper sulphate to prepare the solution for the potatoes he was going to plant between the rows.

Every morning he would go there to watch the maize grow, with its white tassels and tufted ears the colour of wine, swaying in the wind. Earlier he had noticed nothing. Even the tender stems had been cut and carried away! 'Jus' like people 'ad done it,' said Felizardo. But it had been the ants, those direful insects, tiny pirates, that had fallen on his plantation with the rapacity of a Turk . . . He would have to fight back. Quaresma set to work at once, discovered the main trails to the ant-hill and burned a lethal formicide in every one. Days passed, and it seemed that the enemy had been defeated. But one night as he walked to the orchard to admire the starlit night, Quaresma heard a strange noise, as if someone were crumpling dead leaves. There was a crackling sound . . . It came from nearby . . . He lit a match and what did he see . . . Oh God! Almost all the orange trees were black with hordes of enormous ants. There were hundreds of them swarming all over the trunks and branches, moving about like the citizens of a large city along busy, well-ordered streets: some were going up, others were coming down, without a sign of disruption or confusion, all in perfect order as though they were being commanded by bugle calls. The ones at the top were cutting off the leaves at the stalk; the ones below were sawing them into pieces until they were carried off by yet others, held aloft above their tiny heads, moving in long lines along a trail that they had cleared between the undergrowth.

For a moment the major almost gave up. He had not fore-seen this obstacle nor understood how serious it was. It was now clear that he was dealing with an intelligent, organized society that was both persistent and daring. The famous words of Saint-Hilaire[1] came to his mind: 'If we don't drive out the ants, they will drive us out.'

The major didn't remember if these were the exact words, but the meaning was the same, and he was amazed that he hadn't thought of them before.

The next day his confidence had returned. He bought the ingredients and there he was with Mané Candeeiro, clearing tracks, scouring his brains in the effort to find their strong-holds, the underground chambers of the direful insects. Then he bombarded them: the sulphide burned and set off a series of deadly, lethal explosions!

From then on it was a battle with no truce. Whenever a hole

appeared the formicide was immediately applied; if it hadn't
been, no cultivation would have been possible. Even so, once
the ants had been eliminated, in no time ant colonies from
neighbouring farms and public land began clearing pathways
towards his property.

It was a torment, a torture, a sort of Dutch dyke vigil, and
Quaresma realized that only a central authority, the government of a country or an agreement between the farmers could
actually achieve the elimination of that scourge, worse than
frost or hail or drought, ever present, be it winter, summer,
autumn or spring.

Despite this daily fight the major did not lose heart and went
ahead with the harvest of some of the crops he had planted. If
his joy had been great when he sold the fruit, it was far greater
now as he watched the rows of carts set off for the station with
their loads of pumpkins, cassavas and sweet potatoes, in baskets covered with sacks. The avocados had been partly the work
of others: the trees had not been planted by him. But these –
these were the product of *his* sweat, *his* initiative, *his* work!

He even went to the station to see the baskets off, with the
tenderness of a father seeing his son go off to glory and victory
in war. When he received the money a few days later he counted
it and calculated his profit.

He didn't work in the fields that day; the accounting kept
him occupied. He was slow with figures, his concentration had
begun to go, and thus it was almost midday before he could say
to his sister:

'Do you know what the profit was, Adelaide?'

'No. Less than with the avocados?'

'A little more.'

'Well . . . How much?'

'Two thousand five hundred and seventy *réis*,' Quaresma
replied, emphasizing each syllable.

'What?'

'Just that. The freight alone cost me a hundred and forty-two
thousand five hundred.'

Dona Adelaide remained for some time with her eyes fixed
on her sewing, then she looked up and said:

'For heaven's sake, Policarpo, you should give up . . . You've spent a lot of money . . . Just on the ants!'

'Nonsense, Adelaide! Do you think I'm doing this to make money? I'm doing it to set an example, to encourage agriculture, to make use of our incredibly fertile soil . . .'

'Yes, I know! You always want to be the shining example! Have you ever seen the rich and powerful make such sacrifices? Of course you haven't! They plant coffee, which gets government assistance!'

'But *I* make them.'

His sister went back to her sewing. Policarpo got up and went to the window that looked over the chicken pen. The weather was overcast and oppressive. He adjusted his pince-nez and stared out. Suddenly he said:

'Adelaide! Isn't that a dead chicken?'

The old lady took her sewing and went to the window to see for herself:

'Yes. And it's the second one that has died today.'

After this brief exchange Quaresma went back to his study. He was contemplating major agricultural reforms. He had ordered catalogues, which he now planned to study. He already had in mind a double plough, a mechanical hoe, a planter, a grubber and harrows, all made of steel, all American, which would do the work of twenty men. Until then he had not wanted these innovations: the most fertile soil in the world did not require such procedures, which seemed to him artificial, to produce. But he was now prepared to use them as an experiment. In his heart he still resisted fertilizers, however. As Felizardo said: 'Hoed earth, manured earth.' To Quaresma applying nitrates, phosphates or even common manure to Brazilian soil was sacrilege . . . an outrage!

If ever the day came when he thought they were needed, it seemed to him his whole philosophy would collapse, the driving force of his life disappear. He was thus engaged in choosing ploughs and various Planets, Bajacs and Brabants[2] when his servant boy entered to announce the arrival of Doctor Campos.

The councillor now entered, his massive bulk oozing with joviality. He was tall and fat, with a protruding belly; his brown eyes seemed to start out of his face; he had a sloping forehead and his nose was crooked. He was what we call a *caboclo*, with olive-coloured skin and hair that had already gone grey, although he had a curly moustache.[3] He was from Bahia or Sergipe,[4] not from Curuzu, but he had lived there for twenty years, where he had married and prospered thanks to the dowry of his wife and his medical practice. As a doctor he expended little mental effort: having memorized half a dozen prescriptions, he had long since fit all the local ailments into his limited formula.

As chairman of the council he was one of Curuzu's leading dignitaries. Quaresma particularly admired him for his unpretentiousness and his friendly, open manner.

'Well met, major! How is the farm going? Lots of ants? We've got rid of them at home.'

Although Quaresma did not reply with the same enthusiasm and joviality, he was pleased by the doctor's cheerful loquaciousness. He continued with the same spontaneity and lack of inhibition:

'Do you know what brings me here, major? You don't, do you? I need a small favour from you.'

This did not startle the major. He liked the man and immediately offered to help.

'As you know, major . . .' His voice became soft, subtle and insinuating; the sugary, slippery words trickled from his lips: 'As you know, major, in a few days we have the elections. Victory will be ours: all the polling stations are supporting our candidate, except one . . . That is where you come in, major . . .'

'But how can I help? I don't vote here and I don't get involved in politics because I choose not to,' Quaresma said ingenuously.

'*Precisely for that reason*,' replied the doctor in a loud voice, and then more softly: 'The polling station is in your district, in the school. Now if . . .'

'If what?'

'I've got a letter here from Neves, addressed to you. He desires to know if the elections were held in your district. If you could reply (right away would be best) saying that they were not . . . Would you?'

Quaresma looked at the doctor firmly, scratched his beard for a moment and then replied clearly and firmly:

'Certainly not.'

The doctor did not get angry. His voice became softer and more earnest, he gave arguments: it was for the party, the only one that fought for the improvement of farming. Quaresma was inflexible: he said he would not, that he found all such disputes repellent, that he had no party and, even if he had, he would not attest to anything when he did not yet know whether it was true or a lie.

Campos showed no sign of annoyance, he chatted a little about insignificant things and then said goodbye in a friendly way, with as much joviality as he could muster.

His visit was on the Tuesday, when the weather was overcast and oppressive. There was thunder in the afternoon, and it rained heavily. The weather only improved on the Thursday, the day the major was surprised by a visit from a man in an old, decrepit uniform, who brought an official letter for him – 'the owner of "The Haven"', as the man in uniform called him.

'In accordance with municipal legislation,' the document ran, 'Sr Policarpo Quaresma, owner of the farm "The Haven", is hereby notified, under pain of sanctions foreseen in the said legislation, to clear and maintain all stretches of land pertaining to the said farm that adjoin the public highways.'

The major thought for a while. He couldn't believe the notification was real. How could it be? It was a joke! He read through it again and saw the signature of Doctor Campos. It *was* real! But what an absurd notification: to clear and maintain one thousand two hundred metres of road front, because one road ran along the front of his farm and another along the side, for eight hundred metres – could it be *possible*?

It was feudal servitude! Outrageous! Let them confiscate the farm. When he consulted his sister she advised him to speak to Doctor Campos. So Quaresma told her about the conversation he had had with him a few days before.

'Don't you see, Policarpo? He's behind it . . .'

At last he saw the light. That network of laws, ordinances, rules and regulations, in the hands of administrators, political bosses like these, became a rack, an instrument of torture with which to torment their enemies, oppress the people, robbing their initiative and independence, leaving them crushed and demoralized.

In his mind's eye he saw those yellow, haggard faces, lurking outside the food shops, the ragged, dirty children, with downcast eyes, furtively begging on the streets; he saw the abandoned, unproductive land, overrun with weeds and destructive insects; the despair of Felizardo, a good, hard-working man, without the heart to plant a single seed of maize on his own piece of land, spending all the money he earned on drink. All this passed before his eyes, very fast and with an eerie brightness, like a flash of lightning. The flash that was only entirely extinguished when he settled down to read a letter that had come from his goddaughter.

It was a lively, cheerful letter. It gave an account of her affairs, her father's forthcoming trip to Europe, her husband's desperation the day he went out without his ring. She asked for news of her godfather and of Dona Adelaide, and, without wishing to interfere, asked the latter to take special care of the Duchess's luxurious mantle.

The Duchess was a large duck with sleek white feathers, whose slow, majestic gait, with her long neck and firm stride, had earned from Olga this aristocratic nickname. The creature had died a few days before. And what a death! A disease that had carried off two dozen of his ducks had killed the Duchess too. It was a kind of paralysis that affected the legs and then the rest of the body. She had taken three days to die. Lying on her chest with her beak stuck into the ground, attacked by ants, the only sign of life she gave was a slight swaying of the neck around the beak to drive away the flies that tormented her during her final moments.

It was remarkable how, at that moment, he had felt her agony, the suffering and the pain of a life so different from his own.

The chicken pen was like a devastated village; the disease attacked hens, turkeys and ducks, reaping its toll, first under one guise, then under another, until the population was reduced to less than half.

And there was no one who knew how to cure it. In a country whose government had so many schools, that produced so many scholars, not a single one, with their drugs or prescriptions, was able to prevent such a terrible loss.

All these setbacks and hardships did much to dampen the enthusiasm of the first few months, but the idea of abandoning his projects never crossed Quaresma's mind. He bought books on veterinary medicine and was even planning to buy the agricultural machines described in the catalogues.

One afternoon, however, he was waiting for the pair of oxen he had ordered for the ploughing, when a policeman appeared at the door with an official paper. He remembered the notification. He was determined to resist, so he was not too concerned.

He took the paper and read it. It was not from the municipality but from the tax department and contained a notification from the secretary, Antonio Dutra, in which Sr Policarpo Quaresma was ordered to pay a fine of five hundred thousand *réis* for dispatching farm produce without payment of the respective taxes.

He saw clearly how much of this was petty revenge but, given his patriotic inclinations, he immediately began to think of the wider implications.

Forty kilometres from Rio one paid taxes to send a few potatoes to the market? After Turgot,[5] after the Revolution, did inland customs houses still exist?

How could agriculture possibly flourish with so many obstacles and taxes? If one added the monopoly of the middlemen in Rio to the extortionate demands of the state, how was it possible to earn a reasonable living from the land?

And the picture that he'd seen in his mind's eye when he received the intimation from the municipality returned, this time even more sombre and doleful; and he foresaw the time when those people would have to eat toads, snakes and dead animals, like the French peasants in the *ancien régime*.

Quaresma remembered his Tupi, his folklore, his *modinhas* and his attempts at farming – it all now seemed insignificant, childish, immature.

There was far more important work to be done; the entire

administration had to be changed. He imagined a strong government, respected, intelligent, removing all these obstacles and hindrances: Sully and Henri IV[6] implementing wise agricultural laws, protecting the farmer ... Yes indeed! Then the granaries would be full, and the fatherland happy.

Felizardo arrived with the paper he sent him to buy at the station every day.

'Guv'ner, I ain't comin' t' work tommora,' he said.

'Of course not, it's a public holiday. Independence day.'

'Vat ain't ve reason.'

'Why then?'

'Ve guvmen's in trouble. Vey say vey're recruitin'. I'm off t' ve woods ...'

'What trouble?'

'It's all in ve paper, guv'ner.'

He opened the paper and saw the news that ships of the naval fleet had rebelled and ordered the president to resign. He recalled his thoughts of a few moments back: a strong government, even tyrannical ... Agricultural reform ... Sully and Henri IV ...

His eyes shone with hope. He sent Felizardo away and went into the house. He said nothing to his sister, took his hat and headed for the station.

He arrived at the telegraph office and wrote:

'Marshal Floriano, Rio. Stand firm. I'm on my way. Quaresma.'

V

THE TROUBADOUR

'You're right, Albernaz, it can't go on like this. Some fellow gets into a ship, aims his cannons at the coast and says: "Leave, Mr President!" and the president leaves? No sir! An example has to be given!'

'I entirely agree with you, Caldas. We have to consolidate the Republic, make it strong. Brazil needs a government that imposes respect! It's unbelievable! A country like this, so rich, perhaps the richest in the world, being poor, owing money to everyone. Why? Because of the governments we've had, which have no power, no prestige, that's why.'

They were walking along in the shade of the large, majestic trees in the abandoned park.[1] Both were in uniform, with their swords. After a while Albernaz continued:

'Take the emperor, Pedro II. The satirical newspapers used to call him a numbskull, and worse things. He used to head the carnival parade! A scandalous lack of respect! And what happened? He sneaked away like a thief in the night.'

'But he was a good man,' the admiral said. 'He loved his country. Deodoro never realized what he had done.'

They walked on. The admiral stroked one of his sideburns. Albernaz glanced around and lit a cigarette before returning to the conversation:

'He died repentant, refused to be buried in uniform! Just between us – as no one is listening – he was an ungrateful devil, after everything the emperor had done for his family, don't you think?'[2]

'There's no doubt at all! Albernaz, do you want to know

something? We were better off in those days, whatever people may say . . .'

'Who would disagree with you? There was more morale. Where are the likes of a Caxias, a Rio Branco?'[3]

'And more justice too,' the admiral said firmly. 'What I suffered wasn't the old man's fault,[4] it was that rabble's. A band of nonentities!'

'I don't know,' said Albernaz, with particular emphasis, 'why people still want to have children . . . The end is at hand.'

For a moment they watched the old trees of the Imperial Gardens, through which they were walking. They had never contemplated them before. Surrounded by vast stretches of cool, delicious shade, they seemed prouder and more beautiful, calmer and more self-assured than any they had ever seen. It was as if they thrived because they knew that that land was theirs – they could never be ejected from it, hewn down by axes and used for building shacks – and this certainty had given them the strength to flourish and to bloom. The soil where they grew was theirs, and they thanked the earth by stretching out their branches and closely interweaving their leaves so as to give their bountiful mother the coolness of their shade and protect her from the inclemency of the sun.

The mango trees were the most grateful of all. Their long branches, thick with leaves, almost kissed the ground. The jackfruit trees stretched out their limbs. On either side of the path the bamboos swayed, covering the earth with a vaulted arch of green . . .

The old Imperial Palace[5] stood on a small hill. They could see the back of the building, the oldest part, built by Dom João, with the clocktower a short way off, separated from the building itself.

The palace was not beautiful; it had no graceful features. It was in fact uninspired, monotonous. The old-fashioned façade with its low ceilings and poky windows made a poor impression. It had, however, a certain air of self-assurance, a self-confidence that is unusual in our residential buildings, a sort of dignity that stemmed from an awareness that it would be there for many years, for centuries to come ... It was surrounded by palm trees, tall and erect, with their large green fronds, very high up, reaching out into the sky ...

They were like the old imperial guard, proudly fulfilling their role as sentries of the royal residence.

Albernaz broke the silence:

'How will all this end, Caldas?'

'I have no idea.'

'The man[6] must be going crazy ... First it was Rio Grande,[7] now it's Custódio ![8] What a business!'

'It's the price of power, Albernaz.'

They were walking towards São Cristóvão station. They crossed the old imperial park diagonally from the wooden gates to the railway line. It was morning; the day was clear and cool.

They walked with a short, firm step, without haste. As they were about to leave the gardens they saw a soldier sleeping under the bushes. Albernaz decided to wake him: 'Comrade! Comrade!' The soldier drowsily got to his feet; seeing the two senior officers, he quickly pulled himself together and gave the required salute. He kept his hand fixed in that position until it began to flag.

'Lower your hand,' said the general. 'What are you doing here?'

Albernaz spoke sharply, with the voice of command. The private, trembling, explained he had been patrolling the shore all night. The troops had returned to barracks. He had obtained leave to go home but, overcome by sleep, he had rested for a while.

'And how are things going?' the general asked.

'Dunno, sir.'

'Have the rebels given up or haven't they?'

The general contemplated the soldier for a while. He was white, with blondish hair, but a soiled, adulterated blond. His face was ugly – prominent cheekbones, bony forehead – and his whole body was angular and disjointed.

'Where are you from?' Albernaz now asked.

'From Piauí,[9] sir.'

'From the capital?'

'The backlands, sir, from Paranaguá.'

The admiral had not questioned him yet. The soldier was still terrified, stammering his answers. To calm him down, Caldas decided to speak to him kindly.

'Don't you know, comrade, which ships they have?'

'The *Aquidabã* . . . The *Luci*.'[10]

'The *Luci* isn't a ship.'

'You're right, sir. The *Aquidabã* . . . a 'ole lot of 'em, sir.'

The general interrupted. He spoke to him with an almost paternal gentleness, using the informal *tu*, which sounds even kinder and more familiar when coming from a superior:

'Well, rest, my boy. But go home first. Someone might steal your sword, and you're on leave.'

The two generals[11] continued on their way and were soon on the station platform. The little station was busy. A large number of servicemen, including retired and honorary officers, lived in the district, and the government-posted notices ordered them all to present themselves to the competent authorities. Albernaz and Caldas walked along the platform amidst salutes. The general was well known due to the post he held; the admiral was not. As they passed they heard people asking: 'Who is that admiral?' Caldas was pleased; he felt rather proud of his rank and his unknown status.

There was only one female on the platform, a girl. As he looked at her, Albernaz thought of his daughter, Ismênia. Poor child! Would she recover?

Those obsessions! Where would it end? Tears came, but he firmly fought them back.

He had already taken her to half a dozen doctors, but none had managed to restore the power of reason that seemed little by little to be eluding her.

The noise of an express train clattering down the track, whistling furiously, leaving a trail of smoke behind it hanging in the air, drove all thoughts of his daughter from his mind. The monstrous creature went by, weighed down with soldiers in uniform. When it had left, the rails were still quivering.

Bustamante arrived. He lived in the vicinity and had come to take the train to report for duty. He was dressed in his old

Paraguayan uniform,[12] the same design as the fighters in the
Crimean War had used. The cap was a truncated cone that
tilted forward. With his short jacket and purple sash he looked
as if he had escaped from a canvas of Victor Meirelles.[13]

'So you're here? How did you come?' asked the general.

'We came across the park,' the admiral said.

'Quite right, my friends. These trams go very close to the sea.
I don't mind dying, but I want to die fighting. Dying just anywhere, for no reason, not knowing why – that's not for me . . .'

The general was speaking loudly, and the young officers
nearby glanced at him with ill-concealed disapproval. Albernaz
noticed this and added immediately:

'I know all about artillery fire. I've been under fire a lot . . .
Do you know, Bustamante, that at Curuzu . . .'

'That was a terrible business,' Bustamante added.

The train pulled into the station. It crept quietly along. The
locomotive, pitch-black, puffing and oozing with sweat, with
its huge lantern in front like a Cyclops' eye, came forward like
an apparition of the supernatural. On it came. Then the whole
train shuddered and finally came to a halt.

It was full, a lot of officers in uniform. An onlooker would
have thought Rio had a garrison of a hundred thousand men.
The soldiers chatted merrily. The civilians were silent and
downcast, some even terrified. When they spoke it was in whis-
pers, cautiously glancing at the seats behind.

The city was infested with secret agents, members of the
Holy Republican Inquisition, and denunciations were the currency by which positions and rewards were obtained.

The slightest criticism was enough for one to lose one's job,
one's freedom and – who knows – one's life as well. The revolt
was at its inception, but the regime had already shown what it
was capable of. Everyone had been warned. The chief of police
had drawn up the list of suspects. No exclusions were made for
rank or competence. A wretched office boy or an influential
senator, a university professor or a lowly office worker, all were
the targets of the same government persecution. Then came the
petty revenge, the settling of scores. Everyone was giving
orders; everyone had the authority . . .

In the name of Marshal Floriano, any officer, or even civilian, with no government post whatever, could make an arrest, and woe betide any man who was thrown into jail, for there he would stay, abandoned, submitted to the anguish of tortures worthy of the Inquisition. Civil servants vied to outdo each other in fawning and servility. It was a reign of terror, unscrupulous, bloody, duplicitous, with no greatness, no excuse, no justification and no accountability. There were executions, but no Fouquier-Tinville.[14]

The soldiers were cheerful, especially the lower ranks, the ensigns, lieutenants and captains. For most this satisfaction stemmed from their conviction that they would wield more power in their platoons and companies, and over all the civilians. But there were others whose motivation was purer, more disinterested and sincere – the disciples of positivism,[15] that wicked, hypocritical movement whose narrow-minded, tyrannical pedantry justified every act of violence, every murder, every savagery committed in the name of maintaining order, the necessary condition, or so it proposed, for progress and the advent of the ideal regime: the religion of humanity, the worship of Mother Earth, accompanied by a cacophony of trumpets and hideous verses, paradise itself, engraved in phonetic script,[16] with those elected to power wearing boots with rubber soles![17]

The positivists discussed and cited theorems of mechanics to justify their ideas about a government which in every way resembled the emirates and khanates of the east.

The mathematics of positivism was always mere words, words which at that time terrified everyone. There were even people who were convinced that mathematics had been created solely for positivism, as if the Bible had been created solely for the Roman Catholic Church and not for the Anglican as well. Its prestige, however, was huge.

The train sped on, stopped at one more station and pulled into the Praça da República. Admiral Caldas clung to the walls as he made his way through the crowds to the Arsenal; Albernaz and Bustamante went to Army Headquarters. They entered the huge building amidst bugle calls and the jangling of swords.

The vast courtyard was full of soldiers, flags, cannons, rows of rifles and bayonets glistening in the setting sun . . .

On the upper floor, near the minister's office, there was a whirl of gilded, multicoloured uniforms, the military attire of the various companies and militias; and among them the civilians in black suits, as persistent as flies. There were officers from the National Guard, from the police, the navy, the army, the Fire Brigade and from the patriotic battalions that were beginning to appear.

They reported at the same time to the adjutant-general and the minister of war and then stood chatting in the corridors, very contented, as they had just met Lieutenant Fontes, to whom they both enjoyed talking. The general because he was now engaged to his daughter, Lalá, and Bustamante because he had learned from him some of the terminology used for modern weaponry.

Fontes was indignant. He was outraged by the rebels and heartily cursed them, proposing the harshest punishments.

'They'll see soon enough! Pirates! Bandits! If I were the marshal, and I got my hands on them . . . then they'd be sorry!'

The lieutenant was neither harsh nor wicked, he was actually good and even generous. But he was a positivist and saw the Republic as something religious and transcendental. He made it the depository of all human happiness and he would not accept there could be any ideas for its welfare that diverged from his own. Those that thought otherwise were crafty and hypocritical, self-seeking heretics. An inquisitor in a Phrygian cap,[18] furious at not being able to burn them at *autos-da-fé*,[19] he would go red with anger as he saw the vast procession of criminals pass: the penitent, the relapsed, the irredeemable, the devious and the sincere, with no priest in a cassock, but free to just wander about!

Albernaz had no such rage against their opponents. Deep down he even wished them well; he had friends among them. These differences meant nothing to a man of his age and experience.

Nevertheless, he was hopeful the marshal would succeed. In his financial difficulties, his pension and the remuneration he received for his post at the Largo do Moura archives being insufficient for his needs, he was hoping to obtain a further commission to help him meet the cost of Lalá's bridal gown.

The admiral, too, had great confidence in Floriano's talents for war and statesmanship. His lawsuit was not going well. He had lost at the lower court hearing; he was spending a lot of money. The government needed naval officers; nearly all of them had joined the revolt. Perhaps they'd give him a squadron to command! On the other hand . . . Oh, what the hell? A ship would be fine: but he was capable of commanding a squadron. All it needed was the courage to fight.

Bustamante had great faith in Marshal Floriano Peixoto, so much so that to support him and defend his government he was planning to organize a patriotic battalion. He already had the name – 'Southern Cross' – and naturally he would be its commander, with all the benefits that the post of colonel implied.

Genelício, whose profession had nothing to do with war, expected a great deal from the drive and determination of Floriano's government: he hoped to be assistant director, and what other course could an honest, energetic government take, if it wanted to see his department in order?

Such secret ambitions were more common than one might think. People depended on the government, and the revolt had thrown the system of patronage and honorary positions into disarray. Those under suspicion lost their posts, and their attributes and titles were taken over by people who were faithful to the government. Moreover, as the government needed both men and support, it had to invent and create jobs, salaries, promotions and emoluments, and lavishly distribute them.

Even Doctor Armando Borges, Olga's husband, the once prudent, dedicated student, saw the revolt as a means for the realization of his dreams.

He was a doctor and, due to his wife's fortune, rich, but he was not content. He was spurred on by his desire for fame and money. He was already a doctor at the Syrian Hospital, where he went three times a week and saw thirty patients or more in half an hour. He would arrive, the nurse would brief him, and he would go from bed to bed asking: 'How are you?' 'Better, doctor,' the patient would reply in a throaty voice. On his next visit he would ask: 'Feeling better?' After his rounds he would go to the office and give prescriptions: 'Patient no. 1, repeat the prescription. Patient no. 5 . . . which one is that?' 'The one with the beard.' 'Oh yes . . .' And he gave the prescription.

But being a doctor in a private hospital doesn't make anyone famous. The essential thing was a government post, otherwise he would be a mere practitioner. He wanted an official post as a doctor, director or even professor at the Medical School.

This would not be hard provided he managed to get well recommended, because, due to his work and financial resources, he'd already made a certain name for himself.

From time to time he wrote a paper: 'Shingles, Aetiology, Prophylaxis and Treatment' or 'Contribution to the Study of Scabies in Brazil'. He would send the fifty or so pages to the newspapers, which published them two or three times a year: the 'diligent Doctor Armando Borges, the illustrious physician, the skilful doctor of our hospitals', and so on.

He managed this due to the care he had taken as a student to make contact with the young men from the press.

Not content with this, he would write articles, lengthy dissertations, that contained nothing of his own but that were filled with quotations in French, English and German.

The post of professor tempted him most; but he was afraid of the exam. He had contacts, knew the right people, was well thought of by his colleagues, but the idea of the examination terrified him.

Not a day went by that he didn't buy books in French, English and Italian. He even hired a German teacher to acquire some German erudition. But he lacked the stamina for lengthy studies and, due to his comfortable circumstances, he'd already forgotten the little he had learned as a student.

The front room of the high-ceilinged basement had been turned into a library. The walls were lined with shelves groaning beneath the weight of the heavy tomes. At night he opened the shutters, lit all the gas lamps and sat at the table, all dressed in white, with an open book in front of him.

Sleep would overcome him by the end of the fifth page . . . This was awful! He looked through his wife's books. They were French novels: Goncourt, Anatole France, Daudet, Maupassant, but they sent him to sleep just like the medical books. He didn't understand the greatness of their perceptions, the descriptions, the reflections on society, the revelations about the lives, feelings and sufferings of their characters – these novels were a world in themselves! But due to his pedantry, his false erudition and the generally low level of his education, he saw them merely as distractions, pastimes and gossip, especially as reading them sent him to sleep.

However, he needed to deceive himself, and his wife! What was more, people could see him from the street: what if they saw him fast asleep over his books?! He ordered some stories by Paul de Kock[20] with altered titles on the spine and so avoided falling asleep.

In the meantime his practice prospered. In collusion with the patient's guardian he managed to make six *contos*[21] from treating a rich orphan with a very high fever.

His wife had long accepted that his intelligence was a sham, but she was indignant at such a shameful trick. Why should he do such a thing? Wasn't he rich? Wasn't he still young? Didn't he have the advantage of a degree? What he had done seemed to her baser and viler than the usury of a Jew, than a writer who rents out his pen.

It was not contempt or disgust that she felt for her husband. Her feelings were more tranquil and passive: she had lost interest in him and the things that he did. She felt they had broken all the bonds of affection, of the friendship that held them together, in short, all ties of duty.

While still a bride she had seen that those things – his love of study, his interest in science, his desire to make discoveries – were a sham, were just for show, but she had forgiven him. Many people deceived themselves about their strengths and abilities, dreamed about being a Shakespeare, produced vinegar instead of wine. It was understandable: but being a charlatan? That was going too far!

She thought of taking revenge, but what benefit would she get by humiliating him? Other men must all be the same! There was no point in changing one for another . . .

When she reached this conclusion she felt a great relief. Her face brightened up once again. It was as though the cloud that had cast a shadow over the brightness of those eyes had passed.

In his desperate scramble to achieve quick fame, he did not notice how his wife had changed. She disguised her feelings, more out of self-respect and consideration than for any other reason, and he lacked the perception and the subtlety to penetrate the disguise.

They continued living together as if nothing had happened, but in reality so far apart!

This was their situation when the revolt had broken out three days before, three days during which the doctor had been contemplating his social and financial elevation.

His father-in-law had delayed his trip to Europe and that morning, as he usually did after lunch, was lying back in a garden chair, reading the daily papers. The doctor was getting dressed, and Olga was writing her letters, seated at the end of the dining-room table. She had a study, with every amenity – books, bookcases, a writing desk – but in the mornings she preferred to write here, beside her father. She found the room lighter, the backdrop of mountains, looming ominously, helped her concentration, and the room's vast size gave her more freedom to write.

While she was writing and he was reading, her father said:

'Do you know who's coming, Olga?'

'Who?'

'Your godfather. He telegraphed Floriano to say he was coming. It's here in *The Nation*.'

She guessed the reason at once, how the revolt would affect a person with Quaresma's ideas and sentiments. She was inclined to disapprove, to criticize, but then she thought how in character it was, how in tune with the life he had made for himself, and she gave an indulgent smile.

'My godfather . . .'

'He's mad,' said Coleoni. '*Per la madonna*. A man who has a quiet, settled life is coming to get mixed up in this mayhem, this hell on earth!'

The doctor appeared fully dressed, with a sombre black frock coat and a shiny top hat in his hand. He was radiant: all his round face, except for the large moustache, was aglow. He was in time to overhear these last words of his father-in-law, in his broken Portuguese:

'What's happened?' he asked.

Coleoni explained and repeated the remarks he had just made.

'But that's not the point,' the doctor said. 'It's the duty of every patriot! What's age got to do with it? He's in his forties. That's not old. He can still fight for the Republic . . .'

'But he's nothing to gain,' the old man objected.

'Should only people who have something to *gain* fight for the Republic?' the doctor asked.

The girl, who had just finished reading the letter she had written, said without looking up:

'Of course.'

'You and your theories! Patriotism isn't for filling your belly!'

And he gave an artificial smile, made even more artificial by the lacklustre gleam of false teeth.

'Why should you be the only ones to talk about patriotism? And the others? Does your side have a monopoly?' Olga asked.

'Yes we do. If they were patriots they wouldn't be firing on the city, paralysing and demoralizing the legally constituted government!'

'Should they stand by as the arrests continue, the deportations, the executions and all the other horrors that are being committed, here and in the south?'

'In your heart, you're one of the rebels yourself!' the doctor said, putting an end to the argument.

And indeed she was. The sympathy of the Brazilian people, those that weren't looking for personal gain, was for the rebels. This is always the case, in every country, but especially in Brazil, where for a number of reasons it will always be so.

Governments, with their inevitable hypocrisy and acts of violence, soon lose the sympathy of their supporters. Then, unaware that they have neither the power nor the capacity, they start making promises they cannot fulfil. Thus they alienate more and more people, and the demands for change increase.

It is not surprising, then, that Olga sympathized with the rebels. And Coleoni, a foreigner, who knew our authorities from a lifetime's experience, concealed his sympathies with a prudent silence.

'Now you won't do anything to hurt my interests, eh Olga?'

She had risen to accompany him to the door. She stopped for a moment, looked at him with those shining eyes and, with her thin lips slightly tensed, said:

'You know I never hurt your interests.'

The doctor went down the steps from the veranda, crossed the garden and at the gate said goodbye to his wife, who watched him as he left, leaning over the veranda, in accordance with the ritual of couples, whether happily or unhappily married.

Meanwhile, Coração dos Outros was quite unaware of the impending storm.

He was still living in his tenement house in the suburbs, with a view that stretched from Todos os Santos to Piedade, covering a wide stretch of buildings, a panorama of houses and trees.

People no longer mentioned his rival, so the wound had healed.

Now his triumph was uncontested. The entire city held him in such high esteem that he sometimes thought he had reached the height of his fame. Although recognition was still lacking in Botafogo, he was certain of obtaining it.

He had already published more than one volume of songs and was now planning to publish another.

For days he had stayed at home, hardly leaving the house, working on his book. He stayed shut up in his room, drinking coffee that he made himself and eating bread. In the evening he dined at a tavern near the station.

He had noticed that when he arrived the cart drivers and labourers who were eating at the grimy tables lowered their voices and glanced at him suspiciously; but he took no notice . . .

Although he was popular in the district, he had not seen a single acquaintance for the last three days. He avoided talking to people in the house, limiting himself to exchanging 'good mornings' and 'good afternoons' with the neighbours.

He enjoyed spending his days like that, alone with his

thoughts, waiting for inspiration. He didn't read the newspapers so as not to distract his attention from his work. He thought only of his *modinhas* and his songbook, which would be yet another victory for him and his beloved guitar.

That afternoon he was sitting at the table revising one of his songs, one of the newer ones; the one he had written at Quaresma's farm – 'Carola's Lips'.

First of all he read it through, humming along. Then he read it again and, taking up his guitar to create more effect, sang the following lines:

> Prettier than Helena and Margarida,
> She smiles as she waves her fan.
> There's no illusion that makes life sweeter
> In the way Carola's lips can.

He heard a shot, then another, and another . . . What the devil? he thought. They must be firing a salute for some foreign ship. He struck a chord and continued to sing to Carola's lips, the illusion that made life sweet . . .

PART III

PART III

I

THE PATRIOTS

He had been there for over an hour, in one of the great rooms of the palace. From where he stood he could see the marshal, but couldn't speak to him. Almost anyone could get in to see the president, but to speak to him was another matter.

There was an air of informality, almost laxity, about the palace: an eloquent comment on the times. In some of the rooms staff officers, orderlies and messengers could be seen lounging about on sofas, jackets unbuttoned. There was no apparent discipline or order. There were cobwebs in the corners of the ceiling. Beneath the heavy tread of soldiers' feet the carpets sent up clouds of dust, like an unswept street.

Quaresma had been unable to come at once, as his telegram said. He had had to put his affairs in order, find someone to keep his sister company. Dona Adelaide had given a thousand reasons why he shouldn't go: the risks of combat, of a war, were beyond the capacity of a man of his age, beyond his strength. But he had remained firm, refusing to be put off. He was convinced that everything he possessed, all his resolve, intelligence, every drop of energy and vitality, should be put at the disposal of the government, and then . . . Then!

He had used the time to write a report to give to Floriano. In it he explained the measures required for fostering agriculture and outlined all the obstacles: the large estates that were unproductive, the excessive taxation, the high cost of freight, the insufficiency of markets and the political intrigues.

As he clung to his manuscript, the major thought of his house, far off, on the edge of that dismal plain, facing west to where on clear translucent days the rows of mountains could be seen to stretch away. He thought of his sister, of her calm, green eyes as she watched him leave with an impassiveness that was not natural. But above all he remembered Anastácio, his old black servant, the glazed look in his eyes that no longer possessed that passive tenderness of a domestic pet, but were full of foreboding, fear and compassion, rolling in their sockets and showing their whites as he watched him climb into the railway carriage. It was unusual for him to behave like that – as if he had discerned the warning signs of disaster to come. It was as though he could scent a catastrophe . . .

Quaresma had positioned himself in a corner, from where he could watch the people who entered as he waited for the president to summon him. It was just before midday, and Floriano, who had had lunch, still had a toothpick stuck in his mouth.

He spoke first of all to a committee of ladies who had come to offer their strength and their lives in defence of the fatherland and its institutions. The speaker was a small woman, short and chubby, with a large, prominent bosom and a closed fan in her right hand that she waved as she spoke.

It was unclear which colour she was, or at least to which race she belonged; she was a mixture of so many, one concealing the other, that an accurate specification was impossible.

While the little lady spoke, staring at the marshal, sparks flew from her big, round eyes. Floriano looked uncomfortable beneath that ardent gaze. It was as if he were afraid of melting in the heat from that look that burned more with seduction than with patriotism. He pretended to look at her, hung his head like an adolescent, tapped the table with his fingers . . .

When his turn came to speak, he raised his head a little but, without looking straight at her, and with an awkward peasant's smile, declined the offer, as the Republic still had the resources it needed to win.

He spoke this last sentence more slowly, almost ironically. The ladies took their leave. The marshal cast his eyes around the room, and they fell on Quaresma:

'So you're here, Quaresma!' he said in a friendly voice.

The major was about to approach, but he stopped where he was. The dictator had turned his attention to a swarm of petty officers that had surrounded him. He was unable to hear what they were saying. They were whispering into Floriano's ear and tapping him on the shoulder. From the movement of his lips Quaresma saw that the marshal hardly spoke, nodding his head and answering in monosyllables.

They began to leave. They shook the dictator's hand. One of them, the most buoyant of the group, squeezed it with great force as he left, tapping him heartily on the shoulder and saying very loudly:

'Be firm, marshal!'

This was the new republican protocol. It all seemed so natural, so normal, that no one, not even Floriano himself, seemed at all taken aback. On the contrary, some even smiled at the sight of the caliph, the khan, the emir transferring a part of his sanctity to that insolent subaltern. Not all of them left at once. One of them remained behind to exchange confidences with the country's supreme authority. He was a cadet from the Military Academy wearing the turquoise uniform, sword-belt and sabre of young soldiers from the nobility.

The cadets of the Academy were an untouchable military unit.

They had unassailable rights and privileges; they took precedence over ministers at interviews with the dictator and abused their protection from Sulla[1] to create mayhem all over the town.

They had absorbed a few odds and ends of positivism, which they expressed in the form of devout religious sentiment, transforming authority, especially Floriano, and to some extent the Republic, into an article of faith, a magic spell, a Mexican idol, on whose altar every excess and every crime was offered up as a sacrifice for its gratification and perpetuation.

The cadet was still there . . .

Thus Quaresma was able to take a closer look at the features of this man who, for almost a year, was to accumulate the powers of a Roman emperor; casting his shadow over an entire nation, controlling everything, without encountering so much as a token of opposition to the fickleness of his whims and impulses; neither from laws, nor from tradition, nor from common human decency.

He was a contemptible, depressing sight. The sagging moustache, the tuft of hair that clung to his drooping lower lip, the coarse looks and flaccid features. Not even the chin, or the expression, gave any indication of a person of standing. His expression was blank, glazed, without feeling, except for a melancholy that was characteristic more of the race he represented than of the man himself.[2] He appeared spineless, devoid of energy.

The major refused to interpret these signs as any reflection on his intelligence, temperament or character. They were irrelevant, he told himself.

He had great enthusiasm for this political idol, enthusiasm that was genuine and disinterested. He saw him as determined, shrewd, far-sighted, persistent, a man who understood the country's needs – a sort of Louis XI[3] with a smattering of Bismarck. But he was none of these things. He had no intellectual qualities at all. On the contrary, his predominant characteristic was inertia; by temperament he was extremely lazy. His was not a laziness of the ordinary kind, such as we all experience, it was pathological, as if he had no blood in his veins, resulting in a numbness of the nerves. This indolence of his was notorious: everywhere he went he showed his aversion and distaste for performing the duties pertaining to the post he held.

As commander of the navy in Pernambuco he couldn't even be bothered to sign the order of the day and when he was minister of war he didn't go to the ministry for months on end, leaving everything unsigned, 'delegating' to his assistant an overwhelming amount of work.

No one who knows the rigorous discipline with paperwork of a Colbert,[4] a Napoleon, a Philip II, a Kaiser Wilhelm or all great statesmen in general can comprehend the laxness of Floriano's attitude towards issuing orders, towards informing his subordinates of his plans and views. These communications are essential to ensure that respect for the presidency is maintained and to make it possible for government and administrative measures to be implemented.

It was this mental and physical laziness that was the cause of his silence, the mysterious monosyllables that were endowed with oracular status, his famous hesitations and 'perhapses' which so inflamed the public imagination, ever hungry for heroes and greatness.

This pathological laziness was the reason he used to wear slippers and gave him that appearance of superior calm, the calm of a great statesman or an outstanding soldier.

Everyone recalls the first few months of his government. Confronted with the revolt of the prisoners and the lower-rank officers of the fortress of Santa Cruz, he ordered an investigation, which he then repressed, afraid that those who were charged with instigating the revolt would start another one, and, not content with that, he rewarded them liberally with positions and patronage.

Moreover, who can condone a great leader, a Caesar or a Napoleon, permitting, as he did, such undignified intimacies from his subordinates, indulging them to such an extent that he consented to the use of his name as the justification for an endless sequence of every imaginable crime?

One example should suffice. Everyone knows of the hostile atmosphere in which Napoleon took command of the Italian army. Augereau,[5] who called him 'the rabble's general', later admitted that Napoleon had taken him aside and 'made him fear for his life'; thus the Corsican became master of the army, with no shoulder-tapping, no delegation, veiled or explicit, of his authority to irresponsible subordinates.

Furthermore, the slowness with which he repressed the revolt of 6 September[6] clearly shows a lack of certainty and resolution in a man who had such an extraordinary array of resources at his command.

There is another aspect of Marshal Floriano which does much to explain his behaviour, which can be seen in his notion of family – a deep-rooted, patriarchal approach, something that belongs to the past, that civilization has left behind.

As a result of the failure of the crops on two of his properties his financial situation was precarious. And he did not want to die without leaving these rural properties to his family unencumbered by debt.

As he was an honest and upright man, the only hope that

remained to him was the money he could save from his remuner-
ated posts. Hence his mistrust, the need to play a double game,
indispensable for retaining these lucrative positions; hence, too,
the tenacity with which he clung to the presidency. The mortgage
of his two rural properties was his Cleopatra's nose.[7]

Laziness, inertia and the desire to protect his family resulted
in this indecisive figure, who for cultural and social reasons was
transformed by his contemporaries into a statesman, a Rich-
elieu, and was able to repress a serious rebellion, more through
obstinacy than vitality, obtaining the men and the funds he
required, inspiring enthusiasm and even fanaticism.

But the enthusiasm and fanaticism which supported, encouraged and sustained him would not have been possible had he
not been adjutant-general of the Empire, senator and minister –
that is, he first created himself as a legend and then impressed
that legend on the minds of the public.

His conception of government was neither despotism, nor
democracy, nor aristocracy: it was domestic tyranny. If the
baby misbehaves, punish it. On a national scale, misbehaviour
meant opposing him, holding opinions that were different from
his, and the punishment was no longer a spanking, but rather
imprisonment and death. There is no money in the Treasury?
Put used notes into circulation, just like you do at home when
guests arrive and there's not enough soup: you add more water.

Moreover, his military education and rudimentary culture
reinforced this infantile conception, tainting it with violence,
due not so much to his own natural perversity and contempt
for human life, but to his weakness in covering up the fero-
ciousness of his acolytes, instead of restraining it.

All this was very far from Quaresma's mind. Like many honest, sincere men of the time, he had been gripped by the
contagious enthusiasm that Floriano had managed to inspire.
He was thinking of the great work that destiny had reserved for
that placid, melancholy individual, of the radical reforms he
would implement in what was left of the fatherland, the land
that the major had always believed (but had recently started to
doubt) was the richest in all the world.

He would surely fulfil these expectations. His firm hand

would be felt throughout the country's eight million square kilometres, bringing roads, security, protection for the weak, work for the people and wealth for Brazil.

These thoughts were soon interrupted. Seeing the marshal address him so cordially, one of the men who was waiting had begun to take an interest in that small, silent figure with his pince-nez. He quietly made his way towards him and when he arrived said to Quaresma, as if he were revealing some terrible secret:

'They're going to see the *caboclo*! Have you known him long, major?'

Quaresma replied, and the man asked him another question. But now the president was alone, and the major stepped forward.

'So you've come, Quaresma?' Floriano said.

'I have come to offer Your Excellency my humble services.'

For a while the president contemplated the tiny figure and then smiled awkwardly, without concealing a certain satisfaction. Quaresma's presence confirmed the strength of his popularity, or at least the justice of his cause.

'I'm very grateful . . . Where have you been? I know that you left the Arsenal.'

Floriano always remembered the faces, names, positions and circumstances of the subordinates he had dealings with. There was something Asiatic about him: he was cruel and paternal at the same time.

Quaresma told him what he'd been doing and took the opportunity to speak to him about agrarian laws, measures that would disencumber the nation's agriculture and put farming on a new footing. The marshal listened distractedly, a little wrinkle of annoyance appearing at the corners of his mouth.

'I have even brought Your Excellency this report . . .'

The president shrugged ill-temperedly, as if to say 'Don't pester me now,' and then said indifferently:

'Leave it there . . .'

He put the manuscript on a table, and the dictator turned to address Quaresma's companion:

'What's going on, Bustamante? And the battalion, is it ready?'

The man stepped up, a little afraid:

'It's going well, marshal. We need a barracks! If Your Excellency were to give the order . . .'

'Of course. Tell Rufino from me. He'll make the arrangements . . . Or rather, take him this note.'

He tore a piece from one of the first pages of Quaresma's manuscript and, with no more ado, took a blue pencil and scribbled a few words to his minister of war. Only when he had finished did he notice the discourtesy he had committed:

'Oh look! Quaresma. I've torn your report! But not to worry . . . It came off the top, there was no writing there.'

Quaresma verified this, and the president, turning to Bustamante again, said:

'Make use of Quaresma in your battalion. What post do you want?'

'Me?' Quaresma replied in astonishment.

'Well. Decide between yourselves.'

They took their leave of the president and slowly descended the palace steps. Neither spoke until they reached the street. Quaresma felt a little chilly, although the day was hot, with a clear blue sky. The city appeared as busy as ever with its usual turmoil of trams, carriages and carts, but on every face there was an expression of fear and dread: something terrible, something that threatened them all, seemed to be hanging in the air.

Bustamante introduced himself. He was Major Bustamante, now Lieutenant Colonel, an old friend of the marshal's, whom he had fought with in Paraguay.

'But we've met before!' he exclaimed.

Quaresma stared at the old, dark-skinned mulatto, with his shrewd eyes and his long, mosaic beard, but he didn't remember having ever met him before.

'I don't remember . . . Where was it?'

'At General Albernaz's . . . Don't you remember?'

Policarpo remembered vaguely, and Bustamante told him about the founding of his patriotic battalion 'Southern Cross'.

'Would you like to join?'

'Of course,' said Quaresma.

'We have problems . . . Uniforms, boots for the soldiers . . .

We should help the government by meeting these expenses . . . It wouldn't be right to bleed the Treasury, don't you agree?'

'Absolutely!' Quaresma said with enthusiasm.

'I'm delighted you agree with me! I see you're a patriot. So I've decided to divide the cost between the officers, according to rank: a second lieutenant contributes a hundred thousand *réis*, a lieutenant two hundred . . . What rank do you want? But of course, you're a major, aren't you?'

Quaresma then explained why it was that they called him major. A friend with influence in the Interior Ministry had included his name in a list of the National Guard, with that rank. He had never paid the fee but nevertheless everyone started to call him major, and the title had stuck. At first he protested, but as they insisted he let it go.

'Fine,' said Bustamante. 'You can be a major, then.'

'What is my contribution?'

'Four hundred thousand. It's a bit steep, but . . . You understand; it's an important post. Do you agree?'

'Of course.'

Bustamante took out his notebook, noted it down with a piece of lead from a pencil and cheerfully bid the major farewell:

'So, major, six o'clock at the provisional barracks.'

They had been standing at the corner of Rua Larga and the Campo de Sant'Ana. Quaresma planned to take a tram to the centre. He intended to visit his friend Coleoni in Botafogo, to pass the time until his initiation into military service.

The square was quiet: the trams passed by at the slow measured trot of the mules. From time to time a bugle call was heard, the roll of a drum, and from the central gate of the general headquarters a company would emerge, rifles across their backs, bayonets at rest on their shoulders, glittering with a harsh, cruel light.

As he boarded the tram artillery shots were heard, and the muted explosion of rifles. It did not last long: before the tram had reached the Rua da Constituição all noise of the battle had ceased, and anyone who had not heard it would have presumed that everything was as normal.

Quaresma moved along to the middle of the bench and

started to open the newspaper he had bought. As he carefully unfolded it he was interrupted by a tap on the shoulder. He turned around.

'General!'

They greeted each other cordially. General Albernaz loved these occasions. He took a special delight in renewing acquaintanceship with friends with whom he had lost touch for some reason or other. He was wearing the same dilapidated old uniform, with no sword, and his pince-nez still hung from the little gold chain that passed behind his left ear.

'So you've come to see the revolt?'

'Yes. I've already reported to the marshal.'

'They'll soon find out who they're up against. If they think they're dealing with a Deodoro, they've got another think coming! Thank God the Republic has a real leader now. The *caboclo* is a man of steel . . . In Paraguay . . .'

'You met him there, didn't you, general?'

'Well . . . I didn't actually meet him; but Camisão did . . . He's a man of steel. I'm in charge of munitions now. He's clever, that *caboclo*: he didn't want me on the coast. He knows all about me; there's no one who understands munitions like I do! Not a crate leaves the deposit before I have checked it. I have to! In Paraguay there was all sorts of hanky-panky. Did you know they used to send quicklime instead of gunpowder?'

'No, I didn't.'

'Well they did. What I wanted was to be sent to the coast, into battle, but the president wants me in charge of munitions. The captain orders, the sailor obeys. He knows what's right.'

He turned back, adjusted the chain that had slipped off his ear and was silent for a moment.

'How's the family?' Quaresma asked.

'They're well. Did you know that Quinota got married?'

'Yes, Ricardo told me. And how is Dona Ismênia?'

The general's expression became grave, and he answered somewhat reluctantly:

'Just the same.'

A father's sense of propriety prevented him from telling the whole truth. His daughter had gone mad. She spent days on end in a corner, silently gazing at the things around her with the glazed look of a statue, with the inertia and lifelessness of a mental retard. At times she would put on her finest clothes, comb her hair and run to her mother, saying: 'Get me ready, mother. My husband will be here soon ... Today is my wedding day.' At others she would cut up pieces of paper and write out wedding announcements: 'Ismênia de Albernaz and Tom (or Dick, or Harry) hereby announce their wedding engagement.'

The general had consulted dozens of doctors and mediums and had now found a shaman who was promising miracles. But his daughter didn't get better, clinging ever more tightly to her obsession with marriage – the goal of life that society had imposed on her, at which she had failed, with the result that her spirit and her youth had been crushed in the fulness of their bloom.

Her condition cast a pall of gloom over that household, once so festive and gay. They gave fewer balls. When they could not avoid them, such as on birthdays and anniversaries, they coaxed the girl away to her married sister's house, where she remained while the others danced, forgetting for a brief moment their sister's suffering.

Albernaz did not wish to reveal this grief of his old age. He suppressed his emotions and continued in a natural tone – the same familiar, intimate tone he used with everyone:

'It's an outrage, Sr Quaresma. What a setback for the country! And the cost? A port of this size, closed to shipping. How many years will that set us back?'

The major agreed and said how important it was to support the government so as to prevent the insurrections from spreading further.

'Quite right,' the general said. 'There will be no progress, no going forward like this. And abroad, what a terrible impression!'

The tram had arrived at Largo de São Francisco, and the two separated: Quaresma went straight to Largo da Carioca, while Albernaz headed for Rua do Rosário.

Olga did not feel the usual elation as she saw her godfather arrive. It was not indifference she felt; she was taken aback, surprised, almost afraid, even though she knew perfectly well that he was coming. Yet nothing about Quaresma – his face, his body, his whole appearance – had changed; he was the same small, pale figure with the pointed goatee and the penetrating eyes behind the pince-nez. Nor was he more sunburned, and his way of tightening his lips was just as she had always remembered it. But she found him different; it was as though he had been pushed into the room by some occult force, blown in by a whirlwind. Yet when she thought about it, he had come in quite normally with his short, determined step. What was this feeling that made her shrink from him, deprived her of the joy at seeing such a well-loved face? She was at a loss. She was reading in the dining room, and Quaresma came in unannounced. He just strolled in as he always had done. With the same foreboding she now replied:

'Father has gone out, and Armando is writing downstairs.'

He was, in fact, writing, or rather translating a lengthy article on wounds caused by firearms into the 'classical style'. This classical style was his latest intellectual ruse. In this way he intended to distinguish himself from the young authors who wrote stories and novels for the papers. As a scholar, and above all a doctor, it was inappropriate for him to write as they did. His could hardly do justice to his superior knowledge and his academic degree by adhering to the modish expressions and syntax used by aspiring poets and literary neophytes. This was how he got the idea of the classical style. The process was simple: he wrote in the usual way, using everyday words and style; then he inverted the phrases, punctured the sentences with commas, replaced 'bother' with 'disturb', 'around' with 'surrounding', 'the next' with 'the following', 'as big as' with 'the size of', sprinkled the whole text with 'aforesaids' and 'heretofores', and thus obtained the classical style which was already earning the admiration of his peers and the general public.

He was particularly fond of the expression 'in dispute'; he used it the entire time, imagining as he wrote that it endowed his ideas with a transcendent quality, and his style with the power and brilliance of a Pascal. At night he would read Padre Vieira,[8] but after the first few lines sleep overtook him, and he would dream that he was a master physician of the seventeenth century, prescribing bloodletting and hot water, just like Lesage's Doctor Sangrado.[9]

His translation was nearly finished. He was now quite adept, as with time he had acquired the vocabulary he needed, and he wrote down almost half of the first draft from memory. He was a little put out when he received his wife's message that a guest had arrived but, as he was quite unable to think of a classical equivalent for 'orifice', he thought that the interruption might be useful. He had thought of putting 'hole', but it was too vulgar; 'orifice', despite being commonly used, was nevertheless more dignified. Perhaps later he would come up with an answer, he thought, and went up to the dining room. He cheerfully entered the room, with his round face and large flaky moustache, to find his wife and her godfather engaged in a discussion about authority.

She was saying:

'I can't understand this religious respect you have for authority. The divine right of monarchs no longer exists, so why this respect, this veneration with which you want to see our rulers treated?'

The doctor, who had heard the whole sentence, could not refrain from objecting:

'But it's essential ... We know they are men like us, but without the veneration you speak of, society would collapse.'

Quaresma added:

'It's because of the requirements of our society, internal and external ... In the case of ants, in the case of bees ...'

'I accept that. But do bees and ants have rebellions? Is their authority maintained by murder, extortion and violence?'

'Who knows? Perhaps it is ...' Quaresma said evasively.

But the doctor didn't hesitate:

'What have bees got to do with it? Since when do we humans, the pinnacle of creation, have to go to insects to learn how to live?'

'Of course not, my dear doctor,' Quaresma said kindly. 'We observe them to gain an understanding of the laws of existence – its essence, one might say.'

Before he could finish his explanation Olga put in:

'If this new authority had brought any happiness – but it hasn't. So what is it worth?'

'But it will!' Quaresma declared categorically. 'We need to consolidate it.'

They talked for a long time. Quaresma recounted his visit to Floriano, his forthcoming enlistment in the Southern Cross battalion. The doctor felt a little envious when he spoke of the friendly way with which Floriano had treated him. They ate a light meal, and Quaresma left.

He wanted to see the streets again, those narrow streets with their dark shops stretching so far back that the attendants seemed to be moving about in a tunnel. He missed the sinuous Rua dos Ourives, the Rua da Assembleia with its potholes and that short stretch of the Rua do Ouvidor.

Nothing had changed: people standing in groups, young ladies out for a walk, crowds in front of the Café do Rio. These were the radicals, the Jacobins, the self-appointed guardians of the Republic, so intransigent that in their eyes moderation, tolerance, respect for the lives and liberty of others were crimes against the fatherland, a sign of support for the outlawed monarchy, mere pandering to foreigners. By foreigners they meant the Portuguese (which did not prevent some Portuguese editors from devoutly espousing their cause).

Apart from this inflamed, gesticulating group, the Rua do Ouvidor was unchanged. Couples were courting, girls came and went. If a bullet whistled through the bright blue sky overhead, the girls let out little meow-like screams and rushed inside the shops. They waited for a while and then came out smiling, the blood gradually returning to their cheeks, which had gone pale with fright.

Quaresma dined at a restaurant and made his way to the barracks, which were provisionally installed in the Cidade Nova in a rundown rooming house that had been condemned by the Hygiene Department. The house had two storeys, both divided into cubicles the size of ship cabins. On the upper floor there was a veranda with a wooden grille. It was reached by a rickety staircase that swayed and groaned beneath the slightest weight. The office occupied the first room on the ground floor, and the yard, from which the washing lines had been removed but whose flagstones were stained by hydroxide and soapsuds, was used for parading the new recruits. The instructor was a retired sergeant who limped a little, who had been admitted to the battalion as a second lieutenant. He was shouting, majestically pausing between syllables: 'Shoul-der . . . *arms!*'

The major delivered his contribution to the colonel who showed him the pattern for their uniform.

It looked like a rubber tapper's fancy dress costume: the jacket was bottle-green with navy-blue trimmings, gold braid and four silver stars forming a cross beneath the collar.

A sudden uproar was heard, and they went on to the veranda. A man was being dragged in by soldiers, kicking, struggling, imploring. Every now and again one of them hit him with the butt of his rifle.

'It's Ricardo!' Quaresma exclaimed. 'Don't you know him, colonel?' he asked, full of concern and pity.

Bustamante stood at his side, reserved and aloof. After a while he replied:

'Yes, I do. He's an insubordinate volunteer, a patriot turned rebel.'

The soldiers led the 'volunteer' up the stairs. As soon as he saw the major, Ricardo entreated him:

'Save me, major!'

Quaresma took the colonel aside, begged him, implored him, but to no effect. He needed men . . . So he'd made him a corporal.

From the distance Ricardo watched the conversation between the two: he guessed the outcome and cried out:

'I'll serve! I'll serve! But let me have my guitar!'

Bustamante leaned forward and shouted to the soldiers:

'Return Corporal Ricardo's guitar.'

'YOU, QUARESMA, ARE A VISIONARY'

Eight o'clock in the morning, everything still shrouded in mist. Those on the land can barely make out the lower storeys of the buildings nearby. Out at sea an impenetrable grey fog hangs over the ocean, that bastion of foam and darkness, condensing here and there into spectral shapes, ghostlike apparitions. The sea is calm but for a few feeble waves, breaking at intervals. A small stretch of the beach is visible through the mist, covered with debris and seaweed. The dank smell of low tide seems intensified by the fog. To the left and to the right, complete darkness: the Unknown. Yet the dense fog with its hazy light is peopled with sounds. The sound of nearby saws, the whistles of factories and trains, the cranking of cranes on the docks fill the eerie, brooding morning with noise. And at the same time, the measured sound of oars as they cleave the sea. In that dreadful place it can only be Charon, drawing his boat towards one of the shores of the Styx.

Action stations! Everyone stares at the dense curtain of mist. Apprehension is on every face, as though demons were about to emerge from the midst of the fog . . .

The oars are silent: the boat has moved away. Apprehension gives way to relief . . .

It is not night, it is not day: neither dawn nor dusk. It is the time of anguish, the light of uncertainty. At sea, neither sun nor star to guide the vessel; on land the birds fly into the whitewashed walls of the houses and die. We are left the poorer; the absence of the silent orbs that illuminate our lives heightens the awareness of our isolation amidst the vastness of the universe.

The noises continue, but as everything is shrouded in mist they appear to come from the depths of the earth, or to be hallucinations of the ear. The only reality is the visible stretch of sea, the feeble waves breaking at lingering intervals, creeping cautiously towards their encounter with the seaweed-covered strand.

As the boat draws away, groups of soldiers lie down in the grass that borders the beach; some are already asleep. Others strain their eyes to see the sky through the mist, whose dampness clings to their faces.

Corporal Ricardo Coração dos Outros, rifle at his waist, cap on his head, sits alone on a rock, apart from the others, contemplating that morning of dread.

It was the first time he had seen the dense mist that came from the sea with all its power and menace. The daybreaks he knew were tinged with purple – clear, fragrant and soft; this gloom-filled, foggy daybreak was something new to him.

The minstrel is not unhappy in his role as corporal. The freedom of life in the barracks suits his nature; he keeps his guitar there and plays it in his free time, humming softly to himself . . . He mustn't let his fingers get out of practice . . . The only slight setback is not being allowed to sing with his full voice every now and again.

Quaresma is the commander of his unit, perhaps he would allow it . . .

The major is inside the house which they use as a barracks, reading. His favourite subject is now artillery. He has bought textbooks but, as his basic education is lacking, from artillery he turns to ballistics, from ballistics to mechanics, from mechanics to calculus and analytical geometry, continuing down the scale to trigonometry, geometry, algebra and arithmetic. He studies this sequence of interconnected sciences with the spirit of an inventor. After innumerable consultations, going from textbook to textbook, he acquires an extremely basic grasp of the subject. Thus he spends his idle days as a soldier, absorbed in mathematics, that subject so refractory to assimilation by older minds.

The unit has a Krupp cannon. Although he has no say in the use of this deadly weapon, he continues to study artillery. Lieutenant Fontes, who simply ignores the major's orders, is in charge of the cannon. Quaresma is not bothered by this; he continues slowly learning how to use heavy weaponry and submits to the arrogant behaviour of his subordinate.

The commander of the Southern Cross, Bustamante, with his mosaic beard, is always present in the barracks, from where he supervises the battalion. The unit has very few officers and even fewer men, although four hundred appear on the government payroll. Captains are in short supply; the number of second lieutenants is adequate, the number of lieutenants almost so, but they now have a major, Quaresma, and the commander, Bustamante, who modestly appointed himself lieutenant colonel.

The unit that Quaresma commands has forty men, three second lieutenants and two lieutenants, but the officers rarely appear; they are either sick or on leave. Only the former farmer of 'The Haven' and a second lieutenant called Polidoro are at their posts, the latter only at night. A soldier came in:

'May I go for lunch, sir?'

'You may. Call Corporal Ricardo for me.'

The private left, dragging his heavy boots; being obliged to use them was like a chastisement for the wretched fellow. As soon as he entered the woods near his home he took them off, and an expression of relief came over his face at the feeling of freedom.

Quaresma went to the window. The mist was clearing, and the sun had appeared, shining like a pale golden disc.

Ricardo Coração dos Outros arrived. He was a comic sight in his corporal's uniform. The jacket was much too short, with the sleeves very tight above the wrists. The trousers were much too long and trailed along the ground.

'How are you, Ricardo?'

'Well. And you, major?'

'I'm well too.'

With his penetrating eye, Quaresma contemplated his friend and subordinate:

'You haven't been happy lately, have you?'

Ricardo felt pleased by the major's interest:

'Not really . . . How could I be, major? If it is always like it is now, it won't be too bad. But when the shooting starts . . . There *is* one thing, though, major: when I'm free, if I could wander off into the marshes and sing for a bit . . .'

The major scratched his head, stroked his beard and said:

'I don't know . . . It's . . .'

'Singing under one's breath is like practising on a rowing machine . . . They say that in Paraguay . . .'

'All right. You can sing there, but not too loudly, OK?'

They were silent for a moment. Ricardo was about to leave when the major added:

'Tell them to send me my lunch.'

Quaresma had lunch and dinner in the barracks, and he often slept there too. The meals were supplied by a nearby tavern, and he slept in one of the bedrooms of the building that had once been the emperor's pavilion, where his unit was now accommodated. It was located in the former royal park at the Ponta do Cajú, which it shared with the Rio Douro railway station and a large noisy sawmill. Quaresma went to the door and looked out at the dirty beach, amazed that the emperor should have chosen it for bathing. The mist was clearing fast.

Clearly defined objects were emerging from amidst the heavy fog, as though relieved that the nightmare was over. First the lower parts were gradually revealed, and then, all of a sudden, those higher up.

To the right, the districts of Saúde and Gamboa, with the merchant ships, three-masted cargo steamers and proud sailing boats emerging from the mist, momentarily giving the impression of a Dutch landscape. To the left, the Saco da Raposa, Retiro Saudoso, the dreadful Sapucaia, the Ilha do Governador and the Serra dos Orgãos touching the sky. Ahead, the Ilha dos Ferreiros with its heaps of coal. And, looking further out, across the calm waters of the bay, the hills of Niterói, now outlined against the blue sky in the late-morning sun that had broken through the mist.[1]

The mist cleared, and a cock crowed. It was as if joy had

returned to the earth; it was an alleluia. The sawing, the whistling and the creaking assumed a festive note.

Lunch arrived, and the sergeant came to tell Quaresma that two soldiers had deserted.

'Another two?' the major asked in surprise.

'Yes, sir. Numbers a hundred and twenty-five and three hundred and twenty didn't answer at roll-call today.'

'Enter it in the register.'

Quaresma ate lunch. Lieutenant Fontes, the man in charge of the cannon, arrived. He almost never slept there; he spent the nights at home and came during the day to see how things were going.

One morning, when he wasn't there, while it was still very dark, the soldier on sentry duty saw a shadowy form in the distance, gliding across the waters through the gloom. It had no lights; only the movement of its shadowy form and the slight phosphorescence of the water revealed that it was a ship. The soldier gave the alarm. The men from the small detachment ran to their posts, and Quaresma appeared.

'Bring up the cannon,' he ordered. And then, in a nervous voice, he added:

'Wait a moment.'

He rushed back to the house to consult his textbooks and tables. While he was gone the ship got closer. The soldiers were terrified and one of them, taking the initiative, loaded the cannon and fired.

Quaresma rushed back in alarm, panting for breath, and said:

'Did you verify . . . the distance . . . the aim . . . the angle? One must never forget that the aim is to hit the target.'

When Fontes heard of the incident the next day, he roared with laughter:

'Really, major, do you think you're here on a training exercise? Just fire away!'

And so it was. Almost every afternoon there was a bombardment, the ships firing on the fortresses and the fortresses firing on the ships, and both the ships and the forts emerged unscathed from the terrible ordeal.

On one occasion, however, they hit their target, and the newspapers announced: 'Yesterday the Acadêmico Fort fired a magnificent shot, hitting the *Guanabara*.'[2] The following day the newspaper published a correction at the request of the Cais Pharoux[3] saying that the successful shot had been fired by them. A few days later, when the incident had been forgotten, a letter came from Niterói claiming the credit for the shot for the fortress of Santa Cruz.

Lieutenant Fontes arrived and examined the cannon with an expert eye. There was a trench with bales of alfalfa, and the muzzle of the weapon poked out between pieces of straw, looking like the wide-open mouth of a wild beast concealed in the undergrowth.

After carefully examining the cannon, he looked at the horizon and was contemplating the Ilha das Cobras, when he heard the plaintive sound of a guitar and a voice singing:

> By the holy of holies I swear . . .

Making his way to where the sound was coming from, he saw this delightful scene: beneath the shade of a large tree the soldiers were sitting or lying on the ground in a circle around Ricardo Coração dos Outros, who was intoning melancholy verses.

The men, who had just had their lunch and drunk their *cachaça*, were so enthralled by Ricardo's song that they did not notice the arrival of the young officer.

'What's this?' he said severely.

The soldiers jumped to their feet and saluted. And Ricardo, saluting with his right hand and holding on to the guitar which rested on the ground with his left, explained:

'Sir, the major gave us permission. You know we wouldn't disobey the rules if we didn't have permission, sir.'

'That's enough. I don't want any more of this,' the officer said.

'But sir,' Ricardo objected, 'Major Quaresma . . .'

'There's no Major Quaresma here. That's enough, I say!'

The men dispersed, and Lieutenant Fontes made his way to

the old imperial pavilion to talk to the major of the Southern Cross battalion. Quaresma was continuing with his studies, a Sisyphean task, but willingly undertaken for the glory of the fatherland. Fontes came in and said:

'What's this, Sr Quaresma! So now you allow sing-alongs in the unit!'

Quaresma, who had forgotten all about it, was startled by the young man's harsh, sharp manner. He repeated:

'So, sir, you allow your subordinates to sing *modinhas* and play the guitar while they're on duty?'

'But what's the harm? I have heard that during a campaign . . .'

'And what about discipline? What about respect?'

'All right. I'll forbid it,' Quaresma said.

'There's no need. I've already done so.'

Quaresma was not annoyed. He saw no reason to be and replied kindly:

'You did well.'

Then he asked the young officer how to find the square root of a decimal fraction. The young man showed him and they chatted amicably about everyday things. Fontes was engaged to Lalá, General Albernaz's third daughter, and he was waiting for the revolt to end so that he could get married. For an hour or two they talked about this routine family affair, the outcome of which depended on those explosions, those shots, that earnest dispute between two deadly rivals. Suddenly the metallic call of a bugle pierced the air. Fontes listened carefully; the major asked:

'What call is that?'

'The call to action.'

They rushed out, Fontes impeccably dressed, the major tightening his sword belt while managing to trip over the venerable weapon that insisted on getting between his short legs. The men were already in the trenches, guns at hand, the required ammunition in place beside the cannon. A launch was coming slowly towards them, its prow aimed directly at their position. Suddenly thick smoke came billowing from its deck. 'They've fired,' shouted a voice. Everyone ducked. The shell whistled over their heads. The launch continued dauntlessly to advance. As well as the soldiers, there were boys who had come to watch the firing. It was one of these who shouted out: 'They've fired!'

They always came. Sometimes they came right up to where the troops were, to the trenches, getting in everyone's way. At other times, some fellow or other would come up to an officer and ask very politely: 'Would you allow me to fire a shot?' The officer agreed, the men loaded the cannon, the fellow would aim, and the shot went off.

As time passed, the revolt became a festivity, a public entertainment for the city. When a bombardment was announced on a Monday, the promenade of the Passeio Público would be crowded. It was like the old days, when it was fashionable to come out on clear nights to watch the moonlight sparkling on the waters from the gardens of Dom Luis de Vasconcelos.

They rented binoculars, and the young and the old, of both the sexes, watched the bombardment as if it were a play at the theatre: 'The *Santa Cruz* has fired. Now it's the *Aquidabã*. There she goes!' And thus the revolt became just an ordinary thing, one of the city's everyday entertainments and pastimes.

The little boys in the Cais Pharoux – newspaper vendors, shoe-shiners, fruit sellers – used to hide behind the doorways, urinals and trees, from where they watched and waited for the shells to fall; and when one did they would rush out in a gang to collect it, as if it were a coin or piece of chocolate.

Bullets were now the fashion: there were tie-pins, watch straps, mechanical pencils, all made from small rifle bullets. People also collected medium-sized ones, and their metal cases, scoured, scrubbed and polished, were used to decorate display cases in middle-class homes; the large ones, which were nicknamed 'melons' or 'pumpkins', were used to decorate gardens, like enamel vases or statues.

The launch continued firing. Fontes fired a shot. The cannon belched out the projectile, lurching backwards, and was immediately placed in position again. The launch responded.

'They've fired,' yelled the boy.

The enemy fire was always announced by these boys. As

soon as they saw the flash followed by a column of smoke coming from the ship in the distance, they shouted: 'They've fired!'

There was one boy in Niterói who enjoyed a brief moment of fame. They nicknamed him 'Thirty Réis'. The newspapers that covered his escapades even collected money as a tribute to him. He was the hero of the hour. The revolt ended, and he was forgotten, like the *Luci*, a splendid launch that captured the imagination of the whole town, creating enemies as well as admirers.

The launch ceased tormenting the unit at Cajú, and Fontes, after instructing his second-in-command, left for home.

Quaresma went to his room and continued with his studies of weaponry. The rest of the days he spent at that outpost of the city were no different from this one. The same events reoccurred, and the war became a banal affair of repeated episodes.

From time to time, when he felt bored, he would go out. He would go into town and leave Polidoro in charge, or Fontes if he was there.

This rarely occurred during the day, as the most diligent of them, Polidoro, worked as a carpenter in a furniture factory and only came at night.

There was great merriment in the city at night. People had plenty of money, as the government was paying double salaries and sometimes additional compensation; and death was always present. These two things combined were an incentive for people to enjoy themselves. The theatres were full, as were the restaurants that opened at night.

Quaresma, however, avoided the noisy, overcrowded streets. He occasionally went to the theatre in civilian dress and when the play ended returned to his room in the city or to his unit.

Some evenings, as soon as Polidoro had arrived, he would wander through the neighbourhood, along the beaches, to the Campo de São Cristóvão.

He would look at the rows of cemeteries with their white tombstones climbing the hillsides like newly sheared sheep put out to graze, and at the brooding cypresses watching over them, as if they were showing him that that part of the city was the feudal domain of death.[4]

The houses looked funereal, huddled together as if they were trying to hide. The waves broke mournfully against the muddy shore. The palm trees rustled plaintively, and even the bells of the trams had a doleful ring.

The landscape was impregnated with death, and even more so the thoughts of all who passed, reinforcing the funereal aspect of the place.

He walked as far as the 'Campo'. He suddenly had a desire to see his old house again. As he was in the vicinity, he took the opportunity to visit General Albernaz, to whom he owed a visit.

Lieutenant Fontes, Admiral Caldas and Lieutenant Colonel Inocêncio Bustamante, Quaresma's commander, had just finished dining with the general.

Bustamante was an active commander, but there was no one in the barracks who equalled his zeal for bookkeeping, clear handwriting for every entry in the logs, registers, company records and other documents. With their aid the organization of his battalion was irreproachable, and in order to keep an eye on the accounting, from time to time he would pay an unexpected visit to the units of his detachment.

Quaresma had not seen him for ten days. As soon as they greeted each other he asked the major:

'How many desertions?'

'Nine, so far,' said Quaresma.

Bustamante scratched his head in desperation and said:

'I don't understand these people. The desertions never stop. They have no patriotism!'

'They're quite right, if you ask me!' said the admiral.

Caldas was resentful and pessimistic. His petition was going badly; so far the government had given him nothing. The more his hopes of becoming a vice-admiral eluded him, the more his patriotic spirit waned. It was true that the government had not yet organized its fleet, but rumour had it he wouldn't even be commanding a unit. It was iniquitous! He was no longer young, it was true, but, never having had a command, he could muster all the energy of a younger man for the task.

'You shouldn't talk like that, admiral. Allegiance to country ranks immediately below allegiance to mankind.'

'You are young, my dear lieutenant. I understand these things . . .'

'But we mustn't despair. What we are doing is not for us, but for those that come after us,' Fontes continued eloquently.

'What have I got to do with them?' Caldas said irritably.

Bustamante, the general and Quaresma observed the argument in silence, the first two slightly amused by Caldas's rage, as he fidgeted from side to side and stroked his long, white sideburns. The lieutenant replied:

'A great deal, admiral. We must all work for a better future, for a more orderly, moral and happier society.'

'A better future! There never has been one, and there never will be!' Caldas snapped.

'I agree with you,' said Albernaz.

'Things will never change,' added Bustamante sceptically.

The major said nothing; he seemed to take no interest in the conversation. In the face of such opposition, Fontes, unlike his fellow believers would have done, did not respond angrily. He was thin and drawn, his dark-skinned oval face marked by creases of disapproval. After listening to all of them, in a drawn-out, nasal voice, shaking his right hand as though he were speaking from the pulpit, he said sententiously:

'I will give you an example: the Middle Ages.'

Not one of them could contradict him. Quaresma only knew the history of Brazil, and the others, none at all.

In the face of his affirmation, all were silent, although each had his doubts. What period is this, the Middle Ages, with its high moral standards? What years does it cover? If you say: 'Clothair I personally set fire to the hut where his son Chram[5] was hiding with his wife and children,' the positivists will reply: 'The ascendancy of the Church had not yet been completely established.' If you respond by saying, 'St Louis[6] wanted to execute a feudal baron who had ordered three children to be hanged for killing a rabbit on his land,' the orthodox positivist replies: 'Didn't you know that the Middle Ages end with the appearance of the *Divine Comedy*?[7] By St Louis's time they were already in decline.' If you cite the disease, the plagues, the poverty of the peasants, the armed robbery committed by barons, the delusions of the time, Charlemagne's barbaric slaughter of the Saxons, they reply either that the moral ascendancy of the church had not yet been fully established or that it was already in decline.

But no such objections were raised to our young positivist, and the conversation returned to the revolt. The admiral severely criticized the government:

They had no plan. They were just firing off shots. In his opinion, they should have done everything possible to occupy the Ilha das Cobras, even at the cost of rivers of blood. Bustamante was undecided, but both Quaresma and Fontes disagreed: it would be a risky undertaking and would serve no purpose at all. Albernaz had not yet given his opinion, and when he did, it was in the following terms:

'But we reconnoitred Humaitá, and just in time!'

'But you didn't take it,' said Fontes. 'The natural conditions were completely different, and even so the reconnaissance was completely useless . . . Well, you know – you were there!'

'Well, actually . . . I fell sick and returned to Brazil just before, but Camisão told me it was a risky venture.'

Quaresma had fallen silent again. He wanted to see Ismênia. Fontes had told him about her condition, and in a strange way he felt somehow responsible for her illness. He had seen all the family: Dona Maricota, busy as ever; Lalá, glancing at her fiancé, trying to drag him away from that interminable conversation; and the other girls who from time to time would come from the drawing room into the dining room, where he was. Finally he summed up the courage to ask after her. He was told she was at her married sister's house and was getting worse, sinking ever deeper into her obsessions, getting weaker and weaker. The general candidly told Quaresma all this. When he had finished narrating this personal calamity, he sighed deeply and said:

'I don't know, Quaresma . . . I really don't know!'

It was ten o'clock when the major left. He took the tram back to the Ponta do Cajú and walked back to his room. The moonlight was particularly beautiful that night, milky and soft. It had a strange effect on him, as it does on everyone. A feeling of well-being and relaxation came over him. It was as if the material had been stripped away and only the soul was left, bathed in an atmosphere of reverie and dreams. He was scarcely aware of this transcendental sensation, but Quaresma was under the effect of the pale, cool light of the moon. He lay down for a while, fully dressed, not because he felt sleepy, but because the moon had cast its spell on him.

Before long Ricardo came to get him. The marshal was there. Floriano was in the habit of going out at night, sometimes in the early hours, going from post to post. When the public got to know of this they thought it was something wonderful, and it served as yet further proof of what a great statesman the president was.

Quaresma came to meet him. Floriano was wearing a wide-brimmed soft felt hat and a short, shabby overcoat. There was a devious air about him, like an exemplary head of the family engaged in adulterous adventures.

The major greeted him and told him about the attack that had been made on his post a few days before. The marshal looked around and answered languidly, in monosyllables. As he was about to leave he added as if in afterthought:

'You should put a searchlight here.'

Quaresma accompanied him to the tram. They walked across the former pleasure gardens of the emperors. A short way outside the station a locomotive, half illuminated, was puffing out smoke. It seemed to be snoring, fast asleep. Its small carriages, bathed in the moonlight, so peaceful and quiet, seemed to be sleeping too. The old mango trees, some with severed branches, appeared to be covered in silver dust. The moonlight was glorious. As the two men walked, the marshal asked:

'How many men have you got?'

'Forty.'

'That's not many,' he muttered, falling silent again. For a moment Quaresma saw his face illuminated by the light of the moon. The dictator's expression looked kinder. What if he asked him . . .

He prepared the question but did not have the courage to ask it. They continued walking. The major thought: why on earth not? There's no disrespect implied. As they were approaching the gate he thought he heard a noise from behind them. Quaresma looked back, but Floriano scarcely seemed to notice.

The moonlight was so white, the sawmill looked as if it were covered with snow. The major continued to ponder his question. It was urgent, it was vital; the gate was just two steps away. He summoned up all his courage and said:

'Have you read my report, Your Excellency?'

Floriano replied slowly, scarcely moving his drooping lower lip:

'Yes I have.'

Quaresma became quite carried away:

'You see, Your Excellency, how easy it is to make this country progress. All that is needed is to remove all those obstacles that I listed in the report Your Excellency has been kind enough to read. Once the errors of deficient legislation, which is a burden on the country, have been corrected, Your Excellency will see how all this will change, and instead of being dependent on others we will achieve our real independence . . . If Your Excellency would like . . .'

As he spoke, Quaresma became more and more enthusiastic. He couldn't see the dictator's face, which was covered by the brim of his felt hat, but if he could, his enthusiasm would have cooled, because his expression revealed an increasingly dangerous irritation. However much he may wish it, he could not remain unaffected by Quaresma's little speech, his appeal for legislation and government measures. The president was irritated. He suddenly turned to him and said:

'But do you really think, Quaresma, that I'm going to put every one of these vagabonds to work in the fields? Even if I had a whole army of . . .'

Quaresma was astonished. After hesitating for a while he replied:

'But that's not what I meant, marshal. Your Excellency, with your power and prestige, through energetic and appropriate measures, could promote initiatives, regulate the profession, provide incentives to make it profitable . . . All that would be needed, to give an example . . .'

They passed through the gates of the park that had belonged to Dom Pedro I. The moonlight was still beautiful: opalescent, intangible. A large, unfinished building in the street appeared complete, with windows and doorways made of moonlight. It was a palace of dreams.

Floriano now listened to Quaresma with considerable irritation. The tram arrived. As he bid the major farewell he said in his placid voice:

'You, Quaresma, are a visionary . . .'

The tram pulled away. The moonlight poured into the empty spaces, bringing them alive, giving birth to the dreams of the soul, illuminating the whole of life with its borrowed light . . .

. . . AND THEY FELL SILENT

'I've tried *everything*, Quaresma, but what can I say? There's nothing they can do!'

'Have you taken her to a specialist?'

'Yes. I've taken her to doctors, spiritual healers, even sorcerers, Quaresma!'

And the old man's eyes misted over behind his pince-nez. The two had met at the pay-office of the War Ministry and were crossing the Campo de Sant'Ana, walking slowly as they talked. The general was taller than Quaresma, his long neck and erect head contrasting with the major's, sunk between two high shoulders that looked like the stumps of a pair of wings. Albernaz continued:

'And the medicines! Every doctor prescribes something different. The spiritualists are the best: they use homoeopathy. The sorcerers prescribe potions, prayers and smoke cures. I don't know . . .'

And he lifted his eyes towards the leaden sky. He did not, however, remain long in this position: his pince-nez did not permit it, it began to slip.

Quaresma lowered his head and walked along, examining the patterns in the granite stone of the path. After a while he looked up and said:

'Why don't you put her in a nursing home, general?'

'My doctor has already advised me to. My wife doesn't want to, and now, with the state the girl is in, it wouldn't do any good . . .'

He was talking about his daughter, Ismênia, who had got much worse in the last few months, not only in her mental state but in her general health: always feverish, getting weaker, wasting away, walking with a steady step towards the cold embrace of death.

Albernaz was telling the truth: to cure her of her madness and of her recurring illnesses, he had sought help in every direction, accepting any advice, from whatever quarter.

Food for thought indeed: a man like that, a general with a government career, seeking the aid of mediums and witch-doctors to cure his daughter.

Sometimes he even took them home. The mediums would go up to the girl, quivering, with a wild look in their eyes, and shout: 'Leave her, brother!' Then they would vibrate the palms of their hands before the girl's chest with brusque, rapid movements, enveloping the girl with miraculous fluids.[1]

The witch-doctors had other ways of healing with their hands and used long, ceremonial rituals for entering into contact with the occult forces around us. They were usually African blacks. They would arrive and light a clay stove in the bedroom, take a stuffed toad or some other bizarre object from a basket, beat the patient with bundles of herbs and dance around, uttering incomprehensible sounds. The ritual was complex and lasted for a long time.

As he left, Dona Maricota, no longer as bright and active as she had been, looked pleadingly into the sorcerer's large black face, invested with a certain grandeur by a white beard that gave him a somewhat venerable look, and asked:

'Well, little father?'

The black man reflected for a moment, as if receiving a final communication from the unseen spirit world, and then said with African majesty:

'I go see, missus . . . I take off de spell . . .'

She and the general had watched the ceremony; their parents' love, and deep down, the superstition that all of us share, led them to regard him with respect, even with faith.

'Has someone put a spell on my daughter?' the lady asked.

'Dat right, missus.'

'Who?'

'De *orisha* no say.'

And that old enigmatic black man, once a slave, wrenched from the depths of Africa half a century before, slowly withdrew, leaving for a brief moment a gleam of hope in their hearts.

The situation of that old African was remarkable indeed: with the torments of the long years of captivity still fresh in his mind, using his powers to evoke the remnants of his simple tribal beliefs – beliefs that it had cost so dearly to maintain after their forced dislocation to the lands of other gods[2] – using them for the consolation of his former masters. It was as if the gods of his childhood, the gods of his people, those bloodthirsty idols of inscrutable Africa, wished to avenge him by adopting the example of Christ in the Gospels . . .

The patient watched all this without understanding or taking any interest in the gestures and movements of these powerful men, who had spiritual entities at their command, beings from beyond and above our world.

The general recalled all this as he walked beside Quaresma and reflected bitterly on science, on spirits, on magic spells, on God, who little by little was taking his daughter away from him, without mercy or compassion.

Faced with such terrible suffering of a father, the major did not know what to say. Any words of consolation appeared meaningless and foolish. In the end he said:

'General, would you permit me to let a doctor see her?'

'Who is he?'

'My goddaughter's husband. You've met him. He's young. Who knows, he might help, don't you think?'

The general agreed. His wrinkled face brightened at the hope of seeing his daughter cured. With every doctor, spirit healer, sorcerer he consulted, his hopes were raised. He expected a miracle from them all. That same day Quaresma went to find Dr Armando.

The revolt had already lasted more than four months, and the government's position was problematic. In the south the insurrection had reached the gates of São Paulo. Only Lapa resisted firmly in one of the few upright, worthy episodes amidst that flood of passions. The trenches of the little town were commanded with energy and willpower by Colonel Gomes Carneiro, who remained serene, confident and just. He did not degenerate into the violence produced by fear, giving true meaning to the grandiose cliché 'a fight to the death'.[3]

The Ilha do Governador had been occupied and Magé taken, but the insurgents controlled the whole bay and guarded the entrance, from where they came and went, ignoring the vigilance of the forts.

Quaresma had heard of the acts of violence and the crimes that had marked these two military exploits of the government, and he was deeply upset.

On the Ilha do Governador furniture, clothes and other belongings were pillaged. What could not be transported was burned or destroyed by axe.

The occupation left the most abhorrent memories. Even today residents painfully recall a certain Captain Ortiz of the National Guard or a private militia for his ferocity and voracious appetite for pillaging and other abuses. A fisherman passed with a basket of fish, and the captain called the wretched fellow:

'Come here!'

Terrified, the man approached, and Ortiz asked:

'How much do you want for that?'

'Three thousand *réis*, captain.'

He smiled fiendishly and began to bargain:

'Can't you lower the price? It's expensive – they're just Mojarra fish after all.'

'Well, captain, two thousand five hundred, then.'

'Take it inside.'

He waited outside the door. When the fisherman came out and stood waiting for his money, Ortiz shook his head and said mockingly:

'*Money*, eh? Send the bill to Floriano!'

On the other hand Moreira César[4] left good memories. Even today there are people who are grateful for kindnesses shown to them by the famous colonel.

But the rebels continued to show their strength, even after losing two ships. One of these was the *Javari*, which enjoyed enormous respect during the revolt. The land forces in particular hated her. She was a monitor built in France, flat, lying low in the water, like a sort of steel crocodile or turtle. Her artillery was greatly feared, but what most infuriated her adversaries was that she hardly appeared above the surface of the water, floating so low that she easily made her escape when they started to fire. Her engines did not work, so the huge turtle was towed into combat position with the aid of a tug.

Then one day, near Villegagnon,[5] she sank. No one knew why; the reason has never since been discovered. The loyalists said that it was a shot from Gragoatá,[6] while the rebels insisted that it was due to a faulty valve, or some other such accident.

Like that of her sister ship, the *Solimões*, off Cape Polônio,[7] the loss of the *Javari* is still shrouded in mystery.

Quaresma was still with the garrison at Cajú and had come to collect his pay. He had left Polidoro there because the other officers were either sick or on leave, and Fontes, as a sort of inspector-general, had, contrary to his usual habits, spent the night in the imperial bathing pavilion and was going to stay until evening.

Since the day he had been forbidden to play the guitar Ricardo Coração dos Outros had been brooding. They had taken away his life-blood, his reason for living, and he spent his days sullenly leaning against a tree trunk, silently cursing the incomprehension of men and the whims of fate. Fontes had noticed his despondency and to cheer him up had insisted that Bustamante make him a sergeant. This was not easy as the old veteran of the Paraguayan War gave great value to this promotion, only conferring it as a reward for exceptional service or when requested by an influential person.

So the poor minstrel's life was like that of a songbird in a cage. From time to time he wandered a little way off and rehearsed his voice, to check it was still there and had not evaporated like the smoke from the guns.

Knowing that the post was in safe hands, Quaresma decided to stay away longer and, after saying farewell to Albernaz, he made his way to Coleoni's house to keep the promise he had made to the general.

The Italian had still not decided whether to go to Europe. He hesitated, waiting for the end of the rebellion, which did

not seem any closer. It was nothing to do with him; he had told
no one of his opinion. When pressed, he would plead his foreigner's status and maintain a prudent reserve. But it was the
requirement for a passport, obtained from police headquarters,
that alarmed him. At that time everyone was afraid of dealing
with the authorities. There was so much ill-will towards foreigners, so much arrogance on the part of the civil servants that
he was afraid to apply for the document, afraid that a word, a
look or a gesture, misinterpreted by some zealous, dedicated
government employee, could have undesirable consequences
for him.

The fact is he was Italian, and Italy had just given the dictator a demonstration that it was a great power. The case in point
concerned a sailor for whose death, from a shot fired by loyalist forces, Floriano had paid the sum of a hundred *contos de
réis*. However, Coleoni was not a sailor and he did not know, if
he were arrested, whether the diplomatic representatives of his
country would take any interest in freeing him.

What was more, having not declared that he would maintain his nationality when the provisional government issued its
famous naturalization decree,[8] it was quite possible that one
side or other would use this, either to abandon him, or hold
him in the notorious Gallery no. 7 of the Reformatory, transformed at the stroke of a pen into a prison of the state.

It was a time of fear and apprehension, but he could only
speak of his fears to his daughter, as his son-in-law had become
an ever more radical supporter of Floriano, from whose mouth
very often he would hear diatribes against foreigners.

Armando's strategy worked: he had already received a government post. He had been appointed doctor at the Santa
Barbara Hospital in the place of a colleague whom the government had found fit to dismiss as he had visited a friend in
prison. But as the hospital was situated on the island of the
same name in the bay opposite Saúde, and the bay was still
controlled by the rebels, he had nothing to do. The government
had not accepted his offers to assist in treating the wounded.

The major found father and daughter at home. The doctor
had gone out to walk around the town to display his dedication

to the loyalist cause, talking with the most impassioned radicals at the Café do Rio and making sure he was seen in the corridors of Itamarati[9] by the adjutants, secretaries and others who had influence with the president.

When she saw Quaresma come in Olga experienced the same feeling of unease that she had the last time she saw him. This feeling was heightened as she watched him telling stories about his detachment in the war, bullets flying, launches opening fire, as simply and naturally as if they were party entertainments, normal, everyday amusements in which death had no part.

She also thought him apprehensive, revealing by certain remarks that he was despondent, had given up hope.

Indeed, the major was cut to the quick. Floriano's reception of his proposal for reforms had been unworthy of both his enthusiasm and his sincerity, let alone the idea he had had of the dictator. He had set out to find a Henri IV and a Sully and ended up meeting a president who called him a visionary, who did not realize the significance of his projects, who did not even examine them, with no interest in the lofty tasks of government, as if he weren't its highest authority! Was it to support this man that he had left the tranquillity of his home and was risking his life in the trenches? Was it for this man that so many people were dying? What right did he have to the power of life and death over his fellow citizens if he took no interest in their well-being, their happiness and prosperity, the prosperity of the country, the development of its agriculture and the welfare of its rural population?

With such thoughts there were times when he was overcome with despair, with anger against himself. But then he would think: the man's in trouble, he can't do anything now, but he will later on, I'm sure of it . . .

This painful debate never ceased. It was this that caused the apprehension, the despondency and the lack of hope that his goddaughter perceived in his downcast look.

It was not long, however, before Quaresma stopped telling stories about his military life and explained the reason for his visit.

'Which daughter?' Olga asked.

'The second one, Ismênia.'

'The one who was going to marry the dentist?'

'That's right.'

'Hmmm!'

Her 'Hmmm' was long and meaningful. It contained everything that she would like to say on the matter. She well understood the girl's despair, but she understood the cause even better: the obligation that is hammered into girls' minds that they must get married at any cost, making marriage the aim and purpose of life, to the extent that remaining single is a disgrace, an ignominy.

Marriage no longer means love, or maternity; it is neither of these things. It is simply marriage, an empty, meaningless institution, with no relation to human nature or human requirements.

Due to the weakness of her nature, her lack of intellect, her lack of willpower, the flight of her bridegroom had convinced her that she would never now marry, and the consequent despair had led to her total collapse.

Coleoni was concerned and very upset. He had a kind heart. When he was struggling to make his fortune he had made himself hard and stern, but as soon as he found he was rich he had abandoned his harshness. He realized that in order to do good, one must be strong.

Recently the major had shown a little less interest in the girl. He was tormented by his own conflict of conscience. Nevertheless, if his thoughts dwelt less on the affliction of Albernaz's daughter, she still had a place in the general goodness and generosity of his heart.

He did not stay long at Coleoni's house. Before returning to Cajú he wanted to visit his battalion headquarters. He was going to see if he could arrange a short leave to visit his sister, whom he had left at 'The Haven', and from whom he received news by letter three times a week. The letters were good enough, but he felt the need to see both her and Anastácio again, the people he had lived with for so many years, whom he missed and who might, perhaps, help restore his calm and peace of mind.

At that moment he remembered a sentence in the last letter he had received from Dona Adelaide, and smiled: 'Don't expose yourself to risk, Policarpo. Be very careful.' Poor Adelaide! Did she imagine that a shower of bullets was as harmless as rain?

The headquarters was still in the old rooming house, condemned by the Hygiene Department, out at the Cidade Nova.[10] As soon as Quaresma appeared round the corner the sentry let out a great yell and with a resounding clatter of arms he entered, removing his hat, as he was in civilian dress – he had left his top hat behind, afraid that this garment may offend the susceptibilities of the radical republicans.

In the yard the lame instructor was training new volunteers, and his majestic drawn-out shouts – 'Shoul-der ... *arms*! A-bout ... *turn*!' – rose up to the sky and echoed around the walls of the old boarding house.

Bustamante was in his cubicle, more commonly known as his office, immaculate in his bottle-green uniform, golden braid and navy-blue piping. With the aid of a sergeant he was examining the entries in one of the barracks books.

'Red ink, sergeant! That's what it says in the instructions of 1864.'

He was referring to an amendment or some such matter.

As soon as he saw Quaresma come in, the commander exclaimed delightedly:

'You must have guessed, major!'

Quaresma calmly put down his hat, drank a little water, and Colonel Bustamante explained the reason for his contentment:

'You know we've had marching orders?'

'Where to?'

'I don't know ... I received the order from Itamarati.'

He would never say from general headquarters, or even from the War Ministry; it was from Itamarati, from the president, from the supreme authority. In that way it seemed to give more importance to himself and his battalion, making it into a kind of personal guard, the beloved favourite of the dictator.

Quaresma was neither alarmed nor annoyed. He realized that obtaining leave was impossible, and also that he would have to change his studies: from artillery he would have to move to infantry.

'You will command the troop, major. Did you know?'

'No, colonel. Aren't you going to?'

'No,' said Bustamante, stroking his massive beard and speaking out of the side of his mouth. 'I have to complete the organization of the unit and I can't . . . Don't be alarmed, I will come later on . . .'

It was late afternoon when Quaresma left headquarters. The shouts of the lame instructor continued, majestic and drawn-out, 'Shoul-der . . . *arms*!' The clatter of arms was not repeated, as the sentry only noticed Quaresma when he was already a long way off. He went into town, to the post office. There was some intermittent firing; in the Café do Rio the acolytes continued to exchange ideas for the consolidation of the Republic.

Before he reached the post office Quaresma suddenly remembered the march. He rushed to a bookshop and bought books about infantry. He would need the regulations too, he would get them at general headquarters.

Where was he going? To the south, to Magé, to Niterói? He didn't know . . . He didn't know . . . Oh, if this were only for the fulfilment of his desires, his dreams! But who knows? . . . It could be . . . perhaps . . . later on . . .

And he spent the rest of the day tormented by doubts about the use to which he had put his life and his energies.

Olga's husband showed no particular interest in seeing Ismênia. He was quite convinced that all his newly acquired knowledge would achieve a cure. But this was not to be.

The girl got weaker and weaker, and although she seemed less obsessive, her health was failing. She was so thin and feeble, she could hardly sit up in bed. Her mother was her most constant companion. Her sisters lost interest a little – they were young and had other places to go and things to do.

Dona Maricota, who had lost all her former zest for parties and balls, spent her time in her daughter's room, comforting her, consoling her and at times, after contemplating her for some time, feeling a little to blame for her unhappiness.

Her illness had somehow made Ismênia more determined. She was less apathetic, her eyes had lost their vacant look, and her beautiful auburn hair with its streaks of gold looked even lovelier as it offset the pallidness of her face.

She rarely spoke much. So that day Dona Maricota was amazed at her, how much she talked:

'Mother, when is Lalá getting married?'

'When the rebellion is over.'

'Hasn't the rebellion finished yet?'

Her mother answered her, and she remained quiet for a while, staring at the ceiling. After a moment she said:

'Mother . . . I'm going to die . . .'

She spoke the words quietly, naturally, with assurance.

'Don't say that, my child,' Dona Maricota retorted. 'Die! You're going to get well. Your father's going to take you to Minas. You're going to put on weight, get strong . . .'

Her mother said all this slowly, stroking her cheek, as if she were talking to a child. She listened patiently, and then answered serenely:

'No, Mother! I know. I'm going to die, and I have something to ask you . . .'

Her mother was amazed at her seriousness and resolve. She looked round and, seeing the door was half open, she got up to close it. She still hoped to dissuade her daughter from such thoughts, but Ismênia continued repeating them, insistently, softly, serenely:

'I know, Mother!'

'All right. Suppose it were true. What is it you want to ask me?'

'I want to die in my wedding dress.'

Dona Maricota still tried to make light of it, but her daughter turned on her side and fell asleep, her breath coming softly at intervals. Her mother left the room, deeply moved, with tears in her eyes, and the inner certainty that what her daughter said was true.

She was soon proved right. Doctor Armando had visited her that morning for the fourth time. She seemed better; for several days she had spoken intelligibly, sat up in bed and shown pleasure in conversation.

Dona Maricota had gone out and left her sisters in charge of the patient. They had been to her room several times, and she seemed to be asleep. They busied themselves with other things.

Ismênia woke up, and through the half-open door of the
wardrobe she saw her wedding dress. She wanted to see it close
up. She got up, bare-footed, and laid it out on the bed to gaze at.
She felt the desire to put it on. She did so; memories of her wedding that never took place came flooding back. She remembered
her bridegroom Cavalcânti, his prominent nose, his darting eyes.
She did not remember him with hatred, but rather as a place she
had visited long ago that had left a deep impression.

It was the fortune-teller whom she remembered with anger.
She had escaped her mother and had gone with the maid to
consult Mme Sinhá. How coldly she had said: 'He won't come
back!' That had hurt her deeply. What an evil woman! Since
that day . . . As she couldn't find the corset she buttoned up the
dress over her emaciated body and went to the mirror. She was
startled when she glimpsed her bare shoulders and neck; they
were so white! Was she as pale as that? She pinched herself and
then put on the headdress. The veil fluttered around her shoulders like the beating of a butterfly's wings. A spell of weakness
overcame her, she let out a sigh and fell, lying with her back on
the bed and feet on the ground. When her sisters came in she
was dead. She was wearing the veil. A round white breast pro-
truded from her emaciated body.

The burial took place the next day; for two days Albernaz's
house was as full as it used to be during the days of the merriest
parties.

Quaresma went to the funeral. He disliked funerals but he
came and went up to the coffin to see the poor girl, covered
with flowers, dressed as a bride, like an image of the immaculate virgin. She had not changed: she lay inside that wooden
box, the same sorrowful, fragile Ismênia, with her delicate features and beautiful hair. Her slender beauty and childlike looks
had been preserved in death. She went to the grave with the
same inconsequence, the same ingenuousness, the same lack of
self-assertion that she had shown in life.

Contemplating those sad remains, Quaresma imagined the
hearse and coffin at the cemetery gate. It entered the tomb-lined
alleys. The crowd pushed and shoved, jostling for space along
the narrow streets and up the slopes. Some of the tombs seemed

to look fondly at each other as if they desired to draw closer; others showed repugnance at being so close. There were, in that silent laboratory of decay, incomprehensible requests, attraction, repulsion, kindness, hostility. There were tombs that were arrogant, vain, proud, humble, cheerful, sad, and many that concentrated all their powers on denying the equality of death – death which destroys all differences in human conditions and fortunes.

Quaresma continued gazing at the body. The cemetery opened out before him with its profusion of sculptures. There were tombs that had urns, crosses, inscriptions; others with portraits, pyramids of stone, ornate pergolas, extravagant baroque designs: all to escape the anonymity of the tomb, the end of all ends.

There are inscriptions everywhere. Some are long, some are short: Christian names, surnames, parents' names, birth dates, the precise age of the deceased who now lies, unrecognizable, in the putrid mud below.

And the despair at not finding a single familiar name! Not even the name of a famous figure, a name one has known for decades and that continues to live even after its owner has died. They are all anonymous now. It is only those who left no mark, who passed unnoticed through this world that attempt to escape from the tomb and re-enter the memories of the living.[11]

And that was where the young girl was now going, into a dark grave, without having made any mark on life, leaving no impression of her thoughts, her feelings, her soul!

To free himself from these sad visions Quaresma decided to leave the drawing room. He had not spoken to Dona Maricota who was there surrounded by friends. Lulu was dozing in a chair; he was wearing a mourning band on the sleeve of his college uniform. The sisters came and went. The general, silent, was in the dining room with Fontes and other friends at his side.

Caldas and Bustamante were standing apart, talking in low voices. As Quaresma passed by he heard the admiral say:

'No. The government's force is spent. The rebels will be here any moment!'

The major stood at the window that looked over the garden. The clouds had cleared, and the sky was a silky blue. Everything appeared calm and serene . . .

Estefânia, the schoolteacher with the mischievous, sparkling eyes, passed with Lalá, who from time to time lifted her handkerchief to her eyes (although they were dry). She was saying:

'I wouldn't buy there, if I were you. It's expensive. Go to "Bonheur des Dames". They say it has lovely things. And it's cheap.'

The major looked back at the sky above the garden. It seemed indifferent in its tranquillity. Genelício arrived in exaggerated mourning attire. He was dressed in black, and his face had assumed a mask of the deepest grief. Even his blue-tinged pince-nez appeared to be in mourning.

He had had to go to work: some urgent matter had made his presence indispensable.

'The truth is, general,' he said, 'if I'm not there, nothing gets done. Who would get the navy to send the right papers? They're all so lazy . . .'

The general didn't reply; he was too distressed. Bustamante and Caldas continued talking in low voices. The sound of carriage wheels was heard, and Quinota came into the dining room:

'Father, the coach is outside.'

The old man managed to get to his feet and went to the reception room. He spoke to his wife, who rose with an effort, her features greatly altered. Much of her hair was now grey. She tried to take a step forward but collapsed and fell sobbing into a chair. The others looked on without knowing what to do; some of them wept. Genelício took the initiative and started removing the candles from around the coffin. The mother got up and went to the coffin. She kissed the body: 'Daughter!'

Quaresma decided it was time to leave and took his hat. In the corridor he overheard Estefânia comment: 'What a beautiful coach!'

He left. It looked as though there were a party in the street. The children from the neighbourhood were standing around the hearse, admiring the brasses and decorations. The wreaths were brought out and hung at the back of the carriage: 'To my beloved daughter'; 'To my sister'. The purple and black ribbons with golden lettering fluttered in the breeze.

The coffin came out, covered in purple, adorned with shining golden braid – all to be laid beneath the earth. On both sides of the street there were people crowded into the windows. A boy in the house next door shouted out: 'Mother, the girl's funeral procession is leaving!'

Finally the coffin was fastened to the hearse while the chestnut horses, covered in black, impatiently champed at the bit.

The guests who were to go to the cemetery went to their coaches. The coaches pulled out, and the procession set off.

Suddenly, with a loud flutter of wings a bevy of doves from the neighbourhood, immaculately white, flew into the air. The birds of Venus. They circled once around the hearse and then, almost in silence, glided back to the dovecots concealed in the gardens of those bourgeois homes.

IV

BOQUEIRÃO[1]

Quaresma's farm in Curuzu gradually returned to the state of abandon in which he had found it. The weeds had grown and covered everything. The crops he had planted had disappeared, overgrown with brush, thorns and nettles. The area around the house had a dismal look in spite of the efforts of Anastácio, vigorous and hardworking in his old age, but incapable of devising a strategy, incapable of continuity.

He would clear a stretch here, then the next day a stretch there, moving from place to place, so that the results of his work were imperceptible, and the land surrounding the house acquired an abandoned look that in no way reflected his efforts.

The ants returned as well, more terrible and devastating, ploughing their way through every obstacle, destroying everything – stores of grain, newly planted fruit trees – even stripping the guava trees, with an energy and determination that made a mockery of the feeble strategies of the former slave, who was unable to find an effective way to defeat them or drive them off.

But he went on planting. It was an obsession, an addiction, a senile stubbornness. He had a vegetable plot for which he competed daily with the ants. As it was invaded one day by animals from the neighbourhood he doggedly protected it with a fence made of the most extraordinary materials: rolled-out kerosene tins, rafters, coconut leaves and wooden slats from crates, even though there was bamboo everywhere.

He always chose what appeared the easiest way, but was in fact the most torturous. This was true of everything he did, as much when he spoke, never getting to the point, as when he marked out a vegetable plot, broader in one part, narrower in another, avoiding parallel lines and symmetry with an artistic distaste.

The rebellion had had the effect of pacifying local politics. Both parties had become unswerving loyalists, so that the two powerful contenders, Doctor Campos and Lieutenant Antonio, had now come together in reconciliation and mutual understanding. A greater power than the one they had so ferociously disputed had now appeared, one that was a threat to the security of them both. So they watched and waited, temporarily united.

The candidate was imposed by the federal government, and election day came. Elections in the country are a curious thing. It is hard to tell where so many bizarre characters come from. So bizarre, in fact, that they are capable of turning out in breeches, doublets and lace collars, equipped with a rapier. There are waisted overcoats, bell-bottom trousers, silk hats – a whole museum of costumes worn by those country folk, momentarily brought alive amidst the potholed streets and dusty roads of our villages and hamlets. And there is never any lack of ruffians in baggy trousers with large wooden walking sticks, ready for anything.

This procession of museum pieces past the house on their way to the polling station nearby provided a diversion from the monotony of Dona Adelaide's life. In her isolation the days were long and sad. For a long time Felizardo's wife, Sinhá Chica, had kept her company. She was an old *cafuza*,[2] a sort of emaciated Medea, famous throughout the town for her healing powers. No one knew better than she did the prayers for relieving pain, bringing down fever, curing snake rash, or the effects of medicinal herbs: cow's tongue, tree ferns, lead-vine – all those medicines that grow in the fields, in the undergrowth and around the trunks of trees.

Apart from this knowledge, for which she was held in high regard, she was also a midwife. There was not a family in the neighbourhood, whether poor or comfortably off, that did not rely on her skills at the time of birth.

She was truly a sight to behold as she took a knife and shook it repeatedly in the sign of the cross over the spot where the pain or the problem was located, praying in a low voice, muttering incantations that drove away the evil spirit that was there. People told of her miracles and amazing triumphs; proof of her strange, almost magical powers over the occult forces that either plague us or come to our aid.

One of the strangest stories, told by everyone everywhere, was of how she had driven caterpillars away. The insects had invaded a field of beans by the thousands, covering the leaves and the stems. The owner was in despair and thought the crop was lost when he remembered the miraculous powers of Sinhá Chica. The old woman came. She put crosses of kindling wood around the edges of the field, as though supporting a fence of some invisible material; she left an opening at one corner and stood at the other and prayed. It was not long before the miracle occurred. The insects began to leave in a slow, winding procession, as if being driven forward by a shepherd's crook, at first in twos, then fours, fives, tens and twenties until not a single one was left.

This rival aroused no feelings of jealousy on the part of Doctor Campos. He treated the woman's supernatural powers with slight contempt. He did not invoke the arsenal of laws which forbade the practice of spiritual healing: that would make him unpopular – and he was a politician.

These two schools of medicine coexist harmoniously in the country – including locations not far from Rio de Janeiro – meeting the needs of people according to their traditions and economic means.

Sinhá Chica's services were almost free for the poor, people who, due to their customs and culture, still believe in spirits and demons that can be driven away by exorcisms, blessings and fumigations. Her clientele, however, was not restricted to local peasants; they included Italians, Portuguese and Spaniards who were newcomers to the country. They consulted her not so much because she was cheap, or that they had acquired the local belief in her powers, but because of the generalized European belief that all Africans or people of colour have a deep understanding of such matters as discovering malignant forces and the practice of witchcraft.

Whereas Sinhá Chica's spiritual and herbal cures were

sought out by the poor and needy, those of Doctor Campos were sought out by the wealthier and more cultured, whose educated minds required officially accepted medicine.

There were, however, times when the process was inverted: when there were complications, serious, incurable illnesses, which neither the shaman's herbs and prayers nor the doctor's pills and syrups were able to cure.

Sinhá Chica was hardly an agreeable companion. She lived immersed in a mystical daze, lost in an abyss of mysterious magical powers, sitting cross-legged, eyes downcast, staring listlessly, with the withered, dry face and the varnished eyes of a mummy.

She did not, however, forget the saints; the holy mother Church, the commandments, the orthodox prayers. Although she was unable to read she was strong on the catechism and knew stories from the Bible, which she interpreted in her own way, adding picturesque details.

Along with Apolinário, a chaplain famed for his litanies, she was the spiritual leader of the district. The priest was relegated to the role of employee, a sort of notary's clerk in charge of baptisms and marriages, as all communication with God and the Unseen was made through the intermediary of Sinhá Chica or Apolinário. Although marriage was a part of the priest's duties, it hardly need have been, as our poor people have little use for it and in general common-law husbands and wives take the place of this solemn Catholic institution.

Felizardo, her husband, hardly ever appeared at Quaresma's house. When he did it was at night. He spent his days hiding in the woods to avoid recruitment. The moment he arrived he would ask his wife if the revolt had ended.

He lived in constant terror; he slept with his clothes on, leaping out of the window and diving into the undergrowth at the slightest sound.

They had two sons, both pathetic creatures. In addition to the dispirited outlook of their parents they displayed a lack of physical vigour and reprehensible indolence. The older of the two, José, was about twenty. Both were equally idle, devoid of energy and beliefs, even in the prayers, blessings and magic spells that fascinated their mother and had earned their father's respect.

No one had succeeded in teaching them anything or how to stick at a job for any length of time. From time to time, every two weeks or so, they would collect some firewood and sell it to the first innkeeper they found for half of its real price. Then they would go home, very contented, having been given a coloured handkerchief, some eau-de-cologne or a mirror – trinkets that revealed how truly primitive their tastes really were.

They would then spend a week at home, sleeping or wandering around the streets and the shops. But at night, especially on Sundays and public holidays, they would take their accordions out and play, and they played so well that their presence was always in demand at the parties in the neighbourhood.

Although their parents lived in Quaresma's house, they rarely went there. If they did, it was because they had nothing to eat. They were so carefree and negligent that they weren't even afraid of being recruited. Although they were capable of being dedicated, loyal and good, the routine of everyday work was repugnant to them, like a punishment or a prison sentence.

It is this inertia of the Brazilian people, this type of pathological laziness, this lofty disregard for everything practical, that casts a pall of hopelessness over our countryside. It is this that destroys the magic, the poetry and the seductive exuberance of the natural surroundings.

In none of the great oppressed nations, Poland, Ireland or India, do we see the stagnation one finds in Brazil. There, there are rebellions, idealism, debates; here everything is drowsy, everything seems to be dead. Oh! Here we sleep . . .

With Quaresma's absence this torpor of the countryside had pervaded the farm. 'The Haven' seemed to have fallen into an enchanted sleep, waiting for a prince to appear and wake it up.

Farming machinery that had not yet been used was rusting away with the labels still attached. Those ploughs with the steel shears, which had arrived with their blades gleaming with a soft blue light, now lay, ugly and abandoned, reaching anxiously out to a silent sky. In the morning the squawking of fowl no longer came from the chicken run, nor the fluttering of doves; that morning hymn to life, to work and to abundance no longer came to meet the rosy daybreak, to join the joyful chorus of the birds. No one now admired the kapok trees in flower, with their beautiful pink and white blossoms that fell to the ground from time to time like wounded birds.

Dona Adelaide had neither the inclination nor the energy to supervise the farm or enjoy the poetry of the countryside. She missed her brother and lived as though she were in town. She bought food from the grocery store and took no interest in the farm.

She longed for her brother to return. She wrote him desperate letters, to which he replied with promises, telling her to stay calm. However, the tone of his last letter had been different, without his former confidence and enthusiasm. It betrayed discouragement, despondency, even a lack of hope.

Dear Adelaide, only now am I able to reply to the letter I received almost two weeks ago. When it reached me I had just been wounded; a small wound, but nevertheless one that keeps me in bed and will require a long convalescence. What a battle, sister! How terrible! When I remember it I put my hands over my eyes as if to shut out the dreadful vision. It left me with a hatred of war that no one can imagine . . . The turmoil, the infernal whistling of bullets, the ominous flashes, the curses – and all this in the dead of night . . . At times we abandoned our guns and fought each other with bayonets, rifle-butts, axes, knives. A fight between cave men, Adelaide – it was prehistoric! I do not believe, I simply do not believe in the justice of all of this. I do not believe in its cause. I do not believe that it is right or necessary to force our primitive ferocity to the surface, that ferocity that we learned and was imbued in us during thousands of years of fighting with wild animals when we had to protect our land from them. I wasn't looking at modern men; I was looking at Cro-Magnons, Neanderthals armed with flint axes, with no thoughts of compassion, or love, or generosity, just killing, killing, killing . . . Your brother, the brother who is writing this letter, was doing the same. How much brutality, how much ferocity, how much cruelty he discovered inside himself! I killed a man, Adelaide; I killed him! And not content with killing him, I even fired a shot when my enemy lay gasping at my feet. Forgive me! I ask you to forgive me because I need forgiveness and I don't know who to ask, which god, which man – anyone! You have no idea how much this has made me suffer. When I fell beneath a cart, it wasn't the wound that hurt, but my soul, my conscience. And Ricardo, who was wounded and fell at my side, groaning and pleading, 'Captain, my cap, my cap!', seemed to give voice to my very thought, mocking my fate!

This life is absurd and illogical. I am afraid of living now, Adelaide. I am afraid because we do not know where we are going, what we will do tomorrow, in what way we will betray our beliefs . . .

The best thing is to do nothing, Adelaide. As soon as I am released from my duties I will live quietly, as quietly as is humanly possible, so that from the depths within, or the unpredictable nature of things, nothing provokes me into doing things against my will, things that make me suffer and destroy all the sweetness and joy of being alive.

What is more, I believe that all my sacrifice has been wasted. Nothing of what I planned has been achieved, and the blood that I have spilled, the pain that I shall suffer for the rest of my life, have been used, abused, distorted, their moral purpose denied in the service of petty, meaningless political intrigue.

No one understands my aims. No one is interested in examining their significance. I am thought of as mad, foolish, obsessive – and life goes inexorably on. It is hideous and brutal.

As Quaresma said in the letter his wound was not serious, but it was delicate and needed time to heal completely and without risk. Ricardo, however, had been wounded seriously. Whereas Quaresma's suffering was moral, Coração dos Outros's was physical, and he was constantly groaning and cursing the fate that had dragged him on to the battlefield.

They were being treated in hospitals on different sides of the bay, which it was not possible to cross by boat, requiring a twelve-hour journey around the perimeter by train.

Both on the way and on the way back Quaresma, wounded as he was, passed through the station at Curuzu. The train didn't stop. All he could do was take a long, nostalgic look through the window at his 'Haven', with its poor soil and aged trees, where he had dreamed of spending the rest of his life in peace, but which had propelled him into the most dreadful of adventures.

And he asked himself where in this world true peace could be found. Where could he find that rest for body and soul for which he so longed, after all the turmoil he had been through – where? The maps of continents, of countries, of cities passed before his mind, but in no country, or province, or town, or street, did he see that there was peace.

He felt tired, not physically, but morally and intellectually tired. He wanted to stop thinking altogether, to stop embracing life. Yet he still wanted to live, to live physically, simply to feel the sensation of being alive.

And so he convalesced, slowly, sadly, without a single visit, without seeing a friendly face.

Coleoni and his family had left the town. The general had not come to see him, out of laziness and indifference. He spent his gradual convalescence alone, thinking about destiny, about his life, his plans and above all his disillusionments.

Meanwhile the revolt in the bay was coming to an end. Everyone sensed it. It was what they all wanted.

The admiral and Albernaz, for similar reasons, regretted that it was over. The former saw his dream of commanding a squadron slip away, and consequently his return to active service. The latter would lose his commission, and with it the remuneration that had so notably improved his family's situation.

That morning, very early, Dona Maricota had woken her husband:

'Chico, get up. You have to go to the mass for Senator Clarimundo.'

Albernaz got up at once. He must not miss it. His presence was essential and would mean a great deal. Clarimundo had been a traditional republican, an agitator and feared orator during the Empire. Since the founding of the Republic he had proposed nothing of any significance to his peers in the Senate, but his influence had been great. He was considered one of the patriarchs of the Republic. Leading republicans have an insatiable thirst for glory, to be remembered by future generations. They make ceaseless efforts to force themselves on posterity.

Clarimundo was such a figure and during the revolt, no one seemed to know why, his prestige had grown, and it was even thought that he could be the marshal's successor. Albernaz had known him only slightly, but attending his mass was a political statement.

The pain of his daughter's death weighed much less heavily on him now. What had hurt him most was that invalid's existence, immersed in her ailments and madness. Death has the virtue of suddenness, of shock; it does not gnaw away at our loved ones like these long-lasting diseases. Once the shock has passed we are left with our memories, fond pictures of our loved ones as they used to be.

This was the case with Albernaz, and his enjoyment of life and natural cheerfulness gradually returned.

After his wife's reminder he got ready, dressed and went out. Although the rebellion had in no way abated, memorial services were still held in churches in the centre of town. The general arrived on time. There were men in uniforms and top hats, jostling with each other to sign the condolence book, not so much with the intention of offering their commiserations to the family as with the hope of getting their names in the papers.

Albernaz also pushed his way forward to one of the lists on the table in the sacristy. As he was about to sign it someone addressed him. It was the admiral. The mass was about to begin. They both avoided entering the crowded nave and stood in the sacristy window, talking.

'So it'll soon be over, eh?'

'They say the fleet's already left Pernambuco.'

Caldas had spoken first, and the general's reply made him smile ironically as he said:

'At last . . .'

'The bay is surrounded with cannon,' the general continued after a pause, 'and the marshal's going to command them to surrender.'

'About time too,' Caldas replied. 'If I'd been in charge it

would all be over! Taking seven months to beat a few rickety old boats!'

'Don't exaggerate, Caldas. It wasn't as easy as all that. And the battles at sea?'

'What was the fleet doing all that time in Recife? Tell me that. Ah, if your friend here had been in command, it would have left and attacked at once! I'm for quick action.'

Inside the church the priest was still appealing to God for rest for the senator's soul. The mystical smell of incense wafted towards them, but this perfumed offering to the God of peace and goodness did not dissuade them from their discussion of war.

'We've no one of any use,' Caldas added. 'This country has no future. It'll end up a British colony!'

He nervously scratched one of his sideburns and stared at the tiles on the floor. Albernaz retorted, with a touch of sarcasm:

'It won't now. The government has prestige, the Republic has been consolidated – a new era of progress is opening up for Brazil.'

'What! Where did you get the idea we have a government?'

'Not so loud, Caldas.'

'What kind of a government makes no use of talent, abandons it, leaves it to vegetate? And does the same with our natural riches: just lying there unused!'

A bell rang; they glanced at the crowded nave. Through the door they saw a group of men, all dressed in black, kneeling, contrite, beating their breasts, muttering to themselves: *mea culpa, mea maxima culpa* . . .

A beam of sunlight filtered through one of the windows above, illuminating their heads.

Instinctively the two men in the sacristy raised their hands to their breasts and also confessed: *mea culpa, mea maxima culpa* . . .

The mass ended, and they entered the church for the compliments to the family. The scent of incense filled the nave, presaging the peace of eternity.

They all had an air of great contrition: friends, relatives, those who had known the deceased and those who had not all seemed to be suffering equally. As soon as they entered the church Albernaz and Caldas, aware of this atmosphere, adopted suitably grave expressions.

Genelício had also come. He had an addiction for masses for important people, messages of condolence, greetings on people's birthdays. In case his memory failed him he kept a notebook where he entered the dates of birthdays and the addresses as well. The names were entered with the greatest care; there was no mother-in-law, sister-in-law, cousin or aunt of any important figure who did not receive his congratulations on her birthday, or, on death, whose seventh-day memorial mass he failed to attend.

His mourning suit was made from thick, heavy cloth, so that the sight of him recalled some punishment out of Dante.

In the street Genelício, brushing his top hat with the sleeve of his overcoat, said to his father-in-law and the admiral:

'It'll soon be over . . . Soon . . .'

'And if they resist?' the general asked.

'They won't resist! The rumour is they've already proposed surrender. We must organize a rally for the marshal.'

'I don't believe it,' said the admiral. 'I know Saldanha[3] very well. He's too proud to surrender like that.'

Genelício was a little alarmed at his relative's tone. He was afraid he would speak too loudly and be overheard, and that he would be compromised. He said nothing, but Albernaz continued:

'Pride alone can't defeat a stronger fleet.'

'Strong! A few rickety husks you mean!'

With an effort Caldas mastered the fury that welled up inside him. Overhead the sky was calm and blue. Fluffy white clouds floated slowly apart like sails drifting across an infinite sea. Genelício glanced up. Then he admonished his companion:

'Don't talk like that, admiral! Someone might . . .'

'Nonsense! I don't give a damn!'

'Well,' said Genelício, 'I have to go to the Rua Primeiro de Março and . . .'

He said farewell and left in his leaden suit, hunched over, peering at the ground through his blue-tinged pince-nez, moving cautiously, one step at a time.

Albernaz and Caldas remained talking for a while and then

parted, as friendly as ever, each with his own dissatisfaction and disillusionment.

They had been right: the revolt ended a few days later. The loyalist squadron arrived, the rebel officers took refuge aboard Portuguese warships, and Marshal Floriano was master of the bay.

When the squadron arrived, much of the population thought the city would be bombarded and abandoned it, taking refuge in the suburbs, under trees, in the houses of friends or in shelters that the government had built for the purpose.

The terror on their faces, the anguish and anxiety of their expressions, were an unforgettable sight. They brought bundles of clothes, fishing baskets, little cases, children in arms, crying, the family parrot, the pet dog, the songbird that for so many years had been the joy of a poor family home . . .

What terrified them most was the battleship *Niterói*'s notorious dynamite cannon, a showy American invention, a terrible weapon with the capacity to cause earthquakes and shake the very foundations of Rio's granite mountain ranges.

The women and children, even when beyond range, were afraid of the sound of it firing. But this Yankee nightmare, virtually a force of nature in itself, was found abandoned on the docks, ignored and harmless.

The end of the rebellion was a relief. It was becoming monotonous. With the victory the marshal gained almost superhuman status.

Around this time Quaresma was released from hospital, and a detachment from his battalion was sent to garrison the Ilha das Enxadas.[4] Inocêncio Bustamante continued to command the battalion with his habitual zeal from his office in the condemned rooming house which served as its headquarters. All the accounts were up to date, impeccably entered.

Much to his distaste Quaresma was given the role of jailer, because the Ilha das Enxadas was being used as a camp for naval prisoners. His agony of mind was exacerbated by the attributes of this post. He avoided looking at the prisoners; he felt shame and compassion, and it seemed to him that one of them had perceived the secret of his conscience.

Moreover, the whole system of ideas that had led him to get involved in the civil war had collapsed. He had not found a Sully, and much less a Henri IV. He also realized that none of the people he had met had been motivated by these ideals. They had become involved either for puerile political motives or out of self-interest; they had no higher motivation. Even among the young men, and there were many, where self-interest did not exist, a fetishist worship of the Republic prevailed, an exaggeration of its virtues, a tendency towards despotism that his studies and reflections had convinced him were wrong. His disillusionment was great.

The prisoners were crowded into the classrooms and dormitories previously used by the cadets. There were ordinary sailors, non-commissioned officers, clerks, ship hands; whites, blacks, mulattos, *caboclos*, every colour, every motivation; men who had got involved because they were used to obeying orders, men who had no connection at all with the issues at stake; men who had been press-ganged from their homes or off the streets; boys and children; men who'd enlisted because they were poor, simple and uncultivated; men who could be cruel and perverse like ignorant children, or good, as docile as lambs. But none of them were to blame, none had political ambitions, none had acted on their own initiative. They were simply robots in the hands of their leaders and superiors who had abandoned them to the mercy of the winner.

In the evening he would go for walks and look out at the bay. The sea breeze still blew and the gulls still dived for fish. Boats passed. There were smoke-belching launches on their way to the end of the bay; little boats or canoes gently skimming the surface of the water, leaning to one side, then to the other, as if their white, puffed-out sails desired to caress the mirrored surface of the abyss. The mountains gently faded away in the soft violet light; and the rest was blue, an unearthly blue that intoxicated, inebriated like a heady liqueur.

For a long time he would stand and watch. As he returned he would look towards the town as the dusk began to fall, kissed by the blood-red rays of the setting sun.

Night came, and Quaresma would continue his walk along

the shore, reflecting, ruminating, pained by his recollections of the hatred, the bloodshed and the ferocity.

Society and life seemed hateful to him. By their own example, he thought, they produced the crimes that they punished and sought to prevent. His thoughts were black and despairing. He often thought he was going insane.

At these times he was sorry that he was alone, without a companion with whom he could talk, who would enable him to put the dark thoughts that pursued him aside, the thoughts that were becoming an obsession.

Ricardo was garrisoned on the Ilha das Cobras. But even if he were there the rigorous discipline would not permit them to have a real conversation, heart to heart. Night deepened; he was shrouded in silence and darkness.

For many hours Quaresma would stay out-of-doors, thinking, gazing towards the far end of the bay, where there were almost no lights to penetrate the blackness of the night.

He would continue to stare as if he wanted to teach himself to penetrate the indecipherable, to divine the shape of the mountains concealed by black shadows, the outline of the islands covered by night.

He became tired and would return to bed. He rarely slept well. He had insomnia, but when he tried to read he couldn't concentrate. His thoughts wandered far from his book.

One night, when he had managed to fall asleep, he was awakened by a subaltern in the early hours:

'Major, sir, a man from Itamarati is here.'

'Who is it?'

'The officer who has come for the group for Boqueirão.'

Without understanding, Quaresma got up and went to meet the visitor. The man was already inside one of the dormitories. There was an escort at the door. He was accompanied by a few soldiers, one of whom carried a lantern, which illuminated the room with a pallid yellow light.

The vast room was full of bodies, stretched out, half-naked, men of every colour on the human spectrum. Some snored, others slumbered quietly. As Quaresma entered someone groaned in his sleep. Quaresma and the emissary of Itamarati shook hands, but they said nothing. They were both afraid to speak. The officer woke up one of the prisoners and said to the soldiers: 'Take this one.'

He moved on and woke another: 'Where were you?'

'Me?' the sailor replied. 'On the *Guanabara*.'

'You scoundrel!' the man from Itamarati retorted. 'This one too . . . take him!'

The soldiers took him to the door, where they left him and returned.

The officer passed by a number of sleeping men without paying any attention, until he came to a frail white boy who was not asleep. 'Get up,' he yelled. The boy stood up, trembling. 'Where were you?' he asked.

'I was a nurse,' the boy replied. 'A nurse!!' said the officer. 'Take this one too!'

'Please, sir, first let me write to my mother,' the boy pleaded, almost in tears.

'Your mother!' retorted the man from Itamarati. 'Go on. Get out!'

And so a dozen men, chosen at random, by chance, accompanied by the escort, were put aboard a barge that was immediately towed out of the island waters by a launch.

At first Quaresma didn't understand what the scene meant. But when the launch had left, he realized.

Then he wondered by what mysterious force, by what irony of fate, he had become involved in such tenebrous events, assisting with the sinister methods of the regime for its own perpetuation.

The barge was a short way off. The sea moaned. The waves rolled forward to the pebbles on the dock. The ship's wake left a phosphorescent glow. Overhead, serenely, the stars were shining in a vast black sky.

The launch disappeared into the darkness at the end of the bay. Where was it going? To 'Boqueirão' . . .

V

OLGA

How illogical it seemed to him, to be locked away in that poky dungeon. Did he, the gentle Quaresma, the Quaresma of such profoundly patriotic ideals, deserve this sad end? By what devious means had fate dragged him to this place, completely unsuspecting of her dreadful purpose, to all appearances with no connection to the story of his life? Was it he himself who by his past deeds, the sequence of his actions, had allowed the fates to lead him guilelessly towards the execution of that purpose? Or had it been external events that had overpowered him, Quaresma, and enslaved him to the will of the omnipotent divinity? He did not know. The more he thought about it, the more the two became entangled and confused, and no clear answer came.

He had not been there for long. He had been arrested in the morning as soon as he got up. He roughly calculated – he didn't have his watch and, if he had, he wouldn't have been able to consult it in the dim light of the dungeon – that it must be eleven o'clock.

Why was he under arrest? He could not say for certain: the officer who had escorted him had been unwilling to explain, and since he had left the Ilha das Enxadas for the Ilha das Cobras he had not exchanged a word with a soul, nor seen anyone whom he knew along the way, not even Ricardo, who with a look or a gesture could have calmed his fears. But he thought his arrest must be due to the letter he had written to the president protesting against the scene he had witnessed the previous day.

He had been unable to restrain himself. That group of wretches, chosen at random, led off in the early hours of the morning to be butchered at some distant place had pierced him to the depths. It had gone against every principle he held, challenging his moral courage and his solidarity with his fellow men. And he had written the letter with vehemence, passion and indignation. He had spoken his mind fully. He had spelled it out, frankly, without reserve.

That must be the reason that he was there, in that dungeon, caged, locked up, isolated from his fellow men like a wild animal, like a criminal, immersed in the damp darkness pervaded by the stench of his excrement, with no real food . . . How will it end? How will it end? The question persisted amidst the whirl of thoughts provoked by the anguish of his situation. There was no way of knowing. The behaviour of the government was erratic and unpredictable. Anything could happen: he could be set free or put to death, although the latter was far more likely.

The mood was one of death, of slaughter. Everyone was thirsty for blood, to assert the victory all the more, to feel they were personally a part of that great triumph, to share in its honour.

Was he going to die, perhaps that very night? What had he made of his life? Nothing. He had spent it in the pursuit of an illusion, studying his country, because he loved it, with the intention of contributing to its happiness and prosperity. He had dedicated his youth to her, and his manhood too, and now that he was old, what recompense did he receive from her? How did she reward him? With death. And what had he failed to see, to experience, to enjoy to the full in his life? Everything. There had been no fun, no drunken revels, no lovers – he had seen none of that side of life that had seemed so incompatible with his inherent melancholy, experienced none of its delights.

Since he was eighteen patriotism had been his only interest. For its sake he had made the blunder of studying irrelevant nonsense. Why should rivers matter to him? Because they were big? No doubt they were . . . What happiness had knowing the names of Brazilian heroes brought him? None. The important question was: had he been happy? No, he had not. He thought of his interest in Tupi, in folklore, his attempts at farming. Had any of this brought him happiness? No. It had not.

His Tupi had been greeted everywhere with incredulity, laughter, mockery, contempt; it had driven him mad. A disillusion. And the farming? Nothing. The soil wasn't fertile. The books were wrong: it wasn't easy. Another disillusion. And when he had fought for the cause of patriotism, what had he found? Disillusion. Where was the kindness of the Brazilian people? Hadn't he seen them fighting like animals? Hadn't he seen them killing innumerable prisoners? Another disillusion. His life had been a disillusion, or rather a sequence, a series of interconnected disillusions.

The fatherland he had wanted was a myth, a fantasy he had invented in the silence of his study. His conception of it didn't exist, physically, morally, intellectually or politically. What did exist was the Brazil of Lieutenant Antonio, of Doctor Campos, of the man from Itamarati.

And even in its purest form, what was a fatherland anyway? Had he allowed his life to be guided by an illusion, by an irrational notion, with no basis, no proof, a god or goddess whose empire was collapsing? Didn't he know that it stemmed from the belief of the Graeco-Roman peoples that their dead ancestors continued to live as shadows, and that they had to be fed or they would pursue their descendants? He remembered the ideas of Fustel de Coulanges.[1] He remembered that the notion meant nothing to the Menana tribe,[2] among many others. Perhaps the idea had been exploited by colonizers, to manipulate the subservient mentality of the people they conquered, with the intention of serving their own ambitions . . .

He thought of history, how the borders of every country in the old world had changed. He wondered what concept of fatherland a Frenchman, Englishman, Italian or German who had lived for four hundred years would have.

A Frenchman would see his country lose the ancient county of Franche-Comté, and then Alsace, only to regain it and in the end lose it again.

Wasn't Cisplatina a part of Brazil, before we lost it?[3] Yet we don't feel that the spirits of our ancestors dwell there. We aren't troubled on their account.

It was clearly a notion with no rational consistency, which needed to be rethought.

How was it possible that a calm, lucid man like himself had dedicated his time and his life, had grown old, in the pursuit of an illusion? Why had he not perceived the truth sooner, more clearly? How had he allowed himself to be deceived by a false idol that overwhelmed him, to whom he sacrificed his entire existence? It was because of his isolation, his failure to think of himself, and thus he would go to the grave, leaving no mark of his existence – no son, no wife, no lover's kiss, not even an illicit affair!

He was leaving nothing as proof of his existence; and the earth had given him nothing to savour.

But who knew? Perhaps those who followed in his footsteps would be happier. The response came at once. How could they be? How could they be if he had failed to explain his vision, to write it down, to give it form and substance?

And even if he had, what good would it do?

In the end, would transmitting his ideas bring any happiness to the world? For how many years had people far greater than he been giving the world their knowledge, their lives? Yet nothing had changed: life was still plagued by poverty, oppression and grief.

And he reflected that a hundred years before, in that very place, perhaps in the very same dungeon, illustrious, generous-hearted men had been imprisoned because they had wanted to improve the state of the country.[4] Perhaps it was only a dream, but they had suffered for their dream. Had anything resulted from it? Had the general conditions improved? On the surface, yes;[5] but when examined more closely, no.

The trial of those men, accused of a crime that was truly iniquitous under the laws of the time, had taken two years. And he, who had committed no crime at all, wouldn't be heard, or even judged, he would simply be executed.

He had been good, generous, honest and virtuous – he, who had been all this, was to go to his grave without the presence of a relative, a comrade, or even a friend . . .

Where were they all? Would he never see Coração dos Outros again? Innocent Ricardo, with his obsession for the guitar?
How wonderful it would be if he came: through him he could
send a last message to his sister, his farewell to Anastácio, his
love to his goddaughter. He knew now he would never see
them again. Never again!

For a while he wept.

Quaresma was wrong on one point, however. Ricardo had
heard about his arrest and was trying to get him freed. He
knew the exact reason for the arrest, but remained undaunted.
He was quite aware that he was running a serious risk, because
at the palace indignation against Quaresma was widespread.
Victory had made the winners vengeful and merciless. They
saw his protest as an attempt to diminish the strength of their
position. There was no compassion, no kindness, not even any
respect for human life; what was required was to make an
example by committing an Ottoman massacre, but a clandes-
tine one, so that the constituted authority would never be
attacked again, or even questioned. This was the social philosophy of the time, which, like a religion, had its fanatics,
priests and preachers and was applied with all the cruelty of a
doctrine to ensure the happiness of the majority.

Ricardo, however, was not intimidated. He sought out any
friends that could help. He was entering Largo de São Francisco when he met Genelício. The latter was coming from the
mass for the sister of Deputy Castro's mother-in-law. As always
he was wearing a heavy, black overcoat that looked as if it were
made of lead. He was already assistant director. His chief occupation now was thinking up ways and means of becoming
director. It was not easy; but he was working on a book, *The
Courts of Auditors in Asiatic Countries*, with which, through
its superior erudition, he hoped to win the coveted post.

When he saw him Ricardo acted at once. He ran up to him
and said:

'Sir, could I please have a word with you?'

Genelício proudly drew himself up, as though finding it hard
to recall the face of such an insignificant person.

'What is it, comrade?' he asked gravely.

Coração dos Outros was wearing his Southern Cross uniform. Genelício could hardly be seen to be dallying with a mere soldier. In his innocence, Ricardo thought he'd forgotten him.

'Don't you remember me, sir?' he asked.

Genelício squinted at him from behind his blue-tinged pince-nez and said coldly:

'No.'

'I'm Ricardo Coração dos Outros. I sang at your wedding,' Ricardo said humbly.

There was no smile, no sign that he was pleased to see him. He merely said:

'I see. Well, what do you want?'

'Did you know that Major Quaresma has been arrested?'

'Who?'

'Your father-in-law's neighbour.'

'That lunatic! Hmm . . . And?'

'I was wondering if you could intercede . . .'

'I don't interfere in these matters, my friend. The government's always right. Good day.'

And Genelício continued on his way with that cautious tread, as if he wanted to preserve the soles of his boots. Ricardo looked at the square, the passers-by, the lifeless statue, the church, the ugly houses . . . Everything seemed hostile, evil, indifferent; the passers-by looked like wild beasts . . . He almost wept from despair at not being able to save his friend.

But then he remembered Albernaz and hurried off in search of him. It wasn't far to his office, but the general had not yet arrived. He did so an hour later. As soon as he set eyes on Ricardo, he asked:

'What's the matter?'

In a plaintive voice, overcome with emotion, the minstrel explained the whole affair. Albernaz adjusted his pince-nez, placing the little gold chain behind his ear and said kindly:

'My friend, I can't . . . You see, I'm a loyalist, and if I were to intercede for a prisoner it would look as if I'm not loyal enough. I'm very sorry, but . . . There's nothing I can do!'

And with no sign of conscience, sure that he was right, he

entered his office, looking very self-assured in his general's
uniform.

Officers were coming in and out; bells rang; office boys came
and went. Ricardo searched every face in the hope of finding
someone who could help. But there was no one. He was in despair. Who could help him? Who? Then he remembered: the
commander. And he went off to speak to Colonel Bustamante
in the old rooming house that served as headquarters for the
gallant Southern Cross.

The battalion was still training for war. Although the revolt
in the port of Rio de Janeiro was over, troops were needed to
fight in the south.[6] So the battalions had not been disbanded,
and the Southern Cross was one that had been chosen to go.

In the soap-stained yard the lame lieutenant continued his
task of training the new recruits: 'Shoul-der . . . *arms*! A-bout . . .
turn!'

Ricardo went in, ran quickly up the rickety staircase of the
old rooming house and, as soon as he reached the commander's
cubicle, shouted out: 'May I come in, commander?'

Bustamante was in a bad mood. He was not pleased with
this business of going to Paraná. How could he supervise the
battalion's accounts in the heat of battle, amidst the mayhem of
advances and retreats? It was sheer stupidity to put the commander in charge. He should be protected so that he could take
care of the books and overlook the entries.

He was thinking of this when Ricardo asked permission to
enter.

'Come in,' he said.

The valiant colonel was stroking his long mosaic beard. His
jacket was unbuttoned, and he had just pulled on one of his
boots to be more suitably dressed to receive his subaltern.

Ricardo made his request and waited patiently for the
answer. Bustamante was silent. Finally he shook his head and,
giving his inferior a very sharp look, he barked:

'Get out of here, or I'll have you arrested. Now!'

And in a fierce military gesture he pointed his finger at the
door. Ricardo left at once. In the yard the sound of the solemn

commands of the lame instructor, veteran of the Paraguayan War, continued to permeate the crumbling rooming house: 'Shoul-der . . . *arms*! A-bout . . . *turn*!'

Ricardo walked back, sad and despondent. The world seemed devoid of affection and love. He, who had always sung the praises of loyalty, love and friendship in his *modinhas*, now realized that these feelings didn't exist. He'd been pursuing things that weren't real, that were illusions. He looked at the sky overhead. It was peaceful and calm. He looked at the trees, the palms, proudly reaching up in their titanic attempt to touch the sky; he looked at the houses, the churches, the palaces; and he thought of the wars, the bloodshed, the suffering they cost. *This* was how life and history and heroes were made: by violence to others, oppression and pain.

But his thoughts soon returned to the requirement of saving his friend and what to do next. Who could help? He thought deeply. He thought of one person, then another, until finally he remembered Quaresma's goddaughter, and set off for the house in Rua Real Grandeza.

When he arrived he told her what had happened and what he feared. She was alone. Her husband was busier than ever making the most of the spoils of victory. He never missed a chance to impress the right people.

Olga thought of her godfather – his dreams, his gentleness, the tenacity with which he pursued his ideas – as ingenuously as a romantic girl!

For a moment she was overwhelmed by a feeling of such pity that she no longer had the will to act. She felt that her pity would be enough, that in some way it would console her godfather's grief. Then came a vision where she saw him covered in blood – he, who was so generous, so good – and she thought about how she could save him.

'But, dear Sr Ricardo, what can I do? I don't know anyone. I have no contacts. Of my friends, Alice, Doctor Brandão's wife, is away; Cassilda, Castriota's daughter wouldn't be able to help. Oh Lord! I just can't think what to do!'

These last words were spoken in a tone of anguished desperation. They both fell silent. The girl, who was sitting down, put her head between her hands and sank her long, ivory nails into her black hair. Ricardo stood at her side, completely at a loss.

'Oh Lord, what can I do?' she repeated.

For the first time she realized that there were things in life for which there was no solution. She was absolutely determined to save her godfather. She would sacrifice everything. But it was impossible, impossible! There was no expedient by which she could help him. He must go to his execution, his Calvary, without hope of resurrection.

'Perhaps your husband . . .' Ricardo said.

She thought for a while, reflecting on her husband's character: she very soon realized that his egoism, his ambition and his ruthless opportunism would prevent him taking the slightest step.

'Him? No . . .'

Ricardo could not think of what to suggest. He stared vacantly at the furniture and at the tall, dark mountain that could be seen from the window of the room. He wanted to offer some advice or suggestion, but nothing came!

The girl continued to sink her fingernails into her hair, staring down at the table on which her elbows were resting. There was a brooding silence.

Then Ricardo's eyes brightened:

'And if you went there yourself . . .' he said.

She raised her head. And without pausing to think, wide-eyed with fear, her face set rigid, she declared:

'I'll go.'

She went to get dressed. Ricardo was alone in the room.

He sat down. He thought with admiration about that girl who was prepared to expose herself to such dreadful risk purely for friendship. He mused how deeply she was attuned to her inner feelings; feelings so far removed from the selfishness and the baseness of this world! Silently, he saluted her.

She was soon ready. She was buttoning her gloves in the dining room when her husband arrived. He looked very pleased with himself: his big round face with its large moustache was oozing complacency. He ignored Ricardo and turned straight to his wife:

'Are you going out?'

Flushed with anxiety in her desperation to save Quaresma, she answered sharply:

'Yes!'

Armando was amazed by the way she had spoken. He turned to Ricardo as if to ask for an explanation, but then turned back to his wife and barked:

'Where are you going?'

His wife didn't answer immediately, so he turned to Ricardo:

'What are you doing here?'

Coração dos Outros didn't dare reply. He was afraid there would be a violent scene, which he was anxious to avoid. But Olga answered for him:

'He's coming with me to the Itamarati, to save my godfather from being shot. Have you heard?'

Her husband was calmer now. He thought that with a little persuasion he would be able to prevent her doing something that would be so harmful to his interests and ambitions. He said quietly:

'You're doing a foolish thing.'

'Why?' she asked heatedly.

'Because you'll compromise me. You know . . .'

For a while she didn't reply, her large round eyes staring at him in contempt. After staring for a few minutes, she gave a little laugh and said:

'That's just it! Me, me, me! It's always me! *Me* because of this; *me* because of that! You never think of anything else. Life only exists for *you*; everything has to suit *you*. It's ridiculous! And I – yes, I'm talking about *me* now! – I'm not allowed to risk myself, to prove my friendship, for once in my life to do something altruistic! Why do you think I'm so worthless, so utterly worthless – a part of the furniture, an ornament, with no connections, no friends, no character – why?'

At first she spoke slowly, with irony, then heatedly and with passion. Her husband was staggered. They had lived such separate lives, he had never dreamed she was capable of such an outbreak. Was this his little girl? His little plaything? Where had she learned such things? He tried to calm her down:

'The whole house is applauding!' he said sarcastically.

And she retorted:

'Good! Because unselfishness can only be found in the theatre!'

Then she added vehemently:

'Now listen: I'm going because it's my duty, because it's my wish and because it's my right!'

Decisive, erect and dignified, she seized her parasol, straightened her veil and left. He didn't know what to do. He was stunned. He watched in amazement as she walked through the door.

She soon arrived at the palace in Rua Larga. Ricardo didn't come in. He left her on her own and went to wait for her in the Campo de Sant'Ana.

She went up the steps. There was a hubbub of people coming and going. Everyone wanted to attract Floriano's attention, to greet him, to show their dedication, their service to the cause, their contribution to his victory. No means, no plans, no strategies were beneath them to achieve their end. But the dictator, previously so accessible, now avoided them. Some even wanted to kiss his hand, as if he were the pope or an emperor, but he was sick of such servility. The caliph did not consider himself to be sacred; it irked him.

Olga spoke to the palace staff and asked to see the marshal – to no avail. After considerable effort she managed to speak to a secretary and then to an adjutant. But when she explained her reason for coming, the man's routine manner became hostile. With a sudden flash of anger he barked:

'*Quaresma*? That *outlaw*? That *traitor*?'

Then, embarrassed by his vehemence, he said more politely:

'It's out of the question, madam. The marshal won't see you.'

She didn't even wait for him to finish. She rose proudly and turned her back. She was ashamed for having asked, for swallowing her pride, for affronting her godfather's moral standing by her request. It was better to leave him to die, heroically and alone, on some island in the bay, taking his honour, his kindness, his moral character untarnished to the grave, than to have dealings with such people, untarnished by anything she may do that could diminish the injustice of his death or persuade his executioners that they had the right to kill him.

She left and started to walk. She looked at the sky, the breezes, the trees in Santa Teresa. She thought how savage tribes had once roamed these lands, one of whose chiefs had boasted he'd drunk the blood of ten thousand enemies. That was four hundred years ago. She looked back at the sky, the trees, the houses, the churches; she watched the trams go by. A train whistled, a coach drawn by two beautiful horses crossed in front of her, just as she entered the gardens . . . So many great changes had taken place. What had been there before the park? Marshes, perhaps. So many great changes, to the face of the earth, to the climate perhaps . . . Let's wait, she thought, and walked calmly ahead to meet Ricardo.

Notes

PART I

Chapter I: The Guitar Lesson

1. *modinha*: Considered one of the first genuinely Brazilian art forms, *modinhas* were short rhymed verses which were sung to a guitar at public and family gatherings. Their origins can be traced back to the streets of Bahia in the seventeenth century.

2. *Father Caldas*: Domingos Caldas Barbosa (1739–1800) was a Brazilian mulatto who was sent to study at the University of Coimbra in Portugal, where he later became a priest. Credited with inventing the term *modinha*, he was famous in Lisbon for his improvisations to the sound of his viola with wire strings.

3. *Beckford . . . praised it very highly*: The English writer William Beckford (1760–1844) was enchanted by the seductive Brazilian *modinha*, which he heard in Portugal. In a passage from his *Letters from Italy with Sketches of Spain and Portugal* (volume 2, 1835), he wrote: 'Those that have never heard this original sort of music must and will remain ignorant of the most bewitching melodies that ever existed since the days of the Sybarites. They consist of languid, interrupted measures, as if the breath was gone with excess of rapture and the soul panting to meet the kindred soul of some beloved object.'

4. *Brazilian authors or those considered as such*: The writer is referring principally to Portuguese authors, mostly during the colonial period, who later took up residence in Brazil, or those who had lived in Brazil but later returned to Portugal, but the reference also seems to include distinguished Europeans who spent a few years in Brazil, such as the Englishman John Armitage, or those who wrote about it, like Gottfried Handelmann and the British Poet Laureate Robert Southey.

5. *Porto Alegre*: Manuel José de Araújo Porto Alegre (1806–79) was a noted Brazilian writer of the Romantic movement, founder of the *Revista Guanabara* for the dissemination of Romantic literature, as well as a painter, art critic and diplomat.

6. *Magalhães*: Gonçalves de Magalhães (1811–82) was a Brazilian poet and diplomat whose *Suspiros Poéticos* (*Poetic Sighs*, 1836) is considered the first work of Brazilian Romanticism. His epic poem 'A Confederação dos Tamoios' ('The Confederation of the Tamoios'), which recounts the revolt by Indian tribes allied to the French colonizers of Guanabara Bay in 1556–7, was criticized as reactionary by the founder of the Romantic Indianist movement, José de Alencar, but defended by the writer's friend and patron Dom Pedro II.

7. *São Paulo . . . Rio Grande do Sul . . . Pará*: There is a traditional rivalry between the largest states, formerly provinces, of Brazil.

8. *Guanabara*: From the Tupi-Guaraní (see note 16 below) *guanápará* ('the breast of the sea'), this is the name of Rio de Janeiro's bay, considered by many to be the most beautiful natural setting of any city in the world. The name here refers to the bay and its surroundings.

9. *the Paulo Afonso falls*: An impressive series of waterfalls on the São Francisco River in the State of Bahia. The highest are 80 metres high. The falls were painted by the Dutch landscape painter Frans Post in 1649 and are the subject of a poem by Castro Alves written in 1876.

10. *Gonçalves Dias*: Antônio Gonçalves Dias (1823–64), a Romantic poet and playwright who is considered the first truly nationalist Brazilian writer. Along with José de Alencar, he was one of the prime proponents of Indianism, an artistic movement in the second half of the nineteenth century that sought to create a national identity through the romantic depiction of Brazil's indigenous people in the early years of the colony. On receiving the news of his premature death in a shipwreck, Machado de Assis wrote: 'Brazilian poetry is covered in mourning. Gonçalves Dias was its most cherished son.'

11. *Andrade Neves*: Joaquim de Andrade Neves (1807–69) was a Brazilian military officer and hero of the Paraguayan War (1864–70, see note 15 below).

12. *the Southern Cross*: The current flag of Brazil contains twenty-seven stars (one is added for each new state) representing the Brazilian states and the Federal District. The constellation of the Southern Cross (*Crux Australis*) is on the meridian.

13. *Minas*: The province, now state, of Minas Gerais.

14. *the Dutch invasions*: The Dutch first invaded the north-east of Brazil in 1624, where they later established the colony of New Holland. From 1630 onwards they came to control almost half of Brazil from their capital in Recife, where the Dutch West India Company had set up its headquarters. It was only on 6 August 1661 that New Holland was finally ceded to Portugal through the Treaty of The Hague.

15. *the Paraguayan War*: Also known as the War of the Triple Alliance, the war was fought between 1864 and 1870. The cause of the war is popularly attributed to British colonial interests. The direct cause, however, was the expansionist ambitions of Paraguayan president Francisco Solano Lopez and his desire to obtain a port on the Atlantic Ocean by capturing a slice of Brazilian territory. Although the armies of Brazil, Argentina and Uruguay combined were a fraction of the size of the Paraguayan army, the Triple Alliance defeated Paraguay in conventional warfare, leading to its utter defeat. The turning point came when the Brazilian fleet commanded by Admiral Barroso won the naval battle of Riachuelo on 11 June 1865. The casualties of the war were atrocious. Of the 160,000 Brazilians who fought, 60,000 died and a further 1,000 were left crippled. The total Paraguayan losses – through war and disease – have been estimated at 1.2 million people, or 90 per cent of its pre-war population. The war had a devastating personal effect on the emperor, Dom Pedro II, forcing him, in its final phase, into a disastrous alliance with the conservatives. This led to many leading liberals breaking away and forming the Republican Party, which was one of the contributing factors to the overthrow of the monarchy less than twenty years later.

16. *Tupi-Guaraní*: A generic term for the Tupian languages of South America, including the best-known, Guaraní (the second official national language of Paraguay), and Tupi. Many of the indigenous tribes who lived along the coast when the Portuguese arrived in 1500 spoke dialects that belong to the Tupi-Guaraní group. In the exacerbated patriotic view of Policarpo, Tupi-Guaraní constituted an authentic Brazilian language, as opposed to Portuguese, the language imposed by the colonizers.

17. *'the rosy-fingered dawn for radiant Phoebus heralded the way'*: A quotation from Homer's *Iliad* (Phoebus is another name for Apollo, the sun god).

18. *caboclo*: A person of mixed (indigenous) Indian and European

race, physically characterized by copper-coloured or light-brown skin and straight black hair.

19. *Ubirajara*: A popular Indian name, from the Tupi meaning 'lord of the spear'. It is a common man's name in Brazil today, often substituted for the shortened form 'Bira'.

20. *Rocha Pita of the History of Portuguese America*: Sebastião da Rocha Pita (1660–1738), a Brazilian poet and prolific historian. In 1730 he published the monumental *History of Portuguese America from the Year 1500 of Its Discovery to the Year 1724*.

21. *Ricardo Coração dos Outros*: Ricardo's name, Richard 'Heart of Others', is an intentional pun on the name of Richard the Lionheart (Ricardo Coração de Leão) – a slightly sarcastic reference to the heroism (in Ricardo's view) of his quest to be recognized as a patriotic singer/songwriter.

22. *Méier, Piedade and Riachuelo*: Three residential districts of Rio's North Zone, referred to as suburbs. Formerly characterized by quiet streets and villas with gardens, often shaded by mango trees, the decline of these areas began in the 1940s with the move to apartment blocks in the South Zone.

23. *Tamagno*: Francesco Tamagno (1851–1905) was an Italian tenor, a personal friend of Verdi and the first Otello.

24. *Petrópolis and Botafogo*: Petrópolis, the mountain town named after Emperor Dom Pedro II, who built his summer palace there, and Botafogo, the district of Rio's South Zone that stretches back from the bay of the Sugar Loaf towards the Lagoon, were both elite residential areas at the time.

25. *Rua do Ouvidor*: The Rua do Ouvidor, named after the key political post of senior appeals court judge (literally translated 'the listener'), was, throughout the nineteenth and early twentieth centuries, the street of high fashion, at the heart of the centre of Rio, with stores selling luxury imported goods and cafés frequented by the intellectual and political elite. The street today has kept almost none of its previous glamour.

26. *São Cristóvão*: A district in Rio's North Zone, where the National History Museum (previously the emperor's winter palace) and the Quinta de Boa Vista park and zoo (previously the palace gardens) are located. The decline of São Cristóvão as an elegant residential district began in the first decades of the last century.

27. *old lady*: Dona Adelaide was in her late forties.

28. *pigeon peas*: The pigeon pea, *guando* in Portuguese, was originally brought to Brazil from Africa during the slave trade. It is also

known as the no-eye pea, Congo pea, gungo pea (in Jamaica), gandule (in Puerto Rico) and toor dal (in India).

29. *cachaça*: Popularly known as *pinga*, a colourless (when unaged) spirit distilled from sugar-cane, historically central to Brazil's economy and culture, comparable to tequila in Mexico or vodka in Russia. There is still a certain stigma attached to *cachaça* drinking, as an intrinsically working-class habit. The words *cachaceiro* and *pinguço* are derogative terms for 'drunkard'.

30. *Angra*: Angra do Reis, a coastal town and resort on Rio de Janeiro's 'Green Coast', midway between Rio and Paraty, famous for the islands in its bay.

31. *Rio Grande*: Rio Grande do Sul is Brazil's southernmost and only wine-producing state.

32. *Bilac*: Olavo Brás Martins dos Guimarães Bilac (1865–1918) was consecrated as Brazil's leading Parnassian poet with the publication of his *Poems* in 1888. He is not included in the list of poets and fiction writers on Policarpo's shelves, indicating that perhaps Policarpo didn't keep abreast of contemporary developments in Brazilian literature. Bilac, who was a distinguished member of the Brazilian Academy of Letters and a regular contributor to journals like the *Gazeta de Notícias*, still commands a devoted following in Brazil and Portugal.

33. *Raimundo's 'Doves'*: Raimundo Correia (1859–1911) was a Brazilian poet. His early work is Romantic, showing the influence of Fagundes Varela, Casimiro de Abreu and Castro Alves. With his *Sinfonias* in 1883 he entered the ranks of the Parnassians, becoming a part of the so-called Parnassian Triad along with Alberto de Oliveira and Olavo Bilac.

Chapter II: Radical Reforms

1. *taking his first meal of the day at half-past nine in the morning*: Writers of this period, including Machado de Assis, refer to the two main meals of the day as 'lunch' (*almoço*) and 'dinner' (*jantar*). By today's standards people rose and went to bed very early – 'lunch' being the equivalent of a late breakfast and 'dinner' of a late lunch or early tea.

2. *marriage of the princesses*: The reference is to the two daughters of Emperor Dom Pedro II and his wife Dona Teresa Cristina of Bourbon, Princess of the Two Sicilies: Dona Isabel Leopoldina de Bragança e Bourbon, Princess of Brazil (1846–50) and Imperial Princess of Brazil (1850–1921), who married Gaston

d'Orléans, Comte d'Eu, in October 1864; and Dona Leopoldina Teresa de Bragança e Bourbon, Princess of Brazil (1847–71), who married the Comte d'Eu's cousin, Duke Ludwig August of Saxe-Coburg and Gotha. The cousins arrived in Brazil together, each promised to the other sister, but when they met, Gaston and Isabel found each other's company so agreeable that the emperor agreed to invert the previous arrangement.

3. *crash of Souto*: The reference is to the crash of Souto's Bank in 1864, which is said to have shaken the city more than the French invasion (1710), the arrival of the Portuguese court (1808), the declaration of the Paraguayan War (1864) and the Proclamation of the Republic (1889). Every middle-class *carioca* had his savings with the bank, which was popularly considered 'as solid as the Sugar Loaf'. The failure of the bank and the incredulity of the public at the loss of its savings were the talk of the town and dominated the national press.

4. *Cardim*: Fernão Cardim (*c.*1549–1625) was a Portuguese priest who came to Brazil with the Jesuits in 1583. He was appointed attorney general of the province of Brazil in 1598. Throughout the 1580s he wrote treatises and letters about Brazil that cover the climate, the flora and fauna and the customs of its indigenous tribes.

5. *Nóbrega*: Manuel da Nóbrega (1517–70) was a Portuguese Jesuit priest who commanded the first Jesuit mission to the Americas. The letters that he sent to his superiors constitute an important historical document on the colony and the activities of the Jesuits in Brazil.

6. *von den Stein*: The reference is to the German naturalist Karl von den Stein, who headed an expedition to study the Indian tribes along the Xingu River in 1884, which he later narrated in his book *Central Brazil*.

7. *Tangolomango*: The *Tangolomango* is described in the original as a *folia*. *Folia* (equivalent of the French *folie*) is used to refer to the revelry in a carnival parade or *bloco*.

8. *Benfica*: The district of Rio's North Zone that adjoins São Cristóvão. Today the region is a dilapidated residential area characterized by shanty towns and deactivated factories.

9. *Turenne*: Henri de la Tour d'Auvergne, Vicomte de Turenne, usually simply referred to as Turenne (1611–75), was famous for his personal courage and outstanding capacity as a military commander in the final campaigns of the Thirty Years' War and later

in Louis XIV's Dutch War. He was one of only six marshals who have been made marshal general of France.

10. *Gustavus Adolphus*: Gustav II of Sweden (1594–1632), known in English by his Latinized name Gustavus Adolphus, has been nicknamed 'the father of modern warfare'. As king of Sweden during the Thirty Years' War, from 1611 to his death in battle in 1632, he led his country to military supremacy, becoming an important player in the political and religious balance of power in Europe

11. *Lomas Valentinas*: The Lomas Valentinas fortifications were located on the River Piquissiri, an affluent of the Paraguay River, in Paraguayan territory. They were seized by the allied forces in a succession of assaults between 22 and 27 December 1868, on their way to the Paraguayan capital Asunción, in the so-called 'December campaign'.

12. *Pedregulho*: Literally translated, a large rock or boulder. The same word is used for 'gravel'.

13. *our 'national products'*: Iron-ore, marble, granite and semi-precious stones, as opposed to sugar-cane and coffee, which were traditional products.

14. *Dom João VI*: The Prince Regent of Portugal who fled the Napoleonic invasion and brought the Portuguese court to Rio de Janeiro in 1808. He became king of the United Kingdom of Portugal, Brazil and the Algarves on the death of his mother, declared mentally incapable in 1816. Despite the arrival of the court and the opening of the ports marking the most important turning point in the history of Brazil, the monarch (and especially his mother and wife) are frequently depicted with ridicule.

15. *rue*: Rue, *arruda* in Portuguese, is popularly believed to have healing powers, and to provide protection against spells, evil spirits and the evil eye. Today it is still widely used in Afro-Brazilian cults.

16. *Victor Emmanuel*: Vittorio Emanuele II (1820–78), crowned the first king of a united Italy in 1861. At this time popular sentiment in Brazil was still widely monarchist.

17. *'Bumba-meu-Boi'*: A popular dance of Brazilian folklore that originated in the north-east, based around the death and resurrection of an ox. The characters are men and animals, the female roles being danced by men dressed as women. They include the farm owner (Amo), the farm-worker (Chico or Mateus), the farm-worker's black wife Catarina, the ox, as well as cowherds,

Indians and *caboclos*. *Bumba-meu-Boi* festivals are still very popular in towns across the north-east of Brazil.

18. *'Boi Espácio'*: A folklore song from the north-eastern state of Sergipe. Silvio Romero, the great nineteenth-century researcher of Brazilian folklore, included it in his *Popular Songs of Brazil* (1883). A Boi-Espaço is a breed of bull whose horns are at a very wide angle, consequently with a large space between them.

19. *Santa Ana dos Tocos ... São Bonifácio do Cabresto*: The two saints mentioned – St Anne of the Tree-stumps and St Boniface of the Halter – are a slightly ironic comment on the lengths to which the old poet was prepared to go in his study of Brazilian folklore.

20. *Urubu-de-Baixo*: Both in Portugal and Brazil, towns and villages in the mountains are often referred to as *de cima* (above) and towns and villages with the same name in the plains as *de baixo* (below). The name of the town here is another example of the writer's irony: Urubu (from the Tupi for 'vulture') is a very undignified name for a town, let alone Urubu-de-Baixo!

21. *fabliaux*: 'Short metrical tale[s], usually ribald and humorous, popular in medieval France' (The Free Dictionary).

22. *Tupinambás*: The Indian 'nation' that dominated the entire Brazilian coast in the early days of the colony, which included the subgroups Tamoio, Tupiniquim, Potiguara, Tabajara and Caeté. These tribes fought ferocious wars among themselves and were notorious for devouring their captives. The Jesuits compiled a grammar of their language, Tupi, which became the basis of the *lingua franca* spoken for two centuries in the interior of the colony. References to the Tupinambás are often references to the Confederation of the Tamoios, the objective of which was to expel the Portuguese.

23. *Master Valentim's fountain*: Mestre Valentim (1745–1813) was a mulatto artisan placed in charge of public works in the city of Rio de Janeiro during the government of the viceroy Dom Luís de Vasconcelos e Sousa (1779–90). His famous fountain stands at what was the waterfront in the front of the Imperial Palace in modern-day Praça XV de Novembro.

24. *Mistral*: Frédéric Mistral (1830–1914), lexicographer and writer in the Provençal language, co-founder of the Félibrige, a literary society founded in 1854, along with six other Provençal poets to protect French traditional regional cultures and their languages.

25. *the maracá, the inúbia*: The *maracá* is a gourd rattle that was used in the ritual preparation for war. The *inúbia* was an Indian

war trumpet, made from a series of hollow wooden tubes tied together with vines. The major's contempt for the difficulties of the piano compared with that of these truly national instruments is another example of the author's ironic treatment of his hero's exacerbated nationalism.

26. *Léry*: Jean de Léry (1534–1611), a French Calvinist who came with a group of Protestant missionaries to the 'French Antarctic', the colony established by Nicolas de Villegagnon in the Guanabara Bay, which was conquered by Portuguese troops in 1565, when the city of Rio de Janeiro was founded.

Chapter III: Genelício's News

1. *réis*: (Literally 'kings'), the plural of the monetary unit used in Portugal, Brazil and other Portuguese-speaking countries. Due to its tiny monetary value, the expression *conto de réis* was often adopted, corresponding to a million *réis*.

2. *Parque*: The Parque Real ('Royal Park') was a traditional department store in Largo de São Francisco, the square at the end of the fashionable Rua do Ouvidor, which had been famous since the days of the Empire.

3. *Not a soldier?*: In Rio de Janeiro, the Fire Brigade, to which Sigismundo belonged, was (and still is) a military unit.

4. *Porto Alegre*: Manuel Marques de Sousa (1804–75), the first and only Baron, Viscount and Count of Porto Alegre, was an aristocrat and statesman and a leading military figure of the Empire. At the outset of the Paraguayan War he was retired but volunteered for service and went on to lead the allied troops to a number of remarkable victories.

5. *Caxias*: Luís Alves de Lima e Silva, Duque de Caxias (1803–80), who successively held the titles of Baron, Count, Marquis and finally Duke of Caxias (the only title of duke conferred during the Brazilian Empire), was a statesman and the greatest military figure in Brazilian history. He was an active participant in suppressing all the uprisings during the First and Second Empires (1822–1889) and was appointed commander in chief of the Brazilian army in 1866 after the defeat of the allied troops at the battle of Curupaiti during the Paraguayan War. In 1949 his remains were placed in the specially built Duke of Caxias Pantheon in front of the Ministry of War in what was then the federal capital. In 1962 he was declared patron of the Brazilian army. In contemporary Portuguese, if a person is referred to as

caxias it means that he or she can be counted on to be reliable and correct.

6. *isn't everything based on science nowadays?*: The irony is aimed at the philosophy of positivism, espoused wholeheartedly in republican circles. Developed by Auguste Comte (1798–1857), positivism discarded metaphysics, holding that every rationally justifiable assertion can be scientifically proven. The leading early republicans were ardent positivists who attended the Positivist Temple founded by Teixeira Mendes (which still stands today in Rio's Gloria district), where a belief in progress and solidarity between men was preached. The words on the flag of the Brazilian Republic, 'Order and Progress', were taken from the positivist slogan 'Love as the principle, Order as the means, Progress as the end.' (It is ironic, in the light of Lima Barreto's narrative, that of the three components 'love' was excluded.)

7. *Curupaiti*: On 22 September 1866, in the wake of their success at the battle of Curuzu (see Part II, Chapter I, note 6), the allied forces assaulted the fortress of Curupaiti. The area around the fort, however, had been protected with an extensive network of trenches that proved devastating to the allied troops, who were repelled with the loss of 4,000 men. The loss of the battle was devastating for the Brazilian side, both for its negative impact on public opinion and for the virtual withdrawal of the Argentinean and Uruguayan forces from the war. It took another year and a half before the Paraguayans were finally expelled in March 1868, after a persistent campaign led by the Marquis (later Duke) of Caxias to isolate the area and surround it with trenches, preparing the way for the advance on Humaitá (see Part II, Chapter II, note 6).

8. *the Arsenal*: The naval headquarters.

Chapter IV: Disastrous Consequences of a Petition

1. *Aquidauana and Ponta-Porã*: Municipalities in the swamplands of Mato Grosso. Aquidauana (which had first been settled by Brazilian soldiers who had fought in the Paraguayan War) was officially founded on 15 August 1892 (the first year of Policarpo's adventures) by a military committee sent by the federal government to secure the region on the Paraguayan frontier. The same year a garrison from the military colony at Dourados was established in Ponta-Porã.

2. *Benjamin Constant*: (1836–91), known as the 'founder of the Brazilian Republic', was one of the prime articulators of the republican uprising in 1889 and responsible for drawing up the provisional constitution of 1891. An ardent positivist, as a teacher at the military academy on the Praia Vermelha (at the foot of the Sugar Loaf) he was responsible for divulging the philosophical and religious ideals of positivism to the new generation of army officers.

Chapter V: The Statuette

1. *Pinel ... Esquirol*: Philippe Pinel (1745–1826) was a French doctor, the first to consider mental disturbance an illness and to describe and classify its manifestations. His work was continued by his pupil and successor Jean-Étienne Esquirol (1772–1840). Rio's main psychiatric hospital is now housed in a modern building behind the original asylum in which Policarpo (and Lima Barreto himself) were interned (which now belongs to the Federal University of Rio de Janeiro). The institution was called Hospital Pinel until 1994, when its name was changed to Instituto Philippe Pinel. 'Pinel' has found its way into the Portuguese language as a pejorative term meaning 'crazy'.

2. *throwing her pearls to the swine*: In the original text the expression used is 'mistaking the cloud for Juno'. The meaning is to presume that something is much better than it really is (as, although the goddess Juno could take the form of a cloud, that didn't mean that every cloud was Juno).

PART II

Chapter I: At 'The Haven'

1. *jabuticabas*: Sometimes called the Brazilian grape, it is a sweet, cherry-like fruit with black skin that sprouts in clusters from the smooth trunk of the *jabuticaba* tree.

2. *jambos*: A fruit of the guava family, sometimes called 'rose apple' or 'water apple'.

3. *pluviometers, hygrometers and anemometers*: Respectively: a rain gauge, an instrument for measuring the level of vapour in the air and an instrument for measuring the speed of the wind.

4. *chickadee*: The Portuguese for 'chickadee', also imitative of the
    bird's call, is *bem-te-vi* – roughly translated 'I saw you!' – which
    explains the major's annoyance.

5. *fruits*: In Portuguese the word for 'fruit', as in 'edible fruit', is the
    feminine noun *fruta*, whereas the word for 'fruit', as in 'the fruit
    of his labour', is the masculine noun *fruto*. It is the latter, in the
    plural, that the author uses here.

6. *Curuzu*: The town was named as a tribute to the battle of Curuzu,
    which was fought between 1 and 3 September 1866 during the
    Paraguayan War. The fortress of Curuzu was the first of three
    fortifications that constituted the complex of Paraguayan defences
    against access by river to the capital Asunción. The other two,
    Curupaiti and Humaitá, were also the scenes of major battles.
    (Both Curuzu and Curupaiti constituted advanced defences for
    the major fortifications at Humaitá.) At the battle of Curuzu
    defenders had the advantage that the fort was surrounded by
    swamps and thorn bushes. It was finally taken at great cost,
    including the sinking of the battleship *Rio de Janeiro* with the loss
    of fifty men.

Chapter II: Thorns and Roses

1. *clogs*: Wooden sandals called *tamancos* were the most common
    footwear of Brazilian workers until the 1930s.

2. *magic*: The writer is referring to the generalized, though little
    commented, practice of all social classes of consulting shamans,
    or *pais de santo*, belonging to the Afro-Brazilian cults. Such con-
    sultations often result in the placing of 'dispatches' at crossroads,
    waterfalls or beneath certain trees. They usually contain a clay
    dish with food for the deity, a bottle of sweet cider or beer and
    lighted candles.

3. *If I weep . . . the burning sand my tears doth drink*: The quote is
    from *Vozes D'Africa* (*Voices of Africa*) by Castro Alves (1847–
    71), one of Brazil's most admired and best-loved poets, who died
    of tuberculosis at the age of twenty-four. He was known as the
    'Slaves' Poet', and in his short lifetime he achieved recognition
    for his ardent condemnation of slavery.

4. *Padre Caldas*: Domingos Caldas Barbosa (1739–1800), a Brazil-
    ian mulatto priest who went to Portugal to study at the University
    of Coimbra and became the darling of Lisbon society due to his
    talent for improvisation on his viola with wire strings. He is
    credited with inventing the term *modinha*.

5. *Polidoro*: General Polidoro (1792–1878) substituted for General
    Osório (see note 6 below) as commander in chief of the Brazilian
    forces during the Paraguayan War, during his frequent illnesses.
    It was Polidoro who led the Brazilian troops to victory at the
    battle of Curupaiti.
6. *Humaitá*: The fortress of Humaitá, located on the left bank of the
    River Paraguay 430 kilometres from Asunción, controlled access
    to the capital by river and was turned by President Solano Lopez
    into the country's most powerful and feared defensive complex
    during the Paraguayan War. It was finally taken by Brazilian
    troops in July 1868 after General Osório (1808–79), command-
    ing 12,000 men, had seized the Paraguayan garrison to the north
    of the fortress, suffering 3,000 casualties.

Chapter III: Goliath

1. *corbeilles*: *Corbeilles de mariage*, i.e. wedding presents.
2. *'Marechal Deodoro'* . . . *'Marechal Floriano'*: The two streets had
    been renamed after the overthrow of the monarchy in November
    1889. The old street had originally been named Emperor Street in
    honour of Emperor Dom Pedro II (1831–89), and the new one
    Empress Street in honour of his wife, Teresa Cristina de Bourbon.
    They now bore the names of the first and second presidents of the
    Republic, respectively: Marshal Deodoro Street after Deodoro da
    Fonseca (in office 1889–91) and Marshal Floriano Street after Flo-
    riano Peixoto (in office 1891–4). (*The Sad End of Policarpo
    Quaresma* constitutes Lima Barreto's attack on the cult of Floriano
    Peixoto and his military regime, making it one of the great indict-
    ments of authoritarian governments in Latin American literature.)
3. *Rua da Matriz*: The English equivalent would be Church Street.
    The word *matriz*, meaning 'principal' or 'main', is used to refer
    to the parish church.
4. *Praça da República*: The pompous sounding 'Square of the
    Republic' or 'Republic Square' is not without irony for the name
    of this open, probably muddy, space in a rural backwater.
5. *spider buggy*: A light horse-drawn carriage with a single seat and
    only two wheels.
6. *marshal*: Marshal Floriano was Marshal Deodoro's vice-president
    and the second president of the Republic (23 November 1891 to
    15 November 1894). He was nicknamed the 'Iron Marshal', and
    the ruthlessness with which he crushed a series of revolts, includ-
    ing the second Revolt of the Armada and the Federalist Revolution

in the south, led to a nationalistic cult of his personality, known as *Florianismo*. His detractors have seen him as a forerunner of fascism and the twentieth-century military dictatorships in Latin America. In *Policarpo* Lima Barreto compares his regime's repression to the terror of the French Revolution.

7. *the Empire*: Brazil became an empire on the declaration of independence in 1821 and was so termed until the overthrow of the monarchy in 1889.

8. *the uprising of the Fort of Santa Cruz*: The fortress of Santa Cruz da Barra was originally built by Nicolas de Villegagnon (1510–71), who founded French Antarctica, the first European settlement on Guanabara Bay. It was designed to defend the entrance to the bay from the Niterói side. It was later taken by Mem de Sá (1500–1572), the third governor general of Brazil. (He was the uncle of Estácio de Sá, who expelled the French from Guanabara Bay and founded the city of Rio de Janeiro in 1565.) The revolt at the fort was the first demonstration of discontent after Marshal Deodoro was forced to stand down and his vice-president, Floriano, instead of summoning new elections as the constitution of 1891 required, assumed the presidency.

9. *La Bruyère's*: The reference is to a passage from the seventeenth-century French essayist and moralist Jean de La Bruyère (1645–96), describing human existence in the French countryside during the late medieval period: 'sullen animals, male and female, [are] scattered over the country, dark, livid, scorched by the sun, attached to the earth they dig up and turn over with invincible persistence; they have a kind of articulate speech, and when they rise to their feet, they show a human face, and, indeed, they are men. At night they retire to dens where they live on black bread, water, and roots.'

Chapter IV: 'Stand Firm, I'm on My Way'

1. *Saint-Hilaire*: Auguste de Saint-Hilaire (1779–1853), French botanist.

2. *Planets, Bajacs and Brabants*: Brabant and Bajac would appear to refer to the same machine – the Double Brabant Plough invented by Antoine Bajac in 1900. Planet Jr was a trademark of popular gardening tools of the first decades of the twentieth century.

3. *although he had a curly moustache*: The Indians' smooth skin and lack of body hair may explain the reference to the moustache.

4. *Bahia or Sergipe*: Two of Brazil's north-eastern states: the former, the largest state in the north-east with the most political weight, with a large black population; the latter, territorially small but with political influence in the nineteenth century, with a large *caboclo* population.

5. *Turgot*: Anne-Robert-Jacques Turgot, Baron de Laune (1727–81), was a French economist and statesman best remembered as an early advocate for economic liberalism.

6. *Sully and Henri IV*: Maximilien de Béthune, Duc de Sully (1560–1641), was a French statesman and minister of Henri IV (1589–1610).

Chapter V: The Troubadour

1. *the abandoned park*: The park (now called the Quinta de Boa Vista) was previously the gardens of the Imperial Palace in São Cristóvão, which had been abandoned since the military coup that founded the Republic three years earlier.

2. *he was an ungrateful devil ... don't you think?*: Marshal Deodoro was persuaded to lead the coup of 1889, even lied to, against his will. He was a man of declared monarchist sympathies and a personal friend of the monarch, who as recently as 1888 had promoted him to military commander in the province of Mato Grosso.

3. *Rio Branco*: José Maria da Silva Paranhos, Viscount of Rio Branco (1819–80) is considered one the greatest statesmen of the Second Empire (1831–89). Famed for his diplomacy and indefatigable efforts at conciliation, he was largely responsible for the stability of the conservative governments during the reign of Dom Pedro II. Due to his persistence the slave trade was outlawed under the Law of the Freeborn in 1871 (the abolition of slavery itself was to come seventeen years later).

4. *the old man's fault*: The reference is to Dom Pedro II.

5. *Imperial Palace*: Until the foundation of the Republic, the Emperor's Winter Palace and main residence in Rio de Janeiro, now the National Museum in the district of São Cristóvão.

6. *The man*: Marshal Floriano, the second president of the Republic.

7. *Rio Grande*: The reference is to the Federalist Revolution in the
    south aimed at the independence of Brazil's southernmost state,
    Rio Grande do Sul. (See Part III, Chapter III, note 3.)

8. *Custódio*: The reference is to the Revolt of the Armada. Marshal
    Deodoro da Fonseca, who had founded the Republic in 1889,
    was forced to resign only nine months after taking office after he
    had closed the Congress. His place was taken by the second
    president, Marshal Floriano Peixoto. The constitution required
    new elections if the president resigned before completing two
    years of his term. This served as the legal justification for the
    revolt led by senior naval officers who were afraid of the increas-
    ing political domination of the country by the army. One of the
    leaders, Admiral Custódio de Melo (referred to here), was a
    potential candidate for the presidency.

9. *Piauí*: State in the north-east of Brazil, traditionally one of the
    country's poorest. It has a very small coastline, and much of
    the interior is semi-desert and scrubland.

10. *The Aquidabã ... The Luci*: The *Aquidabã* was considered the
    most technically advanced battleship of its time. It had been
    acquired by the Brazilian navy from the British shipbuilders
    Samuda & Brothers in 1885. The *Luci* was a steam launch,
    famed for its speed, built in Rio de Janeiro by a private company
    and used by the rebels during the Revolt of the Armada (1893–
    4).

11. *The two generals*: *Sic*.

12. *Paraguayan uniform*: That is, from the Paraguayan War.

13. *Victor Meirelles*: Victor Meirelles de Lima (1832–1903) was a
    painter of the Romantic school who is particularly noted for his
    magnificent historical scenes. He is considered one of the great-
    est Brazilian painters of the nineteenth century.

14. *There were executions, but no Fouquier-Tinville*: The meaning is
    that no one was held accountable for the executions. Antoine
    Quentin Fouquier-Tinville (1746–95), public prosecutor during
    Robespierre's reign of terror, was responsible for sending, among
    many others, Charlotte Corday, Marie Antoinette and leaders of
    the Girondists and the Dantonists to the guillotine. After the fall
    of Robespierre he was arrested and guillotined for what he had
    done.

15. *positivism*: It is the fanaticism with which the concepts of posi-
    tivism were used to justify the ruthless repression of all opposition
    by Floriano Peixoto that the writer condemns here, rather than
    the philosophy itself.

16. *phonetic script*: Brazilian positivists adopted the phonetic script which they proposed would be a scientific method for promoting literacy in a largely illiterate country.

17. *the religion of humanity . . . rubber soles*: In other words, a ruthless military dictatorship justified by a religion that claimed to uphold scientific and humanitarian ideals.

18. *Phrygian cap*: A conical cap of soft material worn in antiquity that became a symbol of liberty during the French Revolution.

19. *autos-da-fé*: The ritual of public penance of condemned heretics and apostates that took place when the Spanish Inquisition or the Portuguese Inquisition had decided their punishment, followed by the execution by the civil authorities of the sentences imposed. Both *auto de fe* in medieval Spanish and *auto da fé* in Portuguese mean 'act of faith'. In this extended metaphor comparing Fontes, in his positivist zeal, to a member of the Inquisition, the victims are civilians who are either indifferent to or against the recently founded Republic.

20. *Paul de Kock*: Charles Paul de Kock (1793–1871) was a prolific French novelist who depicted Parisian life during the Bourbon restoration.

21. *contos*: The currency had such a tiny value that it was used in units of a thousand, known as *mil-réis*. One *conto de réis*, or simply one *conto*, was one thousand *mil-réis* (that is, one million *réis*).

PART III

Chapter I: The Patriots

1.   *Sulla*: Lucius Cornelius Sulla (*c*.138 BCE–78 CE), who installed himself as dictator after conquering Rome.

2.   *a melancholy that was characteristic more of the race he represented than of the man himself*: A further indication of the writer's low regard for north-easterners – Floriano was from the state of Alagoas – a prejudice that is still widespread in the south-east of Brazil today.

3.   *Louis XI*: (1423–83), 'the spider king', was one of the most successful French kings in uniting the country. His reign was marked by a web of political plots and conspiracies that earned him his nickname.

4.   *Colbert*: Jean-Baptiste Colbert (1619–83) was minister of finance to King Louis XIV. Through persistent hard work and economies

he achieved the recovery of French industry and brought the economy back from the verge of bankruptcy.

5. *Augereau*: Charles Pierre François Augereau, Duc de Castiglion (1757–1816), first fought for Napoleon as a division commander in Italy in 1796 and was later entrusted with important commands during the Napoleonic Wars.

6. *revolt of 6 September*: On 6 September 1893 a group of high-ranking naval officers demanded that new elections be called immediately. They included Custódio de Melo, ex-minister of the navy and candidate for the presidency. His adherence reflected the discontent at the navy's limited power. The movement that included young officers and a large number of monarchists marked the beginning of the Second Revolt of the Armada.

7. *Cleopatra's nose*: The story goes that, while he was on his way to the decisive battle of Actium, Mark Antony was contemplating a statue of Cleopatra and was spellbound by the vividness with which it reflected her beauty. The delay lost him the battle. Pascal later said that had Cleopatra's nose been smaller, history would have been different. The fate of the world hung in the balance, on Cleopatra's nose.

8. *Padre Vieira*: Padre Antônio Vieira (1608–97) was a Jesuit missionary born in Lisbon and who died in Salvador, Bahia. His was an indefatigable opponent of the persecution of Jews and the enslavement of Indians. His harsh criticism of his fellow priests was to bring him into conflict with the Inquisition. Among his many other achievements he was known as a master of classical Portuguese prose. His sermons are still required reading in many universities.

9. *Doctor Sangrado*: A character in *Gil Blas*, the hugely popular picaresque novel by Alain-René Lesage (1668–1747). The character is a parody of the real-life French doctor Philip Hecquest (1661–1737), who was famous for prescribing bleeding and hot water as a remedy.

Chapter II: 'You, Quaresma, Are a Visionary'

1. *To the right . . . through the mist*: Little of what is described here of the city, viewed from inside the Guanabara Bay in 1893, is recognizable today.

2. *Guanabara*: The *Guanabara* had been confiscated from Wilson & Sons (a company that is still active in Rio with offices in the downtown area). The rebels confiscated a number of ships to

fulfil their requirements for fuel, munition and livestock. Vessels were also seized from Lloyd Brasileiro, Navegação Lage and the Companhia Frigorífico Fluminense.

3. *Cais Pharoux*: A building in neo-classical style, built from materials imported from France and Bohemia, still used for the ferry crossings from Rio to Niterói and the Island of Paquetá. It is located on the seafront of Praça XV de Novembro, at the heart of downtown Rio. The docks were used by the royal family, who were transported from the then Largo do Paço by boat to the end of the bay, from where they took the train to Petrópolis, where the emperor's summer palace is located.

4. *feudal domain of death*: Today, as in the nineteenth century, Cajú is characterized by its cemeteries, including a vertical cemetery belonging to the Carmelites and Rio's first crematorium.

5. *Clothair ... Chram*: Chram was the son of Clothair I (497–561 CE), King of the Franks, by his last wife, Chunsina, and became his father's enemy.

6. *St Louis*: (1214–70) reigned as Louis IX of France from 1226 to 1270.

7. *Divine Comedy*: Dante Alighieri wrote the *Divine Comedy* between 1308 and his death in 1321.

Chapter III: ... And They Fell Silent

1. *Leave her, brother ... miraculous fluids*: 'Brother' was their form of address for the 'spirit without light' by whom they thought the patient was possessed. The miraculous fluids are what in current usage is called *ectoplasm*, a healing substance which in spiritualism is believed to emanate from certain parts of the medium's body.

2. *beliefs ... lands of other gods*: During slavery African traditions such as *Candomblé* and *Capoeira* were practised in secret. The discovery of such practices was punished with the utmost brutality. (The abolition of slavery was less than five years old at the time the story is set.)

3. *Only Lapa ... 'a fight to the death'*: The Federalist Revolution (1893–5) in the south coincided with the Second Revolt of the Armada in Rio de Janeiro. The revolutionaries, who planned to overthrow the president (as state governors were then termed) of Rio Grande do Sul, the autocratic Julio Prates de Castilhos, were supported by the anti-Floriano rebels to the north. Lapa (not to be confused with the traditional bohemian district of Rio of the

same name), a small town 60 kilometres south-west of Curitiba (the capital of the southern state of Paraná), heroically held out against federalist troops under the command of Colonel Carneiro (1846–94), who died in action in February 1894 without giving up his position. The failure of the 'Siege of Lapa', as it became known, thwarted the rebels' intentions to march on the capital.

4. *Moreira César*: Colonel Antônio Moreira César (1850–97), well referred to here, was nicknamed the 'head-chopper' for ordering the execution of 100 men during the Federalist Revolution in Santa Catarina. He died in action in Canudos, where he was sent by President Prudente de Morais after three previous military expeditions had failed to crush the revolt. Colonel Moreira César successfully managed to do so, at the cost of entirely destroying the village of Canudos, where 20,000 backlanders were massacred, the prisoners of war had their throats slit, and 5,200 houses were burned to the ground.

5. *Villegagnon*: An island in the bay which today houses the Naval School, named after Nicolas de Villegagnon.

6. *Gragoatá*: A fort on the Niterói side of the bay.

7. *the Solimões, off Cape Polônio*: The *Solimões* didn't take part in the Revolt of the Armada. On 19 May 1892 she sank off Cabo Polônio, a remote cape on the Uruguayan coast.

8. *naturalization decree*: The provisional government was the first government established under Marshal Deodoro after the military coup which ousted the emperor, lasting until the promulgation of the new constitution. As a move to gain popular support (in the last parliamentary elections under the Empire in August 1889, only two Republican Party deputies were elected), a month after it was established, on 14 December 1889, the government issued the Great Naturalization Decree. Under the decree all foreigners resident in Brazil would automatically gain national citizenship unless they opted to declare for the maintenance of their previous nationalities within six months.

9. *Itamarati*: The Palace of Itamarati was the seat of the republican government from 1889 to 1898. From 1899 to 1970 it was the seat of the Foreign Office (more literally the Ministry of Foreign Relations), which is officially known as Itamarati.

10. *Cidade Nova*: Or the New Town, a district of Rio de Janeiro located between the Centre and the North Zone.

11. *And the despair ... memories of the living*: This paragraph is a little obscure. The writer seems to be saying that the more distinguished the person in life, the less requirement for an ostentatious

tomb; only those who achieved nothing while alive attempt to perpetuate their memory in this way.

Chapter IV: Boqueirão

1. *Boqueirão*: A small outlet of a river and often, as in this case, the name of a beach where such an outlet is located. Here it is the name of a beach at the far end of the Guanabara Bay, the sinister significance of which is revealed at the end of the chapter.
2. *cafuza*: Of mixed Indian and African blood.
3. *Saldanha*: Luis Felipe de Saldanha da Gama (1846–95), a decorated war hero and rear admiral in the Brazilian navy, led the Second Revolt of the Armada along with Admirals Eduardo Waldenkolk (1838–1902) and Custódio de Melo (1840–1902). During the government of Floriano's successor, Prudente de Morais, he was brutally murdered by a fanatical supporter of Julio de Castilhos in the last months of the Federalist Revolt.
4. *Ilha das Enxadas*: One of the many islands in the bay – literally translated 'Spadefish Island'.

Chapter V: Olga

1. *Fustel de Coulanges*: Numa Denis Fustel de Coulanges (1830–89) was a French historian. The reference here is to his book *La Cité Antique* (written in 1864 and revised in 1875), in which he demonstrated the role of religion in the political and social evolution of Greece and Rome. Fustel enjoyed a great reputation both as a scholar and as a writer; *La Cité Antique* is considered one of the French language masterpieces of the nineteenth century.
2. *Menana tribe*: The inhabitants of Menana Harena Buluk, a district of the Oromia region of Ethiopia.
3. *Wasn't Cisplatina a part of Brazil, before we lost it?*: Cisplatina is the region located immediately to the south of the present-day Brazilian border. The province was annexed by the United Kingdom of Portugal, Brazil and the Algarves in 1821. The Argentineans laid claim to the territory, which the Brazilian Empire saw as strategically important for the defence of its southern provinces. In 1828 the territory was incorporated into the newly established Oriental Republic of Uruguay.
4. *illustrious, generous-hearted men . . . the state of the country*: The reference is to the conspirators in the independence plot known as the Inconfidência Mineira (the Minas Disloyalty). The

group was betrayed and its members arrested in 1789. The judicial proceedings lasted until 1792. Seven were condemned to perpetual banishment in Africa, and eleven to the gallows; the rest were acquitted. Queen Maria I then commuted the death sentences to perpetual banishment, with the exception of Joaquim José da Silva Xavier (1746–92), nicknamed 'Tiradentes' (literally 'Pull Teeth', as among his other activities he was an amateur dentist), who was less well connected and was made a scapegoat. He was imprisoned in Rio de Janeiro, where he was hanged on 21 April 1792. His body was cut up and the pieces sent to Vila Rica (present-day Ouro Preto) in the captaincy (present-day state) of Minas Gerais, to be displayed in the places he had frequented. The republicans cultivated Tiradentes as one of Brazil's most important national heroes. 21 April is a public holiday.

5. *On the surface, yes*: The meaning would appear to be that it led to the declaration of independence thirty years later.

6. *troops were needed to fight in the south*: i.e. against the Federalist Revolution.

Penguin Classics

THE LOST ESTATE (LE GRAND MEAULNES)
HENRI ALAIN-FOURNIER

*'Meaulnes was everywhere, everything was filled with memories of our adolescence,
now ended'*

When Meaulnes first arrives at the local school in Sologne, everyone is captivated by
his good looks, daring and charisma. But when he disappears for several days, and
returns with tales of a strange party at a mysterious house and a beautiful girl hidden
within it, Meaulnes has been changed forever. In his restless search for his Lost Estate
and the happiness he found there, Meaulnes, observed by his loyal friend François,
may risk losing everything he ever had. Poised between youthful admiration and
adult resignation, Alain-Fournier's compelling narrator carries the reader through this
evocative and often unbearably moving portrayal of desperate friendship and vanished
adolescence.

Robin Buss's major new translation sensitively and accurately renders *Le Grand
Meaulnes*'s poetically charged, expressive and deceptively simple style, while the
introduction by *New Yorker* writer Adam Gopnik discusses the life of Alain-Fournier,
who was killed in the First World War after writing this, his only novel.

'I find its depiction of a golden time and place just as poignant now' Nick Hornby

Translated by Robin Buss
With an introduction by Adam Gopnik

PENGUIN CLASSICS

THE COUNT OF MONTE CRISTO
ALEXANDRE DUMAS

'On what slender threads do life and fortune hang'

Thrown in prison for a crime he has not committed, Edmond Dantes is confined to the grim fortress of If. There he learns of a great hoard of treasure hidden on the Isle of Monte Cristo and he becomes determined not only to escape, but also to unearth the treasure and use it to plot the destruction of the three men responsible for his incarceration. Dumas's epic tale of suffering and retribution, inspired by a real-life case of wrongful imprisonment, was a huge popular success when it was first serialized in the 1840s.

Robin Buss's lively English translation is complete and unabridged, and remains faithful to the style of Dumas's original. This edition includes an introduction, explanatory notes and suggestions for further reading.

'Robin Buss broke new ground with a fresh version of *Monte Cristo* for Penguin'
The Oxford Guide to Literature in English Translation

Translated with an introduction by Robin Buss

PENGUIN CLASSICS

THE ODYSSEY
HOMER

'I long to reach my home and see the day of my return. It is my never-failing wish'

The epic tale of Odysseus and his ten-year journey home after the Trojan War
forms one of the earliest and greatest works of Western literature. Confronted by
natural and supernatural threats – shipwrecks, battles, monsters and the implacable
enmity of the sea-god Poseidon – Odysseus must test his bravery and native
cunning to the full if he is to reach his homeland safely and overcome the obstacles
that, even there, await him.

E. V. Rieu's translation of *The Odyssey* was the very first Penguin Classic to be
published, and has itself achieved classic status. For this edition, his text has been
sensitively revised and a new introduction added to complement E. V. Rieu's
original introduction.

'One of the world's most vital tales. *The Odyssey* remains central to literature'
Malcolm Bradbury.

Translated by E. V. Rieu
Revised translation by D. C. H. Rieu, with an introduction by Peter Jones

PENGUIN CLASSICS

AROUND THE WORLD IN EIGHTY DAYS
JULES VERNE

'To go around the world in such a short time and with the means of transport currently available, was not only impossible, it was madness'

One ill-fated evening at the Reform Club, Phileas Fogg, rashly bets his companions £20,000 that he can travel around the entire globe in just eighty days – and he is determined not to lose. Breaking the well-established routine of his daily life, the reserved Englishman immediately sets off for Dover, accompanied by his hot-blooded French manservant Passepartout. Travelling by train, steamship, sailing boat, sledge and even elephant, they must overcome storms, kidnappings, natural disasters, Sioux attacks and the dogged Inspector Fix of Scotland Yard – who believes that Fogg has robbed the Bank of England – in order to win the extraordinary wager. *Around the World in Eighty Days* gripped audiences on its publication and remains hugely popular, combining exploration, adventure and a thrilling race against time.

Michael Glencross's lively translation is accompanied by an introduction by Brian Aldiss, which places Jules Verne's work in its literary and historical context. There is also a detailed chronology, notes and further reading.

Tranlated with notes by Michael Glencross with an introduction by Brian Aldiss

THE STORY OF PENGUIN CLASSICS

Before 1946 ... 'Classics' are mainly the domain of academics and students; readable editions for everyone else are almost unheard of. This all changes when a little-known classicist, E. V. Rieu, presents Penguin founder Allen Lane with the translation of Homer's *Odyssey* that he has been working on in his spare time.

1946 Penguin Classics debuts with *The Odyssey*, which promptly sells three million copies. Suddenly, classics are no longer for the privileged few.

1950s Rieu, now series editor, turns to professional writers for the best modern, readable translations, including Dorothy L. Sayers's *Inferno* and Robert Graves's unexpurgated *Twelve Caesars*.

1960s The Classics are given the distinctive black covers that have remained a constant throughout the life of the series. Rieu retires in 1964, hailing the Penguin Classics list as 'the greatest educative force of the twentieth century.'

1970s A new generation of translators swells the Penguin Classics ranks, introducing readers of English to classics of world literature from more than twenty languages. The list grows to encompass more history, philosophy, science, religion and politics.

1980s The Penguin American Library launches with titles such as *Uncle Tom's Cabin*, and joins forces with Penguin Classics to provide the most comprehensive library of world literature available from any paperback publisher.

1990s The launch of Penguin Audiobooks brings the classics to a listening audience for the first time, and in 1999 the worldwide launch of the Penguin Classics website extends their reach to the global online community.

The 21st Century Penguin Classics are completely redesigned for the first time in nearly twenty years. This world-famous series now consists of more than 1300 titles, making the widest range of the best books ever written available to millions – and constantly redefining what makes a 'classic'.

The Odyssey continues ...

The best books ever written

PENGUIN CLASSICS

SINCE 1946